Trisha Ashley

Good Husband Material

avon.

Published by AVON
A division of HarperCollins*Publishers* Ltd
1 London Bridge Street
London SE1 9GF

www.harpercollins.co.uk

First published in Great Britain by Judy Piatkus (Publishers) Ltd in 2000
This edition published in Great Britain by HarperCollins*Publishers* in 2013

A catalogue copy of this book is available from the British Library.

ISBN: 978-1-84756-281-4

Typeset in Minion by Palimpsest Book Production Limited, Falkirk, Stirlingshire
Printed and bound in UK by CPI Group (UK) Ltd, Croydon CR0 4YY

MIX
Paper from
responsible sources
FSC™ C007454

Acknowledgements

With special thanks to Judith Murdoch, my agent, for her encouragement and support.

For Mary Turner Long, with love.

Prologue

'The lyrics of the new Goneril single, 'Red-Headed Woman', taken from the album of the same name, show a searing agony of loss and grief. Singer/songwriter Fergal Rocco plumbs new depths of helpless agony and despair in a voice that seems to have been created for that very purpose.'

New Musical Express

Fergal: 1986

My first brief glimpse of Tish seems to have been indelibly imprinted on the inside of my eyelids, for even after almost twelve years and God-knows-how-many women, I only have to close my eyes and there she is: a dryad poised far above me in the shivering green oak leaves, stretching forward with one hand reaching out, her expression intent.

Then the sharp crack as the branch gives way beneath her weight, precipitating her into a long downward swoop towards me, apricot hair flying behind her like a wild Renaissance angel – a mermaid swept by the glassy green waves – a ship's figurehead forging ahead, one out-thrust hand clasping—

Well, not a trident, at any rate, only some small grey thing. It didn't just then make the same impression that Tish was about to: a bolt from the green.

While I'd like to say I caught her, truth compels me to admit I merely broke her fall, ending flat on my back with the angel sprawled across me. Enormous smoke-grey eyes stared apprehensively down into mine from an inch away. I decided to give in without a struggle.

Then something scuttled shiftily up my arm on hot, pronged feet and bit me savagely on the ear.

I swore and the creature let go and gave an evil laugh.

I'm not joking.

When Dad came round the corner of the house to see what all the noise was, he found the angel still sprawled over me, incoherently apologising and dabbing at my bleeding ear with a wadded-up bit of filmy skirt.

A small, evil-looking grey parrot stood nearby (too near) regarding us with interested, mad eyes.

'Always Fergal catches the girls,' Dad said cheerfully, taking the scene in his stride. Then, with his usual aplomb, he removed his jumper and enveloped the parrot in its folds.

The small assassin gave a dismal squawk, echoed by a screech of outrage from behind us. A tiny, well-preserved blonde, like a piece of shellacked fluff, was advancing up the drive with the martial air of one about to rescue her daughter's honour or die in the attempt.

'Leticia – get up at once!'

'Leticia?' I questioned incredulously, looking up into the grey eyes so close to mine. (And feeling as I did so as if I'd been sucked into a Black Hole and squeezed out on the other side like toothpaste.)

Her hand stopped its rather painful and ineffectual dabbing and she glared. 'I don't see that Fergal is any better!' she said defensively. 'And anyway, I'm always Tish.'

'And *I'm* always Fergal, Angel, so you'll just have to get used to it.'

Her eyes widened slightly, then she suddenly removed herself from me in a flutter of flowing green fabric (no wonder I hadn't seen her in the tree) planting her knee unintentionally – I hope – in a delicate part of my anatomy in the process.

'Leticia is a nice name,' Dad said interestedly, giving it an Italian pronunciation. 'And I am Giovanni Rocco, your new neighbour – call me Joe, everyone does. For six months only we rent this house while our own is renovated – the cracks appear, these old houses in London, they are not well built. And this must be your *mamma*?'

'I am Mrs Norwood,' the fluffy little blonde lady said icily, eyeing Dad with the dubiously surprised expression of one meeting a tall, blond, green-eyed Italian for the first time. (*My* Mediterranean darkness I owe entirely to my Irish mother.)

'So pleased to meet you – and your charming daughter. This is my eldest son, Fergal. I have four sons and one daughter. Perhaps you have heard the youngest ones playing in the garden? They love this big garden.'

'Yes, I have heard them. Normally this is such a quiet, select neighbourhood.'

The girl turned pink and began nervously to pleat the folds of her bloodied skirt. 'I – I like to hear children playing,' she ventured shyly. 'I'm glad to meet you, Mr Rocco.'

'Joe.'

'Joe,' she amended. 'And I'm so sorry my parrot bit your son, only he escaped, you see, and I was trying to catch him.'

I hauled myself up from where I'd been sitting on the grass, stunned in more ways than one, and the blood dripped down my once-white T-shirt.

'Oh dear,' she said guiltily. 'But it's only a little bite. Ears bleed a lot, don't they?'

'Mine certainly seems to,' I agreed, smiling down at her, and she blushed again and looked away. 'Perhaps you should come round later and see how I am?' I added cunningly.

'Yes, come for dinner,' said Dad expansively. 'I stay home tonight, so I will cook – and what is one or two more? You too, Mrs Norwood, and Mr Norwood, of course.'

'I am a widow. And I am afraid I am otherwise engaged. And Leticia—'

Seeing she was about to scupper any designs I might have on the angel I interrupted rudely, 'There's some disease you can catch from parrots, isn't there? Psittacosis? Tish really ought to come and check on me.'

'I . . . is there?' stammered Tish, looking frightened. 'Oh dear, then perhaps I had! And you *will* put some antiseptic on it right away, won't you?'

'You can check on that, too – in about an hour?'

She nodded, still looking frightened, until I winked at her, when she blushed again and glanced away, stifling a giggle.

'Leticia!' began Mrs Norwood in a hectoring voice. 'You—'

Whatever she was about to say was silenced by Dad helpfully shoving the wrapped, protesting bundle of parrot into her arms and tucking the jumper as carefully around it as though it were a baby.

She looked even more aghast than she'd done when she

saw her daughter entwined with me on the grass, and they both retreated down the drive, accompanied by muffled squawks.

'Such a pretty girl,' Dad said appreciatively. 'So tall and slender, and the hair like sun-warmed apricots. But very young, Fergal – maybe only sixteen or seventeen. The *mamma* is right to be careful.'

She *was* only seventeen, and I was her first love, but I was twenty-two and should have known that, for her, it wouldn't last for ever.

I suppose I was lucky it lasted a year.

Chapter 1: A Dream of a Man

November 1998

Last night I dreamed I was back in Fergal's arms.

Nothing new there, then.

I often dream about the current heroes of the romantic novels I write, who all bear a definite (physical) resemblance to Fergal. The sort of dreams that make you wake up and feel guilty when you look at your husband.

They certainly add some oomph to my love scenes, though unfortunately only the ones in my novels. I've come to the conclusion it would take a lot more than that to add any oomph to James.

This time the dream was of a different genre, more like a rerun of my last encounter with my first untrue love. Maybe my subconscious thought I didn't suffer enough at the time and decided to run it past me again.

Anyway, there we were entwined like Laocoön in Fergal's beloved second-hand Frog-eyed Sprite sports car (thoroughly cleaned inside and out with anti-bacterial cleanser by myself when he bought it, of course – after all, who knew where it had been?). Birds were singing, the sun was shining and there was a heady smell of engine oil, old leather and disinfectant ... and the equally heady feel of his arms around me as he said confidently in my ear, 'Goneril are going to make it big this time!'

Goneril was (and still is) the name of the rock band he'd formed together with his brother Carlo and a motley assortment of other art students. Why they had to choose a name that sounds like a venereal disease, I don't know.

In the year I'd been going out with Fergal the band had gone from being a casual thing they did for fun and to earn some money, to the point of taking over more and more of their lives and time. And now they'd just been asked at the last minute to go on tour as support to a well-known group, the original support band having pulled out.

It meant leaving for the USA almost immediately: make-or-break time.

I looked up into his amazing green eyes and said adoringly, 'Oh, Fergal, of course you'll make it! But – I'll miss you while you're abroad.'

He pulled away slightly at this, his straight black brows drawn together in a frown. 'Why should you miss me?'

'Of course I'll miss you. You'll be away for months!'

'But – you're coming with me, Tish! I want you with me.'

Gobsmacked wasn't in it. 'M-me?' I stammered. 'Go on tour with you? But I can't do that, Fergal – my university course starts in September. Besides, Mother would have a fit if I trailed around after you like a groupie. And, by the way, you never asked me!'

Fergal's always volatile temper got the better of him at this point and he gave me a little shake. 'You are *my* girl, not a groupie, and I want you with me. And why go to college? What does it matter?'

'What does it matter when you've got *me*?' was what he really meant, and it made me see red.

'Of course it matters! I'm looking forward to the course.'

Well, I had been until then.

Fergal had just finished his MA in Fine Art at the RCA, and the plan was that he should make a name for himself with his painting while I got my degree, so that one day we could live in the country together. He would paint and I would write poetry . . .

Daydreams – but anything seemed possible when I was with Fergal. And of course I hadn't then realised that although I was a poet, I was not a *good* poet.

The fine distinction between turning out reams of seamless drivel like a miniature stream-of-consciousness novel and writing real poetry is sometimes hard for a teenager to grasp. My literary skills, I later discovered, lay elsewhere.

But at the time I was all set to study Modern English Literature in pursuit of this, and I thought he should understand, since he seemed just as dedicated to painting until Goneril started to take off.

'Well – have a year out, then,' he suggested impatiently. 'Isn't it about time you left home and experienced some real life?'

That would look good on my gap-year CV: 'What did you do in your gap year, Miss Norwood?' 'Oh, I just screwed my rock-singer boyfriend over an entire continent. Nothing interesting.' 'And was that with the VSO, Miss Norwood?' etc.

As to experiencing real life, I'd packed more of that into that year with Fergal than I had in all the previous seventeen.

I looked at him in exasperation . . . and my heart softened

a bit. He was absolutely gorgeous, and I loved him so much. But when I remembered how casually he'd assumed I'd just follow him like a little dog at the asking – or the telling – I got angry all over again.

'Look, Fergal, I'll be waiting here for you when you come back: it's not even as if I'm going *away* to college.' (And that was solely to be near him. Otherwise I would have applied for something as far away from Mother as possible – the University of Outer Mongolia Scholarship in Non-Rhyming Glottal Stops, say.)

He held me at arm's length from him, his fingers biting into me. 'Come with me or that's it – finish!'

His eyes were as hard and cold as emeralds in his dark face.

Then I lost my temper and in a state of hurt fury said a few cutting things about how easy he'd found it to abandon his art for Filthy Lucre (well, I was only eighteen and a bit idealistic) and then we had our worst row ever. It wasn't followed by the sort of making-up that healed such spats either, since he took me straight home and dropped me at the gate without another word.

Even then I didn't think he meant it – he was inclined to say that sort of thing in the heat of the moment – but by next day, when he hadn't phoned to apologise, I started to get worried and even seriously contemplated abandoning my pride and ambitions and going with him after all. So maybe it wouldn't last for ever, but wouldn't it be better to have loved and lost than not to have loved at all?

Who knows what might have happened if poor Grandpa hadn't had his heart attack that day, so that instead of

10

chewing my fingernails by the telephone I was travelling to Granny's?

In the end I was there for the whole summer: through the struggle that Grandpa fought and lost, and that of my down-to-earth and stoical grandmother to come to terms with her bereavement.

Mother was entirely useless, of course. She produced one excuse after another as to why she couldn't come up to lend her support, and then crowned it all by being 'too prostrate with grief' to attend the funeral.

'The woman's got the backbone of a wet lettuce,' commented Granny when I told her, and I was glad to see some slight return of her spirits.

Although Mother always disliked Fergal I *had* extracted a promise from her before I left to tell him where I was if he should ring, and to send on all my mail. But, as she almost gleefully reported, there was nothing to send on: he never contacted me again.

He'd meant what he said after all.

The *coup de grâce* was a picture cut from a gossip magazine and helpfully forwarded by Mother showing Fergal coming out of some American nightclub with a well-known and beautiful model draped all over him like clingfilm.

I was so devastated I prayed nightly that she would stab him to death in bed with her hipbones, but nothing happened, except that Mother kept sending me cuttings about all the scandalous things Fergal and the rest of the group got up to, until I told her that I didn't want to know. I didn't even want the *name* Fergal mentioned ever again. I hadn't got time to have a broken heart that summer.

I'd adored Grandpa, and he and Granny had been a mismatched but devoted pair, so I threw myself into helping her in any way I could.

But somehow all the colour seemed to have bled away from my surroundings; having your first close experience of death and your heart broken simultaneously does that, I find. So when Granny decided, in an old-fashioned sackcloth-and-ashes way, to dye every garment she possessed (plus the inside of the washing machine) black, I put all the clothes I had with me in too.

I'd found this dyeing of the clothes a very dramatic gesture – the Dying of the Light, as it were – and I wore nothing but black for years. After all, it stopped all that bother about wondering what to wear, and matching things up, which I really didn't care about any more. There is only one drawback I discovered with black – you can never see whether it is spotlessly clean or not. Wearing black became a habit, one I only really started to break when Mother pointed out that you can't get wedding dresses in that colour.

When I finally went home from Granny's I didn't dye anything else black, just cut all the rest of my clothes up into little pieces – six-inch, three-inch and one-inch, so as not to waste any – and began on my hobby of patchwork.

But my experience with Fickle Fergal at least made me appreciate James's steadier, mature qualities when I met him, so I've no regrets now over what happened so long ago.

And, look on the bright side, at least I didn't wake up after this dream feeling guilty: just angry and tear-stained.

I gave James a poke in the ribs with my elbow, handed him a cup of coffee-bag coffee from the Teasmade, and informed him that it was time to get up.

Isn't it strange that I should hate tea when I adore autumn leaves? But I find I don't wish to drink dead leaf dust.

'Day off,' James grunted, trying to put his head under the duvet.

'Day off to house-hunt, and I've got a feeling we'll find the country cottage of our dreams today – we've just been looking too near London and in the wrong direction. Besides, a day in the country will do us both good. All the leaves have turned gold now, and—'

'You've got enough leaves,' he said hastily, re-emerging.

I don't know why he disapproves of my harmless little hobbies. My patchwork brightens the whole flat up; it's amazing just how much you can make from a wardrobe of old clothes. I'm still at it after all this time, and I'm sure the acreage is more than the sum of the original. Can this be possible? Algebra was never my strong point. Or do my clothes have a Tardis-like quality?

And my leaf collection: James had never minded going for walks in the park or the country while I collected them when we first started going out together, though it transpired that he thought I was going to press them. (And put them in an album perhaps? I know he's quite a bit older than me, but that's *Victorian*!)

'Oh, no,' I'd told him at the time, surprised. 'I like them all curled and natural as they fall. I spread them out to dry, then give them a light coat of acrylic varnish.'

'Varnish?'

'They get dusty. This way I can rinse them off.'

'Oh,' he'd said, obviously struggling with this concept. Tentatively he'd enquired, 'Then I suppose you make arrangements or pictures or something with them?'

'No, I usually just pile them up in baskets and along the window ledges in my room. I like the whispering sound they make when I go in and out.'

He'd given me an affectionate squeeze and said fondly, 'What funny ideas you have, darling – it must be living alone for so long.'

'Oh, no, I've always had them,' I'd assured him, only until then I hadn't thought my little ways were funny.

Still, you can see how harmless my hobbies are, really.

'I need some more oak leaves, James,' I told him now. 'I never seem to find enough of those, and I'd like a whole basketful.' (I'm a basket person but not, I hope, a basket case, whatever James might imply.)

'You know, I can't think why everyone doesn't collect them – they're free, in beautiful colours and shapes, and perfectly hygienic if you varnish them.' (I only collect clean-looking ones anyway, but you can always wipe them over with Dettox.) 'Isn't it strange we don't value them? We could use them as money instead of a lot of germy bits of paper, or—'

There was a gusty sigh from under the bed, which heaved two or three times as if in a heavy swell and I broke off to exclaim indignantly, 'You let that stupid dog in again last night, didn't you? You know I don't like breathing the same air in and out all night, it isn't healthy. Or hygienic. You'd better get up and take her out so we can get off early.'

'Plenty of time,' he muttered, but determinedly I prised him out, assisted by the lure of stopping off for a fat-and-cholesterol-rich breakfast en route.

*　*　*

14

Fergal: 1998

'DOES BRITAIN'S SEXIEST ROCKER HAVE A SAD PAST?'

Trendsetter magazine

Past is the operative word. And while I don't think I could forget Tish if I tried, I don't try, just go on rubbing salt into the old wound so that it never entirely heals.

Angst is so good for an artist . . .

My immaculate, fiery angel is the muse I still draw on for inspiration for both songs and paintings alike.

But that's the Tish I remember. She's probably Mrs Suburban Housewife now, her dreams stuffed into a drawer to moulder. (Or *smoulder* – she had a way with words.)

What has become of her now I neither need – nor want – to know.

Chapter 2: Home, James

'This is it,' I said, with conviction. 'This is *my* cottage!'

'What?' muttered James absently, peering through a grubby windowpane at the small, blonde and bubbly estate agent, who was hovering tactfully outside despite the arctic November wind. Her legs below the short skirt were an interesting shade of blue.

He always gets a bit silly over that type, which makes you wonder why he married me: tall, reserved, and as effervescent as flat Guinness.

Come to that, why didn't he just marry my mother, who is small, determinedly blonde and, if not precisely bubbly, sparkles a bit after the second Martini?

I gave him a nudge with my elbow. 'Concentrate on the house, James. The estate agent is only being charming to you because she hopes to make a sale.'

He looked hurt. 'Don't be silly, darling – I was just thinking about the case I've got on. I really shouldn't have taken a day off to look at houses, and I think I'd better pop into the office for an hour or two after I've dropped you at your mother's.'

The mystery of why he'd chosen to wear one of his

natty dark suits to go house-hunting was now clear. (Though admittedly they do set off his sandy-haired rugged-Highlander good looks a treat, a fact he knows very well.)

'I'm sure Drew, Drune and Tibbs can solicit away without you for one day, James. Especially when it means we've at last found the right cottage.'

'What? You don't mean this one do you, Tish?' His bright blue eyes widened in astonishment. 'I can't imagine why you wanted to view it in the first place – it's too small, and it isn't even detached.'

'It's twice as big as the flat: all these chairs make it look smaller. There are thirty-two.'

'Thirty-two what?'

'Chairs.'

'What's that got to do with anything? Look at the garden – it's a wilderness.'

'A *big* wilderness. There's some sort of shed out there, too, and plenty of room for a garage at the side of the house.'

'But the house is old, dark and probably unsanitary,' he suggested cunningly. 'It belonged to an old man who didn't do anything to it for years, and probably died in it.'

'From an overdose of chairs, perhaps?' I suggested. 'People have died in most old houses. Of course I'd have to scrub it from top to bottom before we brought any of our things in, and all the walls and ceilings need painting, and perhaps the floors sanding down and sealing if they're good enough. Roses round the door . . . pretty curtains . . . And just look at the situation! Only one neighbour – and the agent says that's a sweet little old lady – and the back garden overlooks the parkland of the local big house, so it'll be very peaceful . . .'

I tailed off. James was looking stubborn and sulky, one of his limited repertoire of expressions. (And now I come to think of it, 'indulgent affection' hasn't made many appearances lately, or 'extreme solicitousness denoting a single-minded determination to have sex'.)

'You know, Tish, I've been thinking lately that perhaps we should just look for a small weekend place near the sea instead. Jack's promised to teach us to sail and—'

'No. Absolutely not,' I interrupted firmly. 'My idea of a fun weekend does not entail sitting with my bottom in icy water, while being alternately hit over the head with a piece of wood and slapped by a bit of wet canvas. Besides,' I added, hurt, 'didn't we always plan to move to the country once we could afford it?'

'Well . . . yes, but—'

'And then I can give up working in the library for peanuts – which really makes no sense when you think that I could earn just as much from writing, if I had more time – and we can start a family, and you could commute to work, and get lots of fresh air and exercise in the garden growing our own fruit and vegetables. Isn't that what we've both dreamed of?'

He closed his mouth and said hastily, 'Yes, darling, of course it is. That is, it sounds wonderful, but perhaps we ought to wait for something detached to come up and—'

'We've been married six years, James. I can see the big three-0 coming up, and you were forty last birthday.'

He winced.

'We can afford this house, it's near enough to commute

18

– only about eleven miles to Bedford station. I'll come off the pill as soon as we move, and we'll eat a healthy diet and take long walks to get fit.'

James looked slightly punch-drunk. 'I suppose it *might* be quite nice here,' he conceded reluctantly. 'And,' he added brightening, 'Gerry and Viola live only a few miles away, and I'm sure he drives into work. Must leave pretty early. I'll ask him what it's like.' He put his arm around me. 'I can see you like this place, darling, but don't set your heart on it. I think we ought to look at a few more first, and once I'm a senior partner we could afford something detached.'

'I want this one, a real country cottage, not a detached mock-Tudor somewhere. I want to be a country dweller, with muddy wellingtons and a cottage garden. And you used to like the idea of being self-sufficient – you had all those books about it. I think they're in the back bedroom cupboard. I'll look them out when we get home.'

He didn't look too enthusiastic, but he's a man of short-lived crazes, as I've learned the hard way. While I would have expected someone to warn me had I been about to marry a serial killer, no one felt it necessary to inform me that I was about to marry a serial hobbyist. Perhaps it should be written into the marriage ceremony? Thou Shalt Not Become A Serial Hobbyist. Still, I don't see why he can't have the same one twice, like the measles, with a bit of exposure to the germ.

He was rather dampening when I enumerated the cottage's many advantages on the way back to Mother's house in darkest suburbia for Granny's birthday tea. I'll have to work on him; but I'm in love with my cottage, and am beginning to have distinctly now- or-never feelings about making the move.

I think it's something to do with thirty looming ahead (my birthday is in February) and so few of my ambitions realised. And if I'm going to take the plunge and have a baby, then my sell-by date is just peeping up on the horizon.

One definite plus point to living in the cottage at Nutthill would be that James wouldn't be so tempted to call in at the pub on his way home from work in the evenings if he had such a long drive ahead of him. (Networking, this is called, apparently.) And with so much to do to the house and garden he won't have either the time or the money for his Friday night sessions out with 'the boys', or our regular show or film and restaurant on Saturday nights.

I never feel relaxed in big, pretentious, expensive restaurants anyway, and would always have preferred to save the money towards the cottage. I'm not much of a social animal, in fact. I like a quiet life and time to write after work, and I enjoy a trip to a museum or art gallery more than anything else.

James's friends are all about ten years older than I am, with self-assured, well-dressed, boring wives, against whom I stand out like a macaw among a lot of sparrows. They're all so well-groomed and *taupe*. If they mix two colours together in a scarf they think they're daring.

Living so far out into the country would also distance us from James's appalling old school chum Howard, ageing hippie extraordinaire, who has recently moved back to London after a brief spell crewing on a yacht, where I should think he was as much use as a twist of rotten rope.

He managed to acquire a rich girlfriend in the interval

between jumping ship in Capri and being deported. (I hadn't realised that he knew Comrades came in two sexes, but there you are. She must be deranged.)

James may not immediately see all the cottage's advantages . . .

He dropped me at Mother's in mid-afternoon (and I can hardly wait to put some distance between myself and Mother – another plus) and drove off to the office to pick up some papers (allegedly) though I did tell him that if he wasn't back within the hour I'd kill him.

I stifled the ignoble thought that perhaps he just wanted to see his ex-girlfriend Vanessa, recently reinstalled as secretary. When she got divorced and had to find a job, she pleaded with James to put a word in for her, and he felt so sorry for her he persuaded his uncle Lionel to take her on again.

He explained how it was, so I'm not in the least bit worried or jealous about her being there every day, even though she's another bubbly blonde. From the sound of it, her bubbles may have gone a bit flat; James said her husband was a brute and she's looking very worn and *years* older.

Mother was a bit pensive and hurt when he drove off, and nearly as dismal as James when I described the cottage. She only really cheered up again when he returned and fell like a famished wolf on the rather nursery spread of food she associates with birthdays.

Then the cake was brought out and we had to sing 'Happy Birthday' with James and Mother trying to harmonise, slightly hampered by Granny, who had already loudly announced that she didn't want any fuss made about birthdays at her time of life, ignoring us and turning the TV up loudly, so that a repeat of *Top of the Pops* drowned us out.

Mother keeps trying to persuade everyone that Granny is losing her marbles, but I think anyone who can learn to preset a video recorder deserves Mensa membership, because I've never managed it.

'You can't possibly want to watch that, Maud!' Mother broke off to exclaim crossly.

Granny briefly unglued her boot-button eyes from the screen. 'Why not?' she demanded belligerently. 'All them funny clothes and lewd dancing. Best entertainment on the box.'

She returned her avid gaze to the gyrating row of young men clad in enormously baggy trousers and no tops. 'Eh! There's more hair on the back of my hands than there is on them poor boys' chests. And call that a beard? Bum fluff!'

Mother sighed long-sufferingly and cast her baby-blue eyes heavenwards. 'So vulgar,' she whispered. 'Dear James, she's such a trial to me – and getting more senile by the day.'

I wouldn't agree with that, though she certainly seems to be reverting to her Yorkshire roots at a gallop!

James squeezed Mother's hand. 'At least she has you to look after her, Valerie,' he said, which I thought was pretty rich considering he *knows* Mother is the giddy, spendthrift widow of the two. But Mother is the tiny, fluffy fragile sort who seems to appeal to a certain type of man. (She's tough as old boots really.) She spends large amounts of money she doesn't have on beauty treatments, make-up and clothes, which is mainly why Granny decided to move in and take over.

I'm sure she thought she could sort Mother out and then leave things running smoothly while she moved to the retirement bungalow she'd set her mind on. Only, as she soon discovered, you can't organise fluff, it just drifts away with every passing breath of wind.

She's had to bail Mother out of major financial difficulties at least twice, and even the house itself now belongs to her, so it's fortunate that Grandpa was a jeweller and had lots of what Granny calls 'brass'. He was a warm man, she always says, though she won't say precisely what his thermostat was set to.

Mother has entirely failed to see that she is Granny's pensioner, not vice versa, and tells everyone she's trying to make her declining years a joy to her.

Granny hasn't shown much sign of declining yet, and not much joy either.

So Mother now squeezed James's hand with sincere gratitude and batted long mascara-lagged eyelashes at him: 'Dear James – so understanding. So very wise.'

Granny's deafness has an astonishingly intermittent quality about it unrelated to whether her hearing aid is switched on or off (or even which ear she happens to have plugged it into).

She now remarked without turning her head, 'Dearest James knows which side his bread is buttered on, and so do you. He—'

She broke off so suddenly that I swivelled round in my chair in alarm, only to find her attention riveted by the appearance on the screen of a dark, extremely angular face: a familiar, very masculine face, framed in long, jet-black hair and with eyes as green as shamrocks.

'Well, I never did, Tish!' she gasped. 'It's that Fergus who used to live next door – the one you were sweet on. Now that's what *I* call a man!'

'Fergal,' I corrected automatically. And he'd been what I called a man, too, until fame and fortune had beckoned and he'd gone off without a backward look. It's not what I call him now.

Still, it gave me a peculiar feeling to see him on screen moodily singing, bright eyes remote and hooded. And even more of a funny feeling in the stomach when the guitars crashed in and he started throwing his lithe body about the stage.

Age does not appear to have withered him or staled his infinite variety.

Top of the Pops seemed an unlikely venue, since Goneril has more of a cult following than a mainstream pop one. They sort of blend Celtic folk music and heavy metal and . . . and I'm sounding like a groupie, which I never was.

I became slowly aware that conversation at the tea-table was suspended, and I could feel James's gaze swivelling suspiciously from the TV to me and back again, like some strange radar dish, but until Fergal vanished from the screen to be replaced by shots of the audience, drooling, I couldn't somehow detach my eyes.

The surprise, I suppose.

'You went out with *him*?' demanded James incredulously. 'You never said!'

It was a relief to find I could turn my head again. 'Didn't I? I'm sure I told you I'd been out with someone who let me down badly, and—'

'Yes – but you never said it was *him*.'

'Well, does it matter? It was all ages before I met you. His parents were renting the house next door and I met him when he came to visit them. We . . . sort of bumped into

24

each other. But in the end he got famous and went off, and I went to university and then met you, darling.'

'At least he was a man, and not a big girl's blouse masquerading as one,' Granny said with a scathing look at poor James. 'First time I thought the girl might have some Thorpe blood in her after all, when she took up with him.'

James's outraged stare almost made me giggle.

'So foreign – I never liked him,' Mother said, primly ignoring Granny's remark, although her cheeks had grown slightly pink. 'The whole family was volatile. You could hear his parents shouting six houses away. And look how he's turned out – always in the papers over some scandal, and with a dreadfully cheap girl in tow.'

'He wasn't foreign,' I said weakly (and certainly none of the girls I had ever heard of him being connected with could be described as *cheap*). 'His father is Italian born – Rocco of Rocco's restaurant chain, you know – but his mother is Irish and Fergal was born here in London.'

'That's what I said – foreign,' Mother said triumphantly, recalling unendearingly to my mind all her tactics to blight my romance with Fergal. Not that it would have lasted anyway: Romeo and Juliet fell in love, grew up, argued, and parted. Juliet became a boring suburban housewife getting her kicks from writing romantic novels, and Romeo became a drug-crazed sex-maniac rock star.

Shakespeare for the New Era: not many dead. And all water under the bridge now.

James was still goggling at me as if he'd just noticed for the first time that I'd got two heads, so I smiled rather nervously and hastened to change the subject.

'Are we going to eat this cake now the candle's gone out?

And *Top of the Pops* is finishing, so perhaps Granny would like to open her presents, Mother?'

Easily distracted, she began to bustle about, and the subject of Fergal was thankfully dropped.

In the car James was very quiet, which suited me, since it had made me feel very peculiar seeing the real Fergal in action, as opposed to the fantasy, sanitised version who lives a life of his own in a specially constructed holding-pen in my head, and off whom I've been vampirically feeding for several years to fuel my writing.

Actually, I should be grateful to Fergal for leaving me in that callous way, because it set me on to a really character-forming curve – even though it might have felt like a downward spiral at times – culminating in my having my first romantic novel accepted, and discovering True Worth and Dependability in James's sturdy and attractive form.

It was therefore a bit of a shock when Dear Old Dependable James broke the silence by saying sourly, 'That old boyfriend of yours – what's his name? Rocca?' He laughed but it came out as more of a disgusted snort. 'I suppose they all change their names, but *Rocca*.'

'Rocco, James. And it's his real name.'

'Of course you'd know that, wouldn't you, having been the Great Star's girlfriend? Funny you never mentioned it before, isn't it? If your grandmother hadn't let the cat out of the bag I'd still be in the dark.'

'So would the cat,' said my unfortunate mouth, which doesn't always refer to my brain before uttering.

James's expression became even more sombre, so I

hastened on soothingly, 'And really, James, there was no cat to let out of the bag, if by that you meant a guilty secret. If I'd thought a detailed list of all my old boyfriends would amuse you I'd have given you one.'

'You didn't *have* any other boyfriends. Valerie told me.'

I felt distinctly ruffled both by the idea of him and Mother discussing my suitability (I mean, she probably assured him I'd only been round the block once, low mileage, practically a born-again virgin), and the fact that it should matter who else I'd been out with (or *in* with) if he loved me. I bet she also tried to smooth over my unattractive points: i.e. my height (I always wear flat shoes), the cleft chin (Mother calls it a dimple) and the strange colour of my hair (strawberry blond).

'I wouldn't have thought you were Fergal Rocco's type anyway, since he's so extrovert and wild, and you're as prissy as Snow White and Little Red Riding Hood rolled into one,' he added unforgivably.

'Prissy? I am not prissy!' I exclaimed, hurt and angry. 'Anyway, when you proposed you said it was my being so reserved and home-loving that attracted you in the first place!'

And then, with a sudden flash of belated illumination, it occurred to me that *prissy* was just the sort of wife he'd been looking for and thought he'd found, since I'd been quietly working hard at my course and my writing – and at that time wore sombre clothes, too. I probably seemed exactly the sort of girl his uncle Lionel had told him he ought to marry, since neither of them has the ability to tell 'good girls' from 'bad girls' (possibly because the distinction no longer exists).

A nice, quiet, malleable young girl . . . only he didn't realise I'd been hardened into quietness by fire.

James was scowling blackly ahead over the steering wheel. 'Suddenly discovering that your quiet, librarian wife is the ex-girlfriend of a notorious rock star is a bit unsettling, and I can assure you that Lionel and Honoria wouldn't have welcomed you into the family as warmly as they did if they'd known.'

'If that was warm I wouldn't like to see them meeting someone they disapproved of.'

'You may yet do so if they find out about this.'

'I don't see why they should. Or why their approval should be necessary.'

'Of course it is! A solicitor needs the right kind of wife. They did comment at the time that you had appalling taste in clothes, but it would probably improve with a little guidance.'

'How nice of them!' I said drily.

Honoria always wears things made out of hairy tweed like sacking, and high-necked shirts.

I remembered the first time Lionel and Honoria had met Granny, Mother having managed to keep her hidden until then.

But James must have told them about her, for we had all been bidden to dine at the pretentious and stuffy restaurant they favoured for such jollifications as interrogating future in-laws.

They had seemed mesmerised both by the size and profusion of Granny's diamonds, a selection of which had as usual been pinned and hung at random over her billowing bosom. As she often says: if you've got 'em, flaunt 'em.

This might have had some bearing on the marked effort to be polite to her they made even after she called the waiter over and demanded, pointing at her soup, 'What do you call this?'

'Chicken soup, madam,' he'd replied haughtily.

'If that's chicken, it walked through on stilts.'

'How very droll your dear grandmother is,' Honoria had remarked in an aside to me. 'A true original. You are her only grandchild, aren't you?'

'What? Oh – yes, Dad was her only child.' I'd replied vaguely, wondering why I found Mother embarrassing whereas I never found Granny so.

Granny is clever, sharp, kind and loving, and if she doesn't want to put on airs and graces I don't see why she should. She says herself that Yorkshire folk are as good as any and better than most.

I gave a snort as I recalled James's expression when Granny had written down a recipe for chicken soup and told the waiter to give it to the chef; then I realised he was still burbling on about my dress sense. Lack of, that is.

It wasn't doing much for his driving.

'Not that your taste *has* improved,' he was saying. 'All that black you used to wear was a bit gloomy, but you've gone too far the other way now.'

'Because I'm happy, and I want to wear bright, cheerful colours while I'm still young enough.'

'I suppose Fergal Rocco liked you in gaudy clothes?'

He liked me best in no clothes at all.

I just managed to button my mouth before it got away from me, and after a brief struggle in which my lips writhed silently, managed to say with supreme self-control, 'Look,

29

I only went out with him for a few months, then Goneril went to America and he dropped me like a hot potato. I never saw or heard from him again after he left. Satisfied?'

'You've never seen him since?'

'No!'

Only in my dreams. And let us hope James doesn't get a sudden urge to read one of my books (unlikely though it seems) wherein all the romantic heroes are remodelled and transmogrified versions of Fergal.

Tish the literary vampire.

Frankenstein Tish, creating a new Fergal each time from the best bits of the old (and there were some choice bits), joined to new parts culled from my imagination. (I've got a good one. Lurid, even.)

Wonder if Fergal gets pale and listless every time I write a new novel? I wouldn't like to think I was draining his batteries . . .

Who am I kidding? Yes I would! It would serve him right for breaking my heart.

James pulled up outside the flat with an over-dramatic swerve and stalked silently off without opening my door, one of the little old-world courtesies that first endeared him to me.

I only hope he's not going to brood over this. I don't know why he's so upset about it, since he knew I hadn't lived in an ivory tower before he came along. (A concrete university accommodation tower, actually – the urge to escape Mother overcame me.)

Perhaps it's just that the type of man I went out with doesn't match the image of me he's been cherishing.

Sometimes lately I've thought the image he has of me doesn't match *me* very much either.

You know, even now I'm not quite sure how I came to be married to James!

I wasn't actually looking for Mr Right. Not even for Mr Will-Do-at-a-Push-if-Desperate.

I remember telling him quite plainly that my life was blighted and I intended living quietly in the country devoting myself to my writing, and him saying he'd always wanted to live in the country too (his self-sufficiency phase). Then he just sort of sneaked up on me with flowers and chocolates and stuff. While spontaneity was not his middle name, dependability was: he was always there.

And being older he seemed rather suave and sophisticated. And attractive, even if not exciting, which was a plus point after Fergal: I'd *had* excitement. In fact James had practically had 'Good Husband Material, Ready to Settle Down' stamped on his forehead.

I don't know what was stamped on my forehead, but it must have been misleading.

He was, in many ways, terribly conventional, and I think, looking back, that he thought *I* was too. I was so quiet and stay-at-home (or stay-at-digs) after Fergal.

On this reflection the car door was suddenly wrenched open, and I would have fallen out if I hadn't still been wearing my seat belt.

'Are you going to sit in the car all night daydreaming about your ex-boyfriend, or are you coming into the house?' demanded James with icy sarcasm.

Oh dear.

Over his shoulder I observed something like a giant

animated white hearth rug leap the area railing and bound off into outer darkness.

'Bess is out, James,' I said helpfully.

Fergal: November, 1998

'ROCCO ROCKS ART WORLD.'

Sun

'Is this the face of New Renaissance Man?'

Sunday Times

The painting is four foot square.
Step back, she swims out at you from the green depths.
Step forward, she vanishes.
The lady vanishes.

The gallery is crowded, thanks to the papers who have finally made the link between Fergal Rocco (infamous) singer/song-writer, and Rocco the painter.

At least most of the art critics have been kind. The gallery's been quietly selling my work since I left the Royal College of Art, so there's none of this 'pop singer thinks he can paint' stuff. That would have really pissed me off.

There are two things I'm serious about: my painting and my music.

There used to be three . . .

'Oh, Fergal, you're so clever,' Nerissa sighs, lifting a face like a cream-skinned, innocent flower. 'All these hidden talents.'

She's small, pretty and curvaceous, and, judging from her

short, select list of former conquests, finds fame in a man a powerful aphrodisiac. Nineteen going on immoral, and about as determined to get what she wants as Scarlett O'Hara. Sounds like her too, when she's trying to get round me, all that fake 'lil' ol' me' stuff.

Daddy's bought her everything she's ever wanted – so far. He'd jib a bit at me, though, even if I were for sale, which I'm not – just available for a short loan.

She's about the same age Tish was last time I saw her . . . Tish.

Swimming out of the green paint like a mermaid; walking hesitantly into the gallery as if summoned by my subconscious.

For a minute I really *do* think she's a figment of my imagination as she pauses in the doorway, gazing around. Her eyes seem dazzled by the lights, then they slide over the painting near me and meet mine, and it's as if we are falling into each other all over again.

Someone coming in behind her touches her elbow to get past, breaking the contact, then she turns on her heel and is gone.

I only realise I've taken a stride forward when Nerissa's weight on my arm brings me up like a sheet anchor.

'What is it? Where are you going?'

I realise I've been holding my breath as though I've been swimming underwater for a long distance. 'Nowhere,' I sigh. 'I'm going nowhere.'

Nerissa's eyes flick from the painted girl behind me back to the empty doorway. She's never going to be acclaimed as Intellectual of the Year, but she has her own sharp instinct to guide her.

'That was the one – the girl in the picture, wasn't it?'
'The girl in the picture doesn't exist.'

The lady vanishes.
Again.
She was the one.

Chapter 3: Painted Out

Oh God! What on earth made me call in to see Fergal's exhibition? And how could I have known he would be there, days after the show opened?

It was pure (or impure) curiosity – but I certainly wouldn't have given in to it if it hadn't been for James's constant snide, jealous little remarks since he found out about Fergal. He even shoved the review of the exhibition under my nose, so it is all *his* fault.

My heart is still going like the clappers even now I'm safely home, and there's a feeling like a hot nest of snakes in the pit of my stomach.

He *saw* me too. (Oh, damn and blast!) All those people, and the minute I walk through the door they part between us like the Red Sea before Moses. Like some invisible ley line . . .

(Wow – that's just given me a great idea for a novel title – *Ley Lines to Love!*)

One glimpse of Fergal, and the pain and hurt feel as fresh as yesterday. But also something else, something I'm ashamed of: lust, I think. All those hot snakes. Very biblical.

It's certainly something never stirred in me by James . . .

When our eyes met it was just like the first time, when I fell on him from a great height – except then he felt it too, I know he did.

This time he simply froze, expressionless, with that old painting he did of me right behind him so that I seemed to be swooping out towards myself over his shoulder.

Like coming face to face with your doppelganger (except that he's given me red hair, for some reason, though at least it means that no one will recognise me).

James goes to art galleries only if I force him to, and I certainly won't be doing that with this exhibition.

Poor old James, steady as a rock. I can't let this ridiculous stirring-up of past emotions affect my feelings for him.

I may be racked with anger, lust, whatever – shaken but not stirred – but it can all be safely bottled up and infused into my next book. *Imprisoned by Love* between hard covers.

Dear old James – he's just as handsome in his own way, and if we have the sort of love that grows steadily rather than bursts instantly into flames and dies quickly, that's better, isn't it? And even if he isn't the world's best lover (which is something I wouldn't have realised, I don't suppose, if I hadn't *had* the world's best lover), that isn't his fault.

Is it?

Perhaps he's a bit stuck in his ways sometimes, and admittedly he's been behaving strangely since he found out about my sordid past, pointing out any mention of Fergal in the press or on TV.

There's been quite a lot since the press suddenly discovered that he's been quietly exhibiting paintings and selling them for years. You'd think they'd have connected Rocco the painter with Rocco the singer by now, but apparently not, until he outed himself, as it were, with this one-man exhibition. I always thought he'd abandoned his painting at the same time he'd abandoned me.

I don't know why James has to make all these snide remarks about groupies and rock stars. Do *I* go on and on about his former girlfriend Vanessa, who went off and married someone else after helpfully presenting him with a replacement companion in the form of Bess the Stupid Bitch, *and* then turned up drunk at our wedding reception, where she peered critically at me through a positively funereal wreath of smoke and remarked blightingly, 'He was always looking for a virgin to sacrifice to his career. I suppose you're the next best thing.'

Cow.

Small, blonde and bubbly cow, now back to working for Drew, Drune and Tibbs as a secretary . . . She's a bit tarty. In my head I call her the secretarty and if I'm not careful, one of these days it'll slip right out.

Mind you, one of the things we originally had in common, James and I, was that we'd both been thrown over by someone else.

We seemed to have a lot in common . . . only lately we seem to have more *not* in common, if you see what I mean.

How *did* I get home from the gallery? I've no recollection of it, so I must have been running on automatic pilot, fired by a need to dive into my dark basement like a scared rabbit into its burrow, and be quiet for a while.

Quiet, that is, except for the muffled thumps and howls as Bess alternately throws herself at the kitchen door and vociferates her desire to be with me, and the deafening silence from Toby the parrot, building himself up for the wild eldritch shrieks my eventual appearance will generate.

I can deal with Toby. He can – and often does – manage to open his cage door and escape, but let me see him fight his way out of two layers of candlewick bedspread, that's all I can say.

As for Bess, her idea of silent sympathy is to stuff her wet, germy black nose into my hand, which breaks up the train of thought, since I then have to go and wash the said hand. A dog's nose is so unsanitary: if they haven't got it stuck up another dog's rear they've got it stuck up their own.

It's odd how the mundane weaves its way in among your thoughts when you've had a shock, isn't it?

Thoughts of Bess, and not having defrosted anything for dinner, and what time James would arrive back from seeing his client in Worcester, and whether the spirit would move the extremely evangelical born-again Christian girl on the third floor to try once more to convert me tonight, all performed a sort of mournful morris dance through my mind, bells muffled.

I could always get Bess to drool the girl to death. Death by Drooling would probably make a saint of her. In stained-glass windows she could be depicted dripping, with the sort of wholesome, earnest, sincere expression that makes you want to take pot shots with an air gun . . .

After a while I became aware of the flashing light on the answerphone, reached over and pressed the playback button.

'Hi, James, this is Vanessa. You forgot your Filofax. I'll just drop it in tomorrow morning in case you need it over the weekend. It's no bother – I'm practically round the corner now. Around ten? Byeee!'

'Find your own husband, you cow!' I told the answerphone, and it bleeped thoughtfully.

'Merry and Little!' boasted a gratingly cheery voice.

'Wrong, buster: big and miserable.'

But the next words made me sit up.

'This is Merry and Little estate agents, regarding your offer for 2 Dower Houses, Nutthill. I'm pleased to say your offer has been accepted. Could you call us back at your earliest convenience?'

The cottage?

My cottage?

Part of my brain began to function cohesively. The vendor had accepted the offer we'd made for the cottage – an offer James insisted we made ludicrously low, in the hope, I'm sure, of having it rejected out of hand.

And I had let him, spineless wet object that I am!

It seems to me that rather than going all out for things I want, I've just been passively letting things happen to me. Except for the novels, of course. I'm determined enough there, though I always imagined myself as a writer living in the country, and now the realisation of that ambition is within my grasp.

A rosy vision of Eden beckons enticingly: James, his interest in gardening rekindled, growing vegetables; myself inside, writing busily by the light of a log fire, and a sleeping baby in an antique wooden cradle at my feet. A clock ticking, distant sounds of cows going to be milked, birdsong . . .

A room of my own, even.

Not just a corner of table to work on in a dark dining room, but a whole room just for me. The little bedroom with the gable window, I think, looking out at the park.

It's time to put the past behind me and go forward, with James, towards the future we wanted.

Only it seems to have taken a hell of a long time to get here.

Lost as I was in this healing Elysian dream the sudden clicking on of the light was a painfully dazzling intrusion.

James stood in the doorway, looking almost as startled as I felt.

'Tish? Why are you sitting in the dark? And why is Bess howling in the kitchen?'

As usual he let his coat and briefcase drop where he stood for the little fairies to come and pick up. They do, too: I must be mad.

'Oh – hello, James. I was just – thinking.' I attempted to contort my features into some semblance of a pleased smile, since it wasn't his fault that he suddenly looked sober and unexciting. I've *had* intoxicating and exciting. Been there, seen it, done it, bought the self-igniting T-shirt.

'Do you need darkness for thinking?' he asked, puzzled,

'You certainly don't need light – all these magnolia walls may suit you, but they make the inside of my head twice as worth looking at as anything in the room other than my patchwork.'

Blink! went his sandy lashes, in that 'I register what she just said but it didn't make sense' way of his.

'Has Bess been out? What have you been doing?'

'Bess hasn't been out yet. Isn't she supposed to be your dog? *You* take her out, it's cold out there.'

'But I haven't got time – I'm meeting Gerry and Dave in an hour.'

'Oh, you aren't going out tonight, James! You've only just got back.'

'It's Friday,' he protested, as though it were some immutable law.

It *is* an immutable law: Friday night out with 'the boys'. Not for very much longer, though! And not for much longer will I have to suffer visitations from James's friend Horrible Howard, who infested the flat for a couple of hours the other day. (He's not really one of 'the boys', more one on his own.)

'The offer we made for the cottage at Nutthill has been accepted, there was a message on the answerphone.'

He looked aghast. 'But—'

'Isn't it *wonderful*, darling? Exactly what we want, and at such a low price. You are clever!' (Only the best butter.)

'Well, I—'

'It means we'll have money to spare for decorating, and sanding the floors and things like that. I'll phone first thing tomorrow and give the go-ahead.'

'Yes – but, Tish, look, let's think before we act hastily.'

'I've thought. We're buying it.'

He was still making stupid objections when he went out, so I spiked his guns by immediately phoning the Rosens, a young couple with whom we've conducted an on-off affair *re* selling our flat for the last year or so. They still hadn't found anything they could afford that they liked better, and were delighted to hear that Thunderbirds were Go.

'Sweetness is so excited!' cooed Charlie. (I kid you not – they have to be the most nauseating couple ever.) 'She'd set her little heart on your flat, the poor darling.'

There was a murmur of assent from Sweetness. I'd met them a couple of times (too many) and Sweetness had informed me she was a model, though since she was a five-foot anorexic I can only assume she modelled children's clothes.

'She's absolutely delighted,' confided Charlie.

Girlish cries of glee could indeed be heard in the background.

'Your flat is such a blank canvas for her – she has so many wonderful ideas of what to do with it. We're both over the moon.'

Excuse *me*, I thought, but this blank canvas just happens to be my home! However, it did look very bland and boring except for my patchwork throws, the baskets of dried autumn leaves, and the giant lime-green papier mâché bowl from Ikea.

James may insist on magnolia paintwork, but I just refuse to have a magnolia life from now on. I've been drifting along, thinking I'm going somewhere, and I've finally found where I want to go and when: *now*.

I must write that book plot down before I forget it: *Ley Lines to Love* . . .

Fergal: December 1998

'Fergal Rocco, pictured with his Frog-eyed Sprite sports car. Although it is his favourite, he also has two Mini Coopers and a Morris Traveller among his rather eccentric collection. He is currently looking for a country house with more room to store them . . .'

Drive! magazine

Mr Rooney was a medium-sized nondescript sort of man, with surprisingly sharp blue eyes behind thick glasses, all important assets to a private eye, I expect. He'd come well recommended, at all events.

'What did you find out?' I asked, as he seated himself and began thumbing through his notebook to the right place, a process that involved a damp finger and more time than I could spare.

'Well, Mr Rocco,' he said finally, 'I did a small check on the lady in question as you requested. She's married to a solicitor called James Drew – younger member of Drew, Drune and Tibbs – lives in a basement flat. No children. She has a part-time position in a university library.'

'A librarian?' I repeated. *Tish*?

'And she writes.'

'That's more like it. Poetry, I suppose,' I said, an errant memory flitting through my mind of long afternoons spent in my flat – me painting, Tish wrestling with a poem, or lying on the rug with her A level books spread around her.

So I was surprised when he said, 'Not poetry, Mr Rocco. She writes romantic novels as Marian Plentifold.'

'Romantic novels?'

'She seems to be doing quite well with them, too.'

'Inspired by her husband, no doubt,' I said, and something in my voice made him cast a doubtful glance my way.

'Mr Drew seems to be a respected member of the firm, which was founded by his grandfather. He's older than Mrs Drew by about ten years. His father lives in South Africa with his second wife and family.'

'So – happily married then?'

Mr Rooney emitted a small dry cough. 'General opinion among the office staff – obtained from one of the secretaries, a Miss Sandra Walker – is that there was some disappointment when he married. Hopes had been cherished, especially by one of the secretaries, who'd been having an on/off affair with him for some considerable time. According to Sandra, Mr Lionel Drew, the senior partner, didn't think she was the right material for a solicitor's wife. She married someone else, but she's now divorced and has recently rejoined the firm. Apparently she's been making a play for Mr Drew again, but apart from the occasion of the office Christmas party he hasn't responded.'

'So what did he get up to at the office party?'

'Having drunk a little too much, he retired with Mrs Vanessa Grey into the small photocopier room.'

'I see.'

'There are thirty-four blurred photocopies in existence.' He passed me a folded sheet. 'I expect in the heat of the moment, as it were, the button . . .'

'Yes.' Well, it was a minor peccadillo, I suppose, compared with what I've got up to in the past. But then, *I'm* not a married man.

'He seems to be able to keep his trousers on generally otherwise, then?'

'There was no hint of anything else,' Mr Rooney said primly, 'and he's been trying to distance himself from Mrs Grey ever since – very hangdog and worried his wife will hear.'

I suppose every dog is allowed one bite. Or one photocopy.

'That was the extent of my brief, sir, but if you'd like me to proceed further?'

'No. No, that's fine, thanks,' I assured him.

'Who was that?' enquired Carlo a few minutes later, passing him in the doorway.

'A private eye. I set him on to find out what became of Tish.'

Carlo has big, liquid dark eyes, and can look indescribably sad-spaniel sometimes. It goes over well with the girls. He looked like that now.

'Tish? After all this time you still care about her?'

'No, it's just my curiosity was stirred by seeing her at the gallery – as I suppose hers was in coming to see the show. I just felt I'd like to know how she was, what she was doing.'

'Yeah, and I'm Titania, Queen of the Faeries,' Carlo said sceptically.

I grinned. 'Well, that's what I thought I wanted, only it seems deep down I wanted to find her miserable, separated, divorced – you know? In need of rescue, anyway. So what does that make me? A complete bastard?'

'Human. Do I take it she's happily married and living in suburbia with two point five children?'

'All except the children. And she's turned into a romantic novelist.'

'Really? So, what now? Drop back into her life like a particularly dangerous spider and invite her to jump into your web?'

'No, of course not. I'm going to keep well clear. And I don't think much of your metaphor, though I might just use it. I've got this idea for a song . . .'

'I wonder if she ever feels the drain of you sucking your inspiration from her over so many years? Did the detective comment on whether she looked like the dried-out husk of a woman?'

'Ha, ha!' I laughed hollowly. 'Now I'm some sort of vampire.'

'Don't you find Nerissa something to write about?' he asked curiously.

'She's a distraction, admittedly, and she's got more sticking power than I expected. But Pop's threatening to cut her allowance off if he sees one more tabloid photo of his daughter with her hands all over me.'

'She'll be moving in with you before you know what hit you.'

'No she won't. You know,' I struck a Garbo-esque pose, 'I often vant to be alooone.'

'Yes, and you also often say you want to settle down and raise a family. Speaking of which, you haven't forgotten it's my engagement party tonight?'

'Of course I haven't forgotten. But I just want to rough out this song while it's running through my head.'

Carlo regarded me sombrely. 'OK, as long as you're not going to stay here brooding. It's pointless. You can never go back.'

'Of course not. "That was another country, and besides, the wench is dead?"' I quoted lightly. 'Something like that.'

Dead to me, anyway.

Chapter 4: Wild in the Country

While I didn't *quite* achieve my dream of having my own country cottage before my thirtieth birthday, we moved in only a couple of weeks later, though early on the very first morning, when I was jerked rudely from the sound sleep of exhaustion by a deep coughing roar like a sick cougar, it struck me that Nutthill, and 2 Dower Houses in particular, was not going to be quite the quiet haven of my imaginings.

Heart pounding, I started up and stared wildly round the strange room, where James and I lay marooned among the flotsam of our possessions.

Dismal February light from the uncurtained window greyly furred every outline, but there was no cougar among them, sick or otherwise, and I'd just snuggled thankfully back into the warm embrace of the duvet when the noise was repeated, this time growing ever louder until it rumbled and snarled itself off into the distance.

Must have been a tractor – or something.

This was not the first thing to strike me about country living, though: the sliding door between the bathroom and the kitchen had already done that, very painfully, in the night. This extra barrier was due to some legal hygiene quibble about the two being next to each other, and while I'm all for germs being kept out, I don't see what notice they'll take of a sliding door.

Once the roaring had died away I could hear birds twittering, a muted cackling, and a faint, faraway foghorn of mooing. The walls between us and our only neighbour are so thick that yesterday, while we were moving in, I heard nothing from her, though her front curtains were twitching like mad – but now there was the slam of a door and shuffling footsteps going in the direction of the back garden.

The muted cackling was suddenly released into a cacophony of squawking, clucking and crowing, accompanied by the rattling of a bucket. Then the slow, dragging footsteps retraced their path, the door slammed, and there was silence . . . apart from the newly released hens, of course, and the cows, and the birds . . .

Yes – the birds.

I'd expected – even looked forward to – waking to the sound of birdsong, but whatever was now performing outside my window was unmelodious in the extreme.

A rook, perhaps?

I'll soon know, because I intend learning how to identify all the wild birds, flowers, trees and little woodland creatures . . . except insects. I've absolutely no intention of being At One with Nature in the form of insects.

Snug again, I tried, half-guiltily, to recapture the dream I'd been having when the cougar woke me (back to the usual dreams again, you see) in which I was lying in a woodland glade with a dark, handsome gamekeeper next to me. His warm, lithe body pressed to mine was entirely na—

'Urgh!'

There was a sudden jerk, a porcine grunt, and a sandy head appeared from a tangle of duvet.

'Get up, James,' I snapped crossly, even though it isn't his fault that he's not tall, dark and romantic, those not being the qualities I married him for, after all. (And I'm determined to concentrate on the qualities I *did* marry him for – those that come under the heading of Good Husband Material, like a length of hard-wearing Dralon.) 'We've a lot to do.'

'Whaa?' He briefly exposed a sliver of bright blue eye. Some women get a 'Good morning, darling' or even a cuddle from their husbands first thing, but James is not a morning person.

Come to think of it, he's not even an *evening* person either lately, but the poor thing has been under a lot of pressure at work, and with the house moving and everything, and he's still sulking about the cottage even though we got it so cheaply that it's a positive investment.

He's also been convinced for the last couple of months that he's been followed by a small, anonymous-looking man, sometimes driving a red hatchback. When I soothingly pointed out that, a) every other car on the road is a red hatchback, b) how could he know it was the same man if he was so nondescript?, and c) who on earth would want to dog his boring footsteps unless it was a member of the Drugs Squad investigating Horrible Howard's cronies anyway? he went all huffy. You'd almost think he *wanted* to be followed.

So I snuggled up against him and murmured, 'Oh, darling – the first morning in our very own little country cottage.'

'Mmph,' he muttered, and turned over.

The bedside coffee-maker not having yet been unpacked, I'd no excuse to lie there any longer. As I gingerly lowered my feet on to the icy bare floor Bess scuttled across with a clatter of claws, heaved herself into my warmly vacated half of the bed and lay staring smugly at me from feminine, long-lashed eyes.

'Bitch!'

Retrieving my clothes from the top of a carton I vowed that this time I would not give in to James about the dog. From tonight she's sleeping in the kitchen. Dogs in bedrooms are unhygienic, and anyway, three is a crowd.

Without a bedroom curtain I felt exposed, even though our cottage only backs on to the park of the local big house and we can't see even a chimney of that from here. I just can't suppress a mental image of Hardyesque farmhands draped along our back fence, all clutching anachronistic binoculars focused on my goose-pimpled and shivering flesh.

It's not easy getting jeans and jumper on under your nightie, but I managed it, then went creaking down the steep stairs that complained at every step – and sometimes for no reason at all – to the bathroom.

As I passed through the kitchen, Toby, whose cage had been dumped unceremoniously on the kitchen table, opened one kaleidoscopic eye and began to scream in a crescendo, 'Hello! HEllo! HELLo! HELLO!'

Horrible bird. Even with both doors shut (and I remembered the sliding one this time) I could still hear him. The whole village could probably hear him.

The bathroom has a certain nightmare fascination: peeling, garish vinyl wallpaper, pebble-effect lino floor, and a plastic shower curtain patterned with bulging-eyed goldfish hanging in tatters from a rail round the bath.

I've already disinfected everything, of course, but it will have to wait its turn for further attention, since it's only one of the many things that need to be done before the cottage looks and feels like the country home of our dreams. Or *my* dreams, now I've realised that James's run more to Bloggs' Tudor-style Executive Country Home standards. But he'll change his mind when he sees how nice the cottage looks when we've finished.

It does look a lot bigger without the previous occupant's furniture. All those chairs . . .

After a quick wash – icy, since we await the arrival of a missing Vital Spark for the gas boiler – I metaphorically rolled up my sleeves and went out to get on with things.

After all, James has got only a few days off work, most grudgingly given by Uncle Lionel, and we intend to sand and seal all the floorboards and emulsion the walls. (I have persuaded James into 'Linen', a soft, warm white, rather than magnolia – a small but important change – and I intend the insidious introduction of colour later.)

Toby paused in mid-scream on seeing me again, clinging to the side of his cage and staring at me with mad eyes. Then he gave the lunatic chuckle he usually saves for those glorious moments when he manages to bite someone and that always remind me of the time he took a chunk out of Fergal's ear.

I hastily threw the old bedspread over the cage and silence, except for the annoyed grinding of a beak, reigned over the kitchen.

The sad, cold, cream-coloured Aga seemed to reproach me from the chimney breast, but I'm not messing about with buckets of dirty, spider-infested coal. I'll wait for my nice new gas cooker, due to arrive today. Perhaps the Aga could be converted to gas later, but in the meantime I could make quite a nice feature of it, with copper pans and bunches of dried flowers hanging from the towel rail.

All was quiet and peaceful again, the way I always thought it would be, and while drinking coffee and eating biscuits I listed the most urgent things that need doing in my little red notebook. It's a diary really, but I'm no Pepys (his poor wife!), and James gave it to me at Christmas in a gift set with woolly hat and gloves.

It seemed a strange combination, but one that must appeal to the Great Last-Minute Present-Buying Male, like scratchy red satin and black lace underwear, which all the recipients immediately exchange in the New Year for something less cystitis-inducing.

At least James knows me better than to present me with any of *that* (though now I come to think of it, when did he ever know me to wear a woolly hat?), and the poor old thing compares favourably with Pepys.

The rattle of the letterbox signalled the surprising arrival of a tabloid newspaper (an error, I presume, since we haven't yet arranged for one to be delivered, and even if we had it would be *The Times*). The whole front cover, I saw to my disgust, was devoted to Fergal Rocco's latest exploits, which seemed at a hasty glance to involve a fountain and several wet nuns.

Fearing it would spark off more sulks from James, I hastily stuffed it into the Aga, sure he would never open it.

After this excitement I roused James out and we got to work.

Later, after a scratch lunch of bread and cheese, he went out to buy some more paint and collect the floor sander, and I made my way into the back garden to look for a dustbin.

I had to force my way through a tangle of waist-high dead weeds, and if the dustbin was out there I must have missed it. But the view of the park over the rickety fence was worth beating a trail for: black and white cows grazed the rolling green turf like Noah's Ark toys. Some fine big trees were dotted about, and the occasional copse. (I think I mean copse ... Thick clumps of trees, anyway.) It all rolled up and down into the distance like best Axminster.

It was too penetratingly cold to stand there for long, so when I got back to the house I was amazed to find a note stuck through the front door saying that the gas men had been and, not getting any answer, left my 'appliance' in the front garden.

Sure enough, my lovely new cooker stood forlornly in the sleety drizzle, inadequately draped in a sheet of plastic like a hippie at a wet festival.

They can barely have tapped at the door once, for Bess barks like a hysterical hyena at the least noise, so as soon as I'd covered the cooker up with a bigger plastic sheet I rang to complain.

My temper was not improved by being passed from person to person until I completely snapped and screamed that they'd better come back immediately and put my oven in, or I would take legal action.

What did I mean by that? What could *I* do against a big utility company?

It certainly did the trick, though, for the man on the other end of the line suddenly capitulated from his previous truculent stance and promised to send someone round to install it that afternoon.

'And tell them to knock properly at the door this time,' I added as a parting shot before slamming the phone down with hands trembling with rage.

My temper was not improved when, noticing the message button was flashing, I listened to Vanessa the secretarty ringing with the news that the big office photocopier was in good working order again.

So what?

Strangely enough, James was cross with *me* for not having stayed in the house all the time to listen for the gas men. But if radar-ears bitch didn't hear them I wouldn't have either, unless I'd been standing on the doorstep.

But I forgave him, because he brought back chocolates, flowers and wine – the latter two a conjunction of gifts usually signifying Interesting Intentions . . .

Only an hour later two rather sheepish workmen returned and installed the stove in the kitchen, mangling the quarry tiles in the process. However, I'm thankful to have a stove that works.

As a bonus and, I suspect, as a spin-off from my telephone tantrum, a completely different man came and brought the missing Vital Spark for the boiler not half an hour later, and after some swearing and awful glugging noises, the central heating system became operational.

Who says it doesn't pay to lose your temper?

The first person to phone us in our new home – unless you count Vanessa's message, duly passed on to James, who looked pleased about it. Sad really! – was, of course, Mother, who has very clingfilm ways.

You know, it was such a wonderful relief when I first discovered that James's father, stepmother and several smaller half-siblings lived in South Africa, and that he didn't seem to care if I ever met them, because Mother is family enough. More than enough.

She was not, she now informed me, deeply hurt by my failure to call her for weeks, and she and Granny were managing very well despite this neglect.

'Don't be such a Wet Nellie, Valerie,' Granny screeched in the background. 'The girl's moving house!'

Mother put her hand over the phone – the wrong end, unfortunately – and hissed: 'She can still phone, can't she?'

'I'm sorry I haven't phoned this week, Mother, but I've been so busy with the move.'

'So far away!' she mourned.

It isn't really, but as neither Mother nor I drive it would make the journey a little difficult.

I was going to miss Granny, though.

'I haven't seen my little girlie for months!'

'Two weeks, actually, Mother – my birthday – and yours, too, just before that.' These celebrations come thick and fast in my family. 'And don't forget we're coming over for tea on Sunday as usual. James wouldn't miss it for the world.'

'Dear boy! Such a good, hard-working husband.'

'Namby-pamby!' shouted Granny, and I grinned. James is too polite and even-tempered for her taste. If he was just as rude back to her she'd like him a lot better, but he just carries on being urbane and forgiving.

And if James had had any romantic inclinations for our second night at the cottage, he was too exhausted to do anything about it by the time we went to bed.

The next few days were a blur of paint smells, sawdust and aching muscles, though I did let James off on the Wednesday afternoon to go to an auction.

The former contents of the cottage were to be sold, and although I'm not keen on second-hand furniture (unless it's antique, which is different) I had liked the big kitchen table and dresser. Our little table from the flat looked way too small and quite wrong.

I gave him strict instructions about not going beyond our agreed limit, or buying anything else, but I knew he had when he returned wearing a sheepish expression.

Since he was accompanied by a Man with a Van bearing the dresser and table I was forced to restrain myself until they'd carried the furniture in, and the last thing to come out of the van was an old chair in carved, golden-coloured wood, with an intricately woven cane seat and back. It was rather nice.

'Where do you want the commode?' enquired the Man.

'Commode?' I echoed blankly.

He flipped the seat up to reveal a white china pot painted with posies. 'See? Save many a long and draughty journey, this will!'

'Nice, isn't it?' James said defiantly, coming back out of the house. 'And only five pounds, too.'

'But it's a *commode*, James. People have been *using* it for years!'

'Oh, don't be squeamish, Tish. I'll clean it up, and we can use the china pot to put a plant in.'

'Over my dead body!'

I paid the Man with a Van, who went off grinning, and returned to the battle, but James was quite determined on the thing and went all stubborn and sulky.

Still, he didn't entirely get his own way, for it is to go into the rickety garden shed until it's cleaned and disinfected. Once that's been done and the lid screwed down I don't suppose anyone will ever know that it was once a commode except me, but I'll always see the ghosts of hundreds of former users sitting there with their germy hands resting on the arms. Hygiene wasn't up to much then.

Although by Sunday we'd broken the back of the work (and possibly our own), we were totally exhausted and the last thing we had the time or inclination for was to drive all the way over to Mother's for tea.

As we were getting ready James, brushing his hair at the mirror, suddenly exclaimed, 'Damn, I've still got paint in my hair – look.'

'Don't be silly, James, that's not paint, it's grey hair,' I informed him after a casual glance.

'*Grey hair!*' He blanched, aghast. 'It can't be. Are there any more? Oh my God – I'm too young to go grey!'

'There's only a sprinkling here and there,' I assured him, amused. 'It'll just make you look distinguished – and look on the bright side, at least you aren't going *bald*.'

He didn't seem very comforted, and I caught him examining his hair in the driving mirror a couple of times on the way to Mother's, which certainly didn't do much for his already limited driving skills.

Fergal: February 1999

'*ROCKER IN UNFROCKED NUN SHOCK!*
Does Rocking Rocco have dirty habits?'

Sun

Our publicity's always been outrageous. That first tour in America, after I found out about Tish seeing someone else, I did everything they said I did and more. We all did. That's probably what sobered me – realising my younger brother Carlo, also in the band, was going to Hell with me.

Hywel, our manager, who also does our publicity, played up on the wild image from the beginning and made it part of our hype, and on the whole we all still go along with it even if in real life we're pretty sober types now.

But sometimes Hywel goes just that little bit too far.

At that photo shoot in Rome he really excelled himself, plumbing whole new depths of taste, and it took him some very fast talking and more than a few lire to get me out of gaol after that set-up with the nuns and the fountain.

Of course, they weren't *real* nuns, and yes, they did have dirty habits. (I'm going to sock the next person who asks me that.) Perhaps that's why they all jumped into the fountain with me.

It was supposed to be a reversal of the wet T-shirt shoot – me in the fountain wearing clinging wet clothes – only I ended up wearing six wet nuns.

Do you know what nuns wear under their habits?

Neither do I, but I know what these street-scrapings were wearing under theirs, and it's what the Scotsman's supposed to wear under his kilt. Nothing.

Ma was a bit upset about it all, and half my Italian relatives weren't speaking to me, so I told Hywel if he didn't cool it down I'd be looking for a new manager.

Ma knows Carlo and I aren't as bad as we're painted, but it doesn't mean she doesn't get hurt by seeing all this sex 'n' drugs 'n' rock 'n' roll publicity about her sons.

The rumour that quickly spread that I'd engaged in sexual misconduct with one (or even several) of the 'nuns' in the fountain particularly upset her, but Hy swore he'd had nothing to do with that.

And just think a minute – was it likely? That water was ball-shrivellingly cold, even if I'd had the urge, which I certainly didn't.

What I've never understood is why sexual misconduct is so irresistible to a lot of women?

You wouldn't believe the mail I got.

Chapter 5: The Bourgeois Bitch

After our brief debauch at Mother's we resumed our back-breaking toil until James returned to work.

'It's all right for some people who can stay at home all day doing nothing,' he grumbled at breakfast, before setting off for his office.

This was, as usual, a full cooked breakfast prepared by Yours Truly. It's amazing really that, if carried out by mere wives, cooking isn't real work, nor is laundering, nor cleaning, nor painting and decorating, gardening, childcare, shopping or . . . well, *ad infinitum*.

Why isn't there a minimum wage for housewives? Or a maximum working week?

So it was with something of a snap that I said, 'I've already told you, James, that after this week spent finishing off jobs around the house I'll be writing every morning and most afternoons, so I will in fact be working harder than ever.'

His expression remained disgruntled, since, in his opinion, a nice safe job should be seamlessly followed at the right time by a nice safe pregnancy.

I decided that this was not the moment to inform him that I forgot to take my pill for a couple of days in the bustle of moving and haven't bothered since. You really never know how these things are going to affect men.

It *could* spur him on (but I don't want to get pregnant too soon) or put him off, so I need to invest in some other form of contraception, though all the alternatives are revolting. But if I conceive I'd like it to be a conscious decision, not a sort of Russian roulette.

I must register with a female doctor locally too. I'm not having some man examining my credentials. What good would that do if I get pregnant? His only experience would be from books and we all know that they inform medical students that women feel no pain between the knees and the navel.

Mal de merde.

'. . . charity work,' James was saying. 'Are you listening?'

'What?' I said hastily, sitting up.

'Noelle doesn't go out to work, but she runs a charity and is a Hospital Visitor.'

'Like being visited by the Angel of Death,' I shuddered, conjuring up the awful vision of the severely tailored wife of one of James's drinking acquaintances (otherwise known as 'friends').

'That isn't funny,' he said stiffly.

'It wasn't meant to be,' I assured him. 'Besides, if you think I should be out there doing charity work, I can tell you now that the only charity I'm interested in right now is the Make Tish Drew a Rich and Famous Author Society.'

'I know you aren't serious. When you find how much time you have on your hands you might like to ring Noelle up for a chat.'

Time on my hands? The man is mad! But then, I've never

managed to convince him that writing is serious work and not some dubious hobby that got out of hand, like the patchwork and leaves, and once he gets an idea into his head it's set there for all time like a fly in amber. Writing is my career.

He says I'm only an author with a little 'a' because I write short romantic novels. I suspect he thinks you have to be a man to be a real Author, an attitude he only allowed to come out of hiding after we were married, when he seemed to think I wouldn't need to write any more.

I discovered I had the knack of writing romances in my last year of university, after comfort-reading so many other people's (the literary equivalent of a Mars bar), where the hero wasn't quite right, and certainly didn't suffer enough before the heroine relented and let him marry her.

Fergal Rocco may have been too much for one woman, but he provides a rich vein to draw on: distilled essence of sex appeal. Just as well James has never read any of my novels! I may be a sort of literary vampire, but Fergal *owes* it to me after treating me like that, and anyway, slapping a series of his clones into shape is rather fun.

My pen name is Marian Plentifold and I've been turning out two novels a year ever since college. James annoyingly refers to the money I make from them as 'your pin money' and doesn't like me to tell anyone about them because of their being romance. But I'd like to tell *everyone*, and anyway, Mother knows, which is the same thing.

Funnily enough, he made no objection when I had poetry published, probably because no one he knew read that sort of magazine. (Sometimes I suspect that only poets and aspiring poets read them: all very incestuous.)

62

He might be a bit jealous, too, since he has trouble signing his name on documents, and reads James Bond. Impure escapism.

He's unfortunately not much of a New Man (more of an Old Man lately) and the only help he really gives me is to do the weekly large shop at the supermarket.

I was glad when he'd gone, so I could savour the feeling of being alone in the cottage, now looking amazingly different – light and spacious, with stripped and sealed mellow golden-yellow floors and freshly painted walls and paintwork. Once all my brightly coloured vases, bowls, patchwork cushions and throws are scattered about, it will look a lot livelier. And a basket or two of leaves, and later some bright rugs . . .

It's surprising how little furniture we have considering we've been married for six years but, as I've mentioned, I hate second-hand furniture, except antique. There's something very antiseptic about the expensive gloss of an antique piece.

My dresser and table are scrubbed and sealed, and I at least know where they came from. The commode has had a Total Baptism by stripping solution, and I don't think many germs could stand up to that. James has now waxed and polished it, and I must admit that it looks very nice in the hall.

I got him to remove the bowl and screw down the lid (he suggested seriously that we keep our gloves in it!) and have told him not to mention to anyone what it was. I neither know nor care what he's done with the bowl, except that it isn't in the house.

Later I measured up our bedroom window and made out

the order for some bright curtains (tough luck, James!), then set out with an ecstatic and panting Bess to look for the postbox. I wouldn't have taken the stupid dog except that she can't be trusted not to Do Something in a fit of pique if left behind.

Strangely enough it was the first time I'd walked into the village. All our journeys have been in the car: the supermarket, the DIY centre, the common to give Bess a run. We know that Nutthill has a village shop, infants' school and bus service, and is quite pretty and peaceful, but that's about it.

I can't imagine why it's called Nutthill, either, because it's pretty flat around here.

It was with an unusually exposed feeling that I closed the door and strode off down to the lane, and, glancing across the jungle of our front garden, I was just in time to see next door's curtains twitch and a pallid, moon-shaped face retreat behind the glass.

Bess immediately squatted in an unladylike posture on the narrow country road and assumed a determined expression, so I got as far upwind as the lead would allow and looked around the countryside with its dotting of picture-postcard cottages.

February is perhaps not a time of year when the countryside looks its best – there's a sort of fuzzy greyness over everything, like mould.

In the distance a small squat church tower appeared over the top of some dark and gloomy trees, which might be yew, but little more of it could be glimpsed even when we walked past the churchyard, because the high wall and trees conspired to shut out any further view.

There were some interestingly ancient-looking monuments set among the short green turf, which I would have explored despite the biting wind if I hadn't had Bess with me.

After some searching I spotted the postbox nestling inside a carefully clipped niche in the holly hedge. Gleaming with newly replenished paint, it looked as small and insubstantial as a bird-box on a post, but I pushed the letter in and walked on to look at the shop.

It was one of a row of little cottages, but the original window had been replaced by larger panes of thick greenish glass, and the displaying space was added to by an overflow of assorted goods over the concrete frontage: boxes of vegetables and sacks of potatoes jostled with hoes, rakes and spades, and a large and garishly painted selection of garden gnomes.

The low doorway was festooned with wellingtons on strings, and it all looked a bit Enid Blyton: by rights there ought to have been an elf behind the counter in a long striped apron.

It was dark and, as I halted on the threshold to let my eyes adjust, a voice from the murk instructed briskly, 'No dogs, please! There's a hook outside to tie it to.'

There was, too, half hidden by the onions and potatoes. A little wooden plaque above it, tastefully executed in poker-work, said 'DOGS', with a languorous hand pointing downwards, rather Michelangelo.

'Sit!' I commanded, tying Bess up. She whined and tried to jump up at me, only the lead was too short and she fell back, puzzled.

When I ventured in, a small, wrinkled woman had

appeared behind the wooden counter. She smiled at me, a smile that stretched from earring to earring, showing teeth set singly and far apart, like rosebushes in gravel, but her eyes were sharp and full of curiosity.

'Sorry about that, dear, but it's the Law, you know – no dogs in shops what sell food. I'm a dog-lover myself. What sort would yours be, then?'

'Borzoi,' I replied, taking in the serried ranks of jars and tins and packets jammed from floor to ceiling all round – not to mention all sorts of things hanging from hooks in the ceiling, and the jars of sherbet dabs and other comestibles on the counter.

'Beg pardon?'

'Borzoi.'

'Oh – *Bourgeois*. One of them foreign breeds. Labradors, I like. Nothing like a nice Labrador.'

'She's "an Aristocrat of the Russian Steppes" actually,' I told her, quoting from *The Borzoi Owner's Handbook*, which I had bought in the hope that it would tell me the stupid creature would acquire brain cells when mature.

'A Bourgeois,' she murmured, committing it to memory. 'What can I get you, now?'

Since I'd been drawn inside by sheer curiosity this momentarily stumped me, but then my eye fell on a basket of tangerines and I said hastily, 'Four pounds of tangerines, please.'

Don't ask me why four pounds – it just came into my head.

'Four pounds it is,' said the woman. 'That'll be a lot of tangerines, then?'

'Yes . . .' A picture from my *Complete Book of Home*

Preserving (a recent book club choice) flashed into my brain. 'I'm making tangerine marmalade.'

'Oh, yes?' she said brightly, measuring out tangerines into a large set of scales and then wrapping them up in a bit of newspaper. 'Right, then – you'll be wanting some sugar, I expect? Granulated do?'

Weakly I agreed, and again when she suggested a lemon (why a lemon?). But when she started hauling out expensive-looking Kilner jars from under the counter I hastily said I had lots of empty jars, which I have. I've been collecting them in anticipation of such country pursuits, though I didn't expect to be doing them quite so soon after moving in!

Disappointed, she thrust the jars back with her foot.

'That's all, I think,' I said firmly, but even so, she managed to add two packets of jar labels and waxed discs to my purchases before I got away, having spent rather more than I intended.

I was aware of her absorbed gaze through the window as, hampered by the insecurely wrapped tangerines, which threatened to break out of their newspaper bundle at any moment, I untied Bess, frantic and drooling.

As I made my way along the lane something compelled me to look back; in the distance a small figure stood planted sturdily in front of the shop, staring after me. I gave a kind of half-wave, then, feeling uncomfortably aware of the eyes boring into my back, hurried on.

Even before I turned into our garden gate I could hear faint shouting, high-pitched and very penetrating, and when I got the front door open it revealed the astonishing range and power of a parrot's lungs to the entire village. Possibly even the whole county.

How amazing it is that something the size of an over-stuffed budgie can produce so much noise! I lost no time in rushing into the living room and throwing a cloth over the cage. Bloody bird.

Silence reigned. Sometimes I wish that I could leave him permanently covered, but that would be cruel, even if he is the parrot equivalent of a mental defective.

He was left to me by an elderly neighbour, since I'd looked after the creature once when she was taken into hospital. He came together with a small legacy, and unfortunately I couldn't keep the money and refuse the parrot.

He was supposed to be very ancient, but years have passed and, though the legacy has gone, Toby hasn't. There's nothing more determined on life than a parrot. He's a dirty bundle of grey feathers touched with crimson, noisy and vicious – and doesn't biting the hand that feeds you *prove* he's stupid?

When I came back from the kitchen with a cup of coffee the shrouded, silent cage seemed to reproach me. I uncovered it and cautiously filled up the seed pot with the Super Expensive Parrot Mix he favours, and he rushed up to it on his horrible crinkled grey feet as if he hadn't eaten for a week. All was peaceful – if you can ignore the ghastly grindings and crackings of a busy beak.

Sipping my coffee, I looked up tangerine preserve in the book. I'd make the marmalade this very afternoon, before James could return and point an accusing finger at the psychedelic citrus spoil-heap.

The recipe seemed straightforward enough, and soon I was stirring the bottom half of my pressure cooker, entirely full of liquid with bobbing bags of pips and peel in it. (The book said a muslin bag, but I haven't got one, so in the end I used the feet of a pair of clean tights.)

Then, just at the stage where the marmalade was going critical, Toby decided to treat the world to his full repertoire: Concerto for One Parrot.

I began to feel a bit fraught. Marmalade-making is a surprisingly messy business, and both I and the kitchen seemed to have become horribly sticky. *And* Bess. Do other dogs eat tangerine peel?

As I thankfully slapped the lid on the last jar the doorbell jangled out its vulgar 'Oranges and Lemons' tune (it's got to go!) and, with a muttered curse, I washed my hands and went to answer it.

On the doorstep was a diminutive old lady, ill-dressed against the cold in a cotton dress covered by a flowered pinny, and with long, draggled grey hair tied up in a skittish ponytail with red-spotted ribbon.

Her pink, dough-like face, set with beady black eyes, had an expression of belligerence that seemed natural to it, and which was not helped by the minor landslide that had reshaped the left side of her face, dragging the eye and corner of her mouth with it.

I've seen more attractive old ladies.

'I've come about The Child!' she hissed accusingly out of the good corner of her mouth.

Chapter 6: The Posy Profligate

'Oh, yes?' I answered politely, in case she should prove to be the local lunatic. 'What child?'

'What child! What child!' uttered the old lady scathingly. 'Why, the one I hear screaming and crying night and morning! Morning and night! Hark at it now, the poor thing! It's a disgrace to neglect a child like that – besides going out and leaving it alone in the house, which I seen you do this morning! If it doesn't stop I'm going to complain to the authorities, and so I warn you!'

My mind swung into gear with an almost audible click as I grasped the truth of the matter, for even now there was a raucous screaming coming from the living room.

And this must be the quiet, sweet little old lady from next door! Hardly what the estate agent led us to expect.

'It isn't a child screaming, it's my parrot,' I explained. 'I'm very sorry if it disturbed you.'

She turned on me a look of indescribable contempt. 'A parrot? The child was screaming and sobbing for its mother!'

'Where's Mummy, then? Toby want biccy!' pleaded the feathered encumbrance from the other room.

'Parrot, indeed!'

There was nothing for it but to invite her in to view the wretched bird, and of course Toby immediately shut up and eyed us with malevolence through the bars, turning his head doubtfully from side to side. Then he scratched the back of his head with one foot, before excreting copiously with a horrid 'glop'.

I averted my eyes. He makes me feel quite ill, sometimes.

'He's not very big to be making all that noise, is he?' said my neighbour, unconvinced. 'I thought parrots were them big, colourful birds with curved beaks.'

'I expect you mean macaws, but he *is* a parrot – a South African Grey – and it's surprising just how much noise he can make. I have to cover him up sometimes, just to get a bit of peace, but I can't cover him up all the time.' (Unfortunately.)

'He's not saying anything now, is he?'

We both stared at the silent cage, and Toby stared inimically back.

'But if you really haven't got a child, I suppose it must be him I heard.'

'I haven't got a child hidden away, and I'm really terribly busy just now . . .'

She gave one last, doubtful look at Toby and turned to go.

'Shut that bloody door!' screeched an eldritch voice, and she whirled round as fast as her game leg allowed her.

Toby blinked innocently at her, then gave a fruity chuckle that slowly worked its way up to an evil cackle.

Backing out, still staring, she fell over the chair in the hall. 'I never would have believed it!' she muttered, hauling herself up by the chair back. Then she looked down and added absently, 'Nice commode!'

71

'We like it,' I replied coldly. How on earth did she know? 'Well, I'm glad to have met you at last, Mrs . . . er?'

'Peach.' And the dumpy figure limped away down the drive without another word.

Feeling even more ruffled than before, I closed the door and discovered a long, thin brown envelope lying by the wall, which must have come earlier. Quite a stiff envelope – probably one of the garage brochures we'd sent for.

Ripping open the end, I pulled out the enclosure – and then, with a sharp 'twang!' something brick red sprang out and hit me sharply on the nose. I recoiled backwards onto the commode and wept overwrought tears.

I soon had myself back under control, of course, and discovered that the flying object was a cardboard garage, ingeniously arranged so that it would fold flat to fit in an envelope. Once opened it sprang back into its garage shape by means of a system of elastic bands. The name of the firm was emblazoned on the side.

I put it back in its envelope and went back to the kitchen to label my marmalade and clean up myself and the kitchen, and when James returned home he found me arranging the jars proudly on the dresser, where they glowed like amber.

'What a terribly domestic scene for a rock star's ex-girlfriend!' he sneered, and I was so cross that I handed him the garage envelope, hoping it would hit *him* on the nose too.

No such luck.

'What a promotional brain wave!' he enthused, playing with it.

'Isn't it just,' I said gloomily. 'But they aren't such good

72

value as the brochure that came last week. That had a garage with a white finish that would blend with the rest of the house.'

'Perhaps. Let's wait for the others to arrive before we decide. There's the phone – bet it's your mother.'

With the usual feeling of reluctance – not to mention weariness and a bit of residual stickiness – I picked up the receiver and heard her babbling even before I got it to my ear.

'. . . and I simply can't go on. I just can't carry on like this! She grows more impossible every day!'

'Hello, Mother. What can't you go on with?'

'Mummy, dear – do call me Mummy! Mother is so ageing. And I'm talking about Granny, of course. I just said. And it's not as if I ever liked her!'

'But you asked her to come and stay with you after Grandpa died!'

'I felt I had to. And she never thought I was good enough for her precious son either. Really, I can't see why I should have to like someone just because they happen to be my mother-in-law.'

'No Moth— Mummy.'

'Of course, you and I have always been more like sisters than mother and daughter, haven't we, darling? But I was such a young mother – little more than a child.'

'Yes, Mummy.' A faint, familiar nausea rose in my throat.

'And I need a rest from Granny. I said to the doctor, "I need a rest." And do you know what he said to me? "Don't we all, Mrs Norwood!" Then I said, "What about admitting her into hospital for a week?" And he said she wasn't ill, and besides, there was a waiting list stretching right into next year! Not that I believe him, of course – he's just afraid that I would refuse to have her back again.'

'And would you?'

The words were out before I could help myself.

'I hope I know my duty,' she replied ambiguously after a short pause. 'If my health was up to it I would, of course, be prepared to have her back whatever the strain.'

'Why don't you ask that nice district nurse for her advice when she comes to give Granny her injection? Mrs Durwin, isn't it?'

There was a snort. 'I did. I said to her, "I can't cope any more – it's too much for me," and do you know what she said? She said, "Have you tried soap on the stairs, Mrs Norwood?" and then she laughed, positively roared, until the tears ran down her face. And not five minutes later I heard her repeating it to Granny! These West Indians have a strange sense of humour.'

'So has Granny – that's why they're such good friends. And it *was* just a joke, after all.'

'I can't see anything funny in it. I'm at my wits' end. I need a holiday. Now, if I could just get her off my hands for a week or two I could come and visit your sweet little cottage, couldn't I? I'm just dying to see it. You have got a spare bedroom for Mummy, haven't you?'

Panic gripped my heart and gave it a squeeze. 'Oh, yes – two – but I'm afraid one is completely bare at the moment, and the other is going to be my office.'

'Ah, yes, for your Writing,' she said reverently. 'How is it coming along, dear?'

'It isn't, there's been too much to do. But at least I can have a room to myself here, and I'm about to start the next book.'

'All my friends are so impressed when I tell them my little girl is a Writer!'

I winced, even though I get this sort of thing all the time. Then I braced myself to ask, 'You haven't been – well – drinking again, have you, Mummy?'

'Oh, there's the doorbell!' she said brightly. 'Must go, darling. I'll let you know if I can arrange anything for Granny so that I can come and take a little holiday with you. Bye-ee!' And the line went dead.

I hadn't heard any doorbell, and I replaced the receiver with a feeling of deep depression. Mother generally has that effect on me.

James was immersed in his paper, oblivious both to me and to Bess, who was staring fixedly at the door. (Normal dogs whine.)

'Bess wants to go out, James!' I said loudly, but he pretended not to hear, so with a sigh of resignation I took the lead off the door.

Standing in the icy darkness of the lane waiting for Bess to perform, I thought: What a day!

'You have remembered that I'll be late home tonight, haven't you?' James said casually about a week later, preparing to dash out after breakfast.

He looked pretty good in his natty dark suiting, but I always think he would look even better striding about the heather in a kilt like his forebears did. He has that sort of look. Rugged. (Which he isn't, really.)

'Remember? How can I remember when you never told me in the first place?' I exclaimed in surprise.

'I told you days ago.'

75

'But what about dinner? Just how late will you be?'

He looked annoyed at my perfectly reasonable question: 'Don't wait for me – I'll pick something up.'

'Eating junk food on the run isn't healthy, James.'

'Then I'll go and eat at Howard's afterwards, and stay overnight!'

'Eating at Howard's is even more of a health hazard. It's all takeaways, and too dark to see what's in them, because the electricity's always cut off.'

'I don't know what you've got against Howard!'

'You mean, apart from him being a drug-crazed, free-loading ageing hippie who's never worked in his life?'

'Howard's all right – we were at school together,' he protested, as if that qualified Howard as a member of the human race. 'Anyway, I've decided: I'm staying there tonight.'

I didn't say anything more, because if I hadn't nagged him about junk food he probably would have come home instead. I don't think I handled that too well.

After James had gone (with overnight bag, though Flit gun would have been more to the point) I went into the front garden and hammered the spike of the rotary dryer with unnecessary force into the rough grass. I can't afford to keep using the tumble dryer all the time, although when you hang clothes out in March it's a toss-up whether they are going to dry or be glazed like mutant frozen prawns.

With the first load of washing churning away I went up to my little writing room. I'd been working on the floorboards, which were not good enough to sand and seal, so I'd painted them cream and stencilled roses round the border.

Piled in one corner were light cardboard boxes filled with some of my varnished leaves. (James says two baskets of dead leaves are more than enough in one sitting room.) I had a brain wave, and soon there were drifts of golden leaves along the walls and piled in the corner opposite the door, where they whispered at the least small draught. It looked lovely, though I am very sure that James will say it is a weird idea. He is so stick-in-the-mud and staid about everything *I* do, yet *he* can go off and stay with Horrible Howard who really *is* weird.

By then the washing was done and, as I was hanging it out, the vicar called: a tall, thin, middle-aged man radiating an air of youthful enthusiasm, and wearing a bright purple T-shirt with his dog collar.

As he shambled up the drive with that strange gait some men have – knees turned out as though they have been kicked in the naughty bits and never recovered – I hastily swivelled the rotating dryer round to hide the more ancient and tatty items of my underwear. (I always put my undies in the middle with the shirts and so on round them, but I'd only just started.) The sooner we've tackled the back garden, so that the washing can be hung in decent obscurity, the better! However, the vicar came charging right round, stretching out his hand while still several yards away and, seizing my cold wet one in his, pumped it energetically up and down.

'Strange lady!' he exclaimed, excitedly.

'Oh!' I said doubtfully, taken aback. But it seemed that this was his name – rather an unfortunate one for a vicar.

'Strangelady! And very pleased indeed to welcome you to our little parish. Ah! washing day, I see!' he added, and bestowed a benevolent smile upon my black bra and shabby knickers. I went red as a beetroot.

'Er . . . come in, er . . . Vicar?' I invited, hastily backing away from the washing and opening the front door. (How *do* you address a vicar?)

Still, I recovered my equilibrium over coffee and biscuits while he admired a mercifully silent Toby, and The Bitch drooled adoringly over his knee, shedding long white hairs. ('*The Borzoi is devoted to one person, showing only aloof attention to others.*') She placed her paw on his knee whenever he stopped patting her, and assumed her best Starving Russian Aristocrat look at the sight of the biscuit tin.

(Yes, she really *is* the lost Anastasia.)

The vicar didn't press me to attend church, which I rather expected, though he left me a copy of the times of the services and said we would be very welcome, and a copy of the parish magazine.

Just as he was about to leave, a florist's van pulled up and delivered a bunch of cream roses. I didn't need to read the card to know that it said: 'To my lovely wife, from James,' since he always does this when he's got his own way or upset me. It makes him feel better.

'Your birthday perhaps? An anniversary?' hinted the vicar. 'What lovely roses!'

'Just a house-warming present,' I muttered ungraciously, seeing him off. And the sort of gesture we couldn't afford now – it must have cost a fortune to have them delivered all the way out here, and why *cream* roses? They would be invisible against all the pale walls.

If he wanted to give me a present I'd have preferred that brass stencil of vine leaves from Homebase.

You know, I used to think James's profligacy with posies romantic, but really it's easy enough to phone up a Teleflorist and read your credit card number. Feeling dissatisfied, I rammed the scentless and useless roses into a cream vase and stood them on a cream table against the cream wall, where they vanished.

Fergal: March 1999

'GONERIL: FAREWELL TO ALL THAT?
Fergal Rocco says his next tour really is his last.'
Trendsetter magazine

Not only me – we're all saying it, though no one outside the band seems to believe we really mean it. We're not breaking up, we'll still record together and do the odd gig, but we all have other parts of our lives we want to develop.

And we're sick to death of touring.

Mike and Col want to spend more time with their families, Carlo's getting married, and I want to concentrate on the song-writing and painting for a while.

Funnily enough, it was seeing Tish so suddenly at the gallery that made me really stop and take stock of myself: where I was going with my life. (*And* where I'd been. When I could remember where I'd been.)

She sparked off a whole new series of songs, too, but that's by the bye.

She still looked good . . .

Can I be the only man who finds fiery-haired, militant Pre-Raphaelite angels a big turn on?

Chapter 7: Drained

James came home next day exhausted: some kind of party had developed at Howard's and he had hardly had a wink's sleep all night.

I refrained from comment with some effort (apart from suggesting he go for a shower, since Howard usually lives in some squalid squat fermenting germs), but later I wished I'd let rip when he looked up from the paper and sneered, 'I see your boyfriend's band are going on a farewell tour of seven countries – he must be getting a bit old for all that touring!'

'He's quite a bit younger than you,' I pointed out. ('Your boyfriend' indeed!) 'And age doesn't seem to hinder the Rolling Stones much, does it?'

'I wouldn't know. I don't have your musical interests.'

He doesn't have any musical interests, but that doesn't excuse the cheap gibe.

'Never mind, James,' I said sweetly, 'at least being tone-deaf makes you able to appreciate that busty blonde country singer with the nasal whine.'

He let the subject drop then, but I wish he'd forget it altogether. I'm getting very tired of all these snide little remarks.

Later I had a sneaky look at the paper, and there was Fergal at an airport, looking jetlagged, unshaven and mildly dangerous. I hope the photographer didn't get too close.

I debated whether to cut the article out in case it set James off again, then thought that perhaps a hole where it had been might be even worse, since he'd think I'd cut it out to keep. Besides, why should I pander to his warped imaginings?

Speaking of warped imaginings, I had a dream last night about Fergal: one of those blush-making ones. I know a wholesome drink of water is what I need, but once you've had champagne, part of you still thirsts for it, even if you know it doesn't agree with you. (And I'm not even getting the water lately!)

Usually I feel guilty the morning after, but this time I was still miffed with James and decided he didn't deserve it. I gave him a kiss of the tight-lipped variety and, after he'd gone, retired to the bathroom with the crossword, where, enthroned and mid-clue, I was startled by the sound of men's voices from the garden right beneath the window.

Hastily flushing the loo I went out only to discover, to my complete embarrassment, three men in fluorescent orange waistcoats staring down into the swirling sewage trap from which they had just removed the lid.

I wanted to curl up and die, but they'd seen me, so I brazened it out with a cheery 'Good morning!'

You could have roasted chestnuts on my cheeks (all of them).

The men wore uniformly blank expressions and after an answering chorus of 'Good morning' resumed their absorbed study.

'Blockage isn't here, then?' said one, after some ten minutes of silent scrutiny.

'No, must be further along,' said Second Workman.

'Yes. Must be somewhere else,' said Third Workman.

'Perhaps it's further along,' said the first. 'Funny – I thought it was sure to be this one.'

'Never mind, Dan – it'll be further along.'

And so on until, after another ten or fifteen minutes of this tediously Beckett-like dialogue, they dropped the manhole cover and went off into Mrs Peach's garden to try their luck.

It took copious amounts of coffee to soothe my shattered nerves, and even then I still wanted to cringe. I kept remembering the workmen's blank faces as they peered into the manhole.

Later, the most stupendous thunderstorm broke over the cottage and the Wrath of God in the form of a bolt of lightning flashed down the telephone cable and blasted the answerphone into little melted pieces.

I don't know what I did to deserve that.

Nothing like this ever happened when we lived in the flat.

Chapter 8: Busted Flush

We've been here a whole month now, and I've settled into a more professional working schedule: mornings for the book, afternoons for the house. How nice it is not to feel guilty about writing instead of doing housework, and being able to do it without James's constant interruptions. I don't know how Jane Austen ever managed to write a word with her family coming and going like yo-yos.

My little room is very inviting, with walls of palest pink (not any kind of cream!) though it needs a touch or two of a strong colour – lime green, possibly. When I'd said as much to James, he'd replied, 'Why spoil a good colour scheme?'

He hasn't seen the leaves yet. Or the patchwork curtains.

My desk is set in the little window, with everything neat and tidy: pile of manuscript on one side of the typewriter, unused paper on the other. James says I should be fully computerised, seeing we're hovering on the brink of a new century, but I'm quite happy as I am: I type my first draft, then rewrite it onto my Amstrad word processor and print it out. I suppose publishers will soon refuse to accept type-written manuscripts, as they do now with handwritten ones, but I bet if your name is something bestselling like Archer, they'd accept them written in lipstick on slices of bread.

The present book is going well. The heroine is about to meet the radio ham who heard her distress call when her yacht was sinking and so saved her life, and he's going to be terribly handsome and exciting, although scarred in some way and hiding himself away because of it, only communicating through his radio messages.

I thought *Love on the Waves* would be a good title, but I don't know if Thripp, Thripp and Jameson, my publishers, will like it. Mr Thripp – Mr H. Thripp – has appalling taste in titles and book covers.

I need to go into town and find some books on radio-hamming in the library, since I don't know enough details for even a sketchy outline. It's very tedious not being able to drive, because the bus service isn't all that good, besides being very expensive and taking ages.

Fergal tried to teach me to drive once, but he got so furious when I inadvertently reversed into a bush and got a *tiny* scratch on his beloved sports car, that I refused to try again. He had a thing about that car; he even got cross just because I rubbed Leather Food all over the seats so they made rude raspberry noises when he was being romantic.

As soon as the cottage is sorted out I'll book lessons. Sometimes I feel quite marooned out here, especially since James has now stayed overnight with Howard *three* times when he's had to work late. When I protested, he said, 'Well, that's the price you have to pay for living in the country!' He always comes back next day with chocolates or flowers, but I'd rather he came home, however late.

Really, I don't know what's got into him since we moved

here. He used to talk about growing vegetables and things like that, but he hasn't even *started* planning the garden yet. I'm not sure he's been *in* the garden! And as for helping me with the house – it takes constant badgering just to get him to put up a simple shelf or two.

He says his work is serious and very exhausting, and he needs to relax in his spare time; but he even neglects taking Bess for her daily walk, which would do him good.

I can only hope he's adjusting and will show some interest in the garden once the weather bucks up a bit. And he still has to drive to the supermarket once a week for the shopping, that's something.

If I need any extras, Mrs Deakin at the village shop is very good, and I don't really mind paying a few pence more to save the trek into town, except that she's very persuasive, so I often come out with stuff I never intended to get.

Some things, like natural soya sauce, bran and lentils, I have to buy at the health food shop in Bedford: I'm determined we'll have a Natural Healthy Diet, whatever James says. I bought some recycled paper loo rolls there, too, which were not a complete success since it took three flushes before it was vanquished. And I didn't like the horrible chewing gum colour, even if they did assure me it was all totally hygienic. But there's no point in saving trees if I'm not saving water.

Mrs Peach now delivers our eggs, which she calls 'free-range'. Certainly the hen-runs are free-range, since they're on little wheels so she can move them up and down her garden.

The very day after complaining about Toby screaming she came toiling up the drive pulling a little cart behind her made up of a set of pram wheels with an ark-like wooden structure on top. She wore a black cloth coat, very shiny, and a strange pointed woollen hat in magenta with ear flaps that tied under the chin and ended in huge pom-poms dangling on her slumping frontage.

When I reluctantly opened the front door she was licking the end of a pencil attached to a little notebook by a piece of greasy black string.

'You'll be wanting eggs, then,' she announced tersely, without looking up. 'How many a week?'

Over her shoulder I could see that the Perambulating Ark was stacked with battered egg boxes. 'I get my eggs in town. Free-range ones.' (Nice, clean ones, in new boxes!)

'That's right – free-range brown is what I've got. Save you the journey. How many?'

I capitulated. 'Half a dozen please.'

'Mondays. Save the boxes.' And off she stumped, her ark bouncing on the rutted pathway, and that was that.

Now every Monday she comes, receives her egg boxes and money, hands me the eggs in return and then, with a muttered, 'Let's see that cunning old bird, then!' she stumps right past me into the living room to stare greedily at Toby. Charmed by her attention he invariably runs through his entire repertoire at top speed (and volume).

Then she silently departs, only betraying her enjoyment by the occasional quiver of her collapsed cheek.

I expect she regales the entire village with the awful things he says when she does the rest of the egg round, and everyone will think he learned them from us.

The library did have a couple of radio ham books, although they didn't look very up to date. But I don't suppose it changes that much, and I also managed to buy a magazine on the subject, which James seized when he got home. Then he lay on the bed immersed in it, though he's never shown any interest in that sort of thing before.

I suppose he just wanted something to read – but why can't he come downstairs and do it? I tried snuggling up next to him on the bed, but apart from pointing out one or two interesting passages he took no notice of me, so I went back downstairs and read one of the books instead.

Bess woke me with hysterical whining at the crack of dawn next morning – she must have eaten something that disagreed with her. James pulled the sheet over his head and pretended not to hear her, as usual.

After she'd got the worst of it over I thought we might as well carry on and have our usual little morning walk up the lane. There's an old, overgrown driveway to the Hall further up, and a rough pathway through the tangle where I can let her off.

But as I was about to release her I saw a hare, and it's true what they say about mad March hares, because this one was bouncing all over the place. Then another joined it, and they had just begun a sparring contest when Bess whined and spoiled it; in a flash they were racing off.

Hare today, and gone tomorrow . . .

For some reason they reminded me of the vicar.

Bess seemed fine later, which was just as well, because I had to go up to Town to meet a literary agent who specialises in romance. Having just reached the end of a three-book contract with Thripp, Thripp and Jameson, I thought it would be interesting to see what an agent could do with my next one.

I got him out of *The Writer's and Artist's Yearbook*, although I must admit that I thought Vivyan Dubois was a woman until I got there. He's quite young, eager, intelligent and gay. I liked him immediately.

He's read some of my books and is sure he can get me a better contract with another publisher, and also that there would be a market for them in America!

He was very enthusiastic, and delighted that I'm such a fast writer. I'm to send various contracts for him to pore over, and *Love on the Waves* when it's completed.

After this I was dying to impart the glad news to someone, so popped in to see Mother and Granny.

Granny was in a grumpy mood. 'If you fell into the Leeds-Liverpool canal you'd come up with a trout in your mouth!' she said dourly.

'Aren't you going to give me any credit for hard work, Granny?'

'I'm sure we're very pleased, dear,' Mother said. 'But when you said you had wonderful news I did hope for a moment . . . I mean, I know how much dear James longs for a son, and I'd love a grandchild.'

'Let the girl alone!' snapped Granny. 'She hasn't been in her new house five seconds.'

'But it isn't a *new* house, is it? There are all sorts of hazards in old houses for tiny tots – and they're always damp and unhygienic. I did so much prefer your last home, darling, because at least you knew that no one else had ever lived in it – or died in it!'

'Thank you for sharing that thought, Mother.'

'Mummy, dear. And I only say these things for your own good, Leticia.'

'Tish,' I corrected. Fair is fair.

I set off early for home, calling off to purchase a bottle of inexpensive champagne on the way, then took a taxi from the station (but that was just because my being out for so long puts such a strain on that daft dog's bladder).

However, she'd been good, and was rewarded with biscuits and a walk to the village pond, where she chased the four Muscovy ducks until one turned and gave her a hard stare. Then she slunk off with her feathery tail between her legs.

James was late home, didn't eat much, and said cheap champagne wasn't worth buying. 'Are we celebrating something?'

'Well, we never really celebrated moving in here, darling, and it's almost April already! And you know I went up to see that agent today?'

He nodded, and I told him all about it, though he couldn't seem to grasp the importance of it to me – to *us* – at all.

'But is it worth it? After all,' he said, sloshing down the despised cheap champagne like lemonade, 'once you've got a baby to look after you won't have time for writing, will you? Now I'm a full partner in the firm we can manage without your writing to bring in any little extras.'

My mouth must have dropped open several inches. It took me a few minutes to get my voice back. 'It's more than a little extra! Besides, I like writing, and I can't just turn it off like a tap. I don't want to turn it off!'

'You say that now, and I know how much your little hobby means to you, but when you have a baby to look after—'

'There might not *be* a baby.'

He smiled indulgently. 'I don't see why not; we're both healthy and I don't think we should leave it much longer. I want my sons while I'm young enough to play football with them.'

'Sons? They may be girls, James! Or *girl* – I don't think I want more than one. And my writing isn't a hobby, so I'm not going to stop doing it!'

(I don't think I *could* stop, actually. It would all dam up inside me until I burst.)

We carried on like this for some time, because James couldn't be persuaded out of his old-fashioned, stupid ideas and just kept repeating, 'Wait and see!' in his solicitor's voice.

He'll wait and see for ever, if he keeps this up.

Although the idea of starting a family once we moved to the country was on the agenda, I find now I've got cold feet. I might not – horror of horrors – enjoy motherhood at all! My biological clock seems to have a very quiet tick.

Thinking back, I felt much the same about pets, before the arrival of Toby and then Bess . . .

And just how much of the childcare would James actually be prepared to do?

Still, I suppose babies sleep a lot, and then I would be able to write. I don't know, I've never so much as held a baby and know nothing of them. They sort of fascinate and frighten me at the same time, so goodness knows what sort of mother I'd make!

Not one like mine, at any rate, who is so unsure of my love that she is incapable of letting go for a second. It's pretty sad, really, that she never realises such tactics have the opposite effect to the desired one.

I wish I had a close female friend I could discuss it all with, only I seem to have lost touch with college friends, and my schoolfriends vanished after I met Fergal – no one else existed for me when he was around.

I do have a good friend I made when I joined the Society for Women Writing Romance (there are two organisations for romantic novelists, and I chose to join the SFWWR because my favourite author, Tina Devino, is a member), but Peggy, who is older than I am, lives in Cornwall, so mostly we chat on the phone.

I used to think James and I thought as one on all the important things and that there was nothing we couldn't discuss, but either he's changed or I was seeing him through rose-tinted spectacles . . . He didn't even seem to be aware of the fundamental chasm opening beneath his feet.

Just to round the evening off nicely, I had a peculiar phone call. Not peculiar in the sense of being obscene: just silence, although I was convinced there was someone at the other end of the line. The caller withheld their number.

The Chinese may have the Year of the Rat, but March is clearly Month of the Lavatory.

The fatal day got off to a good start when James forgot to duck under one of the low beams and gave his head such a crack that he was writhing and swearing for a full five minutes, with Toby listening to every juicy word. One day I expect James will become accustomed to the beams, and react automatically like Pavlov's dogs. A sharp blow to the head early in life has been the making of a lot of men – Augustus John springs to mind – but unfortunately I think James is too old now for it to make any difference.

After he'd finally driven off to work, pale, martyred and armed with a whole bottle of paracetamol, I climbed up onto the toilet lid to try to unjam the shower curtains. This proved not to be a great idea, for there was a sudden cracking noise, and I ended up with one very soaked velvet mule and some nasty scratches round my ankle. This was doubly upsetting for, apart from the shock and pain, I'd have all the embarrassment of trying to order a new toilet lid, and since the bathroom is ancient and old-fashioned I'd have to take the remains of the old one with me to ensure I got the right type. I didn't think I could persuade James to do it for me.

I at last unjammed the shower curtains by fetching the kitchen stool, and was standing under the hot spray in my mules, directing the nozzle at the one that went down the loo, when it occurred to me that I hadn't examined myself for lumps recently, what with one thing and another.

So I did, and when I got to that portion of my anatomy where my left breast becomes my armpit, I wished I hadn't, because I felt something. A lumpy quality. A faint tenderness.

Fighting down panic, I felt again, and it was still there . . . The next thing I knew I was sitting on the side of the bath thinking: this sort of thing can't happen to me!

Then I pulled myself together and tried comparing the other side, and there was *definitely* a difference on the left – although surely not that single hard lump you're supposed to look for? Also, I thought I'd read somewhere that there's no pain with breast cancer until it's terminal?

Of course, once I'd let the dreaded words *terminal* and *breast cancer* into my mind, cold, shaky panic crept in too, even though I kept trying to assure myself that I had just pulled a muscle scraping paint or something. I felt perfectly fit and well, after all.

So there was no need to go to a doctor. If it was – if it didn't go away – I didn't want to know . . .

I didn't *think* I wanted to know.

Only that was stupid. I decided to wait and see.

To add to my misery, the fluffy fake fur trimming on my very expensive mules went all stiff and matted like a dead cat, and I didn't feel the same about them any more.

One week of pure hell followed.

James wouldn't notice if I was dragging myself round on crutches, since he's begun a new craze: ham radio. This also foiled my attempts to distract myself by getting on with my writing, since he's cut several things out of my ham radio magazine, and hogs my library books.

I can only hope it is temporary. It's bad enough him slipping back into the habit of meeting his cronies after work in the pub (which is turning dinner into supper practically every evening, now he has so far to drive home), or risking arrest by consorting with Howard, without him having his nose glued to my books whenever he is here and I want him to do something.

Friday morning, the Lump still being present, I went to see my new doctor, which I should have done at the start.

Not that she – brisk, brusque and overworked – was very reassuring.

She said she didn't think it was anything to worry about, but would refer me to the hospital anyway and I'd be sent an appointment.

This meant another wait, although I knew that if she'd only been *pretending* not to be worried by the lump I'd be sent for instantly.

So the longer the wait, the less important she'd found it . . .
It didn't do anything to stop me worrying.

Fergal: April 1999

'WHO IS BRITAIN'S SEXIEST STAR? YOU VOTE!'
Trendsetter magazine

SEXY?

I'm not about to become celibate for life, but seeing Tish like that . . . well, if you crave champagne, then water is just something you quench your thirst with when you can't get what you really want.

Nerissa – the latest thirst-quencher – is turning tricky now I'm losing interest. I don't have much respect for women prepared to lie down at the drop of a famous name, but I don't want to hurt her.

She was just a girl who threw herself at me, and prettier than most. Only now it turns out she used to go to school with Sara, Carlo's fiancée, and she's using that old friendship so that she always knows where I'm going to be next, trying to turn a casual affair into some kind of relationship, though I made sure she knew right from the start that it would never be that.

Now she's always there. Especially after a gig, when I'm on a high . . .

She always seems to be there whenever the cameras flash, too.

Chapter 9: Nutthill Nutria

Two weeks later I found myself sitting in a dingy hospital corridor on a bursting plastic chair, thinking about Life, the Universe, and other more mundane things such as why James hasn't noticed the state of panic I've been in for a fortnight.

He ought to have guessed something was wrong. But even last night, when I was so nervous and in need of a hug that I wound my arms round his neck and kissed him, he just sort of suffered it, then leaned over and pressed the video play button.

If he ever touched me these days he might have noticed the lumpiness himself . . . which is another thing: since the move our love life seems to have pretty well tailed off. (Not that I ever found the sex riveting, but I do miss the cuddles.) Our only physical contact lately seems to be James's absent-minded goodbye kiss in the mornings – when he isn't staying at Horrible Howard's.

Now I've stopped the pill I'm back to the light, erratic periods I had before I started taking it. But I don't really mind – it's only the unpredictability that's irritating, and I'm sure my body is enjoying a holiday from all those chemicals.

James *did* notice I wasn't eating much lately, but thinks I am on a diet. He said if he wanted a wife who looked like a coat hanger with a dress on it, then he would have married one in the first place! I am certainly not *that* thin – I do go in and out in the appropriate places – but perhaps I have become too thin to attract James any more?

Mind you, if *I* am getting thinner, *he* is putting it on – especially round the waist! And his face seems to be losing some of its craggy good looks under a blur of padding and saggy eye pouches. He always looks worse when he's spent the night at Howard's, so he'd be much better off coming home and getting a good night's sleep when he works late.

He was a bit miffed when I asked him if he'd weighed himself lately, and muttered that at least he wasn't a hollow-eyed drug addict like my former boyfriend, which I ignored as beneath contempt. (I mean, have you *seen* Fergal Rocco? You don't acquire a body like that through a syringe!)

With all this to occupy my mind it was some time before I began to resurface and take stock of my fellow sufferers in the waiting room – and a highly unsavoury lot they appeared to be, too, though it could have been the lighting that made everyone look terminally consumptive.

Some were talking quietly, but no one tried to exchange even a nervous smile with me, and eventually I realised that there was something that made me conspicuous from the other women – the brightness of my clothes.

I was the only one wearing anything brighter than beige, and in fact most of them looked as if they'd gone into mourning for themselves already.

James would like me to wear smart Country Casuals-type

stuff and little suits, and he often says I should go and have my hair styled.

What does he mean, *styled*? It is deep gold, naturally curling, and hasn't been cut since I was old enough to resist Mother, although the curls ravel it up like knitting. Isn't *that* a style?

By the time I was summoned an hour later I looked more Edith Cavell than the nurse, since I'd been too afraid of missing my turn to go to the ladies.

She marched me past two men in white coats with their heads together in earnest discussion and threw open the door of a little cell.

'In here,' she ordered bossily. 'Undress. Top half only.'

With the closing of the door the distant rattle of the hospital was abruptly silenced, and I turned to face the narrow room with its couch, washbasin and sliver of frosted window.

I unfastened the straps of my dungarees, took off my shirt with fingers made clumsy from cold and fear, and laid it on the end of the couch.

There was a white cellular hospital blanket folded there, clean, but marked with old stains, and I felt so cold that I draped it round my shoulders and huddled on the couch. My legs dangled, and one shoe fell off on to the chewing-gum-coloured lino. I let the other one drop too, realised my hand was pressed firmly to my Lump, and snatched it away.

After ten interminable minutes a spotty youth in a white coat breezed in. 'Good morning! I'm a student doctor and, if you don't mind, I'm going to examine you first,' he said cheerfully, without looking up from the grubby clipboard he carried, and the nurse materialised from behind him and deftly removed the blanket without waiting for my reply.

He probed long and deep at both breasts like a child searching for the free plastic toy in a box of cereal. Then he straightened and let his breath go in a long sigh.

I looked fearfully at him.

'Yes, there does seem to be the hint of a lump there, doesn't there? I'll just fetch Mr Thomas, the consultant, now – won't be a tick.'

Five minutes later, while I was still visualising my deathbed scene, a small, rotund, elderly doctor with a polka-dot bow tie and an entourage of obsequious nurses swept in.

He wasted no time on polite preliminaries.

'Lift your arm. Left arm. Higher. So?' He probed once, fingers flat and unpleasantly warm. 'Nothing there. You can go.'

And out he marched again.

Blankly I stared at the student doctor hovering in his wake: 'Does that mean – does it mean I'm all right?'

'Yes, if Mr Thomas says so. You can go.'

I exhaled deeply, and colour, warmth and movement flooded back into the world. 'My God! I thought he was about to say I had six months to live, or something.'

'Not this time!' He hurried off after the Master.

The *relief*!

From not wanting to tell anyone about it I swung round to wanting to tell everyone. James just said I was an idiot, and he could have told me there was nothing wrong with me, but since he hasn't got a medical degree it would hardly have been likely to reassure me.

Secretly, I'm still hardly convinced of my reprieve, and

the lumpy tenderness is still there. But I expect I'll live with it, since it's got to be better than the alternative.

It's put me right off checking my breasts, though. How can you spot one rogue marble in a bagful?

James's reaction was such a damp squib that I cast about for someone else to tell, then I thought: why not phone Peggy? She'd understand.

Peggy Mulvaney, my friend from the Society for Women Writing Romance, writes raunchy books under a variety of unlikely pen names, Desdemona Calthrop being the best known of them.

She says she spends a lot of time on research.

I haven't seen much of her since we moved here because it's so difficult to get to SFWWR meetings as a non-driver, and I do miss her and my other friends in the Society. Being accepted as a member when my first book was published did wonders for my self-confidence. And, of course, since my books keep on selling, I do feel I'm a success at *something*.

Anyway, I phoned her up and we had a lovely long chat. She understood perfectly what I'd been going through, because she had a similar scare in the past and they'd told her it was some sort of benign thing and to ignore it, which she did.

She said now she'd put on so much weight it would take her a week to do a check, but Gerry, her current lover, was always willing to try.

I felt much happier after this, and thought Mother might like to know what I'd been through, too. But there was such a very long wait before the phone was picked up that I'd begun to imagine her lying in a pool of cooking sherry in the kitchen before there was a click and a cautious voice quavered, 'She's not in!'

'Hello, Granny!' I shouted. 'It's me – Tish.'

'Who?'

'Tish – your granddaughter.'

'Why are you shouting?'

'Sorry. Where's Mother?'

'Gone to the off-licence. She said the library, but when did she ever go to a library? She doesn't fool me one bit and never has. I answered the phone.'

'I know, I can hear you. I thought you never answered the phone?'

'Yes, I answered the phone, and I never answer it.'

'Then why did you answer it today, Granny?'

'Don't whisper, I can't hear you. I don't know why I bothered to answer this pesky thing. I won't do it again.'

'Granny, I went to the hospital today because I thought I had cancer, but I haven't. Isn't that wonderful?'

'Cancer? I'm Scorpio. Not that I believe in all that nonsense. Your mother does, more fool her. What have you taken up astrology for? I don't want my charts read!'

'But I haven't taken astrology up!'

'Then why did you want to know my birth-sign?' she demanded reasonably. I gave up.

'How are you, Granny?'

'Your mother is trying to kill me.'

'Kill you? But Granny . . . !'

'Yes, kill me! Brown sherry bottles left on brown carpets and green wine bottles left on green carpets. She does it on purpose. Soon I'll be falling over your mother.'

'She's not that bad, surely?'

'"My daughter-in-law drinks," I told the doctor, and do you know what he said? "Drink is necessary to sustain human life, Mrs Norwood." "That may be," I told him, "but sherry isn't!" Then I told him where to stick his stethoscope, the patronising fool!' She cackled evilly, and I winced.

'Oh dear – you really shouldn't have done that, Granny! And I thought you liked Dr Reevey.'

'Stuffed shirt. Said he wasn't going to come and see *me* again. Good riddance!'

'Oh dear!' I said again, helplessly. 'You'll run out of doctors at this rate.'

'No such luck. They breed like flies, and always looking for old people to experiment on. That's what they do in geriatric wards – experiment on old folk. That's why you never hear of them coming out again,' she said darkly.

'I'm sure you're wrong, Granny!'

'Can't hear a word you're saying. Why does everyone whisper at me? Here's your mother coming – I'm off.'

And the phone went suddenly dead.

It rang again almost immediately and I picked it up thinking it would be Mother – only it was just silence.

'That's funny,' I told James as he walked into the room. 'No answer again.'

'Wrong number.'

'N-no . . . the phone wasn't put down and I'm sure there was someone there. That makes four I've had like that, and they always withhold their number.'

'Oh, come on, Tish: it's just a fault on the line! But if it will make you feel better I'll phone British Telecom from work tomorrow and get it checked out. OK? I mean, it wasn't like it was a rude message, or heavy breathing, or anything, was it?'

'No,' I conceded, feeling silly. 'You're right – I'm getting in a state about nothing.' (Mind you, it wasn't me who was imagining they were being followed everywhere, though he does seem to have dropped that idea pretty quickly.)

I managed a smile, since he was looking a bit impatient, but later, when I was standing in the dark lane with Bess, the silent caller gnawed away in the back of my mind like a rat.

I want everything in my Eden to be perfect – no worms in this apple!

As I quietly let myself back in I heard James exclaim crossly, 'Just stop doing it!'

'Stop doing what?' I demanded indignantly, sticking my head round the door, only to find him holding the telephone receiver.

'I'll speak to you tomorrow,' he added, putting the phone down.

'Sorry – I thought you were speaking to me,' I explained. 'Who was that?'

He stared blankly for a moment, then said: 'Howard.'

'What did he want? You sounded a bit terse with him. Stop doing what?'

'Oh, you know Howard! He's been moonlighting behind some pub bar and the Social Security have found out about it. Told him either to stop working or stop claiming benefit.'

I lost interest (except for a faint surprise that Howard's phone wasn't cut off as usual for non-payment of bills) and went to bed, where I had another of those dreams that made me too guilty to look my husband in the face next day. Fergal featured largely in it.

I am *not* responsible for my subconscious.

* * *

Later, I bethought myself of another person I could tell about the Lump who would enter into the spirit of the thing: Mrs Deakin.

She responded to the sordid details of my examination and reprieve with comfortingly horrific mastectomy tales and harrowing deathbed scenes she'd personally witnessed. All her relatives (female) must be either lopsided or dead. Strangely, I felt much better after this.

Then she imparted the astonishing news that wife-swapping is rife in the village on the new estate! While personally disapproving of such goings-on, as a novelist I feel that I should know all about Life, so I pumped her for more details. (I hope the rumour never reaches James's ears – men are so strange about that sort of thing.)

Running out of wife-swapping stories at last, she changed gear and added a lengthy run of village history for good measure.

'There was a man . . .' she began, resting her elbows and bosom on a stack of sugar bags. Most of her best village stories start like that, or, 'There was a woman . . .'

'There was a man,' she continued now, 'lived at Rose Cottage down the other end of the village. His wife, Polly, she died two year ago. Used to teach leatherwork at the WI – a dab hand at making gloves and bags and such, she were, though a strange sort of woman.

'Her husband, Reg, his hobby were breeding fancy guinea pigs, out in the garden shed. A farm worker, and a steady sort of man, you'd have said. Not over-bright, mind, but good-looking in a big, bullish sort of way.

'Then Polly gets suspicious, like, that he was seeing someone else, so one night she creeps out after him when he goes down to the Dog and Duck.'

'What made her suspicious?'

'Clean underpants! Yes, every day he was demanding a clean pair!'

'R-really?'

'She was right, too – he was carrying on with a London widow what had just moved into one of they bungalows. But, as I say, Polly were a strange sort of woman and she didn't say anything at first, thinking this smart London lady would get tired of her Reg soon, and then she could make him suffer for it at her leisure. Only one day she finds all their Post Office saving taken out, and spots the widow swanning along in a new fur jacket, and put two and two together.'

'How awful! What did she do?'

'Threw his traps out into the street and locked the doors against him. A fine row he made when he come back, too! But after a bit he picks his stuff up and goes over to the widow's.

'Next day he comes back for his guinea pigs, but Polly says she sold 'em. He was fair murderous since they was some fancy kind he'd been breeding for years, but that was that.'

Mrs Deakin paused and shifted her weight so that one bosom slid off the sugar bags into the tray of toffee apples.

'But didn't they ever make it up? What happened?'

'After a bit the widow chucks old Reg out and goes off back where she come from, and he moves in with another farm worker in a tied cottage.

'No one seen much of Polly for a long time – preoccupied, she was. Then one day she startles the whole village by appearing in a new fur jacket. Sumptuous it were, the fur all long and glossy and a mighty unusual colour. I never seen one like it. "What sort of fur would that be, Polly?" I asked her, and she give me a strange smile.

'"Nutthill Nutria," she says.'

'B-but surely . . .?' I stammered, startled.

'Just goes to show what weak, untrustworthy creatures men be.' Mrs Deakin fixed me with her bright eye. 'Even the ones what look most steady, like Reg.'

'Not all, though!' I assured her, smiling, for even if he had the time, James would not have the inclination. If you sliced him up you would probably find 'Good Husband Material' running all the way through, like a stick of rock.

'You have to watch them all the time,' she assured me darkly. 'Even if the spirit's willing, the flesh is weak!'

I thought with sudden unease of Vanessa the secretarty, then firmly pushed the idea out of my head.

Mrs Peach would be very bored if she watched James all the time now he's hooked on amateur radio. All sorts of stuff arrives for him with each post. He must have answered every ad in the ham radio magazine, hence all the holes I found cut out of it. He has also joined a nationwide club for enthusiasts and is going to a meeting of the local branch next week, plus some sort of evening class.

If he is so busy that he can't even take me out for a meal, how come he can fit this in? And what about the cost?

Still, perhaps it will be one of his shorter crazes. Photography lasted ten hellish weeks, during which I couldn't move a muscle without appearing in deathless, glossy colour. And he wanted to take pictures of me without my clothes on! But I soon told him what I thought of *that* and added that if he wanted a hobby he should start getting the garden straight, though I have come to the conclusion that he only enjoyed reading about self-sufficiency. When it comes down to rain and muddy wellies he isn't interested.

But we're well into April, after all, and someone has to make a start, so on the first reasonably clement day I went out, notebook in hand, to draw up a plan of campaign.

The front garden didn't take long:

1) Cut hedge.

2) Dig over front garden and returf, I wrote and then, as I turned for a last look, it struck me that what the front of the cottage cried out for (besides repainting) was:

3) Rose, climbing.

Satisfied, I went round the side of the house, soon to be partially blocked by an Instant Garage, and stood, daunted, on the brink of the waist-deep sea of weeds that formed the back garden, already springing back to life after a short winter's nap.

No trace remained of the path I had once beaten to the fence, and I never had found the dustbin. A new plastic one stood forlornly on the edge of the wilderness like the Last Outpost of Civilisation.

I could hear the cackling of Mrs Peach's hens, and when the breeze changed direction, smell them.

Girding up my wellies, I waded out to the garden shed and found it surprisingly complete apart from one cracked and starred window. Inside was a great quantity of cobwebs, with and without occupants, a heap of broken plant pots, a rake with three prongs missing, a heap of mouldering sacking that might contain anything, and the china pot out of the commode. Clearly a job for James.

106

4) Clear out shed, mend window (James).

5) Scythe weeds. (Or sickle weeds? Is there a difference?)

The long, fenced sides of the garden are covered by small, flattened, spreading trees, forming a dense mass of intertwining branches, which look a bit like the espaliered fruit trees I've seen in books. If so, I only hope they aren't as ancient and dead as they look.

It was all very daunting and would take a lot of hard work and yet more money before it became the pretty cottage garden I longed for.

The contrast with the smooth, well-nibbled turf of the park was revolting.

A few days later, when I popped into Mrs Deakin's to buy dried figs, she told me that the Hall had finally been sold, but she hadn't managed to find out who to. Workmen have moved in, but they're not local, and she's further hampered in her investigations by the main entrance and lodge to the house being on the far side of the park in Lower Nutthill. I suppose I'll soon have to stop exercising Bess in the over-grown rear drive, which is a nuisance.

The house is called Greatness Hall, though Mrs Deakin says it was once Great Ness (which makes even less sense to me).

'Some say it's been bought by one of them foreign opera singers,' suggested Mrs Deakin hopefully. 'That Monster Rat Cavaliero.'

'Greatness Hall would certainly sound like the right address,' I agreed, puzzling over who the Monster Rat could be. Then it clicked: Montserrat Caballé.

'They say the Dower House once stood where your

cottages are, but the lady what lived there went mad and set fire to it and perished,' she was blithely continuing.

'How exciting! The surveyor did say that one or two parts of the house walls looked much older than the rest.'

'A touch of Greatness!' she giggled. 'Now, dear, here's your dried figs. Do your insides a world of good.'

'Actually, I'm making fig and sesame seed chewy bars.'

'Doesn't matter what you do with them – clean your tubes out a treat, these will.'

The fig and sesame bars are tasty, but not only do they have the texture of sand-filled sandwiches, they look like something Bess does when she's constipated. I gave Toby a bit and he loved it, but Bess gulped a dropped piece down and then looked as if she wished she hadn't. I sincerely hope they don't clean *her* tubes out.

James came home even later than usual, smelling of beer, and admitted he'd called in at the Dog and Duck for a quick pint.

'If I'd known, I could have met you there!' I said, hurt.

'I didn't plan it,' he said irritably, 'I just felt like a pint on my way past.' He poked around in his curry, then looked up, frowning. 'I can't seem to find the meat in this.'

'There isn't any – it's vegetable.'

He put the fork down. 'Is there any cheese?'

'Don't you like the curry? I thought it came out rather well. And there's protein in the peas and the brown rice, you know.'

He pushed back his chair. 'Never mind, I'm just not hungry. I had a pasty at the pub – corned beef and onion.'

'There doesn't seem much point in my cooking dinner if you are going to spoil your appetite before you even get home!' I snapped. 'Not that I ever know when you're going to deign to arrive these days anyway.'

'I can't help having to work late,' he said sulkily.

'You can help stopping off at pubs on the way home, though!'

'I need to unwind after a hard day at work. And if there was something more appetising than vegetable curry waiting for me when I got back, it might give me a bit more incentive to rush home.'

'There's nothing wrong with vegetable curry! And how do you expect me to cook anything Cordon Bleu when it's got to be kept hot for hours on end waiting for you to get back? I— Where are you going?'

'Out for another pasty!' he said, and slammed off before I could even mention the fresh fruit salad.

I'd gone to bed (with a headache) before he returned, and when I came down next morning discovered that he'd been brewing beer in the kitchen from a kit he'd bought from the supermarket months ago. From the look of it, he'd been drunk when he got the idea.

The top of the cooker was covered in sticky brown goo, with about a pound of coagulated sugar heaped and drifted all over it. In the sink were two of my best, expensive, cast-iron enamelled casseroles in which the goo had hardened to a tight, brown skin, and coiled around them was the run-out hose of the washing machine, also sticky and revolting.

The place smelled like a brewery and the floor stuck to my slippers.

Why doesn't he ever clear up after himself? And when I complained about the mess he went all hurt, and said he thought I'd be pleased that he was making home brew since I didn't like him going out to drink beer.

'When you used to make beer before, it didn't stop you going out drinking as well!' I said without thinking, and he slammed off to work in a rage, and without kissing me. (And God knows, it's our only physical contact these days!)

It took me ages to clean everything up, and I'd only just finished and was sitting down with a cup of coffee before finally going upstairs to get on with my writing, when Bess decided to empty her entire stomach contents in the middle of the clean kitchen floor.

Mornings never used to be like this.

Later, the inevitable flowers arrived, but this time a spring arrangement of daffodils in a basket, which was actually quite nice.

It probably smelled good too, except that the mingled scents of burned malt and dog vomit had permanently invaded my nostrils.

Fergal: April, 1999

'IN THIS ISSUE: an exclusive pin-up of the man you all voted for –
as you've never seen him before!'

Trendsetter magazine

I've never seen me like that before, either. Where did they dig that one up from? I don't have any hang-ups about nudity, but still!

Maybe it's an old picture from my early days with Goneril? I can't honestly say I remember everything I did during that first tour. Or maybe it's some clever computer mock-up?

And that bear rug's a definite cliché. I'm not surprised it's wearing an anguished expression.

Chapter 10: Just Award

James seems to be making more of an effort to come home earlier, or at least tell me when he is going to be late, so I'm rewarding him with boring old meat and two veg meals with apple crumble and custard to follow, the kind of thing he really likes. I can see I will have to introduce Healthy Eating more gradually.

He's taken me down to the pub a couple of times, too, for Dogfish Tail in a Basket. (Scampi, according to the menu – isn't that illegal?)

But he still needs kick-starting before he helps me do anything to the house, and I began to feel like a prize nag before I got him to agree to spend all of the long Easter weekend sorting out the front garden, but it had to be done.

In a moment of inspiration I hired a mini skip and had it delivered to the front of the house, where it proved a magnet for the whole village.

Although we never saw anyone, for they moved under cover of darkness, strange rubbish appeared in the skip every morning – though, to be fair, all sorts of things disappeared as well, from lengths of rotting timber to clapped-out wellies.

We hacked down the privet to a reasonable, though still

private (privetcy?) height, and cleared the front garden for returfing.

It was back-breaking work, and I have blistered hands, but the difference already is amazing!

James spent hours afterwards soaking himself in the bath, because he said he would be permanently fixed into a Hunchback of Notre-Dame posture otherwise. He used all my expensive pine bath oil *and* all the hot water, leaving me to wait nearly an hour for it to heat up again. I tried pointing this out through the bathroom door, but he had the radio on in there full blast and pretended not to hear me, the selfish pig.

Although I'm glad the garden is taking shape, James turned something that should have been hard work but fun into a kind of penance I forced on him, and even when I assured him that all that would be needed when it was finished was a little lawn-mowing and some hedge-trimming, he didn't seem much cheered, so I haven't dared to mention the back garden.

While he was still marinating there was another of the silent phone calls, too – the first for quite a while. It never seems to be James who answers them.

On the Tuesday morning James was still hobbling about groaning, and said work would be a nice rest after all that digging, but I felt quite invigorated by the fresh air and exercise.

For once the postman managed to deliver the mail before James left for work, and among the one and a half tree's worth of junk mail was my invitation to the SFWWR Awards Dinner in June.

'James, do you want to come to the SFWWR dinner this

year?' I enquired. 'It's at the Fitzroy Tower Hotel, so the food will be wonderful!'

I didn't really think he would want to, because the only time he did come he didn't enjoy the experience of being just Marian Plentifold's husband – a mere appendage – at all.

'You don't need me,' he muttered sulkily, buttering toast. 'You always go off with your friends, talking about books.'

'That's what it's for, James – the chance to get together with other people with the same interests. I haven't even been able to go to the ordinary meetings since we moved here, and I really miss them.'

He leaned over suddenly and twitched the invitation out of my fingers, like a Victorian papa scenting a love letter, and let out an indignant howl as he saw the price (very reasonable, I thought). Then he glanced down at the names of the award winners.

I was *so* hoping he wouldn't do that.

'I see! So that's why you're so keen to go! Fergal Rocco is to receive the award from *Trendsetter* magazine for The Man Their Readers Would Most Like To –!'

He looked up, baffled and suspicious: 'Most Like To *what*?'

'Use your imagination, James!'

'That's disgusting!'

'I think it's funny. And anyway, Fergal won't be there.'

'How do you know that?' he snapped, eyes narrowing suspiciously, and the little warning vein in his temple beginning to twitch.

'Because he's currently on a world tour – you showed me the newspaper article yourself! He's hardly going to fly back from Japan just to receive the *Trendsetter* award!'

114

'Japan? How do you know where he is?'

'For goodness' sake, James! I just said the first country that came into my head! What on earth has got into you?'

It turned out that he'd kept the newspaper article, and unfortunately Goneril *were* due to appear in Japan at about that time. But at least he was reassured that Fergal would not therefore be present to receive his award. (And so was I – I wouldn't have gone if I'd thought there was any possibility of meeting him again.)

James slammed off to work, late and in a filthy temper (but that's his problem), and I phoned Peggy Mulvaney and suggested we sit together at the dinner.

'It's a shame Fergal Rocco isn't going to be there,' she said sadly. 'He's nearly as sexy as Robert Plant.'

'Robert Plant?'

'I forget you're younger than me. He was in Led Zeppelin.'

'Oh, yes – I thought the name rang a bell.'

'Funnily enough, I never fancied him when he was younger – all sideboards and legs like a spider – but now, if he came to the door and pleaded with me to have an affair with him I'd have to give it my serious consideration. About two secondsworth,' Peggy said.

'I used to know him.'

'What, Robert Plant?'

'No, you idiot! Fergal Rocco.'

'You knew him? In the biblical sense?'

'Really, Peggy! I used to go out with him years and years ago, and I'm glad he isn't going to be at the dinner, because he treated me rather badly. I don't really want to meet him again.'

'Well, well! No wonder you write good steamy bits in your

novels. And you might not want to meet him, but you could have introduced him to *me*.'

'James only found out I'd gone out with him recently, and he's been extremely odd about it. Jealous. I think it might have sort of given him a disgust of me, because we're supposed to be trying for a baby and he's hardly come near me since we moved here.'

'He's probably just afraid of the comparison – not measuring up. Anyway, you don't want a baby. Nasty, noisy smelly things.'

'Are they? Don't they sleep a lot?'

'Only other people's.'

'Oh. I thought they spent a lot of time asleep, so I could still write and—'

'Forget it. If you're lucky and they do go to sleep, then you spend the time stuffing vomit-stained clothes into the washer, sterilising bottles, putting toys away, and trying to keep things hygienic. If by any miracle you get more than four hours' sleep in one stretch it's sheer bliss.'

'It sounds awful. Is it really that bad?'

'Worse. But you're young – I dare say you could cope. Just have the one, and resign yourself to doing nothing constructive until it goes to nursery.'

'I'm not that young – turned thirty. I think you've put me off.'

'Sorry. It does have its upsides. I loved mine dearly once they stopped lying there like suet puddings. But I wouldn't have had them if my ex hadn't been so set on it, and *I* hadn't been so set on him.'

'James is set on the idea too – or he was until he found out about my murky past.'

'Sons, that's what it is. He's over forty, isn't he? Next

generation. Probably harbouring outdated ideas about producing little replicas of himself.'

'How did you know?'

'Men are so predictable – that's why it's so easy to write male characters. Press knob A, and you get reaction B, as it were.'

'Is Gerry predictable, too?'

'To a certain extent, but he's arty, which gives him a certain depth. And big – big, bearded and silent – got all his own hair and teeth. That's about all the criteria I can expect these days. But he's quite nice.'

'I think he sounds very attractive.'

'He'll do. Anyway, I'll see you at the hotel, then. I'll catch the night train home, so we'll have time to catch up on things in the hotel bar after dinner.'

'Couldn't you stay overnight too?'

'I don't trust Gerry with the cats for more than a day – they terrorise him.'

When I went out to post my ticket application, Mrs Peach's curtains twitched, but I am getting used to it. Apart from her egg round I rarely see her, because when I'm outdoors she stays in to watch me.

She offered to sell me rabbits 'for the pot', but I declined. A revolting idea, even if they came ready to cook, which I doubt. Ugh!

Fergal: April 1999

'TOKYO BOX OFFICE RUSH
Nine people hurt as tickets for the last Japanese performance by Brit band Goneril go on sale . . .'

Sun

117

Don't ask me how Hywel found out that I intended flying back to Britain halfway through the farewell tour just for one night, but he did. I've never actually caught him lying prone with his ear to the ground, but I have my suspicions.

I didn't tell him why, not wanting my personal affairs instantly composted into publicity material.

He pointed out that if I stayed a second night I could very well receive my *Trendsetter* award in person.

'I could – but then I'd have to leave at some unearthly hour of the morning or I wouldn't get back to Japan in time for the next gig.'

'I can book you a room at the hotel where the award is being made,' he said persuasively, 'and you can get your head down for a couple of hours before the flight back.'

'Thanks a lot. But I'd rather go back the day before and let the worst of the jetlag wear off.'

'But just think of the publicity,' wheedled Hy. 'The award is being presented at the annual dinner of the Society for Women Writing Romance – a photograph or two of you surrounded by the Queens of Romance. Good publicity for them, too – and who knows? You might inspire a bit of purple prose!'

He chuckled and his six chins trembled on a Richter scale of four.

'This Romance Society – are they all in that?'

'Most of them, I think. There's going to be about three hundred people there, and a lot of them will be novelists. Why, you don't know any, do you?'

'I might. Could you get a list of all those who are going to be there, if I promise to receive the award in person?'

'Easy – they'll be so pleased you're going to be there they'd probably give you a romantic novelist too, if you asked.'

'I think you overestimate my charms, but I'll bear it in mind. Just a list will do for the moment.'

She probably won't be there – and if she is I shouldn't go . . . But hell, surely we can meet like civilised people after all this time?

'If you told me the name you were interested in?' suggested Hywel innocently.

I gave him a look.

'The Man Most Readers Would Like To . . .' he sniggered, unabashed.

'Don't get carried away. Most of the readers of *Trendsetter* magazine are about fourteen years old, and if they actually came face to face with me would go bright red and stutter. Sometimes I feel like their father.'

'That's certainly not how they see you. Anyway, arrangements for the tour all right?'

'Yes. I've got a message for you about Japan from Carlo, though. He says if you try a stunt like you did last time we went there, sending a fake Geisha girl and a cameraman up to our suite, he'll personally knock your block off. And I'll help him,' I added.

'Carlo's engagement isn't doing his image much good. At least Mike and Col have been married for so long everyone's forgotten about it. Anyway, they aren't front men. Still, look on the bright side – at least *you* aren't getting married.'

'No, I've no plans to get married. But I'm glad this is the last tour. It's time I settled down.'

'You say that every year.'

'Carlo's saying it now, too, and the other two would like to have a bit of normal family life. I'm not saying we want

119

to break up, just that we'd all like to do occasional gigs rather than tours, and have time for other interests.'

'You don't mean it!'

'This is billed as a farewell tour, remember?'

'Yes, but that—'

'So it can be one,' I cut in ruthlessly.

He shook his head slowly. 'Now, Fergal, I can't believe you really mean that! Why, what would you do if you weren't touring?'

'Paint? Write more songs? Get a life?'

He looked up, suddenly alarmed. 'It's not that little American girl, is it? The one who's been following you around?'

'No, not in the way you mean.'

I haven't met a woman yet I've wanted to live with permanently – except one, but Hywel is the last man for confidences like that.

He was relaxing now, smiling expansively: he doesn't think I mean it. But I do mean it – that's the business that's making me fly back briefly from Japan. I'm not going round and round on tour until I'm some sort of parody of myself. I may be the Bad Boy of Rock still to Hy, but I don't want to degenerate into the Naughty Old Man of Rock, oldest swinger in town.

Chapter 11: Nasty in the Woodshed

Today I took the bus to the garden centre and bought a climbing rose and a length of folding white trellis, then fell in love with a rustic bird table and had to phone James and ask him to collect it on the way back from work. That didn't please him much, although it's only a couple of miles out of his way.

'And it's such a waste of money!'

'It seems to be all right for you to spend pounds on alcohol and expensive magazines and books about ham radio, James,' I pointed out. 'So why shouldn't I buy the odd extravagance?' (If you can call a bird table an extravagance!)

He was still sulking when he came home with the bird table, which I have now set up on the little beaten area at the back of the house where the patio will be one day. I can sit in the breakfast nook (oak – everyone has those heavily varnished pine sets) and watch, identification book in hand, though all I seem to see so far are large, brown, boring birds who bounce around the table as if they have rubber legs.

The morning after this little difference of opinion James went off to work without kissing me goodbye again, but out of absent-mindedness rather than the sulks, I think.

The late-night working sessions seem to be increasing steadily again. I wonder if I should mention to Lionel how tired this makes him? Only I feel James will be cross if I do. And Uncle is not exactly friendly: he has a domed bald head and little beady, disapproving eyes, like a squid.

I did quite a lot of *Love on the Waves*, then came down for a cup of coffee, and it was while sitting drinking this that, out of the corner of my eye, I saw something large, brown and very fast run up to the base of the bird table, pick up dropped food, and dash away again.

Excitedly I tried to remember all the kinds of medium-sized brown animals there are in the British Isles. Otters, of course – but don't they live in rivers and eat fish? And stoats.

I tiptoed out and sprinkled a generous portion of food round the table, then went back in and jammed my nose against the window hopefully.

It returned with extreme speed, so that I barely had time to register the glossy brown body, rounded ears and long, naked tail before it had bounded away again.

A horrid doubt – a premonition of evil – immediately shook me. Surely it couldn't be a *rat*?

No – it must be something else that *looked* a little like a rat but was quite harmless . . .

But some sort of in-built race-memory was shrieking warning bells, and after watching the creature paying repeat visits I was quite, quite sure that it was indeed a rat.

Nothing would have induced me to go out of the back door. *Bubonic plague and the Black Death*, I thought, *nosegays and pustules*.

'James!' I demanded, panicking, down the phone. 'What do rats look like?'

His voice became hushed, as if I had imparted the news of a death in the family.

'Rats? Don't tell me we've got rats in the house?'

'No, but there's one living outside, under the shed, I think.'

'Oh, outside!' His voice became louder, more irritable. 'Is that all? That derelict barn next door must be full of them! Let Bess out – she'll frighten it away. Now, if that's all, I'd better get back to work. I'm extremely busy today, and you really shouldn't ring me unless it's something urgent.'

'But it is urgent!' I wailed, but with a casual 'See you later' he rang off.

Pig.

I slammed the receiver down and remained by it, gnawing my fingernails until I realised I was sitting on the commode and, rising hastily, went off to lure the Canine Defender out into the garden.

She was cosily asleep in front of the gas fire like an expensive Norwegian rug and refused to open her eyes even when I lied and said, 'Walkies!'

Then I rang the Pest Control Officer at the Town Hall, but he wasn't interested either, once he knew that the rat wasn't actually sharing the house with me.

There was only one thing for it – I put my coat on and went to consult Mrs Deakin, our local *Enquire Within Upon Everything*.

'Rats?' she said comfortably, adjusting her shoulder straps with a sharp snapping noise. 'Nesting under that old shed of yours?'

I visualised a whole family of voracious rats emerging from the shed to attack me with large, yellowed teeth, and my voice went high-pitched: 'There must be some way of getting rid of them – it!'

'Terrible lot of trouble we had with rats a year or two back when they was putting the new sewers in. Ran about the village street in droves, they did. Squeaking.'

I clung to the edge of the wooden counter, gazing desperately at her.

'You need Bob and his Jack Russells,' she conceded. 'That'll fetch them out of there!'

'Bob and his Jack Russells?' It sounded like a band or punk group or something.

'Little terriers, Jack Russells are, but something terrible on rats. I'll tell him to bring them along tomorrow morning, shall I?'

'Oh, yes, please!' I agreed gratefully. Rats definitely have priority over writing.

'I'll do that. He'll enjoy it, Bob will. He's not more than ten shillings in the pound, mind, but a good biddable lad, as you'll see.'

'Not more than . . .?'

'Seven months child,' she explained. 'And born on the train to London. Ma Slogget wanted to call him Euston, but her husband, Jack, he put his foot down and said if Robert was good enough for his father, it would be good enough for this 'un. But we call him Bob.'

'Oh . . .' I caught myself up with an almost audible grinding of mental gears. 'Oh, well, thank you, Mrs Deakin! Will I have to give him anything? I mean, what—'

'Give him?' she echoed, surprised at my not automatically knowing the right thing. 'Why, give him some old magazines! Loves magazines, he does. Any sort:

comics, ladies' weeklies, old catalogues. It's the coloured pictures.'

I'd never have thought of that!

'Now, what can I get you?' she enquired.

'Er . . . do you have any *Batman* comics?'

James, informed that the Rat Man Cometh, proved very dubious about the success of the scheme, but was unable to suggest anything else and went to work next day leaving me to await the half-wit's arrival in some trepidation.

But I needn't have worried, for he proved to be a resounding success.

Large, curly-haired, and with vacant blue eyes and bashful smile, he presented himself at the back door in mid-morning.

He had, in fact, arrived some time earlier, but had not announced this except by the noise of a large body crashing about in the back garden, yells of encouragement, and barking.

The blond giant on the doorstep whipped one hand from behind his back and held aloft for my inspection an extremely dead rat. He swung it by the tail.

'I got 'un!' he said cheerfully.

Naturally I recoiled a bit, but recovered enough to congratulate him on the dogs' prowess in hunting. The two small, nondescript canines panted happily at his feet.

He showed no sign of leaving, just stood there amiably smiling at me, as one who had all the time in the world, which I dare say he had.

'Stay there a minute,' I said, remembering, 'I've got something for you.'

I returned with two *Batman* comics and a couple of women's magazines. As I hesitantly offered them to the large, masculine figure ruggedly attired in mired corduroy and the biggest boots I'd ever seen, an expression of child-like pleasure crossed his face, and I was so relieved I also pressed on him a Mars bar and two bone-shaped dog biscuits, so that we parted on a note of great friendliness.

As he turned the corner of the house he was thoughtfully sucking the end of one of the dog biscuits, but I don't suppose it will harm him.

I was looking forward to telling James all about it, but dinner was cooked and drying out in the oven before he called from Howard's to tell me he wasn't coming home that night.

'But why didn't you let me know earlier?' I demanded. 'Dinner's ruined, and I was just wondering whether to ring round the hospitals and find out if you'd had an accident!'

'There's no need to get hysterical! I was with a client until late, and then I thought I might as well phone you from here. Sorry about the dinner. Look, I'll pick up a takeaway tomorrow night to make up, how about that? And a bottle of wine.'

Yes, a bottle of very dry red wine, not the medium white I like. And if I don't drink fast these days, he's finished the bottle before I've savoured a mouthful.

'I wish you'd come home,' I said miserably.

'Don't be silly. I'll see you tomorrow. Good night.'

And he rang off.

I gave Bess the dried-out remains of dinner, feeling too depressed to do anything except go to bed, and I even let her come upstairs with me because I felt so lonely. She kept pushing her nose into my hand and sighing, which tickled.

I fell asleep eventually and dreamed that Fergal Rocco, wearing an entirely unsuitable halo and wings (nothing else) told me just how boring I'd become.

'Get off your horse and drink your milk!' he drawled, and then rode off into a Technicolor sunset to the sound of bells.

Phone bells.

I reached out a groggy hand for the receiver. 'Hello?'

There was a smothered giggle, a sudden rustling, and then the phone was slammed down at the other end with some force, leaving me sitting bolt upright with a wildly beating heart.

Was this the next move by the silent caller? Or someone playing a trick on me? Or just a wrong number?

I hadn't considered before that the silent caller might be a woman . . .

After a bit I gave up trying to sleep again and made some cocoa, and when I finally returned to bed I found Bess snoring there almost as loudly as James, but looking more attractive while doing so.

She obligingly moved over to let me get in when I insisted on it (also unlike James).

Eventually I fell asleep over a book, but as soon as I woke this morning I put in a request for an ex-directory number. I don't care what James thinks, I have had enough strange phone calls.

Anyway, he wasn't there to ask.

Fergal: April 1999

'WORLD TOUR A TOTAL SELL-OUT
Rumours strengthen that it really is Goneril's last.
No more tours, but the band goes on, says Fergal Rocco.'
NME

Believe it.

Chapter 12: Mayday!

I was so fed up with James that I ordered another skip for the weekend and ruthlessly herded him out into the back garden on the Saturday morning, despite his mutterings about some class for hams he meant to go to, and the spasmodic April showers.

He did cheer up for a while after I handed him the new scythe I'd bought: the Grin Reaper.

With some gruelling hard work we roughly denuded the long narrow plot from the espaliered fruit trees on Mrs P.'s side (pear, I think), to the vastly overgrown hawthorn hedge on the other.

James began to show vague signs of enthusiasm, despite a whole new set of calluses and a near miss to an extremity with the scythe, and as soon as the ground was cleared he measured it up with my dressmaking tape (getting it very muddy) and bits of string on sticks. At last he is taking some interest in where the patio and flowerbeds are going!

A herd of cows gazed wistfully at us over the fence all afternoon, drooling, which was rather alarming since the fence is not strong and they were pushing at it. I am not afraid of cows, but they are surprisingly big, and I don't want an eyeball-to-eyeball confrontation across the washing line.

The fence is the responsibility of the owners of the Hall, so now it has been sold I can write asking them to repair it as soon as possible. We still don't know who has bought it, though Mrs Deakin increasingly favours the Monster Rat rumour, and if so, I hope we are not going to get some sort of Pavarotti in the Park festivals in the grounds.

I asked Mrs Deakin what the house was like, and she said it was 'old, like, with them funny turrets' which sounds a bit Victorian Gothic.

After tea James went out in the car to get (ostensibly) some cigars, despite my telling him that Mrs Deakin would have them, even if the Dog and Duck didn't. But he said he didn't like other brands, and the ones in the village shop would be mummified remains that had been there for centuries.

He does Mrs D. an injustice there, because she could sell a Centurion tank to a Quaker, and so does not have any problem in turning her stock over quickly.

James gave cigarettes up after a TV programme frightened him, but now smokes expensive and smelly thin cigars instead, which he says are harmless since he doesn't inhale. (He does.) It's very annoying watching good money go up in smoke.

Anyway, off he went without so much as asking me if I would like to go with him, so I'm pretty sure he's meeting some of his friends – probably Rob or Gerry. It's very hurtful that he doesn't want to take me out now, but more so that he's lying to me.

His friends (apart from Howard) are solicitors and accountants and that sort of thing, and they all drink too much and get red in the face and extremely silly, then drive home in that condition. They're all about James's age, and have long-suffering wives with well-maintained faces, who drive big off-road vehicles (*on* the road – they would get muddy, otherwise). It's amazing how many of them live around here.

He crashed into bed at midnight, distinctly sozzled, and informed me that he'd probably got tetanus from the finger he scratched gardening, and all his friends said it was invariably fatal.

'Good,' I said, turning over and going back to sleep. I thought I heard him say, 'Hard-hearted bitch!' but I think he must have been talking to Bess, because she was lying on the bed in the morning looking smug.

It took ages to prise James out of bed, away from the *Sunday Times* and back to digging over the garden while I cut back the hedge, leaving enough to hide the barn. He kept moaning about his hangover, but I wasn't in the mood to be sympathetic.

Then he suddenly threw down his spade, yelled, 'I've found something!' and held aloft a large whitish object.

I took it from him and gingerly brushed away the earth. 'Ugh! It's some kind of tooth – but what a whopper! I wonder what sort of animal it came from?'

'A mammoth, perhaps? Ancient man probably camped here and tossed the remains of his meals over his shoulder.'

'This garden must have been cultivated in the past, so there can't be much left, even if it was a prehistoric picnic site,' I pointed out dubiously. 'Still, we can keep our eyes open – and perhaps I could ask the people at the museum what sort of tooth it is. I'm going in on Monday anyway.'

Digging for the rest of the day revealed nothing more exciting than a rubbish heap buried at the bottom of the garden, including a complete dismantled outside toilet, so it was with some relief that I watched the skip finally depart, complete with a wooden toilet seat balanced precariously on top of the debris.

As it moved slowly into the road, Mrs Peach flew with amazing speed down her front garden and stopped it, scurrying back up the path a moment later clutching the loo seat to her bosom with an expression of what I can only describe as senile triumph.

God knows what she wants it for! To frame her *Monarch of the Glen* print?

We've decided on a garage – James sent the order off. It was nice to see him engrossed in the brochures, even if his enthusiasm for gardening was so short-lived.

On Monday I importantly confided the mammoth tooth to a world-weary curator at the local museum, and was instantly deflated when he just shoved it into a plastic bag labelled with my name and the date, dumped it into a bulging cardboard box, and told me to come back in a couple of weeks.

While I was out at the museum the washing I left running turned pink. Why is this? There were no red or pink items in there. James is not amused by pink handkerchiefs and underwear, but I think he's jolly lucky to have his own personal laundry maid, even if she is highly inefficient!

Bess and I discovered on our evening walk that the overgrown drive to the Hall has been cleared back, and wrought-iron gates were being fitted. The crumbling wall had been repaired too – and this is just an unimportant rear entrance! I told Mrs Deakin and she became almost incandescent with sheer frustrated curiosity. Someone is spending a fortune on the place.

'Depraved May', as Eliot put it, was a-coming in and, primed by Mrs Deakin, my alarm clock went off just before dawn.

James flatly refused to leave his bed before five in the morning to, as he put it, 'Watch a lot of folksy idiots dancing round a painted stick while standing in wet grass.'

'How can they dance and stand in wet grass simultaneously?' I asked, but he just groaned and turned over.

He has no sense of fun any more.

Come to think of it, he never did have much.

Dressed warmly in a striped Peruvian serape and jeans I set off for the village green, leaving the Bourgeois Bitch behind, despite all her blandishments, since she specialises in doing her business in front of the largest possible audience.

Walking briskly up the road, I felt suddenly very, very happy, and at one with the world and all that, for already the sun was gilding outlines, birds sang, and the sky grew bluer every minute. A rabbit scuttered away – even I can recognise one of those! – and bluebells, buttercups and pinky-red things flowered in the hedgerow.

One or two cars passed me as I walked past Mrs Deakin's shuttered shop, strangely naked without its festoons of goods around the door, and lots more were parked near the green.

The sizeable crowd seemed to be made up of village folk with vaguely familiar faces, and what Mrs D. called 'them Folklore Society people', who were clad in mobcaps and shawls or beards and woolly hats, according to gender.

Moving among this disparate collection were two strangely

dressed figures, one all in green-fronded material from head to toe, giving a loose-leafy kind of effect, and another in top hat and tails and knee-breeches, with odd-coloured stockings and pumps with bows.

A fiddler struck up a few notes and at this signal all the people fell back into a circle around the maypole. On the brightening grass the pole's tall shadow was joined by the elongated wraiths of the leaping, jingling morris men.

There was something essentially right about it all – that this ceremony should take place on this day, year after year, as it always had and always would . . .

Or the first convenient Saturday, anyway.

The Green Man and the top-hatted one circled the crowd and sometimes joined in with the morris men, until they danced a final round with a decided air and walked off, leaving the fiddler alone, refreshing himself from a pint mug. An accordionist joined him, and the crowd made expectant noises.

After a minute or two they struck up some music together, the accordionist shouted something, and suddenly everyone was dancing in a huge circle round the pole, with myself swept up with them.

After a few stumbling minutes I got the hang of it, happy to be a part of it all.

Mrs Deakin, flushed and diminutive, was also whirling through the dance, her flowered pinny discarded in favour of a dress of apple-green and white checks.

After the dancing the morris men gave a final performance, and then a collection taken by the man dressed in green fronds signalled the end of the festivities.

I sat on a dead elm to get my breath back and to watch

the little groups cluster and disperse to their cars, which one by one pulled away from the rutted grass until quiet descended once more on the green.

Then, looking up into the perfect golden morning, I saw a great pink and silver hot-air balloon, delicate as a mirage, drifting with awesome silence across a clear sky.

Closer and closer it drew, becoming steadily larger, but still blending into the dawn until it was near enough to make out the advertisement emblazoned along its sides, ending in the immortal words: 'Lip-smackin' good!'

'Oh hell!' My idyll rudely shattered, I turned my back on the apparition, which was by now low enough to be heard making the raspberry noises and strange abdominal creakings of its kind, and strode briskly homeward.

James was just getting up, not at all interested in May Day celebrations.

'You've been ages, and I've got appointments this morning.'

'But it's Saturday – and this is the first I've heard of it!'

'Well, I'm telling you now, then. Haven't you ironed any shirts? What's for breakfast?'

You'd think I was the housekeeper! It struck me suddenly as absolutely ludicrous that one adult human being (if you could call James adult) should expect another to cook for them, and wash their clothes, and nanny them.

He was now attiring himself in natty grey suiting and striped tie (all pressed and ready for him) and had nothing more strenuous to do than sit and have his breakfast brought to him, before driving off to Important Appointments, leaving a greasy pile of washing-up behind him and his dirty clothes on the bedroom floor.

Something suddenly snapped in my head. 'Oh, get your

own damned breakfast for once!' I yelled at him, and slammed off to my writing room.

I knew he wouldn't cook himself anything, and after a bit there was a tentative tapping on my door.

'Tish? I'm going now. I hope you feel better when I get home.'

I flung open the door. 'Better? Why should I feel better? There's nothing wrong with me – I'm just fed up with doing everything around here! You expect to be waited on hand and foot.'

He looked as taken aback as if his teddy bear had bitten him. 'You don't think I want to work on a Saturday, do you?' he demanded, aggrieved. 'I have to do these things to bring in enough money – which *you* don't seem to have any trouble spending.'

'I work too, you know: not only writing but all the housework, the gardening, the cooking, the laundry . . . not to mention looking after Bess, who's supposed to be your dog!'

'But it isn't real work – you can do it any time. *I* have a very responsible job. And I don't know what you're fussing about – most women would be glad to stay at home doing nothing. You've got it made.'

'I dare say you think so. But my writing is my profession, James – not a hobby! Why should I be your housekeeper while you continue to do nothing around the house? You used to help me before I left the library.'

'Let's not argue, Tish. After all, I bought you your country cottage, didn't I?'

'*We* bought a country cottage with *our* money. You wanted it as much as I did.'

'It doesn't matter much to me where we live, except that

135

you seem to have been ratty ever since we moved here. You never used to be like this. I can't think what's got into you!'

My lips ached to say, 'Well, it certainly hasn't been you for the last couple of months, James!' but I just managed to prevent them from uttering such a vulgarity.

'You never used to be like this either,' I said instead, my newly opened eyes seeing a selfish, complacent stranger.

'Hell, I'm going to be late – for God's sake have some aspirin and lie down. You're overwrought.'

The door slammed and he was off.

He obviously thinks it's that time of the month and all this is a little emotional outpouring resulting therefrom. (*A Womb with a View*?) I blame the Sunday Supplements.

And it isn't that time of the month, because now I'm off the pill there doesn't seem to *be* any particular time; my periods have reverted to being totally erratic.

Why do matrimonial arguments always vanish down the same holes, like the rabbit in *Alice*? It's hardly worth starting one when you know where it's going.

I made a pot of coffee and was just eating my muesli when Bess greeted the arrival of the postman with hyena-like rapture.

Ten minutes later I was toasting myself in cooking sherry. I'm going to be sold in America! Lovecall Hot Editions want *everything* of mine they can get. It looks like my earnings may be overtaking James's at any second and he can't call it pin money then, can he?

Flown with this excitement I put in a good morning's work on the novel, then started on the bathroom. I'm going to enclose the bath in tongue-and-groove pine, which looks quite easy in the book.

When I prised the plastic side off the bath, woodlice like tiny armadillos scattered in all directions, and it took me ages to scoop them up in the dustpan, because they kept curling into tiny balls and rolling away.

James arrived back very late and very drunk, so he wasn't working all day. Goodness knows where he'd been, but I wish he wouldn't drink and drive.

So I never did get round to telling him about the letter from the agent. Or about Vivyan's other suggestion that, since the editor of Lovecall was going to be the speaker at the SFWWR dinner and would like to meet me for a working breakfast next morning (apparently an American concept), before flying back, he thought I might as well book a room overnight at the hotel.

This is all very exciting – and scary. But Vivyan will be at the dinner and the breakfast too to support me.

James is bound to disapprove, but I don't care – I'm going!

What do you wear to a working breakfast? Pinstriped pyjamas?

Tongue-and-groove pining is more difficult than I thought, and James is very critical; but what does it matter if the framework is nailed together? No one is going to see it, it'll be covered in pine.

There's only one pattern of shower curtain material with toning roller blind and wallpaper that I really like, and it's very expensive. But at least it's a small bathroom. I've hung the shower curtains already, having had more than enough of the bulgy-eyed fish.

James found the brochure and moaned about the price, but I pointed out to him that it actually costs much the same as he spends on alcohol in a month, and would give me infinitely more pleasure.

Then I suggested that he cut out the middle man and pour the wine straight down the toilet; or better still, just flush the money he'd have spent on it down the toilet. He said he was profoundly disgusted at my crudity and sarcasm.

He was very disappointed when the museum said his mammoth tooth was only a horse tooth, too, and of no interest. It interested *me*, though. Just imagine, a horse can carry a full set of those and still hold its head up! But why did it die in my garden? I hope we don't find the rest.

One morning I arrived home from a shopping expedition via the chancy and erratic local bus service, to find the front garden looking as if several cement mixers had rolled all over it, and there was no sign of the workmen who were supposed to be laying the garage foundations.

The garage base itself seemed to be nearly finished but the cement mixer was still in business, so I followed the sound of voices out to the back garden and found them laying a second garage base near the shed.

They were deeply aggrieved when I demanded to know what on earth they were doing and showed me their instructions, which allowed for a second, smaller foundation to be laid.

A sudden, horrible suspicion entered my head as I recalled how carefully James had measured this area, and I left the workmen standing defensively round the wet concrete while I went to phone him.

My suspicions were justified – he'd ordered another building without telling me! He knows how I hate hire-purchase, and paying for the garage will be bad enough.

'What on earth do you want another shed for?' I demanded

angrily. 'Why didn't you tell me what you were doing before you signed for it?'

'It was when I was filling in the form for the garage – the catalogue had just what I needed, so I added it. The payments aren't increased by much and anyway, I'm the one who goes out to work, so I'm entitled to spend a bit of money how I like!'

'I earn money too, James, but I would never have spent so much without consulting you first! What do you want it for, anyway? There's nothing wrong with the shed.'

'It's a Hobby Home – like a detached room. I'm going to run electricity across to it.'

'What for? Your only hobby lately seems to be drinking too much and staying out late. Unless you've decided to do it in solitary confinement?'

'I can't discuss it now, I've got a client coming in,' he said stiffly, and rang off.

Twelve thirty. Some client!

Later, when I looked out of the kitchen window, there was only a new stretch of whitish concrete, some bits of wood and the sound of the cement mixer being driven away.

James arrived home early, ready for battle. Before he came in he went and looked at his expensive foundations – the hut will cost nearly as much as the garage!

During the ensuing argument I had the deadly feeling that we'd said the same things before: James insisting he earned his money and was entitled to spend some of it on himself, and me pointing out that I earned money too, and I didn't go and spend large sums without consulting him, etc.

'What about clothes?' he demanded. 'You're always buying clothes! And it's not as if they were really nice ones – always jeans. You've never worn that suit I bought you for your birthday.'

'I dress to be comfortable, not to please you.'

'Obviously!'

'I'd look ridiculous wearing smart clothes in the country, and all I've bought since we came here is one pair of jeans, which I *needed*.' (And a new outfit for the SFWWR dinner, but he doesn't know about that yet.) 'What about your new suit?'

'Necessary for work.'

'And your silk ties?'

'I have to look smart, you know.'

'Your clients wouldn't turn away in disgust if you weren't wearing a silk tie. Anyway, all this is beside the point: what do you want a Hobby Home for?'

'To set up my amateur radio equipment in,' he said sulkily.

'What!' I screamed. 'You mean you're going to be a ham? But, James, we can't really afford a Hobby Home, and we certainly can't afford all that expensive equipment.'

'Don't exaggerate. Anybody would think we were on the breadline, the way you talk about money. We'll hardly notice the monthly payments for the garage and workshop, and I've arranged a bank loan for the radio gear – the order's already been sent off.'

I sat down feeling limp: this was going to set us back a small fortune. And a bank loan – without telling me!

'But why?' I asked miserably. 'Why didn't you talk it over with me first?'

'I knew you'd make a fuss, and it has nothing to do with you really.'

'Nothing to do with me? So if I'd gone out one day and bought a computer, that would be none of your business?'

'You don't need one – it's time you were giving up all this scribbling and having a baby. Derek Wyman's wife is pregnant.'

I might have pointed out that unless I became pregnant by Spontaneous Combustion there wasn't much hope of that these days anyway, but decided it was too low a blow.

'James, how often do I have to tell you before it gets through your thick skull? My "scribbling" is earning a lot of money, and this new contract my agent has got for me means I'll end up earning more than you do!'

That did it. I don't know where he gets such old-fashioned ideas from, but the thought was like a red rag to a bull. Most men would be overjoyed if their wives earned lots of money, but not James.

In the end I said I was going to keep all my money in a separate bank account, except for a proportion which I would pay into our joint account, and he slammed out of the house saying I could do what the hell I liked.

Oh dear! We used to be happy before we moved here . . . and I don't think *I* have changed all that much – or have I? I'm not sure James has, either. I'm beginning to think he always had these ideas entrenched somewhere, but he's only revealing them now.

I couldn't help crying, I felt so unhappy.

Fergal: May 1999

'Fergal Rocco pictured with his constant companion, Miss Nerissa Bright, daughter of American Computer Tycoon, Curtis Bright . . .'

Exposé magazine

It made Nerissa sound like a guide dog, but she seemed quite pleased with it, as she seems pleased with any article that couples our names together, as if they could help to build a relationship like so many bricks.

My little limpet.

She has amazing sticking power. Thought she'd have moved on to pastures new by now, especially since I've refused to be flaunted round the 'In' circle, like some captured tiger.

And how do you define companion? Hanger-on?

I'm sort of used to having her around, and she has done one useful thing. When she knew I was looking for a house she got details of everything within easy distance of her father's place at Lavenham, and among them was a real gem . . . the house I've always dreamed of.

As to Nerissa, I don't want to be unkind. I think she'll find someone else while we are away on tour. I really hope so. It's not fair to her either – what she can give me I can find anywhere.

(And often do.)

Chapter 13: And the Beet Goes on

For three days we exchanged the minimum of communications, and I opened a separate bank account. Actually, I'd always left the paperwork and finances to James, so it took a bit of working out, but it was quite interesting seeing where the money had been going, and I concluded that James was an expensive luxury.

Then, with the hurt and puzzled air of one who is wrongly accused but willing to be friends, he started making overtures of reconciliation, though chocolates and flowers don't go a long way to healing that sort of breach of trust. Like putting a Disney sticking plaster over a broken leg.

It's odd – I don't think James is changing, just showing his true colours, and they're colours I don't like (and I'm not talking magnolia here).

We keep off tricky subjects, and I'm not closing my separate account if he is going to do sneaky things. It's probably a good idea anyway, now I'm hoping to earn so much more. I'll just go on paying my half of everything (except the Hobby Home and the bank loan payments for the ham equipment) out of it.

In some small retaliation (petty but satisfying) I finally

informed him that I would be staying the night at the hotel after the Awards dinner, which nearly scuttled the reconciliation, but I don't care.

Mother has been snively on the subject of 'when will I ever be a grandmother?'. She says all her friends have grandchildren, but I didn't think she had any friends outside Transylvania. James must have put her up to it, as he tends to phone her from the office when displeased with me (another sneaky habit).

Since I'm now convinced that the baby would be left entirely to me to look after, as well as everything else, and provide another excuse for James to leave me behind when he goes out, it doesn't inspire me to reproduce.

Mother also revealed her hopes of having Granny declared senile or something, so that she can get at her cash and jewellery, using some of it to incarcerate her in an old people's home . . . Power of attorney, that's it.

Of the two, Granny is definitely the saner and more competent, so Mother's scheme is clearly doomed to fail. Even Granny's diabetes doesn't noticeably impede her, and there's really nothing wrong with her mind – it was always like that.

Her only mistake was moving in to look after Mother after Grandpa died, out of some grim Northern sense of duty.

I wonder if I could get power of attorney over James.

The Hobby Home and garage were erected in a day, and he's already run electricity across to his palatial shed, bought curtains and even ordered carpet. I'm saying nothing any more about the expense; if he gets into difficulties, it's not my affair any longer.

He then graciously informed me that he's going to have an enormous aerial fixed to the house, which will look dreadful, and surely they won't allow such an eyesore in a nice village like this? But he still has to pass some sort of exam or test before they let him loose on the airwaves, so I can only hope he fails dismally and takes up something more reasonable, like stamp collecting.

On my next duty visit to Deepest Suburbia I entertained Granny with an account of the May Day revels, which sent her off into a spate of reminiscence, her accent even more infused with Yorkshire.

'May Day? I were Keighley Queen of the May. My Bernard were passing through and he said to me: "What's a pretty lass like you doing in a daft hat like that?" Only he put it a bit different, being posh and from down South.'

Mother rolled her eyes up and went out to put the kettle on.

'Was it love at first sight, Granny?'

'Aye, but I made him wait!' She heaved a sigh. 'Well, we had a good life even if we did just have the one child, and that without the backbone of a gnat!'

'Dad wasn't—'

'Your father was a soft, easy-going fool – took after Bernard's side more than mine. Not that he wasn't a loving, good-hearted soul, mind, and a good son, though Bernard was disappointed that he didn't want to go into the business. But there – he was happy enough in his bank.'

'Who do I take after?' I asked curiously.

'Lord knows! And your father had the mumps bad right after he got married, so we didn't think . . .'

She tailed off into silence and I thought that was it until

she suddenly added, 'I said to Valerie when I saw you: "If that's yours it's a changeling – there's no red hair in my family!"'

'I haven't got red hair! It's deep gold.'

'Then that Vanessa Redgrave was blonde, too. Valerie was light-haired, mind – real pale blonde.'

'She still is,' I said, as Mother reappeared with a tray.

'Comes out of a bottle.'

'What does?' enquired Mother brightly.

'Never mind,' I said quickly. 'Did you make these lovely scones?'

Easily distracted, she preened. 'Yes, I made lots because Dr Reevey came to call earlier.'

'You aren't ill, are you?'

'Oh, no!' She smiled smugly. 'He's not *my* doctor. That would be quite unsuitable! It was Granny who used to be his patient. This was just a little social visit. We were arranging to go out line dancing.'

'Line dancing?'

I looked at her with more attention than usual. She's a little fluffy blonde with big blue eyes and is pretty well preserved for forty-nine. But her rather fairy-off-the-tree appearance hides a will of iron and a rigid adherence to respectability (whatever that is). She's always had one or two devoted admirers, usually elderly. Dr Reevey isn't much older than she is. I noticed she was looking a bit different – heavier on the eye make-up, for one thing.

'*I* went out!' Granny declared rather thickly through a mouthful of scone. 'Didn't want to play gooseberry, so I called a taxi and went to visit that old rogue Herries. Calls himself a solicitor!'

'But didn't Mr Herries retire ages ago?'

'Climbs out of his crypt especially for me!'

'So that's where you went!' Mother exclaimed, and added more casually as she poured tea into delicate, fluted cups, 'What did you need to see him about?'

I took the cup of horridly pallid coffee she'd made me.

'Wouldn't you like to know!' rejoined Granny crudely.

'Not really; I'm sure I've no interest in your affairs.' Mother tossed her head. 'I only thought that I could have taken a message for you if I'd known you wanted to tell him something, and saved you a journey.'

'Enjoyed the visit, it did me good. I'm in better shape than he is, diabetes or no!'

I drank the coffee quickly, to get it over with, then ate the last bit of my scone, which was excellent.

If there's one thing Mother is good at, other than interfering, it's baking.

'I'd better be off, or I'll miss the train. I really must find a driving instructor. I keep saying I will, and then not getting round to it.'

'Can't dear James come and collect you? It's ages since I saw him.'

'No, he's gone to see a client in Bradford.'

'Ah, the Jewel of the North!' said Granny cheerily, and Mother gave her a dirty look. She's never been further north than Luton.

As she was letting me out I remembered what Granny had been saying earlier, and asked, 'Who do I get my shade of hair from, Mother, and my grey eyes? Is it your side of the family?'

For a moment her baby-blue eyes were startled, then with

a light laugh she said, 'Oh, I expect so. My mother died when I was a small child, but I think she had your shade of hair.'

'You never talk about when you were growing up or say much about your sister. Did she look like me?'

'Really, Leticia darling! If you want to delve into the family history we can't do it on the doorstep. And Glenda looked very much like me, as I recall – though, after all, it's over twenty years since I last saw her.'

You don't forget what your only sister looks like, though, surely? However, poor Glenda blotted her copy-book at sixteen by running off with someone else's husband, and Mother is always reluctant to acknowledge her existence.

I was about to ask her if she had a photograph of Glenda, but seeing she was looking ruffled I left the subject and, pressing a kiss on the powdered surface of her cheek (like kissing a floury bap, only scented) set off on the circuitous route home.

Definitely driving lessons.

James spent the weekend making his shed into a luxury home from home, while I papered the bathroom, having finished the tongue-and-grooving. (Wouldn't Tongue and Grooving make a good name for a pop group?)

Then, on the Monday, something strange and wondrous happened that cheered me up no end – I discovered that Mrs Peach is a sun worshipper!

I was looking idly out of the bedroom window, noting that since pruning the pear trees I can partly see in to the next-door garden. It stretches further than ours and has an orchard at the bottom as well as all the peripatetic hen coops.

There was the slam of a door and Mrs Peach appeared,

back from her egg round, in her woollen hat and sombre cloth coat.

Wandering slowly down the garden on her stumpy little legs she first tugged off her coat and threw it over the nearest bush, which happened to be lavender, kicked off her shoes, and then kept on toddling down the pathway shedding items of clothing as she went.

When I lost sight of her she was clad only in voluminous shiny pink bloomers, and was tugging at the fastenings of a monumental bra as she headed for the orchard.

I sank down on the bed in amazement, hardly able to believe my own eyes. But when I looked out again the clothes were still scattered on the bushes like a gypsy washday, and the extra-wide-fitting glacé leather shoes lay abandoned in the grass.

Of the elderly dryad there was no sign.

Fancy Mrs P. communing with Nature in the raw! I expect the hens are used to it.

I could hardly wait to tell James, but he was disappointingly unamused.

I still can't believe it when I see her dumpy little figure stumping down the pathway with her trolley of eggs. Can this be the same person as the porcine nymph who threw off her clothes like confetti in the garden? But she did it again next morning when she got back from her round, so evidently it's a habit – unless May's brought her out, like blossom?

Mrs Deakin can't know about it or she would surely have told me. It's a strange thing knowing something about the village she doesn't, but I couldn't possibly tell her. It would be a sort of betrayal.

I wish I had someone to share it with, though, who'd appreciate it.

Mrs Deakin persuaded me into buying the ingredients for making pickled beetroot when I called in after lunch for mineral water, and I emerged carrying pickling vinegar, peppercorns and a large and insecurely wrapped parcel of beetroot, which came undone halfway home. I was impeded in picking them up by the Bourgeois Bitch whom I'd rashly taken with me, and the beetroot acquired even more mud than they were originally coated with. (I noticed that Mrs Deakin made no allowance for that caked mud when she weighed them.)

I was just staring down at the newspaper wrapping, which had a picture of Fergal Rocco and a pretty girl on it (partly obscured by mud – quite appropriate), when a smartly dressed woman coming out of a nearby cottage very kindly stopped to help me, and we fell into conversation.

Her name is Margaret Wrekin, and she sounds Awfully County, but is very pleasant. Her clothes were the sort of thing James would like me to wear – a straight skirt and long jacket, with low-heeled court shoes, and her dark hair sort of straight and angular. She's about my age.

Her cottage is one of those thatched ones without a hair out of place – indeed, the thatch is covered in a sort of wire hairnet – but when I said how Olde Worlde and charming it was, she revealed that it was just a façade since the rest had fallen down and at the back it was a big modern house.

She admired the Bourgeois Bitch, who fawned, and invited me to go for coffee tomorrow to meet some of her friends, which was very nice of her, but I explained that I wrote every morning.

She was very interested and said I must tell her all about it, only just now she had to dash to Mrs Deakin's for a tin of artichoke hearts.

It was very heartening meeting someone here at last.

The beetroot pickling was awful – the ghastly red juice and the awful smell of vinegar – and my rubber gloves had vanished.

It took hours, and by the time I'd filled up the last jar I was covered from head to foot in splashes of bright red, with matching hands and wrists: never again!

Before I could clean myself up, the doorbell went. Why do doorbells invariably ring at moments like this? I answered it with my hands cupped in front of me like a surgeon.

The vicar recoiled.

I suppose I did look rather gory, dripping on the step. Hastily wiping my hands on my apron I smiled reassurance: 'Just pickling beetroot, Vicar! Won't you come in?'

'Ah – beetroot!' he breathed, visibly relaxing. 'Yes indeed – beetroot.' He straightened his collar nervously. 'No, I won't come in just now, thank you. The fact of the matter is that I'm collecting items for the church bazaar and fête. It's on June the twenty-sixth – by the church if fine, in the church hall if wet.'

'Church bazaar?'

'And fête. Proceeds towards renovating the east window this year. I always ask everyone to contribute, even if not regular attenders. I think a church in a village like Nutthill is a heritage for all the people, don't you?'

'Oh, yes,' I said vaguely. 'Er . . . what sort of things did you have in mind?'

'Well, there's the raffle. Any tins of food, and so on. And the bottle stall – any sort of bottle. Or the white elephant—'

'Any sort of elephant?' I suggested and he gave me a weak smile.

'Ha, ha! Very good.'

In the end I donated a bottle of the ghastly, expensive French perfume Mother gives me every Christmas. He was highly pleased with this, and the packet of wrapped guest soaps left over from Christmas presents.

When I told James later about meeting Margaret Wrekin, he said he thought he'd seen her husband in the Dog and Duck once or twice when he'd stopped on the way home for a quick pint.

I don't know why he does that, when he could come home and take me for a quick pint. (Well, not a *pint* perhaps, but a drink.)

He added, 'The Wrekins are the type of people we want to make friends with here. Suitable people.'

'Suitable for what?' I enquired, astounded. 'I don't choose my friends for their accents, social status or wealth, James! I just thought she was nice.'

'You don't want to get on close terms with any Tom, Dick or Harry when you live in a small village, like you are with that shopkeeper woman. When we have children we'll have to be more fussy about who we know.'

'Why? She'll go to the village school and mix with everyone anyway.'

'*He*,' corrected James firmly, 'will go to a good school – though the village one might do for the first year or two.'

'I hope by "good" you don't mean boarding school,' I said, astonished, 'because if so I can tell you now that if I go through childbirth it will not be so I can shuffle my offspring away from home at the first available opportunity. Not that we could afford it anyway!'

'Lionel would help.'

'Why? He's never given you the least help other than a start in the firm.'

'It's a family thing – you wouldn't understand. I went to Eshington School, and so did Dad, and so did Uncle Lionel . . . and so will my sons.'

And Horrible Howard too, until they threw him out for a misdemeanour unspecified!

'Your half-brother Robert hasn't gone there, has he?'

'He's still very young. After all, Dad didn't remarry until just before we did, and his wife is not much older than you.'

'It's funny to think you've a stepmother and half-siblings you've never seen. And I've never even met your father!'

'He talked about coming over to visit in his last letter.'

'He always does.'

We had rather got away from the subject in hand, but I let it go for the moment. I needed to think this one out, it was another new aspect of James I hadn't expected and didn't particularly like.

When I got back from taking Bess for her evening walk, I could hear James's voice on the phone, but as soon as I came in he put the receiver down.

'Howard again?' I enquired.

He nodded. 'Just a chat, nothing important.'

'Not been caught moonlighting again, then?'

'Moonlighting?' he echoed, as though he'd never heard of such a thing.

'Yes, moonlighting. Isn't that what he wanted to ask you about last time he rang?'

'Oh, yes. No, it was just – a chat,' he said, but he looked decidedly shifty.

I hope he and Howard aren't plotting something.

Chapter 14: In the Drink

The astounding and therapeutic amount of money I spent on an emerald silk shantung trouser suit with a long Nehru jacket for the SFWWR dinner was worth it, and my newest jeans and good silk shirt would just have to do for the Working Breakfast. I'm glad Vivyan will be present.

James went sulky when I reminded him that he'd have to get home early on Friday in order to feed and exercise Bess, and didn't answer at all when I explained what I'd left in the freezer for him to eat.

He might just find Bess had deposited a little Welcome Home present for him, since she looked decidedly worried when I left with a suitcase (late, because the postman arrived just as I was leaving).

I took my mail with me to read on the train, but there was nothing of much interest until I came to a bulky brown envelope containing a big, folded sheet of paper. When I opened it out, I found it was one of those huge photocopies, only of *what* I was unsure. I tried it different ways up and the only thing it reminded me of was . . .

No.

It's like that ink-blot test where your subconscious makes

you see things that aren't there, like butterflies, when it's just a big blob. Big blobs and a long thing, in this case . . .

James's office has a big photocopier, for plans and documents.

No, it must be a mistake, sent to me in error. I checked the envelope again: definitely addressed to Mrs L. Drew.

Then I tried holding it the other way up again, but it made no difference because the more I looked at it . . .

And didn't Vanessa phone just after we moved to Nutthill with some inane news about a photocopier? The big photocopier was back in working order, or some such thing?

The man opposite was looking curiously at me over the top of his *Times*. Slowly I folded the sheet up and put it back in its envelope.

Vanessa?

He wouldn't – would he?

But I'm sure she's been chasing him and, as Mrs Deakin once said of men, their spirit may be willing but their flesh is weak, especially if tempted.

No – he wouldn't.

But I *could* just pop casually into the office on the way to the hotel and show him the photocopy, because once I've seen that he's just as puzzled by it as I am, I'll feel a lot better. Back to gritty reality again.

Not that James is gritty – more crumbly, lately. But he might be pleased to see me even though he's never encouraged me to drop in at the office. (I don't usually want to – it's all dark and gloomy, and the receptionist is a snooty bitch who knows where to put her make-up.)

I took a taxi from the station and we were almost at the turn to the quiet cul-de-sac where Drew, Drune and Tibbs hung out, when I spotted Drew Junior walking along the crowded pavement towards me on the far side of the road.

Only he *wasn't* alone.

A small blonde nestled in the shelter of his arm and their heads were close together. I couldn't see her face, but it was Vanessa the secretarty. I *knew* it!

As the taxi slowed outside the offices, I leaned forward and said quickly, 'I've changed my mind – don't stop here after all.'

'Where to, then?' the driver asked, executing a quick turn and setting off again. There was no sign of James this time.

'Where to?' he repeated.

My mind went totally blank. Where? Where was I? Where was I going?

'Could you just sort of drive around for five minutes please, while I decide?'

He shrugged and pulled out into the main road.

There are lots of good reasons why James might be in such a position – very good reasons . . . It was just seeing them – and then the photocopy and . . . I trusted him!

No, of course he isn't seeing someone else, he simply isn't the type! It's stupid to feel the foundations of my life are crumbling and bubbling like quicklime.

'Made your mind up yet?' enquired the driver who had, I now noticed, a face like a prize-fighter. But since he was sporting a small gold cross in one ear I expect he was a nice man really.

'Yes. Fitzroy Tower Hotel, please.'

Thank God I'd remembered where I was going.

I just had time to check in, change, and meet Vivyan in the bar for a quick pre-prandial drink – very quick, in my case, because I downed it in one.

'You look under the weather,' he commented kindly. 'Pale and interesting.'

'I'm OK really, Vivyan, it's just that I've had a bit of a shock. I – I've just seen my husband walking down the street with his arm around his old girlfriend.'

'The bastard!' he said comfortably.

'Oh, no,' I smiled weakly. 'He's really not like that at all. There must be a perfectly reasonable explanation.'

'Of course there is. Have another drink.'

As the second drink hit the cold, empty chasm of my stomach, I began to feel a lot better and sure I'd jumped to the wrong conclusions. I decided I'd worry about it tomorrow.

Then Vivyan leaned across and whispered conspiratorially, 'Here's something to bring the colour back to a maiden's cheeks. Fergal Rocco will be making a surprise appearance tonight.'

'What? But I thought he was in Japan.'

'He's supposed to be – he's flying back there early tomorrow morning. Excited?'

'Delirious!' I replied weakly. That was *all* I needed.

Fortunately Peggy and I were a long way from the top table (much to her disgust) and Peggy is large enough to hide behind. (Rubens would have loved her.)

Not that Fergal could have spotted me anyway, in such a dark corner, and I intended leaving the minute I could. *I* could only just see *him*, hemmed in by the Illustrious, but Peggy gave me a running commentary on his finer points.

We shared a bottle of wine with dinner, and I began to feel even better about things. Well, perhaps not *better*, more numbed.

Peggy *would* go and try to meet Fergal afterwards (along

with about ninety per cent of the other women present) so I said I'd see her in the bar when she could tear herself away, and scuttled off.

'That man,' she said dreamily when she joined me some time later, 'has the sexiest voice I've ever heard. It's positively knicker-quivering!'

'Peggy!'

She eyed me thoughtfully. 'And to think you once had all that within your grasp! I'm seeing you in a different light.'

Red, probably.

It was a mistake to try to match her drink for drink – she has hollow legs – for the next thing I knew, Vivyan had taken her place and was suggesting that I got a good night's sleep, since I was going to meet the Lovecall editor in the morning.

When he added that Fergal Rocco was also spending the night – or part of it – at the hotel, all my instincts said: 'Run for cover.'

Lurch for cover proved to be the best I could manage.

The journey to my room was a bit surreal – trying not to slide down the side of the lift wall – the corridor undulating as I walked along it – the dark, menacing shadows outside my room . . .

As I fumbled with my key, one of the shadows detached itself from the wall and loomed over me. I gave a strangled shriek and my knees gave way.

'At last!' said the husky, familiar voice that Peggy had just described so aptly to me. 'I thought you were never coming. I want to talk to you.'

A hand like a vice closed on my arm, the key was wrested from my nerveless fingers, and I found myself inside my room with Fergal Rocco.

It occurred to me as I gazed with mesmerised fascination at his angry face (and why he should be angry I'd no idea) lit by alternating bands of colour from the signs outside the hotel, that there must be few women who wouldn't like to find Fergal Rocco in their bedroom; but if talking was what he wanted, I didn't think I was capable of it. My mouth has a tenuous connection to my brain at the best of times, let's face it.

My knees felt as if they were slowly liquefying, and it seemed like a good idea to stop myself falling down by putting my free arm around him and leaning my head on his chest.

Under my hand I felt the muscles on his back shiver.

'Tish,' he said softly, in a changed voice.

Fergal: June 1999

'FERGAL FLIES IN!
Hysteria at airport as Fergal Rocco makes surprise visit to receive Trendsetter *award.*'

Sun

I spotted Tish almost immediately, although she was about as far away from me as it was possible to get and still be present at the dinner, and she was also trying to hide behind a large, flamboyant-looking lady. But that unmistakable red-gold hair shining in the light of the chandeliers gave her away.

All through the dinner and the award presentation (a singularly tasteless trophy) I was acutely conscious of her eyes on me, and wondered what she was thinking.

160

I should have resisted the urge to be here tonight, to see her again, but I didn't mean to try and speak to her until she positively leaped from the table at the end of the meal and scuttled from the room.

Just because we once went out together, it doesn't mean we can't meet in a civilised manner . . . does it?

Only I found I wasn't feeling very civilised. I wanted to follow after her and drag her back by the hair.

It was a real effort to be pleasant to the people besieging me, until I spotted the large dark lady clad in flowing cherry red who had been sitting next to Tish among them.

Ten minutes later I was in possession of the information that Tish was actually putting up at the hotel that night, that her friend knew she had once gone out with me, but that she hadn't thought I would be there that night and didn't want to meet me. Also that the small sprightly man circling the edge of the group around me was Tish's agent, Vivyan Dubois.

I was also in possession of the lady's phone number. She said she really preferred blond men, but was always willing to make an exception in a good cause!

I decided I was going to speak with Tish – be cool and show her that I didn't mind meeting her – how little she meant to me.

Nothing else, just a 'How are you, well, nice to see you again' conversation.

In private.

It took less than five minutes for me to obtain Tish's room number from her agent: he reminded me of Hywel.

Chapter 15: Brief Encounter

'Oh God!' I groaned, starting awake with a pounding heart, throbbing head and dry mouth and staring wildly about the hotel room, empty apart from myself and a scattering of clothes. I felt as if I'd gone three rounds with a grizzly, and the sheets were tied into one big knot.

For a minute I thought I'd just had the lurid dream to end all dreams – and then it all began to come back to me. I *had* gone three rounds with a grizzly, and I had the aches in strange places to prove it.

I went hot from my feet to my head in one giant wave: Miz Scarlett.

What had I done? *Had* I done . . .? Did I . . .?

What the hell did I drink last night?

I clutched my head and tried to remember. Vivyan. Wine with dinner. Drinks with Peggy in the bar . . . trying to stay upright as I walked the undulating corridor to my room.

I'd have been all right if Fergal hadn't been waiting for me, if when he touched me I hadn't . . .

Did I *really*?

He must have *seen* I'd had too much to drink and taken advantage of me . . . except I have this awful feeling that *I* took advantage of *him*. I remember touching him and feeling that I just wanted to wrap myself in him for comfort, like a duvet.

Some duvet.

I think my body's wearing a smirk, even if the rest of me is Disgusted, Ashamed and Mortified.

It's all James's fault – it was the shock of seeing him with Vanessa that sent me off the rails. But now, in the cold light of day, perhaps I made too much of it. There must be a perfectly reasonable explanation. James is not like that.

But then – *I* am not like *this*. Am I?

Not that infidelity with Fergal really *is* infidelity, since I knew him first . . . so it sort of doesn't count. Well, you know what I mean.

But when I apply that to James and Vanessa, it does count – if they are – if they *did* . . .?

I wished my head would stop pounding so I could *think*.

A knock on the door signalled a big pot of coffee, which Vivyan must have arranged, because I'm sure I wasn't capable of thinking about it last night. I must apologise to him for getting in such a state.

After the coffee, some aspirins out of my handbag and a long shower, I began to think I'd live after all. I even began to wonder if I'd dreamed the whole sorry episode, since there was no sign that Fergal had ever been in the room, apart from the odd slight bruise (very odd). No message, nothing.

But the photocopy, which I do remember crumpling up and hurling away before I went down to dinner, had been smoothed out and now lay on the carpet like a small, strange rug. Ikea might find a market for that design.

While I was puzzling over the implications of this, the phone rang and it was James.

'Tish? It's me. Where's my green and terracotta silk tie?'

He sounded normal (cross). I cleared my throat and suggested, 'The tie rack?'

'Are you all right? Your voice sounds a bit strange.'

'I drank a bit too much last night.'

'Welcome to the human race!'

'I hadn't realised drinking yourself senseless was the qualification,' I said coldly.

'Look, Tish, I'll have to go or I'll be late—'

'I saw you yesterday on my way to the hotel – with a blonde woman. You had your arm round her,' I blurted, quite without meaning to. (Mouth out of Control Again syndrome.)

There was a pause short enough for me to think I'd imagined it, then he said aggrievedly, 'You did? Then I wish you'd stopped! I needed a taxi, and there's never one when you want one. I was taking Beryl home.'

'Beryl?'

'You know, the clerk. Small, blonde, plump, wears glasses. What's the matter with you? You surely didn't think . . .? You *did*, didn't you! You thought you'd caught me out! If this is all the trust you have in me, I—'

'Why,' I interrupted, clasping my aching brow with my free hand, 'did you have your arm round her? And I *don't* remember Beryl.'

'She had a terrible migraine – spots before the eyes and all that. Couldn't have got home alone. If you'd stopped and asked, instead of swanning off to your hotel thinking the worst, we could have used your taxi.'

'She looked exactly like Vanessa!'

'Vanessa? Vanessa isn't blonde.'

'I've seen Vanessa, James – at our wedding – remember? She is blonde.'

'She was, but she's let it go back to its natural colour, a sort of reddish brown.'

'She – she isn't blonde?' Suddenly I started to feel seriously ill again. 'Oh! Well – well, I'm sorry, James, but it did look suggestive, you must admit.'

'You shouldn't jump to conclusions,' he informed me coldly. 'It was Beryl, and she's years older than me, with two teenage children. Look, I'll have to go. Don't wait dinner for me tonight, I might have to work late.'

'But, James!'

The phone went dead. My stomach had gone back to feeling like a big, shivering pit, but by the time Vivyan knocked I was outwardly in control again.

I'm sorry I misjudged James like that, when he was just being nice to his clerk, but how was I to know? And anyway, I haven't had an explanation for the photocopy yet. (What *did* Fergal make of it, if anything?)

And I refuse to feel ashamed about last night, even if it makes me go hot and cold to remember – mostly hot – because if I had a sex life at home, then I don't suppose I'd have reacted like that.

But I never want to see Fergal Rocco again. *Ever.*

On my way home, like some callow teenager on her first heavy date, my heart lurched as I remembered: no pills. Then it plummeted like a pebble into an abyss when I thought of the horrible diseases Fergal could have picked up from all those women he's been with.

I certainly wasn't thinking about precautions. I wasn't

thinking, just going on (basic) instinct – and I don't think I gave *him* time to think either, did I? (Oh God – I must be a late-onset nymphomaniac.)

Perhaps he's so used to having women throw themselves at him he comes permanently pre-packaged?

Ever-ready.

The second worry is worse than the first, for it's been months since I came off the pill and nothing's happened, so I'm probably barren. Also, I've been reading up about these things and I don't think this is the right time of month anyway.

Realising I needed to ask him about the risks of infection, at least, as soon as I got home I sent him a communication, double-enveloped, via his father's flagship restaurant.

It said: 'Have you any communicable diseases? T.'

I gave c/o Vivyan Dubois as the return address, since I don't want him to know where I live.

After this, I bathed in mild disinfectant and then had another long shower. Guilt may be indelible, but germs aren't.

When I heard James's car I had to brace myself to be normal, which isn't easy when you feel as if the Sword of Damocles is suspended above your head by a thread.

He was late, and looking very martyred St Sebastian, but when he nobly said he forgave me, since he could understand how my suddenly seeing him in a compromising-looking position with another woman could have upset me, it had the contrary effect of making me lose any vestiges of guilt and feel cross instead.

Even the mad urge to Confess All, which had been trying to take over my lips, forsook me at this point.

He didn't ask me how the meeting went, either. (Very well, considering my state.) But a day or two later he arrived back from work early, strode in and slapped down a torn-out photograph.

'Fergal Rocco makes flying visit to receive award' read the caption, but I averted my eyes from Fergal's dark visage. I couldn't even look a photograph of him in the eyes at the moment and I just knew I'd turned a guilty pink. 'I didn't know you read *Trendsetter* magazine, James.'

'I don't, as you know very well. The junior typist had this stuck up on her filing cabinet.'

'You'd better take it back – she might be upset when she finds it gone!'

In answer he crushed it into a ball and tossed it in the general direction of the wastepaper basket. 'I suppose you knew he was going to turn up all the time!'

'For goodness' sake, James! No one knew until the last minute! Urgent business called him back to London.'

'I suppose he told you that?'

'He told *everyone* that.'

James eyed me closely. 'So you didn't talk to him?'

'We exchanged no conversation,' I said truthfully. (Bodily fluids, maybe.) 'And I don't know why you keep harping on about Fergal, when I've never given you the least cause for jealousy. Yet when I quite reasonably asked you why you had your arm round someone else you—'

'That was quite different!' he blustered. 'My life is an open book, but you're so secretive. I mean, you go out with one of the most infamous of rock stars and don't even mention it in six years of marriage and—'

'He wasn't a rock star, infamous or otherwise, then,' I interrupted, but there was no reasoning with him.

He only shut up after I remembered the photocopy and

showed it to him. He denied all knowledge of it at first, but eventually admitted there had been some horseplay at the office Christmas party, though he swore that 'nothing really happened', and I would have to trust him. He said Vanessa had probably sent me the photocopy because of his virtuous refusal to take up with her again.

It sounds quite probable, so I suppose I'll have to forgive him, even if I feel like dipping *him* in Dettol too, just in case.

After this I felt the guilt and suspicion stakes were about equal, and stopped being extra nice to him.

I'm still worrying about strange diseases, but no longer about pregnancy, since three days after my Brief Encounter I had one of my Brief Periods.

For some reason I just cried and cried. I don't know why. Yes I do.

I've been feeling so mixed about getting pregnant and yet the thought of carrying Fergal's baby was not totally repulsive to some part of me – though how I would have explained a black-haired and possibly olive-skinned infant away to James, I can't imagine.

So just as well I'm not going to be called on to do it, isn't it?

Fergal: June 1999

ROCCO K.O.s REPORTER IN AIRPORT FRACAS!'
Sun

What did I think when Tish threw herself so unexpectedly into my arms? Nothing – I only felt.

When she touched me every nerve in my body stood up and shivered. (Everything stood up and shivered.)

It felt right.

I did have some vestige of control left: enough to ask her if she was sure, for instance . . .

She seemed pretty damned sure.

And it's just as well that leading a dissolute life means taking precautions comes automatically.

Afterwards I just might have let the plane leave without me if Tish hadn't stirred in my arms and murmured, 'James?' with a sad catch in her voice, stirring my conscience, because contrary to public opinion, I do have morals and yet here I was in bed with another man's wife – or she was in bed with me.

If she hadn't started it . . .

It wasn't really like her . . . though how do I know what she's like now?

When I disentangled myself and switched on the bedside lamp she was dead to the world – Venus asleep.

Maybe she'd had a bit too much to drink. But she'd seemed . . . purposeful was the only word for it.

'Tish?' I shook her shoulder and she fluttered her eyelashes and murmured.

Would she regret it when she woke? I needed to leave her some message . . . I needed to get out of there before I started all over again!

I got up and retrieved my scattered clothes, dislodging a crumpled paper from under my shirt. I smoothed it out, and one look at that familiar photocopy told me she'd found out about her husband and his tart.

If she'd seen this, then consoled herself with drink and then me – was I just revenge?

169

I felt used. (Well used, but used.) Then my eye fell on the clock. 'Oh my God!'

Ten minutes later, clean, changed but unshaven, I was on my way out of the hotel.

Awaiting me at the airport were Hywel, Nerissa, a cameraman and a reporter. I blinked as the light flashed right in my eyes just as Nerissa flung herself at me and hung from my neck like a small, scented sloth.

'Darling – I've missed you so much! Why didn't you tell me you were going to be here?'

I pushed her off and socked the reporter trying to shove a microphone up my nose.

My temper was never that good. And I'd been hoping Nerissa would attach herself to someone else in my absence. I certainly didn't tell her I was making this trip back.

Hywel was looking smug. This was his idea of good publicity.

I shook them off and headed for the check-in.

Chapter 16: Cat's Paw

That airport photograph made me feel sick: out of my bed and straight into a clinch with his girlfriend, the bastard!

I expect he was just in need of a bit, and I was handy and willing. But I thought . . .

Are all men tomcats at heart?

He did answer my note, though, eventually. Vivyan phoned me the other day to tell me he'd just had the strangest phone call. 'A man's voice – didn't give a name but very husky and attractive and sort of familiar. Left a message for you.'

'What did he say?' I broke in urgently.

'He said, "Tell Tish: No I haven't, and anyway, I'm like the Boy Scouts, I always come prepared." Then he rang off. Does that make sense, darling?'

'Yes.' I suddenly felt a bit better. (No diseases.) But, strangely enough, piqued that he was thinking clearly enough to take precautions when I certainly hadn't been! 'Yes it does, thank you, Vivyan – thank you very much.'

'You're welcome – but what *have* you been up to? I think you're very mysterious! Now I'll just go on and on wondering where I've heard that voice before.'

As long as he doesn't guess.

* * *

James and I are being terribly nice to each other. I'm convinced Vanessa tried to seduce him at the Christmas party, but I'll have to forgive him since I—

And I'm sure he didn't *actually* . . . he wouldn't.

We'll start again with a clean slate. Only I can no longer regard James as the dependable cornerstone of my life, now I can see he's more like a patch of quicksand you know the path across.

Bit like the gardening: I've long since stopped expecting James to show any interest in that, so I came to an arrangement with Bob's parents through Mrs Deakin, who suggested it, and he now comes regularly. (Well, *irregularly* – he seems to spend more and more of his time here.) James disapproved, but he couldn't really complain about it since he didn't do it himself.

This afternoon Bob was working cheerfully away at the back garden, in which he is producing a row of neat deep beds full of unidentifiable vegetables. He seems to know what he's doing, but if I make any suggestions he just smiles, nods and ignores them.

After making him a mug of tea (in a giant enamel mug I bought specially, so it doesn't get broken), I went with a parcel of book proofs to catch the bus into the next village. I once asked Mrs Deakin why she didn't have a Post Office counter in her shop, and she said darkly that she'd had it and lost it, then laughed and added that that was the story of her life.

There was a pretty tabby cat sitting on the wall near the bus stop, and as I drew level it stalked up to me with distinct signs of friendliness. Flattered, I bent down to stroke it, but saw to my horror that each front paw boasted such a multitude of toes that they could furnish a spare cat with the usual number without being noticeably missed.

Recoiling, I was wiping my hands on my jeans when there was a ripe, senile chuckle from behind me. A fat old man was leaning over a gate watching from watering blue eyes.

'Surprised you, dinnit? Should have seen your face! Always tickles me, it does, to watch strangers seeing Tibby's feet for the first time.'

'I'm glad to amuse you,' I said coldly, fighting down queasiness. That sort of thing has upset me ever since I paid at a fair to see the pig with six legs, and it was some disgusting little white corpse floating round in a jar of formaldehyde.

'Is it your cat? What a pity it's deformed, because it's so pretty otherwise. I suppose that's why it wasn't put down when it was born?'

'Put down?' he quavered, agitatedly mumbling his false teeth, which seemed rather too big for his mouth. 'What need to kill 'un? Lots of Nutthill cats got extra toes and always have had – don't do 'em any harm. Some says there's summat in the water round here that does it, but that's daft – if it were true every other creature would have more toes than it oughter.'

'Something in the water?' My blood ran cold, until common sense reasserted itself, and I realised that this was just a genetic freak among the village cats that had been nurtured instead of stamped out.

'Well, she has very handsome markings,' I conceded magnanimously, preparing to go on my way.

He gave an evil smile. 'I'll save a kitten for you next time, if she have one the same. Her generally do.'

As I began to hotly deny any desire to own a multi-toed

feline, the bus appeared round the bend and I had to run, so I only hope the senile old fool forgets all about his promise.

The bus was surprisingly full, but as we approached the next village all was explained by banners advertising a country fair and, while waiting my turn at the post office, I read a small poster describing the delights on offer: demonstrations of sheep-shearing, spinning and weaving, beer tent, antiques, handmade clothes . . .

Irresistible!

Shortly I was walking up the lane to the farm where it was being held. I say 'farm', but it was more of a small manor house.

There were lots of little stalls around the edge of the courtyard, where I bought honey, homemade fudge and a picture formed from pressed local wild flowers.

The sheep-shearing was surprisingly gory, long snicks appearing as the sheep grew pinkly naked, so I wandered past the little fair and inflatable castle, and into the beer tent.

Hot and tired, I sat in its grass-scented darkness with a nice chilly lager and lime until it was time for the next bus.

There was one stall just at the exit where you couldn't really get out of buying a ticket ('a prize every time'), but I discovered, unsurprised, that my numbers were not winners. As I turned away, the youth behind the counter suddenly thrust a plastic bag containing a very small goldfish into my hand. I recoiled and tried to hand it back.

'But I didn't win anything! Besides, I don't want it.'

He fielded the bag away. 'Consolation prize.'

Irresolutely, I stood on the hot field. The fish was very small and already the plastic bag was warm to the touch.

I wandered disconsolately away, trying to adjust all my

small, awkwardly shaped parcels without capsizing the fish, but in the end had to go back and purchase a patchwork holdall. Once everything was in it, I managed to hold the goldfish bag so that it hung down inside, which at least gave the poor thing some shade.

By now I'd missed the bus and had to start the long trek home, wishing I hadn't gone to the fair at all. The bag was filled with lead, the goldfish gasped, and I felt hot and sticky.

When I made a stop to let some air into the goldfish bag, a car full of youths pulled up, shouting: 'Frying tonight!' and other witticisms, and then persistently offered me a lift. I repelled them, but then another car pulled up behind me only ten minutes later, and I turned with a stream of hot invective on my lips only to discover the vicar in an aged green half-timbered Morris 1000. I changed my scowl into a weak smile and gratefully climbed in.

The vehicle was totally unrestored and very noisy, which meant we drove mainly without conversation. He declined my invitation to come in, saying his wife awaited him with afternoon tea, which sounded very vicar's wife-ish to me.

Bob was still working in the back garden and his shallow blue eyes lit up at the sight of the goldfish glassily circling its bag.

'Go-fish!' he said delightedly, prodding the bag with an earthy finger. 'Go-fish!' But I knew that in the ungrateful manner of its kind, it would soon turn into a Stop-fish.

Then an idea of amazing brilliance struck me. 'Bob, would you like the goldfish? To take home?'

'To keep? Me?' He capered delightedly.

I handed the small prisoner over. 'Here you are, then. Now, wait a minute while I get the envelope for your mother.'

I came back with his (very reasonable) wages sealed in an envelope. 'There. Be careful not to lose it, and give it straight to your mother when you get home.'

His eyes, hideously magnified through the bag of water, remained as blank and clear as usual, then he nodded slowly and lowered the fish.

'Envelope for Mum. Go-fish for Bob.'

'That's right. Goodbye, Bob.' I retreated into the cool kitchen with relief.

His lumbering footsteps went off round the side of the house and he seemed to be talking to someone: probably the goldfish.

There can be no more blissful feeling on earth than taking off your sandals and pressing your hot swollen feet onto cold quarry tiles: practically orgasmic.

And I swear the glass of water hissed going down.

James, when he came home, ate all my fudge.

Tomorrow being Saturday I wanted him to drive me in to buy tiles for the bathroom, and then chip off the old ones; but he informs me he'll be too busy setting up his radio equipment. He's knee-deep in transmitters, manuals and things, and is constantly coming and going between the house and what he now calls his Shack. I'm still deeply hurt by his underhand attitude in ordering the things and arranging a bank loan without telling me about it (and he called *me* secretive!), and now he won't even help me with the house.

I was so annoyed that I phoned Mother – I had to talk to someone. But it was no good, because Golden Boy had got in first. I'm sure she likes him more than she likes me. In fact sometimes she doesn't seem to like me at all.

But I suppose that's silly, because she's smothered me with intense possessiveness since birth. ('This is my doll and you can't play with it.') I'm sure she was disappointed that I wasn't a conventional, fluffy little clone of herself.

Anyway, Mother burbled on about men needing a hobby, and how it gave them an interest at home (at home, with half the garden between us?) and she was obviously the worse for drink: at the careful, garrulous stage.

James came back from the Shack at midnight and let the Bourgeois Bitch into the bedroom.

On Monday Mrs Peach delivered her eggs as usual and went to take a look at Toby, who was, as ever, delighted to see her.

'Bloody hell!' he screamed, bobbing his head and shifting up and down his perch in a dance of joy. 'Bloody hell!'

Then, as she was leaving, she turned to ask abruptly, 'How's yer Old Fertilities?'

'What?' I said blankly, thinking that surely James hadn't been discussing our marital affairs down at the pub with all the village listening in.

'Them Old Fertility pear trees out back,' she elucidated. 'They may look past it, but they bear wonderful. I noticed you'd pruned them right back.'

That was ages ago! 'They look all right to me, Mrs Peach, but we'll just have to wait and see, won't we?'

She didn't say anything else, but went off. I can put up with her strange ways now I know her secret.

This was another day when James forgot to kiss me goodbye. He's done it a few times now. No kisses, no cuddles . . . I don't feel loved.

I wish I had a close friend I could talk everything over

with, but perhaps I could tell the doctor about some of it? I ought to see her about stopping the pill and irregular periods and things anyway. Last time I was too worried about the Lump to think of it.

I made an extra effort at dinner that evening – chilli con carne – but James was very disgruntled because it wasn't meat and two veg, although I told him less meat and more beans was healthier. He said red beans are poisonous, and anyway, he'd rather stay unhealthy than eat this sort of rubbish.

I was hurt, since I'd never made chilli con carne before and thought it was very good, though a bit hot. Bess liked it, too.

Later, when I found an enormous spider in the bath, James flatly refused to come back from the Shack and remove it, so I had to deal with it myself.

First I warned it (from the doorway): 'Spider, if you aren't out of the house in two minutes I'm going to kill you!'

It wasn't, so I bludgeoned it to death with a leftover piece of tongue and groove pine and disposed of the remains down the toilet.

Ugh!

Next day James and Bess were both suffering appalling flat-ulence, which James insisted was due to the poisonous red beans in my chilli. But I was perfectly all right.

Bess kept exploding awful stenches and then looking at me accusingly, which made me a bit doubtful about accepting Margaret Wrekin's invitation to go back with her for coffee when we bumped into her again in the village.

I hoped the worst was over.

There really is only a front bit of old cottage with an

enormous modern house built on the back, and in the garden two dark-haired, pretty little girls played with a ball, watched over by a small Malaysian woman in a swinging hammock. Margaret let Bess out to play with them, to my relief.

The woman cowered in the corner of the swing seat – not one of Nature's Dog Lovers. I can sympathise with that.

'That's May, the mother's help,' Margaret explained, and I almost said, 'Yes, and I'm Mrs Bun the Baker's Wife,' but restrained myself.

'This house is so big that I said to Ray, "I just can't manage with only a cleaner," so we advertised and got May. She's the sweetest girl, and her English is coming on beautifully. The girls love her.'

I accepted coffee in a fine porcelain cup, and one of those yummy French coffee-iced biscuits. 'I didn't realise before that you had children.'

'You don't have any yourself?'

I shook my head. 'Not yet, anyway.'

We exchanged a smile.

'Plenty of time – and if you have girls like me they're as good as gold! I hardly know they're there.'

That was probably due to May, the martyred help, but I doubt if we could afford a mother's help, or any other kind of help, and anyway, as I pointed out to James when he was waffling on about boarding schools, there doesn't seem much point in having children if you don't want them around. What had Margaret had children for?

What did *anyone* have children for?

The inside of the house is very lush, with quilted Designers Guild curtains, huge showy tassels, and the biggest rose Dralon sofa in the world.

I felt distinctly grubby in my dog-haired tartan trousers and green T-shirt, but Margaret was so impressed and enthusiastic about my being Marian Plentifold the author that I relaxed and we had a nice long chat.

I think we might become friends in time; I hope so.

Mind you, I nearly didn't live long enough to make friends with anyone, because when I got home and went to hang Bess's lead up, I fell into the Underworld.

Well, that's what it felt like at the time, but it was actually a secret cellar – and only secret to us, at that, because it's obvious the last owner of the cottage knew about it.

The door is what I thought was just wooden panelling at the back of the cupboard under the stairs, until I overbalanced and nearly broke something falling down a flight of stone steps.

When I recovered from the shock, I got the big torch out and shone it down into the cold, stale blackness, feeling much as Howard Carter did at the entrance to Tutankhamen's tomb.

Little shelves at the side contained the last owner's collection of Wondrous Things: bits of old candle stump, a rusty tin box, and a broken umbrella.

Without even taking the basic precaution of pushing Toby ahead first to test the air, down I went, with Bess following hard on my heels, shivering, her cold wet nose pressed into my hand.

At the bottom was a little arch-roofed cellar with a flagged floor, stone slab shelves, and a vast stone table, which must have had the house built around it since it wouldn't have fitted down those stairs.

The whole thing was obviously older than the cottage and must have been part of the Dower House originally – Mrs Deakin was right, as usual. I could see where arched doorways had been blocked off on two sides.

It was entirely empty and, while I admit to a slight disappointment that it wasn't filled with treasure, equally I would have been highly aggrieved had I found a skeleton chained to the wall.

How on earth did the surveyor miss it? You can sue for compensation if your house turns out to be smaller than its description, but what do you do if it is significantly larger?

James was amazed.

He stalked around like a cat marking its territory, then looked lingeringly at the stone slab table with a very strange expression on his face and remarked that the cellar would make an original party room.

'Not for the sort of parties I go to,' I informed him coldly.

'Well, then, a wine cellar.'

'You don't seem able to keep a bottle of wine in the house for more than a day at a time, James, though I suppose you could use it to store the empties.'

'Anyone would think I was an alcoholic to hear you talk!' he exclaimed, his voice muffled since he was examining the shelves for forgotten treasure.

But I'd already found it: the tin box at the top of the stairs contained forty-three silver threepenny bits.

Even if I can't think of a use for the cellar at the moment I can have electricity run down there and give it a good vacuum.

I've given the spiders notice.

*   *   *

Fergal: June 1999

'THE SHOW MUST GO ON
Goneril go onstage in USA as heiress girlfriend of
lead singer Fergal Rocco is rushed into hospital . . .'
                                                    Exposé magazine

I told Nerissa before I went on tour that I thought she should find someone else, and my brusque – if not brutal – brush-off at the airport must have given her some hint that I meant it, you'd think.

Her only response was to threaten to kill herself if I didn't carry on seeing her.

I don't like being manipulated.

It's lucky Sara warned me it's a device she's used in the past, especially to bring her father to heel, but there's no way I would believe she'd destroy herself anyway. Her body is her temple and she worships it constantly.

We were about to go on stage for the last American show when I got a telegram from her father, saying what had happened and that it was all my fault for breaking his little girl's heart and I must fly back immediately.

I sent one back, saying, 'Get Well Soon, see you in a couple of days when we're back.' He showed it to the papers, who had a field day with it.

I did go and see her the day we got back and she looked pretty pathetic – like a little girl sitting up in bed with her long loose hair and a fringe. She was all ready to play a big scene, but I kept it short and brisk. Said if she tried a stunt like this again I wouldn't come at all, but being a soft touch I didn't say that I was totally bored with her juvenile ways and never wanted to see her again, just gave her the 'let's just see each other as friends sometimes' spiel.

Since then she's been underfoot whenever she can find where I'm going to be, despite my swearing Sara into secrecy on the subject. Persistence should be her middle name.

But I'm holding out now for something more than she can be, and surely there must be other women out there who have the same effect on me as Tish still does? All I have to do is find one. But I'm determined never to come within temptation's reach of Tish again, that's for sure.

Chapter 17: A Fête Worse than Death

June the twenty-sixth, the day of the church fête, dawned hot and sunny (the power of prayer?) and I decided to grace the event with my presence.

The church field was transformed by stalls, acres of faded bunting, and another of those inflatable castles. There was also an awful band composed of small children playing instruments unsuited to their age, size, or mental abilities.

The place swarmed with piranha-like raffle-ticket sellers and I ended up with a fistful of different colours.

The stalls sold everything from knitted garments to second-hand books, and lots of those frilly little aprons and peg-bags shaped like dresses on coat-hangers so dear to the supporters of church bazaars, but I resisted all blandishments to buy any of these ghastly things, or try to throw a hoop over a bottle, or put a dart in the middle of a board.

I kept bumping into the vicar, who seemed to be everywhere at once, radiating enthusiasm and carrying a starting pistol. One of his toes was poking through his plimsolls. His large, jolly wife made her presence felt in every corner of the field by means of a megaphone.

All the children were marshalled into races of various

kinds, including Margaret's two dark-haired moppets, watched over by May (but no sign of Margaret, the Missing Mother).

Then there was an exhibition of folk dancing by local children, followed by a woman who clog-danced on a wooden board. I must tell Granny about that.

Feeling I'd done more than my duty by buying all those raffle tickets, I was about to call it a day when they announced that Lady Somebody was going to give the raffle prizes, so I thought I might as well hang on even though I never win anything.

She dispensed all sorts of really good prizes: a basket of fruit, a bottle of bubbly, etc., and I thought she'd finished when she suddenly read out a green raffle ticket number which I recognised as being one of mine. I didn't quite believe it, but she read the number out again, and it was!

It was highly embarrassing going up for my prize in front of all those people. Lady Somebody shook me by the hand, murmured something that smelled of sherry, and handed me a painting.

A painting!

Of course, I didn't stop to look at it until I was back in the anonymity of the crowd. It was in oils and depicted a seaside scene, probably Cornwall (aren't they all?), and it wasn't bad, either. On the back was a label: 'By Claude Sturgeon: Foot Painter.'

And then it went on about there being a whole group of disabled artists who paint with their feet, and I was a bit more impressed with it after that, because I couldn't have painted it with my hands, let alone anything else.

What a feat!

Sorry.

Mrs Deakin materialised at my side like a small flowered Dalek and admired it so greatly I almost gave it to her, but then decided that the first thing I'd ever won should really stay in the family, and Mother would love it.

Mrs Deakin said she'd closed the shop in order to attend the last half-hour of the fête, but she intended staying open extra late this evening to make up. 'And those are *my* knitted scarves and gloves over there,' she pointedly remarked, having observed my lack of trophies (other than the picture).

'Really? They seem to be selling very well.' Especially to the colour blind. I began to edge away: 'Is that the time? I really must go and—'

But her eyes, fixed on something over my left shoulder, glazed over and the small predatory claw that she had laid on my arm tightened.

There was a strange prickling sensation down my spine. I turned slowly and with a sense of the inevitability of my doom watched a tall, dark and unwelcome figure stride determinedly through the crowd in my direction, like Moses parting the Red Sea.

His presence there was so surreal I thought for a minute I was having one of my peculiar dreams, and he would snatch me up in his arms at any minute and do unspeakably pleasurable things . . .

Shame on me!

Then I remembered that we'd *done* the unspeakably pleasurable things, and some instinct for self-preservation made me try to turn and flee, my heart flopping about like a dying fish and my face burning, before all the blood literally drained out of it. (Into my feet, I think, which is why I didn't get very far before Mrs D. brought me up like my own personal anchor.)

His greeting was not that of one softened by the recollection of a tender moment – or even a hot, sweaty couple of hours.

'What the hell are you doing here?' he snarled, coming to a stop so close that I had to tip my head back to look at him.

Blue lights sparked in his long black hair, his skin was tanned an even dark olive against the soft white of his shirt, and his glacial green eyes froze me to the spot.

Anger loosened my tongue. 'How nice to see you too, Fergal!'

Becoming aware for the first time of the small, chestnut-haired girl clutching his arm and panting from the exertion of being towed along, I added politely, 'Hi!'

Then I took a second look: she was the girl in the airport photograph, the one he was embracing not an hour after he left me.

Her pansy-brown eyes stared inimically back: no one seemed pleased to see me, except possibly the vicar, beaming away on Fergal's other side.

To say we were the centre of all eyes was an understatement. Mrs Deakin's faculties were set to Maximum Receptivity Point, and I'd never known her silent for so long.

Fergal looked down his long nose at me. 'I didn't expect to find *you* here!'

I tried a cool smile, since I couldn't think why he was looking so angry about it. He certainly couldn't want a snake in his Eden any less than I did. 'Why should you? And I could say the same about you: this is hardly your sort of thing, is it?'

'You know each other?' the vicar said, with an air of doubtful discovery.

'We certainly did – once.' The green eyes scanned me thoughtfully from head to foot. 'You've changed a lot, Angel.'

Clearly this was not meant as a compliment, despite my old pet name.

'Older and wiser,' I said sweetly.

'Vicar,' Mrs Deakin broke in, unable to contain her curiosity a moment longer. 'Who? What?'

The vicar took pity on her. 'This is Fergal Rocco, Mrs Deakin, who, I'm reliably informed, is a rock star of note!'

He waited for polite laughter at his little pun, which Mrs D. supplied solo, before adding with éclat: 'And the new owner of Greatness Hall!'

'Some inherit Greatness,' my mouth said, going it solo as usual, 'and some have Greatness thrust upon them!' Then I took a hasty step backwards, because I thought Fergal was about to commit violence on my person. Age doesn't seem to have mellowed him.

'Say, who is this?' drawled the girl, still clinging to his arm like a furled bat (only the right way up) and giving me the Evil Eye. 'An old flame, Fergal honey?' she added disparagingly: 'An *old*, old flame!'

Cow.

Fergal ignored her. 'What are you doing here, Tish?' he said more moderately.

'I live in Nutthill.' (And of all the villages in all the world, you had to choose this one!)

'Really?' He sounded less than delighted at the prospect. 'Coincidences never cease, do they? I'm just moving in. Did

I introduce Nerissa? Never mind, I don't suppose you'll ever meet again.'

Nerissa was pouting, and the vicar had the uncertain look of a puppy who doesn't know if he's done the right thing or not. Fergal began to turn away. 'Nice to have met you again, Tish . . . Mrs . . .'

'Deakin,' she supplied eagerly. 'Of Nutthill Home Stores. Anything you want, you come to me. No need to go to they nasty supermarkets!'

For a moment I thought his face might crack open into a grin, but no. 'I'll bear it in mind,' he said gravely, and began to walk off.

With one mighty bound my mouth was free. 'Oh, Fergal!'

He paused and scowled back at me over his shoulder.

'There's a letter in the post to you – well, to the new owner of the Hall, I didn't know it was you – about the fence dividing your park from my garden. You're responsible for it and the cows are trying to break through. Do you think you can have someone fix it?'

'Fergal, honey, will you buy me one of these cute little teddy bears?' Nerissa broke in rudely, batting her dark eyelashes at him. 'The fête is going to close soon, and we haven't seen anything yet.'

'I'll attend to it!' Fergal Honey snapped in my direction, and strode off with Nerissa still clamped to his side.

The Human Poultice strikes again.

She's definitely the girl from the airport. The future Mrs Rocco? She looks as if she intends to be, and that soft accent, big brown eyes and iron will might just do it. OK – and the marvellous figure and pretty face. And she can't be more than twenty, if that.

He must have been desperate to make do with me that night. Any port in a storm, I suppose. Or perhaps *he* was drunk too?

How on earth am I going to cope with having him living in Nutthill?

I avoided Mrs Deakin's questions (for the moment) by the simple expedient of walking off without another word, feeling churned up and confused. Why on earth was he angry at finding me in Nutthill? Unless he was as afraid of his girlfriend finding out about his illicit session with me, as I was of James discovering it?

Or perhaps he's angry with himself for seducing me when I was drunk and (almost) incapable. So why come tearing across merely to freeze me to death and be rude?

I spent ages trying to frame a casual way of telling James that Fergal Rocco was the new Lord of the Manor, but I needn't have bothered, because a couple of days later he picked up a copy of the local rag in the pub, which he carried home to brandish under my nose like Exhibit A.

'Perhaps you'd like to explain *that*!' he roared, his face an unbecoming shade of puce. It did not go well with sandy hair.

The large photograph on the front page showed Fergal and me gazing longingly into each other's eyes from an extremely close range.

'Funny, I didn't notice a photographer.'

'Obviously – I'm surprised you noticed anything except each other. I suppose you told him where you lived when you met in London?'

'James! I've already told you I didn't have a conversation with him.'

Unfortunately my face burned guiltily, even though it was the truth: the odd word does *not* constitute a conversation. 'What are you being so cross about? I swear I didn't know he'd bought the Hall until that day. It was a surprise to both of us, and I was just exchanging polite—'

'Polite! You're staring at him as if he was every hero in your stupid books rolled into one.'

That was pretty imaginative for James, though I resented the word 'stupid'.

'It's the angle of the camera. See that hand at the edge of the picture there, clinging to Fergal's arm? It belongs to the very young, very pretty American girl he was with.'

James gave me a suspicious glare and bent to examine the evidence. The vein in his temple ceased to twitch and his colour subsided to something approaching normal.

'All this is quite ridiculous and you ought to know me better by now, James.'

'I felt ridiculous down at the pub when they were showing me the photograph and asking me how my wife came to be on such familiar terms with a rock star,' he muttered disagreeably.

'We are not on familiar terms, and I wouldn't describe him as a rock star, exactly.'

'You're the expert,' he said nastily, but with a little less conviction.

'Since Mrs Deakin observed the whole of this eventful meeting, I expect the correct version is known by everyone within five miles. The men were just teasing you, and you rose to it beautifully. I don't suppose it occurred to you to defend me?'

He looked a bit shamefaced then, but did not apologise.

When he'd gone out to the Shack, I looked at the paper again. It just goes to show that the camera can lie – as also, apparently, can the photocopier.

I'd better give Mrs D. a brief outline of my youthful romance before other more lurid rumours begin to spread.

James woke me up much later by falling over the bedroom furniture and Bess, which was a pity since I'd only just dropped off. (Every time I closed my eyes I saw Fergal's dark, face staring at me: rather unsettling.) Once awake I couldn't get back to sleep again, and all my worries rose like black scum to the surface of my mind.

It had been possible almost to forget my fling with Fergal when I never expected to see him again, but not now, with him actually living here, when I could run into him any day of the week. Walking Nemesis.

Then there's James: what's the matter with him since we moved here? Is he having some sort of premature mid-life crisis? If he isn't in the Shack he's at the pub, or Howard's, or with his cronies.

I used to look forward to our weekends, but now all we seem to do is bicker when we bump into one another on one of James's rare visits to the house. And I'm doing all the house renovating and gardening (helped by Bob).

It's strange that James is so jealous of Fergal, yet doesn't seem to want me physically himself. Perhaps I've let myself go a bit since we came here and should make the effort to dress up when he's home. (Not that he makes the effort to *be* home that much, so it would be wasted.) I could try a bit, though.

It would certainly make me feel better about running into

Fergal, if James and I were presenting a United Marital Front, even though it may be a bit hollow at the heart.

That made me remember some queen who wanted her heart buried at Calais, of all places. It's probably under a hypermarket by now.

Fergal: June 1999

'*I'M JUST LOOKING FOR A QUIET LIFE,*'
says rocker. Seen talking to an old friend,
Mrs Leticia Drew, at the Nutthill Church Fête.'
Nutthill District Advertiser

Life is stranger than fiction, they say. Mine certainly is.

I wouldn't have chosen a house here if I'd known – and yet . . .

Is she happy? She looked thin and tired, with dark circles under her eyes. Has she forgiven her husband for his lapse with the secretary? Does she regret sleeping with me?

She must – she looked so horrified when she saw me and, perversely, it made me feel angry, because if I can't have her, I don't want to see her around all the time.

But I'll have to, and pretend what happened meant nothing to me, that *she* means nothing to me. I'm no marriage wrecker.

Nerissa, who tagged along, recognised Tish from the gallery and is busy putting two and two together and making ten or more.

Life's a bugger sometimes.

Chapter 18: Fencing

Had a terse note in Fergal's instantly familiar scrawly handwriting, saying he would look into the matter of the boundary fence as soon as he could, 'Yours, F. Rocco'.

Up yours too, buster.

I now know all about his girlfriend courtesy of Mrs D., and it sounds like they were made for each other.

'Her dad's a Yank, and they live over at Lavingham. Rolling in it, they are. "Bright's Computers Are the Best" and all that, you know?' she informed me.

I nodded, which was all the encouragement she needed.

'She – this Nerissa they called her – she's a handful. Ran off from school when she was just sixteen with a fairground worker and her dad didn't find her for a fortnight. School wouldn't have her back, so she had to go to a different, stricter one, and then she was finished.'

'Finished?'

From the sound of it, she'd barely begun!

'Went abroad somewhere to learn the language and cook fancy foreign food. When she came back she was in the mags every week with a different man, and none of them what you might call a nice, steady boy. All actors and pop singers, and that footballer – well, his last girlfriend may say she walked into a door, but it was one with a fist attached to it if I'm any judge. But there, I don't suppose she'll listen to any advice, for she's proper wild, for all she looks such a sweet, innocent young thing.'

'She should suit Fergal Rocco very well then,' I told her, slightly tartly. 'They can compare their misspent pasts on long, dark, winter evenings.'

'I suppose she may be settling down,' Mrs D. suggested doubtfully. 'After all, it's been going on for quite a while now, and if he's bought the Hall I expect he may be thinking of marrying? But I don't suppose her dad will like him any better than the others, and he's quite a bit older than she is, too. You know,' she added, resting her bosom comfortably on the sugar bags, 'it's funny, but it's a bit hard to believe those stories about Mr Rocco when you're talking to him. He's ever so pleasant. Sort of – warm.'

Hot, more like.

'A man can smile and smile yet still be a villain,' I quoted. (Or misquoted. It was probably Shakespeare, most quotations seem to be.)

'Oh, yes, that's true, dear, as I well know. And it must have been right about those nuns in the fountain because I saw the photos myself in *Exposé* magazine.'

She gave me one of those oblique glances, sharp enough to lance a boil at fifty paces, and added, 'I still can't get over you knowing him.'

I tried to look bored with the subject. (Practice makes perfect.) 'Oh – it's so many years ago that I'm surprised he recognised me again.'

After this conversation I went home and gave the kitchen

the sort of thorough cleaning that includes scraping between the tiles with a toothpick. I was in that sort of mood.

Maybe it's because I can never quite cleanse myself of the taint of adultery. I'm a walking Whited Sepulchre.

Speaking of Whited Sepulchres, James got awful sunburn through spending the first really hot Sunday of the year lying on a garden chair wearing his squash shorts, thus exposing a pair of corpse-like white legs. Anyone with a modicum of common sense would at least have basted them before going out and roasting them: but not James!

Now he blames me for not telling him to put oil on. Am I my husband's keeper? (Apparently, yes!)

Soon after he came in his legs started to turn strawberry-coloured and sore, and he vanished for ages into the bathroom, where he smeared nearly a whole pot of my expensive face cream over them.

At bedtime he was annoyed when I laughed at him because he looked as though he was wearing scarlet leg warmers – though that was before I found out about the face cream.

Today he's lying on the bed moaning that his legs hurt too much for him to move. I had to call Lionel and explain why he wasn't coming in, which didn't go down too well, Uncle obviously considering that anything short of amputation shouldn't stop business.

However, I seized the opportunity to inform him that James could do with a rest anyway, working all these late nights and Saturdays, and that seemed to silence him. Perhaps he'll be a bit more considerate of the workload he asks him to take on.

Then I had to dash into town (having already run up and down the stairs for hours with drinks, cigars and food) to find something a bit less expensive and more effective than face cream for the invalid to anoint himself with. *And* some more face cream for me, since he's now had the lot.

But unfortunately for James, no sooner had he smeared on the cod-liver oil ointment recommended by the chemist, than Bess leaped on him with loud cries of delight and began frantically licking it off again, making him scream with pain. He insisted that I shut her out of the bedroom (as though it was me who allowed her upstairs in the first place).

This was the high spot of an otherwise very tedious day. The bedroom was so unbearably full of cigar smoke at bedtime that I had to open all the windows, letting horrible flying things in. Then, after a night largely spent listening to Nature's Wonderful Creations slaughter each other in the garden, I was woken at dawn as usual by the tractor starting up, followed by Mrs Peach's hen chorus.

Oh, the joys of country living!

Still, on the upside, there was a hand-delivered invitation to a barbecue on the mat from Margaret Wrekin, addressed to 'Marian Plentifold and husband', which made James a bit sour.

It's on Friday night at eight thirty. 'Come and meet your neighbours,' she'd written, and I do think it's very nice of them to invite us. Perhaps we'll meet lots of nice local people and have a (joint) social life again.

Then a workman appeared at the end of the garden and started measuring up the fence, and it seems Fergal has ordered a curved, white-painted metal paling to be installed, one strong enough to keep the cows out but not impede my view (of his park).

It was thoughtful of Fergal, because if he just wished to put a barrier between us he could simply have had a high wall built, and I wished I hadn't been quite so rude to him (though he started it). But James went all jealous and peculiar, as he does at any mention of the dreaded name.

I don't know what this dog-in-the-manger attitude is all about – he may be guarding the bone, but he doesn't seem very interested in it otherwise.

Is the Right Wife just a possession like the Right House, Right Friends and Right School?

While chatting to the workman at the bottom of the garden I discovered that Bob had dug up all the pretty pinkish-purple flowers that I'd been training up the fence, but he told me that it was bindweed and very persistent. Well, not in those words he didn't, just said it was 'turrible stuff' and ground it under his heel. I looked it up in my wildflower book. Gardener's Bane.

I'll have sweet peas next year.

I finally made an appointment to see the doctor, where I told her about stopping the pill, and how my periods have been sporadic and slight ever since, just like they used to be before I started taking it. I mean, my last one lasted two days and was hardly worth mentioning! (Perhaps drinking to excess the night of the SFWWR dinner affected it? But I didn't like to ask that.)

'Perfectly normal. They'll settle down in time.'

'Oh – right. Er . . .'

Actually, what I *really* wanted to ask was whether my ambiguous feelings about motherhood were normal. And is *James* entirely normal in wanting only sons? Where does he get such feudal notions? He seems to be slowly reverting to some horribly chauvinistic ancestor. Possession, perhaps?

'Anything else?' she asked briskly.

'I – I was thinking of having a baby, doctor, but—'

'Well, you don't need my help for that, do you?'

I tried to explain my confused feelings, but she was looking down all the time and writing, and after a bit I petered out, without even mentioning James's lack of libido.

'All perfectly natural. Balanced diet. Relax. Good luck.' Then she went back to her writing.

I leaned over as I left to see what it was: *The Times* crossword.

This was all highly unsatisfactory, so I attempted to discuss how I felt with James, and he looked so shocked that he obviously felt I was unnatural, if not actually insane.

Nor did he want to discuss why our sex life has gone from being a series of reconciliations with longer and longer gaps in between, to non-existent, except to say that he's always tired since we moved here, working such late hours, and then the commuting, and doing things to the house. (What things? *I* do them all.)

Perhaps a baby would bring us closer together. I've never seen James with a baby – perhaps he'd love it, since he goes on about it so much, and share in looking after it.

Or am I deluding myself? At any rate, you can't ignore a baby, can you?

I made the long journey in to see Mother, since we missed Sunday, but she was on her way out when I arrived, accompanied by a man I only managed, after a struggle, to identify as Dr Reevey, one of Granny's discarded medicos.

Duncan (as he jovially invited me to call him) was attired in checked shirt, denim jeans and Cuban-heeled boots, which had the merit only of making Mother's garb not look quite so odd.

No, I'm wrong, they *both* looked very odd.

'We're just going line dancing, dear,' Mother explained. 'So we can't stop. Such good exercise!'

They teetered off together. Dr Reevey is a short man, so I suppose he quite relishes the chance to put on the high heels occasionally. Perhaps Mother being so tiny is also part of her attraction for him.

Could this be *lurve*?

'It's me, Granny!' I called as I went in.

'She's not in,' Granny greeted me, offering me a chocolate from a small gilt and white box. 'Gone to a hoe-down or some such with that doctor, and dressed like an extra from *Oklahoma!*'

'Line dancing.'

Granny had lost interest. 'What have *you* got on? Makes you look like an Avon lady.'

'It's the suit James bought me for my birthday as a surprise. I don't like it either, but I thought I'd just try it and see if I could sort of get used to the idea of Smart. Only going out in a skirt above my knees makes me feel like a Transvestite after all these years of long skirts and jeans.'

'Always look perfectly all right to me,' Granny said decidedly. 'Wouldn't bother, if I were you.'

I threw my arms around her and gave her a big hug. 'Granny, I do love you!'

'Eh, well, you big daft ha'porth. Maybe there's some Thorpe in you after all,' she said, pleased.

'There must be – though I don't look like Dad, do I?'

'No, though sometimes I think there's a look . . . but there, even a dog and its master look alike.'

'Anyway, I don't look like Mother, as she's always reminding me,' I said ruefully.

'You're very well as you are, so stop trying to be what other people want, especially that big girl's blouse you married. Wear bright colours – I like a bit of colour now I'm over yer grandpa's death – and if I see one more taupe twinset I'm going to puke.'

Granny herself that day was wearing a shiny, deep green shift of tubular construction, with a black velvet coatee and a bracelet of tiny Fabergé eggs.

On her feet were tartan slippers with gay red pompoms, and her legs were encased in matching Black Watch tartan.

'I like your stockings, Granny.'

'Tights, they are. Only a masochist would wear a suspender belt when they could wear tights.'

'Are suspender belts uncomfortable?'

'Contraption of the Devil. In the war I painted my legs with gravy browning, only the family dog kept trying to lick it off. He had a warm tongue.'

That reminded me to tell her about James and the cod-liver oil ointment, which made her laugh.

Two of us against the sartorial world isn't bad, so I have given up my half-hearted attempts to be alluring, which were not working anyway, and reverted to type. (Slob, I think.)

Fergal: July 1999

FURIOUS FERGAL IN PATERNITY ROW AFTER NUN FUN!

Sun

That I'm furious is the only true thing about the story: she wasn't a nun, we didn't have fun, and if she's pregnant, it's nothing to do with me.

Things have been quiet lately, so perhaps it's another of Hywel's schemes, but if so then he can damned well pay for the DNA check, or pay her off, because I'm not.

Nerissa seems to believe it. Unfortunately, the worse I'm painted, the more attractive she seems to find me, and living near her parents' house doesn't help, because she's always on the damned doorstep.

I only hope Tish doesn't see the nun story . . .

Have I any infectious diseases, indeed!

That's Tish.

Chapter 19: One Big Ham

I never thought James would get permission to put that enormous, unsightly radio aerial up on the house, but he did. He said his uncle Lionel knew someone in the planning department, or somewhere. He would. It looks awful, really awful.

Now his radio equipment is functioning (I'm glad something is!) he spends most evenings in the Shack, and his friends visit him there, bypassing the house completely. They do say 'Hi!' if they happen to catch sight of me in the garden, except Horrible Howard, who just smirks.

If I'm very lucky I get to give James an evening meal between his arrival home (at an undisclosed time), and his going over to the Shack: this is what my married life has degenerated into. Not quite how I envisaged our rural idyll, I must admit.

Sometimes ghostly-sounding voices waft over on the night air from the little hut, and crackling noises, but when it all goes silent I know they've adjourned to the pub.

I don't know what Mrs Peach is making of all this. She hasn't said anything when she comes round with the eggs and to see Toby. He increasingly avidly anticipates her arrival, and gets very excited – as soon as he hears the doorbell he starts to scream hello. It's a true communion of souls. (Pity I can't give her the bloody bird, but I'm not sure that I wouldn't forfeit the legacy, which has long since been spent . . . and I suppose I am sort of used to having him around after all this time.)

One evening James actually came home early, but it was only because he was in a panic and wanted to ring the doctor up for reassurance. One of the junior partners has gone down with mumps.

'I don't suppose you'll get it anyway,' I consoled him. 'It sounds such a childish sort of ailment.'

'You can kiss goodbye to any chance of having children if I do!' he retorted melodramatically.

'What do you mean?'

'It often leaves men infertile.' Sweat broke out on his forehead.

I didn't know that, although something about mumps did ring a bell somewhere at the back of my mind. Then I remembered: 'It can't always have that effect, James, because Granny told me once that Dad had it just after he married Mother, and they still had me!'

'They didn't have any more, though, did they?' he pointed out unarguably, but actually, I've always thought that was because Mother disliked the whole messy, undignified business.

'And I've got this rash under my arms,' he added as a clincher.

'You know very well that's heat rash, James,' I said unsympathetically. 'You always get it in the summer.'

Fortunately the first flush of fear (and the rash) had worn off by the night of the Wrekins' barbecue on the ninth of July.

I wore a new pair of designer-label jeans, a short-sleeved silk blouse, and my one and only cashmere cardigan (twenty-first birthday present from Mother), in case it got chilly when the sun went down. Also the sandals with high heels that James hates, because they make me nearly as tall as he is – but nuts to him.

When I came downstairs ready he was dressed in a lumber-jack shirt with the sleeves rolled up and a very old pair of corduroy trousers.

'Good God, Tish! You aren't going to a Garden Party, you know!'

'At least I don't look as if I've spent the evening cleaning the sewers!' I retorted, annoyed. He goes from one sartorial extreme to another.

We walked there in silence (once we were out of earshot of Bess's anguished howls.)

The Wrekins' doorbell plays 'Oranges and Lemons' like the one I just got rid of.

A head popped over the garden wall. It had a beaky nose set between chubby cheeks and a tonsure of hair. Rather like a squished-up André Previn.

'Hi! Come round the back – there's a gate here. Like the doorbell? Amusing, isn't it? Hear it at the bottom of the garden!' He gave a snort and vanished.

Our host, presumably.

He proved to be a very small Welshman, and had been standing on a beer crate to look over the wall. I was glad he wasn't one of those extremely tall, thin people with very small heads, because I find that type physically very repulsive, like spiders.

There were about twenty other people there on an

enormous patio with an assortment of swinging seats and lounging chairs. Margaret emerged briefly from behind the barbecue and introduced us generally as 'Marian Plentifold, the novelist – I told you all she was coming – and her husband, of course . . .?'

'James,' I said, not daring to look at him. 'I'm really Tish Drew. Marian Plentifold is only my pen name.'

James hissed furiously at me, 'Now look what you've done! Everyone here knows your name and the sort of drivel you write.'

'I don't write drivel!' I hissed back, equally furiously, and then was drawn away from him by the interested questions of all the other women there who could, of course, have written novels every bit as good, 'if only they had the time'.

I expect some of them could, but several looked as if they had abandoned such minor skills as writing (other than cheques) once they'd acquired a husband.

But I'd misjudged them, for it transpired that they'd all read at least one of my books, which was gratifying. One haggard older woman said that there ought to be more sex in them – they were too tame – and I wondered if she'd enrolled in the Wife Swappers yet. But her husband is a desiccated shrimp of a man with glasses an inch thick, so I don't think there would be much call to swap anyone's husband for him.

Once we'd divided up into male and female camps, the women got down to grilling me about Fergal Rocco, and seemed a bit disappointed when I told them that I knew him only briefly years ago.

'He's so sexy!' sighed the haggard woman.

'He certainly is! He can leave his slippers under my bed

any time,' agreed a horsy-looking girl. 'Do you think it's true about those six nuns in Rome? You know, when they said he—'

'I've absolutely no idea,' I said shortly. 'And, what's more, I'm not very interested.'

They eventually gave up in disgust.

There was an enormous bowl of punch and all the ladies had been automatically handed great tumblers of the stuff as they arrived, which were constantly replenished by the Welsh gnome. It contained fruit salad, and a Sargasso of strange purple flowers floated on top.

I was just wondering what the flowers were, and whether they were supposed to be eaten or not, when James lost his footing and fell into a prickly bush and I inadvertently swallowed one.

He was not so terribly drunk that the shock of being picked out of the prickly bush and dusted down didn't sober him quite a bit. Then the kebabs and pitta bread were handed round, which gave his stomach a respite from an almost totally fluid diet.

Margaret wandered up with a plate of little sausages on sticks and, to my horror and embarrassment, James suddenly said in an all-too-audible aside to me, 'Pricks on sticks!'

Luckily Margaret burst out laughing, then told everyone else, as though it was the most amusing thing she'd heard for years. (Maybe it was.)

After that everyone went round offering each other 'a prick on a stick' and being very vulgar about comparing length and width, and telling James how frightfully witty he was.

I expect he might seem to be, if you're not married to

him, and I do seem vaguely to recall his exerting his charm on me in the way he now does only with other women, too.

'You are lucky being married to such a handsome, romantic man!' sighed the haggard woman, whose one-strap trousered garment was in danger of becoming a no-strap one at any minute, since there wasn't much up-front to stop its downward progress, as it were. 'It's easy to see what inspires you to write your novels.'

Romance? There isn't a drop in his veins! (There may have been, once, but it has all been well flushed out since.)

Margaret's husband insisted on taking me for a tour of the garden in the half dark, where I floundered reluctantly about in the loose earth in my high heels with Ray hanging off my arm like a folded raincoat. I was glad to get back to the light and solidity of the patio, particularly since he is the sort of man who must touch women if he is near one – the hand on the arm, the pat on the rear, the hand sliding round the waist. Ugh!

(Though come to think of it, that's better than the ones who check their crotches right in front of you every five minutes, as though afraid something might have fallen off.) More kebabs were circulated and, as it was getting really dark, flares on sticks were lit all round the garden, which looked very pretty. I couldn't see what was in this kebab, and I suspect I got some grease on my silk blouse. I hope not.

My glass had been refilled to brimming point, and the trouble with punch is that you don't know what's in it: it always tastes innocuous, even when it isn't.

Ray Wrekin had an inexhaustible fund of ghastly jokes with which to bore the assembled throng between rushing in and out of the house changing records. (Why did he bother? One Barry Manilow sounds very like another.) Everyone else laughed at the jokes just before the punch line, so they'd probably been just as amused last time he told them.

Margaret, tall and stately, towered fondly above him, reminding me of a picture I'd once seen of a zoo giraffe whose favoured and inseparable companion was a pygmy goat.

I felt a sudden need to sit down, and fortunately there was an empty swinging seat behind me. It rocked danger-ously, and I hastily drained my glass before it spilled, then put my feet up and sat drowsily listening to all the murmuring voices.

James was nowhere to be seen. The Welsh comedian hadn't been in evidence for a bit either . . . and I had definitely had more than enough to drink without intending to. I closed my eyes.

'Oh, there you are!' said James, and I woke with a start, feeling stiff and a bit sick.

'Where have you been, James? I haven't seen you for ages.'

'Oh, Ray wanted to see my radio set-up. I wasn't away very long. He's coming round tomorrow too. Come on – everyone's going.'

And indeed, the garden was emptying fast and the flares were beginning to gutter.

We thanked our hosts and tottered out (well, I tottered, but that was the high heels rather than anything) into the night, where the sound of voices in inebriated conversation and the slamming of car doors enlivened the previously peaceful and sleeping village.

As we walked, he put his arm round me and we talked to each other as we haven't done for ages about all kinds of things, like what Bob had done in the garden, and whether to have wrought-iron furniture or wooden on the patio (when we have a patio), and whether Bess was capable of being obedience-trained, and things like that.

Neither of us mentioned the sticky subjects like radio hams, novels, money, Fergal or babies, and so we went to bed in perfect amity.

Then I woke up at five with awful indigestion (probably those purple flowers in the punch) and had to go down and root in the kitchen for milk of magnesia.

Bess glared dolefully at me.

James didn't let her come upstairs with us last night, though from what I recall of the proceedings they were so routine, boring and inconclusive that she might have been able to offer some good advice.

When I got up for the second time I felt much better, but James refused to speak to me, and when I brought him some tea and toast he put a pillow over his head.

I left him to his misery and went down to Mrs Deakin's for some more milk of magnesia, since I'd finished ours and I could see it would be all my fault if James couldn't find anything to dose himself with.

'I'm not surprised at you wanting this,' she remarked, reaching the blue bottle down from a high shelf with the aid of a little pair of steps. 'You was eating offal last night, and that's a thing I don't never do.'

'Offal? But I never eat offal!'

'If you ate them kebab things you did.' (Mrs D. knows everything!) 'Mrs Wrekin herself told me what was going on them – peppers and courgettes and tomatoes she got here, and liver and bacon she got in town, though some was to be lamb, too, I think she said.'

No wonder I felt ill! Fancy someone like Margaret Wrekin serving offal to her guests. I wouldn't dream of buying liver except to give to Bess.

'The trouble is, everything just tasted of barbecue.'

'Seems silly to me.' Mrs Deakin brushed dust off a card of bootlaces with her pinny. 'I mean, why go cooking outside over a little smoky fire, when you've got a good electric oven indoors? And then sitting about in the nasty night air, bitten by midges and getting grease down you.'

'That reminds me! Do you know how to get grease off a silk blouse?'

'I've got just the thing,' she said.

Fergal: July 1999

'*STAND BY YOUR MAN*
Girlfriend of shock rocker Fergal Rocco
says she'll stand by him in nuns row.'

Sun

I don't know how you define girlfriend – but how nice of Nerissa to stand by me for something I didn't do. It seems to me she doesn't care what I get up to provided she can present herself as my girlfriend.

She's haunting me, although it must be obvious I've long since lost interest in her body and I never was interested in her mind. If she's got one.

No, that's unfair: she may have the intellectual depth of

a very small puddle, but she'd win *Mastermind* on the subjects of fashion, or Who's Who in the In crowd.

Maybe I'm just getting old.

Still, Nerissa provides a smokescreen in case Tish suspects I have any interest in her, there is that . . . and I realise I may not sound like a very nice person, but I did make it clear from the start I wasn't looking for any kind of relationship and, given her track record, it had seemed unlikely that Nerissa was, either.

I really hate people trying to manipulate me.

Chapter 20: No Change

I thought the night of the barbecue would change things between James and me a bit, but it hasn't really – in fact, I don't think he remembers very much about it. (Not, admittedly, that it *was* very memorable. And I'm so out of practice with James that it felt rather more adulterous than my lapse with Fergal.) He's seen more of Ray Wrekin in the last couple of weeks than he has of me! They've struck up some sort of friendship and Ray is constantly round at the Shack in the evenings.

Mother has been labouring under the misapprehension that James has taken up amateur theatricals. I thought her reaction to my telling her he'd become a ham was strange, but then, so is Mother.

She is stupid (but cunning). Where can I have got my brains from? Dad can't have been all that bright, or he wouldn't have married her.

Fortunately she hasn't found a hospital geriatric ward willing to take Granny for a 'holiday'. I'm not surprised, since there's nothing wrong with her except the diabetes and an unpleasant sense of humour, and there's no way in which Mother could have got her into hospital other than in a straitjacket.

Nor was it a good move to try to get power of attorney, either.

'Is that you, Leticia darling?' she screeched wildly down the phone on her return from her latest abortive foray. 'Oh, I've been so humiliated! That terrible Mr Herries! I'm going to move my affairs to a respectable firm of solicitors, and so I told him. Calling me unfit to have the care of a "delicate old lady"! Delicate as old boots!'

'Mother, why should Mr Herries insult you?' I enquired, keeping my voice calm. 'I thought you got on well with him.'

'I didn't know his true nature. I went to see him this morning about Granny – you know how strange she has been getting lately – quite senile, poor thing . . .'

Do I?

'And I told him he had better arrange for me to have control of her affairs, since she was obviously incapable; and he said that she was as sane as he was, and not much older, and only needed the sort of caring attention any daughter-in-law should be glad to give! What cheek!'

She paused to gulp down something – probably sherry.

'Where was I? Oh, yes! I asked Granny as soon as I got back when she had been in to see him again, and she told me that she'd called a taxi last week while I was out and gone to make a new will. Secretive! It's all part of the process of senility, though Mr Herries is obviously going the same way himself.'

Mr Herries, who is indeed a near contemporary of Granny's, has known her since her marriage, so it was not startlingly tactful of Mother to approach him in this way.

Any legal adviser worth his salt would also realise that, with Mother managing her affairs, Granny would be destitute within a year.

Not that any of us knows exactly what she has stashed away in the bank because she isn't telling, and she has been fighting Mother off her jewellery box for years. Mother's latest ploy was to offer to take it all to be cleaned at her own expense, but Granny is too fly to be taken in by that one.

'Are you still there?' demanded Mother peevishly.

'Yes. I'm still here, Mother—'

'Mummy, dear – Mummy.'

'Sorry, Mummy. Look here, why don't you explain to Granny that you would like a little rest, and see if she'll hire a nurse to stay with her while you go away somewhere?' (Anywhere but here!)

'I have. She says she doesn't need a nurse, and she doesn't need me, and I can go whenever I like!'

'Well, she isn't exactly helpless, is she? Though she does need someone to keep an eye on her in case she falls and can't get up, or anything, and to make sure she gets a proper diet. Look, if you really can't stand it any more, why don't you move into a little flat of your own, where you could pop in and see her every day?'

'Oh, I couldn't do that! And anyway, I couldn't afford it . . . we have an arrangement about the bills.'

Yes, I thought, Granny pays them!

'But what's really annoying, Leticia darling, is that when I phoned Mr Herries to tell him a few home truths I thought up on the way home, Granny was listening in on the extension, and now she won't speak to me except to give me orders as if I were the housekeeper!'

'Never mind, Mother, she'll get over it.'

'Mummy, dear – you keep calling me Mother again, and it sounds so hard and unfeeling from my little girlie.'

'Sorry, Mummy. But I really don't think you should have approached Mr Herries about Granny, because she isn't that bad, is she? I mean, she's always been a bit strange in her ways, though it must be very trying for you, of course.'

'You just can't understand my feelings, dear, can you? I gave James a ring at his office earlier, and he was so sympathetic, though he said he couldn't do anything personally to help, because of being family. Professional etiquette, I expect. And he hardly said a word against you, though you've been a trial to him lately, haven't you? Jealous of the little bit of time he spends with his radio thing and his friends. And I do so agree with him that children are more important to a woman than a career.'

'Then it may interest you and dear, sweet, understanding James to know that I'm never going to stop writing novels so long as they sell!' And I slammed the phone down and stood positively trembling with rage.

Of course, this conversation totally destroyed any faint increase in amity between James and me since the barbecue, though that wasn't much anyway. More a *laissez-faire* policy. And it was mostly me who'd been doing the trying – I'd conscientiously not been snarling at him when he came in at dawn after being out with his friends all evening, and then boring the world into the early hours through the miracle of radio waves.

But *he* has asked after the progress of my book! (Devious pig.)

Obviously he doesn't intend to change and, after hearing what he has been saying to Mother, I find myself almost – yes – *disliking* him!

I sat in the hall on the commode (it will always be a

commode to me) and the tears came into my eyes. We should be so happy – we're both young and healthy, and doing well in our respective careers. Any other man would be proud of having a wife who, if not a famous literary name, at least sold vast numbers of books.

And until we moved here, to the cottage we'd dreamed of (though did we both dream of living in the country, or did James just agree with me because he didn't care where he lived?), we *were* happy.

We never quarrelled, possibly because I gave in all the time to please James, because I loved and admired him – or the man I thought he was.

Everything we planned for our future, the sort of things we wanted, were the same. Except for my secret misgivings about motherhood, and James's assumption that I would give up my 'hobby' of writing once he was earning enough money, and I thought time would allay the one and alter the second.

How differently I feel now! My most overwhelming feeling towards him at the moment seems to be resentment. He treats me like a housekeeper. And all his habits have begun to annoy me.

Do I really love this selfish, chauvinistic idiot? Did I ever? The old Tish certainly thought she did: what happened to her?

I wonder if he still loves me. I can't recall the last time he said anything even remotely affectionate. I'm afraid to ask, in case he says 'no'.

What if he asked me? I really don't know what I'd answer, but probably 'yes' from sheer panic. How would I manage alone?

Alone . . . but when do I have his company now? For a few hours of the night, so late that I'm usually asleep before he comes to bed, and at breakfast, which I'm expected to produce punctually and without thanks, and at which he reads the paper and says nothing except, 'Where are the aspirins?' or 'Isn't there any more coffee?'

Our evening meal together is a thing of the past. He often stays out with friends after work, then comes home and doesn't understand why I didn't know exactly the time of his arrival and so haven't got a meal ready and waiting, when I've given him up and had beans on toast hours before.

If I complain he goes off to his Shack with a sandwich, or down to the pub with Ray Wrekin, who has now decided to become a fellow ham and is busily setting himself up in a Shack of his own, far more palatial than James's.

Margaret (we're becoming quite friendly) says she is so glad he has a little hobby, because it keeps him from getting under her feet all the time.

James keeps throwing her into the conversation as a glowing example of motherhood, because she has two children and an immaculate house and garden. (An Immaculate Concept?) She also has a gardener and a live-in mother's help, so I don't see how he can compare our situations. Come to that, I don't remember ever seeing her with the children.

I am really fed up.

That's put the lid on it! James discovered I'd complained to Lionel about his expecting too many late nights and weekends, and more or less told me to keep my nose out of his business. If it isn't my business too, I don't know what that makes me.

Slave?

So we are now back to pre-barbecue status, only worse.

Added to this, I feel thoroughly off-colour and bloated, and I haven't had a period since the scanty one just after the SFWWR dinner. But it would be silly to start imagining I am pregnant just because of one rather inconclusive encounter with James.

Perhaps I am a little run down? I must get some multi-vitamins-and-minerals from the health food shop.

Fergal's workmen have started replacing the garden fence with an elegant metal railing, and one of them is going to come and make me a little patio, very cheaply.

I've only seen Fergal once or twice in the distance, and each time he has turned and walked away.

I don't want a baby.

Surely I can't be pregnant.

This is the moment of truth, isn't it, to know for certain I don't want to be pregnant, when there's the possibility I might be?

Feeling very guilty I had a hot bath and drank a lot of whisky. But apart from looking like a lobster and smelling like a distillery when James came home, it made no difference. *He* didn't notice.

After this panic-induced episode I gave myself a good talking-to, for all the symptoms I have – bloated tummy, tension round the forehead, general feeling of being not quite well – are all those I've had once or twice before when overdue and the doctor did say it might take a while for my system to settle down again after stopping the pill.

As soon as I relax and try to put my worries out of my mind, everything will be just as usual.

Those untraceable silent phone calls have started again! James must have been giving our ex-directory number out to all and sundry, though he says he only gives it to clients who might need to reach him at home. However, he's hardly ever here, so it might be more practical if he just handed out his radio frequency.

At least he's stopped checking himself daily for signs of mumps. I was beginning to wonder if he ever would.

This mumps thing has been niggling at my mind too, but in a different way. So I phoned Granny at a time when I knew Mother would be out lunching with Dr Reevey (an affair that seems to be advancing, though I'm not sure where to).

I had to let it ring for ages, of course, before she reluctantly answered it, and then we had to establish who I was, who she was, and where Mother was.

'Granny,' I said finally, 'do you remember telling me about Dad having the mumps just after he married Mother?'

'I might have!' she agreed cautiously.

'Well, did he?'

'Yes – he were took very bad. Valerie was in a state – as much use as a wet lettuce.'

'Someone told me recently that having mumps at that age can – can lead to not having children.'

'It can,' she admitted, with what sounded like reluctance, but was probably just her usual dislike of the telephone.

'But obviously it can't have affected Dad, can it, because I came along afterwards.'

There was a short pause, and then just as I was preparing to repeat my remark in a louder voice she spoke. 'We were that surprised when we got back from Russia and saw you!'

'Did you say Russia, Granny? You and Grandpa were in Russia when I was born?'

'Grand tour! Bernard – your grandpa – were that romantic! Wanted to tread the streets where that Fabergé lived. We did, too, and there were a lot of them. The food's something dreadful over there, and the signs aren't written in any Christian language.'

There was a pause.

'It was what they call a "fate acumply".'

'What was?' I was still trying to picture Granny, small, dark and determined, in Russia.

'You were. We got back, and Valerie was as slim as a lath just like she was when we went. "Sometimes it happens like that," I said to Bernard, "but it was funny it happened when she was on holiday, like, and why did she go alone?" He said: "Desmond's happy, leave well alone." He always liked you.'

'Do you mean I was a surprise? You didn't know Mother was preg—'

Granny's voice rolled relentlessly on. 'And, after all, there was the certificate for all to see, and no point in worrying about it at this late date.'

'Worrying about what? Granny!'

'Though I would have liked to know.'

'Know what? Granny! If I come when Mother isn't there, will you tell me all about it?'

'About what?'

'When I was born!'

'I wasn't there. I just said, I was in Russia, and bloody cold it is there too! I bought a fur hat.'

'But you could—'

'I've got photos!'

'What of?' I enquired, with more patience than I felt.

'Russia. I've got an album. I'll show you.'

'Thank you, Granny!'

It was like trying to grasp an eel, following the thread of a conversation with Granny, but she really had seemed to suspect something odd about my birth . . .

Though, as she said, she wasn't there! If I saw-the birth certificate perhaps I'd stop having such very strange thoughts?

Perhaps.

I was still sitting on the commode half an hour later when Mother rang to tell me all about her date with the doctor.

Chapter 21: Through a Glass, Darkly

I'm making too much of Granny's hints.

Mother hadn't been married to Dad all that long when she had me . . . but mumps doesn't always lead to infertility, and people do have babies without realising they're pregnant.

Speaking of which, *I'm* not pregnant after all. The loss was amazingly slight and lasted only a day or so, but what a relief! And I feel suddenly so much better all round, in fact – it must be the vitamins.

Every morning, as soon as James has gone, I sit down at my desk with the window open so that all the delicious warm, scented grassy smells of summer can waft around me as I write.

Having completed *Love on the Waves* I've begun a new book about a female explorer missing in the desert while searching for a lost city. She's rescued by a handsome safari tour operator, who turns out to be in the Secret Service (or whatever they call it these days – I'll have to find out).

Vivyan is delighted with *Love on the Waves*, but I've taken a dislike to it since it caused James to become a ham. Maybe when I start getting books on deserts he will become a

Nomad, fold up his tent and steal away? That's quite an appealing thought.

Margaret brought one of my books round for me to sign, for her mother's birthday present. I do think she could have afforded the hardback but she said she was a bit broke, because she'd just bought a marvellous epergne.

I was a bit guarded in my response, since I didn't know whether you ate, drank or wore an epergne, but when I looked it up in the dictionary it was a table centrepiece. I was so glad I hadn't said, 'That should be tasty, then,' or something else equally stupid.

Fancy getting all excited over a table decoration! And I expect Margaret's idea of being broke is not as we know it in real life.

After she'd gone I thought I'd ask Bob to teach me the names of the local wild birds, but when I pointed to one hopping around the strawberry bed and asked, 'What do you call that, Bob?' he just said, 'Little bleeder!' and threw a stone at it, so I cleaned out the cellar instead.

Mrs Deakin (who'd known about my 'secret' cellar and was surprised that I hadn't) sent an amiable, pony-tailed youth called Gary round to run electricity to it, and it now looks a lot less spooky.

I made two discoveries down there. The first was that Bess thinks spiders are Snacks on Legs, which is the first useful quality I've ever discovered in her.

The second caused me to pounce excitedly on James the minute he got home, shoving my treasure-trove under his nose. 'Look – I found this while I was cleaning out the cellar!'

'You might let me get through the door first!' he grumbled,

taking the bent, battered and dirt-encrusted object reluctantly from my hand.

'It's a ring. And it was wedged right down into a crack in the floor, so it's probably been there for centuries!'

James was unimpressed. 'More likely to have come out of a cracker.'

'But I'm sure it's old!'

'All right – a very *old* Christmas cracker. What's for dinner?'

Rather deflated, I went to put on the casserole. (Here's One I Made Earlier.)

But I took the ring to the museum anyway, for an expert opinion.

The bus ride made me feel quite nauseous, so I think I must have some sort of tummy bug. James seems all right, and he hasn't noticed that I'm feeling seedy and off my food. Nor am I sleeping very well, either, so I've got these interesting dark circles round my eyes like a marmoset.

He phoned at lunchtime to say we've been invited by Horrible Howard to a party tonight, but he didn't suppose I would want to go, so he would only be home long enough to grab a bite to eat and change.

He was right – I didn't want to go. It must be evident even to James that I loathe Howard, who is very Red, hasn't stopped being a hippie yet, despite balding and developing a paunch, and insists on wearing the remains of his hair in long oily wisps and buying flared Levi jeans that flap round his spindly legs.

Also they smoke pot, which smells disgusting, and then lose all interest in good conversation or anything else, just sitting around looking glazed. James will be struck off or something if he's ever caught in a house where that sort of thing goes on. He should think about these things, but he'll do anything to be one of the boys, regardless of who 'the boys' happen to be at the time.

When I reminded James about being struck off and all that, he said I was fast becoming a middle-class reactionary bore. I thought a middle-class reactionary bore was just the kind of wife he did want.

'You might make an occasional effort to take me somewhere I do want to go,' I said crossly.

'I often want to take you out, but you never want to go.'

'No you don't! I don't want to tag along when you go to pubs with the boys, I want us to go out together somewhere nice, like we used to.'

'I thought you might want to see Alice's new baby.'

'Who's Alice?' I asked, confused by this sudden change of front.

'Howard's girlfriend. I told you she was living with him, ages ago.'

'No, you didn't. It's a complete surprise to me!'

'It's the girl he met while he was crewing that yacht off Capri.'

That did ring a bell, but it was astounding that they were still together. 'Are they getting married?'

'No. Why should they? The party is to celebrate the baby's birth. Alice is nice – you'd like her.'

That's what he said about Vanessa.

I don't place much faith in James's ideas of the sort of people I'll like – especially women – but I admit my curiosity was stirred. Not stirred enough to go through with one of Howard's interminable parties, though, so I said I wouldn't go.

'Please yourself,' he replied, not sounding bothered. 'I'll be home about seven to change.'

The fact that he really didn't care if I went with him or not was worrying. What if he met Someone Else, or did something silly? And I've always gone to these things and pretended to enjoy myself. But why should I, when he never makes the same effort for me?

At six thirty I suddenly decided, in the interests of marriage-preservation, to make the effort, and dashed down to Mrs Deakin's.

'Have you got anything I could give as a present to a new baby?' I gasped hopefully. (He? She? It? With Howard for a father, probably an It.)

'Certainly. Hang on while I pop into the stockroom.'

This is the cupboard under the stairs, which is crammed full of cardboard boxes.

'Plastic pants . . . potties . . . dummies . . . Here we are!' She held up a card of brightly coloured rattles. 'One of these and a packet of terry bibs would make a good present, dear.'

The dreadfully garish rattles were shaped like no animals I'd ever seen. 'They're very bright,' I began dubiously.

'That's what babies like – the brighter the better. You take my word,' she added firmly.

So I did. I expect she's right, she usually is. I bought one with a vague resemblance to a lamb (or a llama) and a pack of three Mickey Mouse bibs. Then she found me some wrapping paper and a gift tag, though I'd already got a sheet of tissue paper at home that would have done.

When James got back he seemed pretty stunned that I'd changed my mind, but I expect he was pleased really. While he went to the pub to get a bottle to take with us, I went up to change.

I'd probably have to sit on a dog-hairy (or worse) floor, or at best a grimy floor cushion, and most of Howard's friends are closet hippies who emerge draped in nostalgia and limp cheesecloth at the word 'party', so anything light-coloured or smart was out.

My paint-stained jeans, old Indian cotton embroidered blouse, and a pair of thonged sandals seemed about right.

James changed his pinstripes for the Levi's I keep trying to put in the jumble, and a washed-out T-shirt, ditto, printed with the slogan, 'The only safe fast breeder is a rabbit.'

We arrived at a tall, thin mid-terraced house in a slummy part of town, bigger inside than it looked, since it went back and back in a series of little rooms. The last time I'd visited Howard he was living in a bedsit in a run-down house full of very peculiar people, but James said that this house belonged to Alice's father.

We walked straight in through the open front door, exchanging Miasma of Hot, Dirty July Pavement for Odour of Hot, Dark, Dirty House, then wandered in and out of the dimly lit rooms like everyone else, looking for Howard or Alice (or the baby). The only illumination came from candles in green glass tubes made from chopped-off bottles.

All the rooms contained people sitting about in corners holding glasses, cups and/or cigarettes, and not saying much. Probably because the walls were throbbing with music so loudly that it would take a pair of lip-readers with night sight to hold a decent conversation.

We went back into the hall and through a door right at the back. Here the music was even louder, and a couple were standing in the middle of the room shaking their heads up and down wildly in time to it. There was also a suspicious smell and the red glowing circle of a joint being passed from hand to hand.

Disgusting – you could catch *anything*.

James plonked our bottle of wine on to a table loaded with various kinds of booze, mostly cheap wine, and paper cups. It also bore a large, pink and obscene candle, which grew even more obscene and revolting as it burned and rivers of pink wax began to flow downwards.

Howard lurched out of the darkness as I was examining the paper cups to make sure I had a new one.

'Hi!' he said vaguely, reaching over my shoulder to pick up the good bottle of wine we'd brought, and that I was about to pour into my cup.

He was holding a pint glass tankard half-full of something, and he filled it to the brim with wine. It frothed.

I took the bottle from his hand before he could go off with it, though he seemed disinclined to do anything except goggle down at his frothing glass.

He's tall and lugubrious, with a nose like an aubergine, and had tied a long floating scarf in a band round his head. The end kept trailing dangerously near the candle.

'Congratulations!' I shouted.

He smiled into his glass.

'Where's Alice?' mouthed James.

'Alice?' muttered Howard, then looked up and suddenly shouted, 'Hey! Great to see you! How's life? Long time, no see, Tish! Have a drink – there's all sorts of booze there – no, not that one, Tish, it tastes kind of weird . . .'

'That's because you poured it onto beer,' I pointed out

coldly, but he was already on his way out of the room with James in tow. I'm long accustomed to being abandoned at parties. I was lucky James hadn't gone off at the front door.

Making out the outline of a sofa against one wall, I went and sat on the end of it. A girl was sitting on the other, leaning back with her eyes closed; but as I sat down with rather more force than I intended to, there being a deceptive lack of springs or padding under the sofa cover, she opened them and looked at me.

My eyes were now accustomed to the darkness, and I smiled at her nervously. She had large, dull eyes set deeply under bony brows in a haggard face, and hair parted in the middle and draped like seaweed over her shoulders and into her lap.

She examined me incuriously, and I half-expected a lizard-tongue to dart out from between those thin lips. Someone passed the glowing red eye of the joint to her and she bent forward, cupping her hands to it, before passing it to me.

I took it more to stop her setting me on fire than anything and, gingerly holding it at arm's length, passed it on to more willing hands.

After I had done this for the second time the girl's opaque eyes examined me again and she said perceptively: 'You don't smoke.'

It was not a question.

'Do you like cake?'

'What?' I said, confused. Was this a new name for some other unspeakable substance?

'Seed cake. I've made a nice seed cake,' said the girl, coming closer and hissing the remark down my ear.

'Lovely,' I said, pushing a slither of dank hair from my

face and edging back. 'But perhaps not just at the moment, thanks . . .'

She extricated herself from the sofa's clutches in a flutter of cheesecloth and a reek of patchouli.

Could she really have said that she'd made a seed cake? It seemed an unlikely, Victorian high-tea sort of thing for her to offer. And, of course, she must be Alice.

She bore down on me again carrying a plate on which reposed an enormous cake with a single flickering candle, and passed me a slice with her hand. Thank God the lights were off, because I don't suppose she washes her hands more than once a week. But I'm probably being uncharitable.

I nibbled the edge, and it was seed cake – but a very dry, peculiar sort. I'd have hidden it somewhere, if she hadn't reseated herself next to me and watched me eat, while devouring a large slice herself. The plate with the remains vanished on unseen hands into the Greater Darkness.

James reappeared suddenly at my elbow, bearing a bottle, and tried to refill my cup, which was already full.

'Hi, Alice! I see you found Alice, Tish,' he said in a slurry voice, swaying slightly.

'Are you James's wife?' she screamed, sounding surprised. (I don't know why.)

'Yes – congratulations about the baby. Oh . . .' I remembered the present and fished it out of my bag. 'Here.'

She seemed inordinately pleased with the rattle and bibs, peering at them in the gloom and murmuring brokenly, 'Mickey Mouse! Mickey Mouse!' Finally, still muttering 'Mickey Mmmmouse . . .' she fell back against the sofa, apparently asleep.

James had disappeared again and, although I thought of

trying to find him to tell him not to drink any more or take anything he shouldn't, I began to feel a little strange . . . but then, I've had this funny tummy for ages now. I ought to see the doctor about it. It wasn't the wine, because I only took a few sips to take the taste of the horrible seed cake out of my mouth.

Strange how the candle flames seemed to grow larger and larger and dance with a strange vitality of their own! I couldn't take my eyes off them. Then someone put on George Melly singing 'The Joint Is Jumpin'' and it struck me as so funny that I laughed until I cried, though no one heard me since the music was too loud.

I must have closed my eyes for a minute then, because when I opened them there was a Pekinese dog with long blond ears glaring down at me.

I blinked, and the Pekinese resolved itself hazily into a snub-nosed girl with long, light hair who straightened and, still with her eyes fixed on me, began to back slowly away until she vanished into the blackness beyond the candle flame.

As I said, there were some strange people at Howard's party.

Then a thin wailing began, piercing even through the music and the strange barrier between me and reality, and turning my head with infinite slowness I saw Alice reach down into the darkness beside the sofa and produce a wrapped bundle of baby.

The wailing seemed to go on for ever, but at last Alice managed to locate the front opening of her dress through a plethora of limp frill, and, casually attaching her offspring, sank back again with closed eyes.

After about ten minutes or so she woke with a start, looked down with a puzzled air at the baby, which had fallen away from her breast, then just as casually clapped it like a poultice to the other side.

I was amazed by her lack of attention to the poor thing, not to mention exposing herself so openly in a room full of people. I know it is all entirely natural and everything, but I wouldn't do that so indiscreetly for the world, even if it was semi-dark!

James suddenly plonked himself down on the sofa and put his arm round me. He watched Alice and I felt quite embarrassed for her, but she didn't seem to notice. After a bit he turned to me and said: ''S' lovely baby. Isn't it a lovely baby?'

I nodded and tried to smile, and he looked more closely at me, breathing a wine-laden gust so that I recoiled.

'Whasser matter? You all right?'

'I'm not feeling very well,' I admitted.

''S' not like you to get pissed!' He laughed unfeelingly.

'I'm not! I think it's just because it's so stuffy in here, and I don't think Alice's seed cake agreed with me.'

He began to laugh.

'What's the matter?'

'You – eating Alice's seed cake!'

'Shh! She'll hear you! Anyway, what's so funny about that?'

'Special seed cake! You know . . .' He nudged me, grinning. 'Perhaps you'd better ask her for the recipe.' And he started his silly giggling again, while it dawned on me that I'd probably been eating nicely baked cannabis resin or something.

I grabbed his arm and shook him. 'Where's the loo?'

'The loo?'

'Come on – I feel sick!'

'First door at the top of the shtairs . . . but look here, Tish—'

233

I left him babbling and stumbled over legs and bodies to the hall and up the stairs. There was a solitary candle in a saucer on the floor outside the loo, and since the light switch wasn't working I took it in with me. I didn't actually feel as if I was going to be sick, just queasy and a strange sensation about the head.

I quickly stuck two fingers down my throat, but this was not entirely satisfactory since quite a time had elapsed since I ate the cake, but after I'd washed my face in cold water and dried it on the hem of my blouse, I felt a bit better.

But angry – very, very angry. I thought of popping out to the telephone and tipping the police off about the goings-on here just before we left, but this is not a very salubrious area to go looking for a phone box in. I expect they've all been vandalised and used as urinals.

But it's a nasty thing to force that sort of drug on your unsuspecting guests disguised as cake.

I went back downstairs, determined on sobering James up enough to drive me home, and found him still slumped on the sofa next to Alice. I went looking for the kitchen to make some coffee, but it was disgustingly filthy, with what looked like years' worth of unwashed dishes piled in the sink. There were only candles in here too, and I discovered that the electricity was off when I tried to plug the kettle in.

He would probably have caught typhoid or hepatitis from the cup anyway (though that would have served him right).

So I gave up the coffee idea and shook him awake. He was very reluctant to leave, but when I looked at my watch it was a quarter to three. I seemed to have lost about three hours somewhere.

I wanted to call a taxi, but as usual he insisted that he was perfectly all right, the idiot. Another occasion when I wished that I could drive.

We were silent until halfway home, when I remembered something. 'There was a peculiar blonde girl there tonight, James – staring at me.'

The car wavered. 'What? Blonde girl? Staring at you?' parroted James. 'When? Where? What do you mean?'

'At the party. I'd fallen asleep – that awful cake I expect – and when I opened my eyes there was this girl glaring at me.'

'You dreamed it.'

'No, I didn't.'

'Oh, come on, Tish! You're imagining it. Or – I know – maybe it was Alice's sister trying to find her in the dark. She's blonde, though I didn't think she was there tonight.'

'Alice's sister?'

'Her younger sister, Wendy. She's a fashion student, so she lives with them during the week. I expect she's been helping Alice with the new baby.'

'I suppose you could be right,' I conceded slowly. After that cake it was a bit hard dividing the real from the imagined. 'Do you think you could slow down a bit?'

His driving had become even more erratic than when we started out, if that was possible, and I felt queasy again.

'I'm not driving fast!' he protested, but ten miles an hour would be too fast when you've drunk that much.

This is it: I'm never going to be a passenger in the car when James has had a drink again. If I can't persuade him not to drink and drive, I can at least not be a party to it.

The Bourgeois Bitch had left a great steaming Welcome Home gift in the hall from sheer pique at being left behind.

James stepped straight over it and carried on upstairs, saying he had to go to work in the morning and it was very late.

Dealing with that didn't make me feel any better, but afterwards, when I'd cleared up and let the silly bitch into the garden, propitiated Toby with a biscuit, and disinfected my hands – then I sat for a while in my lovely clean kitchen, drinking coffee out of a clean porcelain mug, feeling better at last.

But I'm never going to one of Howard's parties again!

Fergal: July 1999

'BAND ON THE RUN:
Goneril take the plunge with naked Nordic blondes'
Exposé magazine

I absolve Hywel from this one. We all wanted to try the sauna/jumping in the icy lake bit after our gig in Stockholm, and someone set the girls on to us.

As they streamed naked into the sauna we all bolted for the lake and jumped in, and they followed us.

I have this affinity for water . . .

'What the hell do we do now?' Carlo yelled, surfacing next to me like a wet seal.

'Try and rise to the occasion?' I suggested, treading water.

The boys have got some explaining to do to their wives/girlfriends. The camera doesn't exactly lie, but it can certainly be manipulated to show a parallel universe.

Nordic Blondes – what every swimmer is wearing this year.

Chapter 22: Bugged

I think I'm managing to shake off the tummy bug at last. My diet should certainly be healthy enough, with all this stuff Bob produces in the garden. He seems to have gone overboard with lettuce: we've had lettuce soup, braised lettuce, and salad, salad, salad. I wonder if you can make lettuce wine?

James hates salad (and anything else remotely good for him), and I've sent Margaret so much lettuce via Ray that she is probably sick of it too.

(Ray and James have had T-shirts printed with the slogan: 'NUTTHILL HAMS.' How can they be seen like that?)

Then I had a brain wave and sent Bob with a note asking Mrs Peach if she'd like the excess lettuce for her rabbits, and she returned it with 'many thanks – will reciprocate in kind later' written on the bottom.

Does this mean she's going to give me her excess vegetables? I didn't think she grew much.

Bob was quite amenable to all this trotting to and fro with messages. Bob, in fact, is amenable to most things, although he has very stubborn notions about what he's going to grow in *my* garden. We have an unspoken agreement about produce: he divides everything ripe into two portions and takes one lot home after presenting me with the other.

So as not to hurt his feelings I frequently have to sneak down and feed excess vegetables to the cows at dusk over the garden fence, which is what I was doing this evening when my Lurid Past came striding out of the small spinney in the park towards me.

He was wearing a dull green chambray shirt and black jeans, and for once his long black hair was not pulled tightly back into a ponytail, but loose and blowing about his angular face. He looked like an updated Red Indian Brave, and from his scowl when he caught sight of me I wasn't sure if he was going to take my scalp or just sheer off.

Guiltily I hid the lettuce behind my back. Stupid, really – the cows all had stalks dangling from their mouths, which was a dead giveaway.

'So that's why they nearly had that old fence over!' he remarked coolly, coming to a stop before me with his hands thrust into his jeans pockets.

'I've only just started doing it,' I said, thrown on to the defensive. 'Bob produces so much stuff that I don't know what else to do with it.'

Black brows twitched together in a frown: 'Who's Bob? The husband?'

'No, that's James. Bob does some gardening for me.'

'Why doesn't James do it?'

'He's too – too busy. And I don't know what business it is of yours, anyway.'

'I'm told he's a radio ham. That where his stuff is?' He nodded over to the Shack.

'You're very well informed!'

'I've furthered my acquaintance with the excellent Mrs Deakin, Proprietoress of the Nutthill Home Stores.'

All was revealed, then – or if it wasn't, it very soon would be.

'Poor Mrs D. was getting terribly frustrated at not being able to find out anything about you,' I told him.

A smile softened his mouth and radiated little lines around his eyes that I hadn't noticed before. He was older, of course . . . we were both older. But he had rather more years of hard living under his (admittedly narrow) belt than I did.

'The vicar told me she was the local *Enquire Within Upon Everything*, so I asked her about cleaning ladies. I now know large amounts of information about all sorts of local people – including you.'

'Oh – *us*!' I said brightly. 'There's not a lot to tell about us.' Surely even Mrs Deakin can't know what is happening under the skin of my Idyllic Marriage? 'We planned to move to the country ever since we got married, so living here is just a dream come true.'

'Really?'

I met those cool, clever, jade-green eyes and looked hastily away.

'Strange then, that I got the feeling in London that you weren't entirely happy. A little – desperate, even. But then, we didn't really have a chance to talk, did we, Angel?'

I went so hot my skin sizzled. 'No, I don't think we talked at all, because it must have been obvious that I'd had so much to drink I didn't know what I was doing!'

'On the contrary, you seemed to know *exactly* what you were doing. And I didn't think you'd had that much to drink. *I* only intended killing an hour or two before my flight by having a little chat with you about old times, I wasn't expecting to have to re-enact them.'

I clenched my fists and glared at him in impotent, red-faced fury.

'And you did speak to me, you know – mostly short sentences like, "Yes, oh *yes*, Fergal," that kind of thing.'

'I didn't! And if you were a gentleman, you'd never mention a sordid episode that I deeply regret.'

'How Victorian of you,' he mocked. 'Do I take it you haven't confessed all to James yet?'

'There's no reason why I should risk harming my very happy marriage by confessing to doing something so stupid as getting drunk and letting myself be seduced by you!' I snarled.

'Ah, yes, your blissfully happy rural idyll. And as a bonus to all that, you're a romantic novelist, I hear.'

'A very successful one.'

'Everything in the garden is lovely, then,' the husky voice said lightly.

'Yes, perfect.' Ungraciously I added, 'And thank you for the fence – it's much nicer than the old one.'

'Don't mention it. Well, I'd better get back.'

'To Nerissa, wasn't it?' (Unless he'd traded her in for a new model.)

'Yes, Nerissa . . .' he said thoughtfully. 'And you'd better get back to your James.'

'Oh, he won't be home yet.'

'Well, someone's glaring at me from the window. Or is that his normal expression?'

My heart sank as I turned. James was indeed home and, instead of coming out to be introduced, was glowering like a schoolboy through the casement.

'He – didn't like that picture of us at the fête in the local paper,' I explained lamely.

'Funny, Nerissa wasn't too keen either. But the photographer deserves a prize for producing something out of nothing, don't you think?'

'Let's hope it hasn't been syndicated for worldwide publication!' I snapped.

'It wouldn't do me any harm, but your husband might not feel the same.'

'Oh, James quite understands, now I've explained it all.'

'Not *quite* all, I take it.'

'I've told him any interest I ever had in you vanished permanently a long time ago. What did you tell your girlfriend?'

'Much the same.'

I became very conscious of James's eyes on my back and wished he wouldn't behave like such a prat.

'It's unfortunate that we should end up as neighbours again,' I said, 'but these coincidences do happen, and we'll just have to behave in a civilised manner.'

'Never mind, Tish, I don't suppose our paths will cross much.'

'No . . . Are your family well?'

'Fine. Mother had little Bianca after we moved, and Dad has now got six restaurants and is busier than ever. Lucia is married – three children – and it would take for ever to tell you what the rest are up to. Carlo, of course, is still in the band, but he's more interested now in the production side.'

I remembered Lucia and Carlo, of course, but Bianca was a surprise. His voice had softened when he said the little girl's name: he'd always shown a very Italian love of babies and small children, which might have astonished his fans.

'Your mother is well?' he enquired politely, though I'm sure he didn't give a damn.

'Much the same. My grandmother lives with her now.'

His smile was genuine this time. 'Wonderful old lady! You used to be a bit like her – until you let your mother stamp you out in the same prissy mould as herself.'

'Prissy! I am *not*—'

With resolution I pulled myself up. 'Well, it's been nice catching up with you, Fergal, but I think I hear my husband calling me. Good night!'

He detained me by laying his long, strong fingers over mine on the fence.

'Are you well? You didn't look so thin in London . . . or so tired.'

'Quite well,' I snapped, wishing I didn't have dishevelled hair and eyes ringed like a marmoset's from sleeplessness, and he let go my hand and stepped back, his face becoming a remote mask.

'Good night!' And off I marched. Even with my back to him I knew the very moment when he turned and walked away.

'I suppose you weren't expecting me this early?' James greeted me. 'Do you often have these little tête-à-têtes with your ex-boyfriends when I'm not about?'

'I was feeding leftover vegetables to the cows, and Fergal just happened to walk that way.'

'You seemed to have a lot to say to each other.'

'He was asking after Mother,' I said lamely.

'How kind!' he sneered. 'I suppose you've both got a lot of catching up to do? Or did you do that in London?'

'I've already *told* you I didn't speak to him in London. Why didn't you come out and be introduced, instead of lurking in here in that silly way?'

'I might have felt a bit superfluous. Of course,' he added, rocking backwards on the kitchen chair in a way that would weaken its legs, 'you wouldn't have known he'd bought the Hall, when you insisted on living here?'

'Of course not. You're being totally ridiculous. I didn't even know Greatness Hall existed until we'd moved here, let alone that it was for sale. And I'm sure Fergal hasn't given me a thought for years.'

'He's a few years older than you – it can't have been the boy-and-girl affair you try to make it seem.'

'Not much older,' I said wearily. (And he's worn pretty well . . . as slim-hipped and lithe as ever.)

Hasn't it ever occurred to James that he could drive me into feeling that I might as well be hung for a sheep as a lamb? (Baa!) I think I'm feeling less guilty by the minute, though still angry with myself for becoming one more easy conquest for Fergal Rocco.

'What does it matter anyway?' I said drearily, turning away. 'It's all long finished. Now, I've made a tasty lentil casserole for supper, and there's a fresh fruit salad and cream to follow—'

'Lentil casserole!' howled James as though it were the final straw, and staggered up, sending his chair skidding over on the quarry tiles. 'Damn your lentil casserole! A man wants more than a few lentils when he gets home.'

He swayed and focused blearily. 'I'm off to the Dog and Duck for something a bit more substantial!' And off he went.

When I picked up the chair, Bess oozed out from the narrow gap beside the Aga like ectoplasm and reformed into a Borzoi.

I poured myself a stiff glass of cooking sherry and opened a box of chocolates, a habit I probably inherited from Granny.

Who needs men when they can have chocolate?

Who needs sex when they can have chocolate, come to that . . .

Fergal: August 1999

'LOCAL HEIRESS IN PUB BRAWL'
                         Nutthill District Advertiser

I walked on after seeing Tish, feeling angry, but with myself rather than her. Why does she have to be the one to turn my knees to water? She can't be unique – can she? And I may still fancy her, but she was the most irritating girl I ever went out with and she doesn't seem to have changed a bit.

Except that she doesn't look too well – verging on the thin, instead of the slender. I hope that boor of a husband is behaving himself.

Finding myself outside the pub, I went in, which was a mistake, as it turned out, because Nerissa was in there with some bunch of Hooray Henrys, all pretty well oiled.

'Honey!' she shrieked. 'Where have you been? We all drove over to visit you and you weren't there.'

She turned to her crowd and added, with an unpleasant laugh, 'He's got an old girlfriend tucked away in Nutthill, you know.'

'How old?' said the beardless youth on her right, and

sniggered. Since I couldn't hit Nerissa, I socked him one instead, then walked out.

From the rumpus behind me you'd think a small massacre had taken place.

I carried on down to Mrs Deakin, who insisted on putting a Mickey Mouse sticking plaster on my bleeding knuckles at no extra charge, then told me lots of interesting things about Tish and her husband without any prompting at all, before pumping me mercilessly about Nerissa the Nubile.

Chapter 23: Love Goes West

The Museum says my ring is late eighteenth century!

It certainly looks better now it's been straightened a little and the worst of the encrusted filth cleaned off. The stone is a heart-shaped, faceted sapphire, and there's an inscription enamelled inside saying '*Fidelité Mérite Amour*', which I dare say it may, but it doesn't often get it.

Who does it legally belong to? Since it was in the cellar of what was once the Dower House, it was likely to have been lost by one of the family from the Hall, so does that make Fergal, as the new owner of Greatness, the owner of my ring too?

By the time I got off the bus and went into Mrs Deakin's I was totally confused and asked her opinion. She said she thought Finders was Keepers, but I don't want to be underhand, especially with Fergal, so I thought the best thing would be to send the ring to him and let him sort it out . . . only then Nerissa will probably pounce on it, and it's the dearest little ring, really.

Perhaps I muttered something, for Mrs Deakin suddenly remarked: 'That Nerissa Bright don't live up at the Hall.'

'Doesn't she?' I asked innocently.

'No, though I think she'd like to. Her car keeps going up to the Hall, but most of the time it comes right on back!' She laughed wheezily.

'Perhaps it's when he's away.'

'No, it's not then.'

'How on earth do you know that, Mrs Deakin?'

'He's had the lodge done up for the gardener: my cousin Rose's husband's stepbrother.'

All was explained.

I was not, of course, in the least interested in Fergal's affairs, so it was with some surprise that I heard my voice saying, 'I did wonder if perhaps she might be going to be Mrs Rocco . . .?'

Mrs Deakin gave this her serious consideration. 'Well, it's obvious she's got her designs on him, like, and I seen pictures of them together in magazines, but it seems to me she's doing all the running. But he would have told you if they were engaged, surely – you being such old friends?'

'I really know nothing about Mr Rocco these days. I'm hardly likely to move in the same circles.'

'No,' she agreed regretfully. 'I expect there'll be some rare goings-on at the Hall soon as he starts entertaining!' And then she added that nothing this exciting had happened since the previous vicar had fallen down a disused well in the rectory garden and had to be pulled out by his feet, half asphyxiated.

'I suppose one of them rich pop stars can have his pick of girls, can't he? Though he seems nice enough, and comes in regular. He's been in the Dog and Duck a few times too, though he don't stay long. He took that Nerissa in there once, though they left separate, like in their own cars.'

'He has?' Strange James hadn't mentioned that. 'Doesn't everyone stare at him? He's quite well known, you know.'

Notorious might be a better word!

'Funny – I asked him the very same thing. He said everyone would soon get used to seeing him about, being boring and ordinary.'

Boring? Ordinary? Fergal used to turn heads in the street long before he was famous. (Or infamous!)

'Hitting someone can't be that ordinary,' I said drily, having seen the local paper.

She shrugged. 'Oh, these young men – flare up in a minute, they do, when the sap's rising. No one took much notice.'

I bought some tomatoes and then suddenly succumbed to the lure of a jar of sherbet dips. I can't think what got into me, for I was never keen on them as a child, but today I was dying for one. I could practically taste it.

'I didn't know you fancied that sort of thing?' said Mrs Deakin curiously. 'You've never bought sweets before.'

'Oh – just a sudden whim, you know,' I said, feeling stupid.

'Oh, yes? I like a bit of sherbet myself, but I prefer the Rainbow Crystals.' She gestured to a large jar filled with poisonously colourful layers of extremely large granules, like washing soda. 'Lovely stuff. Like to try a bit?'

'Oh – no, thanks, I think I'll stick to the sherbet dips.'

'Stick to the sherbet dips!' she cackled. 'You are a one for a joke, aren't you?'

I smiled half-heartedly. I don't know why she thinks I'm witty, but she usually finds something funny in what I say to her. 'I think that'll be everything.'

'Right you are. Mrs Wrekin come in this morning – well, calls herself Mrs, though she's no more a Mrs than my cat is!'

'What!' I was so startled I dropped ten pence and it rolled under a sack of potatoes.

'Over there – I can see it,' she gestured helpfully.

I stooped, and she continued where she'd left off in a comfortable, chatty voice: 'Yes, her calls herself Mrs Wrekin, but she's not married to him.'

'But she must be! I mean, she doesn't look the type – and they've got two children!' (And an epergne.)

'Not his. They're from her first marriage, and her divorce hasn't come through yet. Suppose they might get married when it does, but till then – well, it's like I said – she's no better than my cat.'

This was all very surprising, but Mrs Deakin is usually right.

'She's got the money, you know,' she approved. 'Not that he hasn't got a good job himself, but it's her as pays for the icing on the cake – and the cherry too!'

'Really?'

But she'd exhausted that topic. 'I've got some of your books in,' she informed me, pointing to a heap of paperbacks on the corner of the counter.

I went pink. 'But surely they won't sell? I mean, you can't have much demand for books, can you?'

'They sell all right when I tells them they was written by you. Full of curiosity, they are then. I read one myself.'

'Did you? Did you – like it?'

'Yes, I like a good romance, so long as the ending's happy. I read it, and then I sold it, but I had to let it go reduced because I got cocoa on it.'

'I'm sorry about that,' I apologised, although I don't know why. It wasn't me who spilled the cocoa.

'Vicar bought it. He said it were for his wife, but I know better. He can't keep his hands off a good love story, can't Vicar.'

'The vicar? Our vicar? I really wouldn't have thought it to look at him! How do you know?'

'Mobile library van,' she said succinctly. 'Mr Rocco bought a copy of all of your books that I had, too.'

'What! Which ones?'

She enumerated on her fingers: '*Love Is on the Outside, Love Goes West* . . .'

'Not *Love Goes West!*' I wailed. That was one of my earliest ones, and the hero is tall, black-haired and green-eyed. My only hope is that whatever curiosity drove him to buy them peters out before the end of the first page.

I felt out of sorts this morning again, but that was explained when my period started. Then it stopped again almost immediately. Really, I seem to be getting all sorts of funny little symptoms lately – I hope they don't all add up to some horrible disease.

And James went off to work without even mentioning our anniversary, so he must have forgotten. Mother, of course, sent a big soppy card listing them all, like Ruby, Silver, etc., but the seventh was something boring like tin or cork – or maybe it was lino. Mundane and non-precious, anyway.

Margaret popped in after lunch and we had coffee in the kitchen because I wanted to keep an eye on the man laying the patio. (Cash on completion – some kind of tax dodge, I think.)

Bob was also keeping a fascinated eye on him, but I've

come to the conclusion that he'll watch any event with the same avid interest, including paint drying.

Margaret and I chatted about all kinds of things and the time just flew by. Although she seems to have a lot of local acquaintances, she is, I think, probably as in need of a good friend as I am.

I offered her a home-made fig bar (the same recipe as before, but with sunflower seeds instead of sesame, which made them much less gritty), and she asked me to write down the recipe.

Just after she left James phoned to say he would definitely be home for six tonight – so he *has* remembered our anniversary! I decided to make a special effort and took steak out of the freezer to defrost, which I will grill with garlic butter. The only snag is that he likes his steak bloody on the inside, and it's awfully hard to gauge when it's like that. And he has to have chips with it.

I'm going to set it all out on the dining table, with candles and low music, and we can have a nice, relaxed evening and talk over everything when we're feeling a bit more mellow.

I'll even put a (sober!) dress on.

Surely our differences can be resolved, with a bit of effort and mutual co-operation?

I am in an absolute rage!

The candles have long since guttered and gone out, I've played the same CD six times, and the steaks are lying in a bloody pool in the kitchen. The red wine has had so long to breathe, it's probably hyperventilated.

I'm so angry and miserable, so frustrated with rage, I really feel like smashing something. I must have been mad to think I could cram all our problems back into the Pandora's box they escaped from! Why hasn't he at least phoned, to say he'll be late? Where the hell is he?

I'm going to bed. I'll leave the table and the food and everything, the wilting salad, dead candles and the CD player switched on, so he'll know what he's done when he comes in.

If he comes in.

Fergal: August 1999

> '*Now available from Nutthill Home Stores!*
> *Novels by famous local author Marian Plentifold!*'
> Advert, *Nutthill District Advertiser*

I couldn't resist buying them, though I don't know if I'll read them.

Still, there's one in my luggage – *Love Goes West* – in case the urge comes over me.

That probably makes me a very, very sad man.

Chapter 24: Reciprocations

Woke up to find James in bed next to me wearing only a loosely knotted tie, which I was tempted to tighten.

How did he get his shirt off?

He looked dreadfully green, unshaven and baggy-eyed by the light of the Teasmade, and groaned, 'Put that light out!' as I poured my coffee.

I ignored him. Frankly. I don't feel that I ever want to speak to him again, and I don't particularly mind if I never *see* him again, either.

As I got up I trod on Bess, who must have come up with him, and she yelped loudly, causing James to groan again and put his head under the pillow.

I apologised to Bess and she watched me dolefully as I put on my dressing gown, because she knows I don't go for walks wearing that. 'Come on down, Bess.'

I let her out into the garden and as I stumbled rather blearily into the bathroom, I thought I heard a rather un-Toby-like noise from the living room.

On my return, slightly more alert, I heard it again and opened the door, revealing Horrible Howard, in a pair of sordid, once-white underpants, sitting on my lovely pale cream sofa with his head in his hands.

'What the hell are *you* doing here?' I demanded, in quite reasonable tones considering that I wanted to kick him off my sofa and have it fumigated.

'Don't shout, man!' he whimpered.

'I'm not a man, and I wasn't shouting. I just asked why you're here. Why are you here?'

'Oh God!' he groaned and, turning his spindly shanks, clambered back into the crumpled pink sleeping bag behind him, like a snail returning to its shell, and didn't reply to anything else I said.

It was *my* sleeping bag.

Upstairs I shook James until he was awake enough to answer my demands as to where he was last night, and what Howard was doing in *my* sleeping bag, on *my* sofa, in *my* house.

'We had a drink . . . came back here, had some whisky . . .' he muttered blearily. 'I lent Howard a sleeping bag – too late to go home . . . anyway, he came in my car. Look, Tish, I feel awful! Get me an Alka-Seltzer, will you?'

'Get your own bloody Alka-Seltzer!' I screamed, and slammed out of the room, a gesture only spoiled by my having to go back in to get my clothes.

James seemed to have lost consciousness again. (Wish it was permanent.)

I dressed hurriedly and then took Bess for a long walk. I was so angry that I just went on and on, mulling everything over and feeling very reluctant to go back and see James ever again. Not to mention my cream sofa.

And he even gave Howard my sleeping bag to put his grimy body and disgusting underpants into!

'This is the end!' I told Bess, who wagged her tail with vague approval. 'Positively the end! I'm *sick* of James.'

I mean it: this has made me realise that I really don't feel anything for him any more except anger – and boredom – and frustration! *And* distaste. He's tiresome, and I'm thoroughly tired of him. And if he really cared about me he wouldn't behave the way he does.

If only he'd said he was sorry for once, and meant it. Or showed me, even occasionally, some signs of tenderness or affection – not just sex or nothing (mostly nothing, since we moved here).

Can this be love? Can this ever truly have been love?

And when I did try to save our marriage by conforming to his idea of a good wife, all he said was that he was glad I'd come out of the dumps because I was becoming a real pain in the fundament.

But *he* hasn't even tried, just carried on as usual, treating the house like a hotel and me as its housekeeper.

Even when I've practically prostituted myself to get his attention it had no result, except to make me feel ashamed.

'He for God only, she for God in him . . .' How that annoyed me when I read it for A level! Stuff Milton: Paradise is definitely lost.

I feel so used . . .

Are all men the same underneath? Cheap pine carcasses and fancy veneers?

James's must be Bog Oak.

Large, cold splashes of rain eventually woke me to the realisation that I was miles from home under a black sky, with an exhausted and complaining dog.

By the time we got back my sodden anorak clung to me

and my jeans hung dark and heavy round my legs. Rivulets ran down my nose and dripped off the end like loathsome dewdrops, and I felt utterly cold and miserable.

Stumbling into the empty kitchen I pulled off my jacket and the equally sodden sweatshirt underneath came with it, leaving me standing under the fluorescent strip light exposed to the world (usually only the herd of cows at the bottom of the garden) in my new Near-Nude bra.

Something – an innate feeling that I was being watched – made me look up: Howard's pallid face was goggling at me through the rain from the Shack's window.

Clutching my soggy rags and the shreds of my dignity I ran upstairs and locked myself in the bedroom, then sobbed with misery as I towelled myself dry.

Bess, who I'd shut into the garage to shake off the worst of the rain, howled dismally and I felt like joining in.

And who would have thought rain could be so icily cold in August?

This is really The End.

I didn't go downstairs until James had driven away, presumably to return Howard to his lair. He'd let Bess back into the kitchen and she was so exhausted she barely raised an eyelid when I went in. I must have walked an awfully long way.

Everything else was just as I'd left it the previous night, so I cleaned up and put my sleeping bag in a bin liner: I don't fancy it any more.

Toby was still asleep, with his head under his wing, groaning – his water pot had been strongly spiked with whisky.

There's nothing you can give a parrot for a hangover.

* * *

256

My communications with James since our anniversary have been terse, to say the least. He's preserving an air of hurt innocence, and has never once mentioned the remains of that ruined dinner. What does he expect? That *I* will apologise for *his* behaviour?

I used to think we had so much in common, and now I can't think of a single thing.

We can't go on like this. The worry's really affecting my health. I was sleeping poorly before, but now I lie awake for several hours every night, turning it all over in my mind.

So it was that I neither felt nor looked my best when I opened my door early one sultry dog day (or bitch day, as it turned out), to find Nerissa, fresh as the dawn of Creation, on the doorstep.

'Hi! Remember me?' she cooed, all her perfect little straight white teeth bared in a friendly smile. 'Hope you don't mind me dropping in, but when Fergal told me how you'd grown up together, I just couldn't resist a little girl-to-girl chat.'

Barbie speaks!

What could I do but let her in? (Other than wish I was wearing something other than old jeans and a lumberjack shirt that used to belong to James.)

'How . . . nice! Do come in. I was just about to make some coffee.'

'Great. I'll come with you, shall I? I just love your little old house! And I hope you'll say if I'm a nuisance. I was so excited when I found out you were Marian Plentifold! My stepmom is a big fan of yours.'

That put me firmly in the Oldies bracket! 'Oh, good . . .' I muttered ungraciously.

Bess oozed out from behind the Aga and fixed my visitor

with the aloof, slightly puzzled stare that signifies an attempt to connect her two brain cells.

Nerissa gave a gasp and backed away. 'I – I'm not real keen on dogs!'

'She's quite harmless,' I assured her. But when I turned back with the (best) coffee mugs she was still staring at Bess like a mesmerised rabbit, so I had to put her into the garden, where Bob would talk to her. (Bess, I mean, though Bob isn't fussy.)

'Oh thank you! I guess you must think me a real coward.'

'It's difficult when you have a phobia about something. I've one about spiders,' I said, warming to her just a fraction, from below zero, to nearly tepid.

'It's not real bad – my analyst's helping me overcome it.'

'Oh?'

'Yes. I had to do something because poor Fergal's holding back from getting a dog just because of Silly Little Ol' Me.' She fluttered incredibly long, dark eyelashes. 'I thought I'd surprise him with a puppy for a wedding present.'

'You're getting married?' I don't know why I felt so stunned and I only hoped it didn't register on my face. 'Congratulations!'

'Why, thanks! But I really shouldn't have said anything, because we haven't set a date yet. To tell the truth, Pop isn't too keen on the idea – but when he knows Fergal like I do he'll soon change his mind.'

Her big brown eyes didn't quite meet mine, so it did cross my mind that this might be just a way of telling me that she'd staked a claim on Fergal. But no, she can't see all his old girlfriends as a threat, surely?

'I promise not to tell anyone until it's all official,' I assured her, wondering cynically if she would still want him if he were not rich and famous. But then, he has obvious charms (and obvious defects, too, like a terrible temper) and Nerissa has Rich Man's Daughter stamped all over her peach suede suit.

'And what do you do?' I enquired politely, pouring out more coffee.

'Do?' Her eyes looked blank. 'Oh – *do*. Well, charity work, you know,' she said vaguely. 'But I don't suppose I'll be able to carry on with that after I'm married. Fergal may think now he wants to quit touring and vegetate down here, but he'll soon be bored and itching to be off again.'

'Oh? But he's making his own recording studio at Greatness, isn't he?'

'Yes – he's been so occupied with it I've hardly seen him for weeks, but once it's finished I just know he'll find it too dull stuck down here all the time.'

Certainly I got the feeling it would be too dull for Nerissa! I wondered how old she was. Despite her sophisticated veneer it wouldn't surprise me if she wasn't much more than twenty. I wondered about something else, too, and before I knew it, it was out.

'Nerissa, your accent – I mean, sometimes you sound all Southern Belle, and other times, quite English . . .?'

She gave me the very same look of feminine complicity that I've surprised on Bess's face before now. 'Oh, you know, all that "little ol' me" Scarlett O'Hara stuff goes down with the men, and I kind of forget I'm doing it.' She shrugged. 'It makes my stepmom mad.'

She changed tack. 'Fergal told me all about your cute little boy-and-girl romance!'

If he has I'll be wearing his guts for garters.

259

I smiled back guilelessly. 'Did he? The boy next door! What ages ago it all seems.'

'And now here you are, living next door again! It's a real strange coincidence.'

'Hardly next door.'

'Still, it is a coincidence' she insisted, watching me over her coffee cup.

'They happen,' I shrugged. 'Actually, it was my husband who found this cottage.'

'Oh? I hope I'll meet him one day. Is he like Fergal?'

Is Mickey Mouse like Vlad the Impaler?

'No, not at all. You must come over and meet him one evening,' I suggested. I can always direct her to the Shack.

'That will be lovely. Gosh, is that the time? I'd better go.'

It was somehow soothing to see Bess's hairs clinging fondly to Nerissa's peach suede rear as she walked out of the door: just a little something to remind you of us.

After that it was very hard to get back into the novel, and the lingering reek of musky perfume worried Bess no end.

Later I found a Mafia-like parcel on the doorstep containing a dead rabbit with its fur on and everything, which was nearly as welcome as Nerissa.

A blood-stained note thanked me for the lettuces: Mrs P. has reciprocated.

I gave the rabbit to Bob.

James has been complaining to Mother again about my 'unreasonable conduct' and she has naturally taken his side. I'm only her daughter, after all – I think! No, unfortunately, I'm *sure*, though I still need to get Granny alone and see just what it was about my birth that's confused her, for she wouldn't say these things maliciously.

I'd already been feeling lonely and depressed, and this treachery made me feel even worse, so that I cried silently all through dinner while James sat there tight-lipped. I didn't want to cry, but I just couldn't stop.

When I saw he was going out again straight afterwards I snapped and started screaming at him, and he shouted back, just like a low-class soap opera.

'Just don't expect me to be here when you get back!' I yelled finally.

'Good!' he snarled, and slammed out.

But why should *I* leave when I'm the one who's done all the work on the cottage and loves it? It would be much better if *he* didn't come back . . .

But of course, he will.

Bess came up looking anxious and laid her paw on my knee. That dog has more sensitivity and affection in her than my husband. Come to that, she might be more intelligent, too.

An attempt to anaesthetise myself with wine was unsuccessful. It made me feel sadder and I don't even seem to like the taste of it any more.

I wish I could stop crying. I wish I didn't feel so desperately alone. I feel so alone that I could almost convince myself I still love him.

Almost.

Is loneliness better? But am I not already alone?

Oh God – I can't think straight – I'm going to bed.

James didn't come back last night, or even ring me from work, which was the final straw. He just reappeared without a word of apology or explanation next evening, expecting to be fed.

Straight afterwards, before he could escape to the Shack, I tackled him. 'I want to talk to you, James!'

He shifted impatiently from foot to foot: 'What about? Ray's coming over in a minute, and—'

'It's important.'

Sighing, he sat back down at the table. 'Oh, very well, but make it quick. What's up? Washing machine broken?'

'No, the washing machine is that thing in front of you with a window, and clothes going round and round.'

'There's no need to be sarcastic. You've become a damned unpleasant woman to live with lately.'

'And you've become a very unpleasant man, James.' I swallowed hard. 'This isn't very easy to say, but I feel our marriage isn't working and I want a separation.'

He looked *totally* flabbergasted, but surely he must have had some teensy-weensy little inkling of how bad things were?

'Separation? What the hell are you maundering on about, woman?' he snarled, a form of address that did nothing to endear him to me; in fact it helped to stiffen my resolve.

'Just what I say. I've given a great deal of thought to – to us lately. I haven't been happy for a long time and I just don't want to live with you any more. And I don't really think you want me. I'm just convenient.'

He turned scarlet and the angry vein in his temple throbbed merrily away like a mad worm. 'Don't be so bloody stupid! Until we moved here and you started getting all these ideas everything was fine.'

'You've changed since we moved here, James, and not for

the better. Or perhaps you started to change even before that. Do you remember how we used to do things together? Go out together, stay in together, decide how we spent the money together, plan our future together? Now we don't discuss anything, and I hardly ever even see you.'

'You're being totally unreasonable! Not only do I have all this extra commuting, but being a senior partner in the firm entails a lot more work. I mean, you don't get Margaret Wrekin moaning when Ray is away on business, or round here in the Shack, do you?'

With a visible effort he softened his tone and conceded magnanimously, 'But perhaps I've been a bit inconsiderate lately – though if you made a push not to be such a misery it might give me some incentive to stay home.'

'Misery! If I'm a misery, it's because you've made me one! You're so selfish, James – out all hours, expecting hot meals at your bidding, laundry done . . . I feel like a land-lady. And you care about me so little you've even told everyone our ex-directory number, so I keep having those scary silent calls.'

'You always make a fuss over nothing. Of course I have to give people my number. Now, have you quite finished? I think I hear Ray coming.'

'No, I haven't quite finished. Don't you understand that I want a separation – a divorce, even. I certainly don't want to live with you any more!'

'You're hysterical!' he said coldly. 'We'll talk again when you are calmer.' And out he went, slamming the door.

Could I have put it plainer than that? And I *wasn't* hysterical.

I put the camp bed up in my writing room and retired

there. James must have let Bess upstairs when he came back, because she came and scratched at my door until I let her in, but he made no comment that I heard; he certainly didn't scratch at the door himself.

Around midnight Bess found that jumping on the end of the camp bed caused the legs to fold, precipitating us both downhill rapidly.

It was not a popular discovery.

At breakfast James informed me that I was having a nervous breakdown, probably due to writing rubbishy novels instead of being a good little Stepford Wife and having babies, and he'd expect to hear that I'd seen the doctor when he came home that evening. (And, possibly, seen the light.)

I replied calmly, on the outside at least, that I wasn't having a breakdown, but had made my considered decision that I didn't want to share a house (or a life) with him any longer, so perhaps *he* should see the doctor since he seemed to be going through some prolonged mid-life crisis, or second adolescence, or something.

'And, by the way, make the most of that cooked breakfast: from tomorrow you'll have to get up earlier and cook your own. And if you want dinner in the evening, you'll have to be home by seven, when I have mine.'

'Are you quite mad? You're my wife! You'd better snap out of this before it's too late, because you could never manage on your own – you'd be begging me to take you back before the end of the first week. And where would you go? Unless,' he added with sudden suspicion in his narrowed eyes, 'you've got Another Man?'

'Don't be silly,' I said crisply. 'You know very well I haven't.'

'Do I? When your old lover moves right in next door? Some coincidence! And now I come to think of it, you were all right until *he* arrived.'

'Oh, get serious, James! It's you who's changed, not me. Fergal has nothing to do with it. Why should he look at me, when he can have any girl he wants?'

He stared at me, and made a discovery. 'That's true – you look terrible! Too thin . . . and those rings round your eyes . . . You've let yourself go.'

'Thanks!'

'I'm just telling you for your own good. These stupid fancies you have are all part of your nervous breakdown and you must see the doctor.'

I sighed wearily. '*You* see the doctor. I'm fine – just sick of you. You'd better get used to the idea of our marriage ending, James, because I'm quite serious.'

He pushed his chair back so hard it bounced off the dresser. 'All this nonsense has made me late and I don't want to hear any more of it when I get back! See the doctor, then go and get your hair fixed and buy something pretty to wear, or whatever girls do to cheer themselves up. I'll give you the cash.'

'I can pay for anything I want myself!' I shouted (except happiness – Money Can't Buy You Love) but he was already on his way out, falling over Bess en route.

A week later I was wondering what on earth I could do to drive my intentions into his thick skull. Absolutely nothing I said or did altered his conviction that I'm losing my grip on reality.

Much more of this, and I may lose my grip on *something*.

He even made a doctor's appointment for me, but I cancelled it, and then he got Uncle Lionel to phone and tell me I was being foolish, I wouldn't find a better husband than James, and I shouldn't resent him working hard when I benefited from it – he did it all for me.

When I replied that mostly he seemed to do it because he wanted to buy more radio equipment or a flashier car, or a newer CD player, Uncle coldly said that he'd been mistaken in me. He'd thought me a nice, sensible girl.

Nice sensible doormat?

No, self-preservation alone demands that we part. But I've nowhere to go – and why should *I* go anywhere? I'm quite happy here.

It's James who doesn't fit, and I couldn't be unhappier without him than I am now with him. I really, really don't want him any more – and, what's more, I don't even need him financially either, since I can now support myself by my pen (I think)!

I see now I was wrong to try to change myself, but at least I tried. He didn't even do that, just went on getting more and more selfish.

I need to take some drastic action to shake him into realising I mean what I say.

He's already said he's staying at Howard's on Wednesday for a 'bit of peace' (I would have thought Howard's was the last place for that), so I suggested quite reasonably that he consider taking his things there and moving in permanently.

He didn't answer, but he only took an overnight bag.

Shock tactics are called for.

* * *

266

Fergal: September: 1999

'The last show of the Goneril Farewell Tour played to a packed and emotional audience.'

Trendsetter magazine

That's that.

Wish I could say the same about Nerissa. She's like a leech, except she doesn't drop off when she's satiated.

Doesn't matter what I do – I told her I'd had sex with six consecutive Nordic blondes and she said she understood, I only did it to satisfy a need when she wasn't there.

Is she mad, or suffering from amnesia? I haven't touched her for months and anyway, do I look like Superman?

Pity she *wasn't* there, actually; I could have held her under the water until she stopped bubbling.

I long to get back home to Nutthill. Snippets of information trickle back, just enough to whet my appetite for more . . .

I want to see Tish and, like a scab, pick at my feelings to see if they've healed.

And I'd like to know why the tricky, devious bastard in her novel *Love Goes West* has black hair and green eyes . . .

Chapter 25: Blood and Roses

In the early hours of Friday morning I was jerked awake by the fumbling of a key in the door, followed by swearing.

I'd been beginning to think he wasn't coming back after all.

The noise was repeated from the kitchen door and I crept to the window and looked down, but he was too close to the house to be visible despite a fairly bright moon.

A handful of small stones rattled the glass next to my cheek, making me jump, and an aggrieved voice wailed, 'Tish! Tish!'

I unlatched the window and leaned out, an unwilling Rapunzel. 'What do you want?'

'Want? I want to get in, you daft cow!'

'Don't you use that sort of language to me!'

'Look, I'm sorry – I'm a bit tired, that's all, and none of the doors will open.'

'That's because I had the locks changed.'

'What on earth for? Look – come down and let me in, then you can tell me about it.'

'But I had them changed to keep *you* out.'

'To keep me out? Good God, Tish, whatever are you

drivelling on about? I live here – this is my house. I'm your husband, James!'

'You did live here, but I've had enough. I kept telling you and telling you, and you wouldn't listen.'

He ranted and raved a bit, sounding much angrier than I'd ever heard him before. I was glad he was out there in the darkness and I was safely in here.

'I've had enough of this,' he shouted at last. 'I'm going to break the bathroom window!'

This was only alarming until I compared the size of the small windows downstairs with his burgeoning beer gut. All was by no means lost.

But I did feel terrified when the sound of breaking glass was followed by a blood-curdling yell. He staggered back round the corner clutching one wrist.

'Tish, help me! I've cut my wrist on the damned glass – it's pouring blood – probably an artery! Let me in before I bleed to death!'

'Go and bleed over the rose bushes, they're supposed to thrive on it,' I suggested heartlessly. He was by now directly underneath me and I couldn't see any sign of draining arteries.

'You heartless bitch!' he raged, which was more like the James I'd come to know and didn't love.

A fruity chuckle on my left warned me that we had an avid audience.

'Good morning, Mrs Peach!'

The chuckle turned into a hoarse wheeze. 'So it is! So it is! My poor hens will be off laying for a week at least, after this.'

'Mrs Peach!' implored the white upturned disc of James's

face. 'Look here! You're a compassionate woman. I've cut my wrist badly and Tish won't let me in. Would you see to it for me? I think I'm in shock!'

'What, have a man in my house this time of night? Not I! You'd best go to roost in your little house in the garden, and maybe you'll not get tetanus – this time.'

And with this jovial sally she withdrew her head and shut the window.

'Good night, James,' I said, preparing to follow suit.

'Tish – wait!' he begged, but I firmly closed the window and returned to the (ex) marital bed, where the ex-marital dog was snugly curled, she having succeeded in opening the door to the stairs and creeping up.

I shoved her off, then lay drowsily listening to James's shouts and the occasional rattle of gravel getting fainter and fainter, until they faded away, and I slept.

Later that morning I cautiously opened the back door and peered out, but there was no sign of occupancy from the Shack. For a few minutes I imagined his blood-drained corpse stretched out behind the blackcurrants, and even went so far as to look, while Bess capered round me like a furred clown; but common sense told me you don't bleed to death from little cuts, and there were no great congealed arterial pools dotted about – not even a splash.

There was a bit on the edge of the broken window – I must get someone out to fix that.

I wonder where he spent the night. The plan had worked well. Perhaps I wouldn't manage to keep him out permanently this time, but at least he could see that I mean business and set about finding somewhere else to live, like Howard's.

270

What will his next move be and where do I stand legally? If we divorce (which might be best, though I, at least, never intend to marry again) would we have to sell the house and everything, and divide the proceeds up?

I'd hate to lose the cottage, because I do love it despite everything going wrong since we moved here. The furniture's no problem – I could replace that, and I'm beginning to think it might look better with antique cottage pieces anyway.

Perhaps I could take over the mortgage? I suppose I would then have to pay James something for the amount the house has appreciated by.

I need an independent solicitor.

It was nice not to have to rush about waiting on James, and I thought if he didn't come back, then I would be able to relax more, sleep better and stop looking such a scarecrow. James was right about my looks – I seem to be getting scrawnier everywhere cxcept round the middle, which is probably water retention. Surprisingly enough, I did a good morning's work on the book, which is going well (fortunately, since I will soon need all the money I can get).

At lunchtime the phone went, and I picked it up with that sinking feeling.

'Tish?'

'Hello, James.'

'How can you sound so calm – as if nothing has happened? Are you out of your mind? I'm beginning to think you must be. First you lock me out of my own home, then you say, "Hello James" as if you hardly knew me! What's going on?'

'If you'd been listening to me lately you'd know. I've resigned from my position as nanny and housekeeper. How often do I have to explain? I want a separation.'

'Come on, Tish! It isn't that bad. I'm happy enough, or I was until you started getting all these strange ideas into your head. Though I'm not saying I didn't wish you could cook better, and – but never mind that now. Look, let's discuss things, at least. You can't just expect me to disappear when the house is as much mine as yours – more so, because I worked for it!'

'You have a serious blind spot where money's concerned, James. I've been paying an equal share of all our expenses since we married, and we both worked and saved for the cottage.'

'Let's not squabble over it. I'll be home at the usual time tonight and we can talk sensibly about it. Perhaps I've been out too much lately and you've got lonely. We can work things out.'

The unbearably self-satisfied tones of someone confident of their own infallibility reasoning with a hysterical idiot made my blood boil.

'That's what *I* suggested only a few weeks ago, only you wouldn't listen. But now I don't even want to try and work things out – I just want to be on my own. Don't bother coming home tonight, because I'm not letting you in.'

'You can't keep me out of my own home. I've got a perfect right to live there!'

'How can you call it your "home" when you've used it like a lodging house?'

'Look, Tish, this is getting us nowhere. I'll talk to you tonight.'

My determination hardened. 'I've said all I want to say, James, but I don't want to argue. I'll meet you somewhere neutral tomorrow, if you like, to discuss arrangements.'

'Arrangements? Stuff your fucking arrangements!' he bellowed, and slammed the phone down.

My hands shook slightly as I replaced the receiver, but otherwise I felt quite calm. Just cold . . . very cold. A chilly breeze was winding itself around my legs like a cat.

A breeze?

Galvanised, I ran to the back door, which was ajar – and the silly bitch was missing. Just as she's coming into season, too!

'Bess! Bess!' I yelled, dragging on a coat and running out, but I had to go all the way to the pond, calling and rattling her lead, before I spotted her romping in great joyous circles with the entire male dog population of the county in hot pursuit.

When I called her she rushed across to me, wet and muddy, with her long pink tongue hanging out of the side of her mouth. I put her on the lead, fending off the advances of the other mutts with my foot, and began to drag her home.

The other dogs followed, trying disgustingly to leap on her from behind, until I found a large branch and beat them off.

In this undignified way we finally reached home, and I tied Bess to the table leg until I could deal with her.

But first I filled two buckets with cold water and poured them over the assembled dogs from an upstairs window, to cool their ardour. A smell of wet dog arose and they fled, yelping. I suppose they'll be back.

I didn't think Bess had been out long enough to have actually *done* anything, so I washed all the mud off her under the shower, and dried her long, silky fur.

She'll be murder to brush tomorrow. I was almost tempted

to eject her for James to collect, but I think I need a dog if I'm going to live alone, and it might as well be Bess. He might want her back, though (not that he's ever done anything for her).

The dogs returned and hung around all afternoon, while Bess lay on the mat snuffling and making shameless moaning noises, until I tied her to the table leg again.

Perhaps I should have taken her to the vet – only it's such a long way, when you don't drive.

I really will have to learn now. I wonder if Mrs Deakin knows a good driving instructor? I didn't much feel like wading through the dogs to find out, but I'll definitely ask next time I'm in.

As the evening advanced I began to feel twitchy. What if James showed up? I didn't regret what I'd done, but I did feel a tiny little bit sorry for him, because I don't think he's capable of understanding why I don't want to live with him any more.

But he didn't turn up – Margaret Wrekin did instead.

'Hello, Tish!' she said breathlessly, looking at me strangely. 'Can I come in?'

'Of course.' I wondered if something had upset her, for it was an unusual time for her to visit, and she did look a bit odd. 'Go through to the kitchen, if you don't mind.'

But she watched me bolt and bar the door first.

'There are such a lot of strange people about lately,' I explained (and I should know – I'm married to one of them).

The kitchen was warm and spiced with the scent of rock cakes and coffee. Margaret seated herself gingerly on the edge of a chair.

'Are you all right, Margaret? You look a bit tense.'

She opened and shut her mouth silently a few times like a goldfish, then stammered, to my complete astonishment, 'It's James . . . I've come . . . James asked me to come and talk to you.'

'*James!*'

'Y-yes. He stayed with us last night, you see, and he told us that you wouldn't let him in. And well . . . he feels . . . er . . . that it might be better if I talked to you instead of him.'

Under my incredulous stare she flushed and dropped her eyes, as well she might.

Fancy retailing all our private affairs to people we've only just got to know and then sending Margaret round to talk me into having him back!

'I suppose he's told you that I'm off my head, just because I don't want to live with him any more? Well, if not wanting to live with him is a sign of insanity, then I'm guilty as charged, but personally, I just think I've come to my senses at last.'

'But, Tish, I'm terribly sorry to butt in, and all that – but James did ask me, and I like you both so much! It would be awful if you split up over some little misunderstanding.'

'There is no little misunderstanding. On the contrary, I understand everything perfectly for the first time. I no longer wish to live with James. I've had enough of James. I've reached saturation point with James. Since he didn't seem able to grasp this concept I had the locks changed. There: that's all very simple, isn't it? I told James again today, but he just can't seem to get the hang of it.'

Her eyes became all sad and accusing. 'Oh, Tish, I didn't think you could be so hard! Poor James says you've always been perfectly happy together until the last couple of months when you've become a little . . . a little strange . . .'

She took a scared look at my face, gulped, and finished in a rush, 'He says you've started getting some very odd ideas!'

'Oh, I have! Odd ideas like not wanting to wait on him hand and foot any more, or give up writing and have children.'

'But surely you can get together and sort it out?'

I don't think she can have been listening.

'No,' I said patiently. 'And if James ever listened to me, then he wouldn't be so surprised now.' I thought *she* was a fine one to preach to me about leaving my husband – only she doesn't know that I know all about her.

She eyed me with mournful amazement. 'You really mean it? You don't want him back? And you aren't even going to discuss it with him, hear his side?'

'I told him I'd meet him somewhere neutral if he liked, to work out arrangements. He can come and collect his things later – I'll pack them up and put them on the door-step.'

I took a reviving swig of coffee. Margaret's cup was still full and untasted and she had spurned my offer of a fresh rock cake.

'How vindictive you are!' she sighed softly. 'I hadn't realised you knew. But this can't all be because you're tired of him, can it?'

'Knew what?'

She reached across and touched my hand. 'Look, Tish, I know all about that blonde he's been seeing, and you can talk about it to me. Really, it meant nothing.'

'What blonde?' I asked blankly.

Hazel eyes goggling with horror, she clapped her hands over her mouth. 'You mean you didn't know? Until I just *said*? Oh God!'

Everything inside me stopped like a dead clock and then, joltingly, restarted, leaving me cold, sick and empty.

'No, I didn't know,' I said evenly. 'Unless – do you mean Vanessa? But he swore it was nothing more than a bit of drunken horseplay at the office party! And she isn't blonde.' (Mind you, I've only James's word for it she isn't blonde . . .)

'No – no, I don't think it's anyone at the office.'

'How long has it been going on?'

'It's not – still going on, I mean,' she babbled miserably. 'I only saw him with her once, and Ray said it was a girl James had met at a party in a friend's house, but it was nothing.'

I bet he did. But if he did meet her at a friend's house . . .

My mind began sluggishly to weave threads together into an unlovely cloth. If it *really* wasn't Vanessa, and he did meet the girl at a party, was it one of Howard's? And all those nights when he stayed there, or was out practically till dawn . . .

'You don't know who she is, Margaret? Her name?'

'No idea, but she was small with long blonde hair.'

So was the girl at Howard's party who'd glared at me. Alice's sister? Wendy, was it?

How could he, the pig! That just about puts the lid on it! I did have one or two guilty pangs, throwing him out just because I'd had enough of him – but now I'd like to take a hatchet to him!

Horrible images of him with this strange girl flitted through my mind like the remnants of a nightmare. No

277

wonder he hadn't touched me for months and was always so exhausted (apart from the night of the barbecue, and the thought of that revolts me now). I only hope that girl hasn't got some unmentionable disease! But I hope she now gets syphilis and *both* their noses fall off.

All those presents when he stayed overnight at Howard's – conscience money?

Margaret was snivelling into a bit of pink tissue. 'I wish I hadn't come!' she sobbed. 'I've only made it worse, and I meant to help!'

'But I'm glad you came,' I assured her sincerely. 'It was a shock, but at least I can now carry on with a clear conscience. Tell James I'll pack his clothes and things, and leave the cases in the front garden. He can pick them up when he likes. I'll send him a letter about the rest of the stuff.'

'But, Tish! What will he say when he knows I told you about his girlfriend? He doesn't know that I know about her.'

'Tell him I already knew. Now, I'm afraid I'll have to get on with the packing.'

She took the hint and got up to go, still snuffling dolefully and pink about the eyes and nose.

I wish *I* had a real Burberry.

She turned plaintively at the door. 'We will still be friends, won't we?'

'That might be difficult while James is staying in your house and telling everyone I'm unhinged. You can't run with the hare and hunt with the hounds. Good night!'

Several pairs of eyes gleamed wolfishly at us from the darkness: Bess's admirers.

Running upstairs, I began tossing James's things into three large suitcases, crammed his brush, razor, etc. on top, and then added any odds and ends of his I found lying around.

It was surprising just how much I could get in there. I couldn't quite expunge all of him from the house in one go, of course, but it was a pretty good start.

After checking to see he wasn't lurking in the garden, I shoved all the cases out of the front door; but actually it was quite late when he signalled his arrival by a lot of rather drunken shouting and a few yelps.

'Tish! Tish!'

I opened the little living-room window, which he couldn't possibly get through unless he'd turned into a complete worm.

'What are all these bloody dogs doing here?'

'Bess is in season.'

'Thass another thing! Take my house, my money – now my dog!'

'I've taken nothing, and I've been looking after Bess ever since we married. Do you want her back?'

'Yes, I damned well do! Hand her over.'

'Now? Don't be silly. The Wrekins won't want her galumphing all over their house.'

'Thass all you know!' he retaliated childishly. 'They're letting me have the granny flat over the garage until all this is sh-sorted out. Now gimme my dog!'

Bess got excited when she heard her lead. 'Stand well back!' I called. 'I'm putting her out and I don't want you coming in here in that condition.'

His pale face receded, and I quickly pushed Bess through the front door and relocked it.

There was a crescendo of yaps, barks and swearing, and

I got back to my window just in time to watch James drag Bess away, while fending her beaux off with one of the suitcases.

I didn't hear him come back for the other two, but they weren't there an hour later when I went to bed.

Perhaps he sent Margaret for them.

I miss that stupid dog more than I ever thought possible. I suppose I ought to get another one if I'm going to live alone, though not a canine moron like Bess.

And I don't know why I bothered going to bed at all, because as soon as I lay down and closed my eyes the whole sham of our marriage swept before me, in Inglorious Technicolor. What a blind, trusting fool I'd been – and I'd never really known him at all. Or he me, come to that.

Was this girl even the first one? And what about the silent phone calls – was it the girl doing it, trying to get James? Or just trying to unsettle me? (She succeeded.)

I spent a largely sleepless night turning these unsavoury possibilities over, and as soon as it began to get light got up to my strangely quiet and empty house. The only sound was Toby, morosely cracking sunflower seeds and spitting the shells out.

Without even stopping to have any breakfast, I went through the house room by room with my handy little red book, listing the contents, and any melancholy this might have engendered was banished by the thought of That Woman.

The James I chose things with, lived with, thought I loved, either only ever lived in my imagination or has transmuted into something unpalatable.

I wonder what That Woman is really like?

The list was surprisingly long, and I copied it out for James with suggestions on dividing everything equally. Then I went through all the figures for the mortgage and other overheads, wondering if I could manage on my own.

I think I can, though it's pretty alarming since my income is irregular. (Promising, but irregular.) If the house has increased in value, it's because of my hard work.

A thought: I must find out how much all the radio stuff cost, and the Shack. I'm sure that was all a fortune, and will have to come out of his share, as will the car . . .

He might end up owing *me* money!

I wrote him a letter appending the list and stating my terms, and hoping we could settle everything in a civilised manner. It was very restrained, considering the sort of thing I would really like to say to him now I've discovered he has the fidelity quotient of a tomcat.

If he agrees to it, then I'll have an agreement drawn up by a solicitor of my own who can get started on the divorce right away, for I now want to divest myself of James permanently.

When I went out to post the letter, I automatically reached for Bess's lead.

What would I do if James broke into the house while I was out? I suppose he has a perfect right? Or does he?

However, there was no sign of him when I returned, so I forced myself to stop worrying about it all and do some work.

I'm typing out the final draft of *Love Lies Bleeding*, but don't like the Bleeding title.

Mother phoned in the evening, but I'd been expecting James to go and bleat out his version to her first, so I wasn't too surprised when she took his part. She said I was hard-hearted, and the Other Woman was all a misunderstanding.

Pretty much what I expected really.

Fergal: September 1999

'THE NUN'S TALE
Baby not Rocco's, rules judge.'

Exposé magazine

I already knew that. So far as I know I haven't got any offspring – I've always been too careful. When I have children I want to be around.

As soon as I got back to Nutthill I went straight down to the horse's mouth. I knew Mrs Deakin would tell me any news going.

And she did, too. Word is that Tish has thrown James out and he's staying with some friends in the village.

She said it was probably over another woman – it usually was.

I wouldn't bust up a marriage, but if he's fool enough to bust up his own . . .? And, love me or hate me, she isn't indifferent to me. A fling with me could be just what she needs.

Could be just the medicine *I* need too: Tish – take regularly until symptoms vanish.

Chapter 26: Pregnant Pause

First thing next morning I phoned the office and asked to speak to Vanessa Grey.

'Mr Oliver Drew's personal assistant?' said the voice.

Why do all receptionists sound snooty? PA? That's one up from being a secretarty, I suppose.

'Vanessa Grey,' said a familiar voice.

'This is Tish Drew – James's wife.'

There was a small pause. 'One minute,' she said, and there was the sound of a door closing before she came back on. 'Yes?'

'What colour is your hair?'

'What?'

'Your hair – what colour is it?'

'Chestnut brown. Why?'

'How long has it been that colour?'

'About a year. It's my natural colour. I got tired of being a dumb blonde. Do I take it from these strange questions that you've at last found out about James's bit on the side, and thought it was me?'

'I just wanted to be certain. Anyway, there was the office Christmas party, wasn't there? Someone sent me a photocopy.'

'Oh, that was me. I thought someone ought to put you on your guard. Not that there was anything much in that – James isn't exactly the world's best lover, is he? And anyway, I've got other, bigger and better fish to fry now.'

'*You* sent it?'

'To be quite honest, I thought it would cause a bit of trouble and you'd find out about this girl he's been seeing. It was obvious to me as soon as I came back here that he was bored with you. It was just a friendly warning.'

'Thank you!'

'I did think at first I might get him back, but then – well, someone else came along. And then I saw him with that tarty-looking bit. She used to hang around outside the office, sometimes, waiting for him.'

Takes one to know one.

'But did you and James – at the Christmas party—' I began, but the phone went dead.

Really, I suppose it doesn't matter now whether he was unfaithful with *one* girl or hordes . . . and my suspicions are growing that the Bit On The Side may be Alice's sister.

After this I popped down to Mrs D.'s for some essential supplies. I was still afraid James would get in, but I mustn't get paranoid about it.

I made myself walk on as far as the village pond for some air first, though. The bottom of it is coated with leaves like a golden bowl set in mud. There didn't seem much point in walking further without Bess.

Bob's mother had sent me a big basket of cooking apples and I'd decided to make apple chutney with them, so I needed a bottle of malt vinegar and some sultanas, though as usual I came out of Mrs Deakin's with more than I intended to buy.

As I turned into the drive with my shopping, I was startled to see Fergal sitting on the doorstep, looking like an expensive advert for something: Sex Appeal, possibly.

He was holding a small cardboard box and, at the sound of my feet – and my shopping bag hitting the ground – he looked up, grinning. 'Someone's left you a present.'

Bemused by the beguiling grin (so different from the last time we met), I accepted the box as he rose lithely to his feet. 'A present?'

The box moved suddenly in my hands like a jumping bean and said, crossly, 'Mmrrow!'

I nearly dropped it.

Fergal proffered a grubby bit of lined paper. 'This was underneath it.'

Clutching the rocking box to my bosom I read the following words with mounting horror: 'ONE OF TIBBY'S KITTENS AS PROMISED. JARED SMITH.'

Tibby!

'Oh, no!' I moaned, my knees beginning to sag. 'I can't – not if it's got millions of toes . . .'

Fergal neatly caught the sliding box and supported me with his other arm.

'Millions of what?' he asked, then added quickly, 'Never mind, you aren't well. Where's your key?'

Things seemed to be spinning a bit, so I shut my eyes, grateful for the feel of a muscular arm around me, and when I opened them again I was sitting in a kitchen chair.

'Here – drink this.' He handed me a glass of water.

'I don't want—' I began, looked at his face and meekly reached out a hand for the glass.

'That's better. I thought you were going to pass out on me. What's the matter? Pregnant?'

I gave a startled gasp and burst into tears. 'No! Yes! I – I might be, but—'

A gentle hand fleetingly touched my hair. 'I thought so. Don't forget I come from a big family, and there's a certain look . . .'

'I – is there?' I mopped my eyes and sat up. 'I'm sorry, I can't think what got into me.'

'It takes you like that, so I'm told. Congratulations – I expect your husband's delighted?'

'He – he doesn't know. I'm not even sure myself, so – so would you mind not mentioning it to anyone yet?'

He gave me a long, uncomfortably searching look, and I went pink. But if he hasn't heard about our Great Schism I don't feel up to telling him about it just now. I'm not playing for sympathy with Fergal Rocco.

'All right,' he agreed coolly. 'But you don't look very well. I thought so last time I saw you.'

'I'm OK.' I managed a shaky smile and ran my fingers through my dishevelled locks. The chimera of pregnancy was thrust back into its pit until I could deal with it. I sat straighter. 'It was just the heat, and then the kitten . . .'

'The dust, the flies, the natives?' He smiled sardonically. 'Didn't you want a kitten?'

I looked with a shudder at the box, which was now on the table. 'No, especially not one of Tibby's! She's a deformed village cat, and an awful old man did threaten to give me one of her next litter.'

He began opening the lid of the box. 'Just because the mother's deformed, it doesn't follow that the kitten is.'

Inserting his hand he removed a spitting ball of black fluff. A pink mouth opened in a tiny meow.

'There doesn't look to be much wrong with that.'

'How many toes has it got?'

'Toes?' He captured a small foot. 'One, two, three . . .' He paused. 'Six. That can't be right, can it? Not that I've ever counted a cat's toes before, but—'

'It's just like Tibby! She's got about twenty on each foot!'

'You couldn't fit twenty on a cat's foot,' he pointed out.

'Well, that's how many it looks like!' I snapped sulkily. 'And I don't want it.'

'If you're pregnant, it's not a good time to house-train a kitten anyway – there's some bug they can pass on if you aren't careful with the litter trays. I remember my sister Lucia telling me.'

'Is there? But what on earth shall I do with it, then?' I mean, it might look quite sweet, really, but . . .

'I'll have it. God knows, there's enough room up at the Hall for a hundred cats, and just think how interesting the pawprints will look on the new cement.'

The kitten, resisting to the last, was thrust back into the box.

'Thank you, Fergal. I'm very grateful – I really couldn't have coped.'

'Yes you could. You were already starting to weaken. You're too soft-hearted to do anything else. At least, I used to *think* you were.'

He slanted a considering glance at me from those devastating green eyes and added abruptly, 'Why didn't you answer my letters?'

'What? Which letters?' I stammered, confused. 'Do you mean the one about the fence?'

'Not that one, stupid! The letters I wrote to you from America, after you refused to come with me. God, they must have been *really* memorable!'

My jaw nearly hit the table. 'But you never sent me any letters!'

'I did.'

'But – you can't have done!'

'Are you trying to tell me you never got them?' he demanded incredulously.

'Of course I never got them,' I said shakily. 'You know I would have answered if you'd written to me.'

Turning away, he stared out of the window, shoulders tense, while I cast my mind back to that terrible summer.

'The day after we argued, Grandpa had a heart attack and I went up to stay with Granny – you know how useless Mother is in a crisis. Grandpa had another heart attack later and died ... so I was there right up to the start of the university term.'

'I'm sorry. I liked your grandpa.'

'Mother promised to tell me if you tried to get in touch with me, and send any letters on.'

'Did she? And did she happen to mention the phone calls?' he enquired bleakly, turning to face me.

'Phone calls?' I faltered.

'Phone calls. The ones I made when you didn't reply to my letters. You were never there – she told me you were going out with someone else and didn't want anything to do with me.'

'Of course I was never there – I was at Granny's! And I certainly wasn't seeing anyone else. She did send me a cutting from a magazine, though – you and that American model coming out of a nightclub ... How could you, Fergal!'

He shrugged. 'I'm only human, and if you didn't want me . . . or that's what I thought, anyway. Your mother should be put in a sack and drowned,' he added pleasantly.

There were a couple of things I'd like to do to her personally before she went in the bag.

'I even went round to your house when I got back from America, you know, and your mother told me you were living in college, and she was sorry but you'd found someone else almost immediately. I should have suspected something when she was so nice to me!'

'She always thought you were too unsteady – she was afraid I'd get hurt.'

'And were you hurt?'

I looked away, blinking rapidly, and tried to summon a smile. 'It's all water under the bridge now, isn't it? But you should have known I'd have answered your letters.'

'And you should have come to America with me when I asked you.'

'Asked? You never *asked* me! You just assumed I was going with you.'

'I can't have been *that* arrogant, Tish,' he protested, looking taken aback.

'Yes, you were! That's what made me so cross, I suppose, though if you'd asked me again next day I would have changed my mind, I think. Still, it wouldn't have lasted, would it? You need someone more glamorous and sophisticated – like Nerissa.'

'And you need someone steady and dull and safe, like your James? You didn't waste much time, did you?'

'But I didn't even meet James until the final year of my course, and we only got married after I finished college!'

I got up and wandered abstractedly about the kitchen, the pain of reopened wounds warring with the underlying spectre of pregnancy that Fergal had dragged, kicking and screaming, out of my subconscious. And yet, my heart was warmed by the thought that he *had* cared about me after all. Even our arguing had a cosy familiarity about it.

He took me by the shoulders and turned me to face him, gazing deeply into my eyes. I never could look away when he did that. 'I suppose I should have known you better,' he muttered. 'But you were so young . . . I should have realised.'

He let me go so suddenly I staggered. 'So you settled for respectable dullness, Angel, while I settled for—'

'Disreputable excitement!' I finished for him, rather tartly. 'And I don't know why you think my life is dull – especially since we moved here.' (That was true at least!) 'Anyway, I'd rather have dullness than be a hanger-on on the fringes of the sort of life you lead.'

'You know nothing about the sort of life I lead.'

'The papers and magazines—'

'So you were interested enough to keep track of me?'

I flushed. 'Not on purpose! But you can't open a magazine without seeing your goings-on plastered all over it.'

'Publicity stunts, most of them. And, as you've discovered, the camera – and journalists – can lie.'

'And is buying a country house a publicity stunt, too?'

'No. It's a mark of the parting of the ways. The band haven't exactly split, since we're still going to record new material together, but we all want to go our separate ways. I'm settling down – I've had more than enough of life on the road. And when I saw the Hall . . . Have you seen it?'

'No.'

'I'll show you round sometime.'

'Does Nerissa like it?' I blurted, then bit my lip. I hadn't meant to ask that.

The arrogant black eyebrows twitched into a frown. 'What does it matter?'

'She told me you were engaged, so it must matter to her!'

'When did she tell you that?'

'She called round a few days ago.'

He smiled, rather unpleasantly. 'She's a pretty little thing, isn't she? But I've no intention of marrying her, as she knows very well.'

'How very trendy!'

'Don't be sarcastic,' he said absently. He seemed to be thinking something over. 'You'd recommend marriage, would you, Tish? Everything in the garden coming up roses?'

Watchful green eyes . . .

'Lettuce and peas mostly!' I hoped my smile was convincing. 'Yes, I have everything I ever dreamed of.' (Except Fergal and/or a faithful husband.)

Since he was still watching me, I babbled on, 'But I didn't ask you – did you get that ring I sent you?'

'That's why I came.' He patted the pockets of his black jeans and produced a small blue velvet box. (Amazing – I wouldn't have thought there was room left for a door key in there, let alone a box.) 'Here it is.'

I opened it to a gentle sparkle of blue and gold, and exclaimed in surprise, 'Oh, how pretty! You wouldn't think it was the same dirty, twisted bit of metal I picked up.'

'I've had it restored, and taken advice about who owns it, and it's yours.'

'M-mine? I'm sure that can't be right! Besides, you must have paid for it to be restored.'

He shrugged. 'You found it, and you ought to have it – and wear it. The motto suits you: fidelity does deserve love.'

I eyed him suspiciously, but he looked quite serious, so I thanked him and slid the ring on to my finger, where it looked and felt strangely familiar. 'Well, thank you, Fergal. I hope this means that we're friends again?' I ventured.

'Friends?' He savoured the word. 'Is there room in your cosy little life for anyone except your wonderful husband?'

'Of course!' I said lightly. 'I – oh, are you going?'

'I have to see a lady about some cat food,' he replied, picking up the box from which we'd been serenaded throughout our conversation with soft sounds of distress and temper: very appropriate really.

'Mrs Deakin? She'll also sell you a cat tray, bowl and flea powder!'

'So she will.' He smiled as he went past me. 'But she can supply me with everything I need, don't you think? Including the most up-to-date village gossip.'

Oh God, I hope not! I don't want him to feel sorry for me (or know I've been lying through my teeth).

He paused on the doorstep and demanded abruptly, 'Tish, just how pregnant are you?'

'I'm not even sure that I am yet.'

'That early?' He scowled down at me. 'Go and see your doctor. You're too pale, and you don't look well – and tell your husband he should be looking after you.'

Why does everyone want me to see a doctor? I don't look that bad!

'I'm just not sleeping very well.' With a disintegrating marriage, who would?

'You're not worrying about anything?'

'Me? No! Not a care in the world,' I assured him, not quite meeting his eyes.

'Then when you come up soon and see Greatness Hall, I expect you'll be looking much better.'

'See the Hall?'

'Yes. I'll show you round.'

'Well – thank you,' I began.

'You can see how the cat is doing.' He favoured me with one of his more enigmatic smiles. '*Ciao*, Angel.'

Later, when I'd calmed myself somewhat by making several jars of apple chutney (I don't know why I find this kind of thing soothing, but I do), I discovered that Toby had let himself out of his cage and was chewing the corner of the cloth that covered the table it stood on, in a bored kind of way.

'Hello?' he said, fixing me with a beady gaze. 'Toby want biccy.'

You'd swear he knew what he was saying sometimes!

As I lured him back into his cage with a trail of leftover sultanas, it occurred to me how very difficult it would have been having a cat about, when Toby might escape at any time.

So really, I should be feeling even more grateful to Fergal . . . only I'm not exactly sure what I feel about him at the moment, and it's probably much better not even to try to find out.

* * *

Fergal: September 1999

'Fergal Rocco – First exclusive pictures of the star's new country home . . .'

Trendsetter magazine

Once Tish's husband knows about the baby, he's bound to see sense and come running, and I'll have to back off, even if I don't think he deserves her.

And what makes me vain enough to think she'd have an affair with me, just because I caught her in a weak (and drunken) moment in London?

Do I think I'm so irresistible?

And why is she still so irresistible to me? Pregnant, and another man's wife, and I only have to touch her, like yesterday, and I want her . . .

Why her? She's not even really beautiful (unique, yes), she's got prissy little ways, and one week in her company and I'd be so clean I'd squeak . . .

Chapter 27: Similar Conditions

It's disconcerting having the real Fergal about, especially now I know he didn't behave quite so badly to me. And he's been kind. Perhaps he really isn't as black as he's been painted. (Just darkish grey.)

I bet he knows all about my marital difficulties now too. Maybe he did before and *that's* why he was so kind.

But he could be wrong about the pregnancy. He's only a man, how on earth could he tell from my face? I'm not even going to consider the idea. There's already too much to think of without such a remote possibility.

Like that box belonging to James I found in the attic, when I was searching for the one containing all the old possessions I couldn't throw out, but didn't want around the house, including some mementoes of Fergal. Suddenly I needed to see them again – it was either that or go and strangle my interfering, impossible mother.

I might do that later.

As I pushed my box towards the hatchway I caught sight of another behind it, and remembered that James had stored some old things up there too, so I thought I might as well get those down while I was at it.

Compared to the several months' fuzz of dust on my box, his was singularly free of it; clearly he'd been in it for something recently. I wondered what, and lifted the lid.

The top layer was crammed with letters: love letters. And the very first one I looked at was signed 'Little Snookums Wendy' – the bitch! I was right then, because I'm sure Wendy was the name of Alice's sister. It all ties in.

Once I'd read all the letters I could see the double life that James had been leading since soon after we moved here, without stupid, credulous old me ever realising it.

But who would have thought he was clever enough to conceal it? I didn't think he had such deviousness in him. And why on earth didn't he keep his letters at the office, when I can see from the envelopes that that's where they were sent?

Wendy's letters show an increasing determination to hang onto him, and quite a bit of jealousy of me. I bet that's why she made those silent calls.

And the day of the SFWWR dinner I'd seen him with her and he'd made *me* feel guilty!

Swine.

If I could be so deceived in the man I married, how could I ever trust anyone again? What with Fergal's revelations and James's infidelities, it's as though my whole life has been shaken up like a kaleidoscope into a totally different pattern.

I received an answer to the letter I wrote to James before I found his hoard, suggesting that 'now I've had a chance to cool off' I'd be amenable to settling our trifling differences and resuming our marriage, so I sent him a postcard asking what he wanted me to do with all the love letters from his mistress. That should circulate round the village in record time.

Later I saw Bess in the distance with Margaret, but I turned and walked away through the whirling bronze leaves. Early autumn was always my favourite time of year . . .

The kitchen cupboards are still full of tins of dog food. I wonder if I could get a refund . . .

It's no use, I simply can't hide my head in the sand any longer. My abdomen is becoming spherical and I have a strange sensation round my bust . . . which is growing.

Fergal might be right.

I certainly don't need this worry on top of all the others, so I've got a pregnancy testing kit – rather a pretty thing to put to so sordid a use. There were simpler kits, but who'd trust some sort of dipstick?

I've added an early-morning sample and must leave it for two hours: please let it be negative!

It wasn't: it was blatantly positive.

I am shaking like a leaf at the thought of something – and something I don't want – growing inside me, with nothing I can do about it.

There is abortion, but since it was my carelessness that caused the baby in the first place, I can't very well murder the poor little thing, can I?

It must have been the barbecue – it's the only possible time – which means I'm getting on for three months pregnant, I think, so it now has all its little fingers and toes and a heart beating in time with mine . . .

No, I can't murder it.

But I just know when James finds out he'll put my decision to throw him out down to softening of the brain caused by the pregnancy. I must press on with the divorce before he finds out – and I suppose I must see my doctor.

The doctor confirmed that I was pregnant, and seemed surprised when I told her the exact date of the conception. (Perhaps I should name the infant 'Kebab' or 'Punch'?)

When I broke down and wept that I didn't want it – I'd left my husband (sort of) and would make an awful mother, she went all Catholic and started waffling on about the Sanctity of Human Life.

The hospital antenatal clinic will send for me for a thorough going-over, and I get the impression my partially suppressed periods were not good news, though at least they have now ceased altogether.

I was in such a state I took a taxi home, where I was met on the doorstep by a thin, shivering, muddy Bess. Her frantic, affectionate and messy greetings were just what I needed to thaw my numb state of shock. I showered her, then poured half my bottle of conditioner over her, since I could see she'd be hell to brush. I still had to cut one or two really bad snarls out, but she looked a lot better afterwards, and wolfed down an enormous dinner. (Just as well I hadn't returned the dog food!)

Considering how thin she is, her tummy really is a funny shape. I only hope we aren't sharing a Similar Condition. It would be too ironic for words.

Since I'd forgotten to lock the door in the surprise of finding her, James just walked straight in later and demanded, 'Have you taken Bess?'

Funnily enough, now I had the pregnancy to worry about, I'd ceased to be nervous about James: it was like looking at an alien but harmless being from another planet.

'I haven't taken her. When I got home she was waiting on the doorstep in a terrible state! What on earth have you been doing to her?'

'Nothing! The silly bitch seems to have gone dotty, or something. Perhaps it's catching?' he added nastily, but the remark just slid off me. 'She wouldn't eat, she wanders round the flat howling when I'm at work, and Margaret can't do a thing with her. You must have spoiled her.'

'I spoiled her? I thought she was *your* dog?'

'So did I,' he sighed, and deflated a bit, like my soufflé the only time I tried making one. 'But I suppose I was wrong about that and about a lot of other things too. Look, Tish, couldn't we talk over a cup of coffee?'

I hesitated, but he seemed suddenly so unimportant and diminished that I led him into the kitchen.

Bess promptly tried to hide behind the Aga. He gave her a look of disgust. 'That creature might as well stay with you, since it's clear she doesn't want anything to do with me any more. I don't seem to be having much luck with females lately.'

'Oh, I don't know,' I mused, getting out a second-best mug for his coffee, 'you still have little Wendikins and Margaret to sympathise with you, and Mother to complain to.'

'But – look here, Tish, you ought to let me explain about Wendy! The girl was nothing. She's Alice's sister, you know, and she made all the running. And I'm not seeing her any more.'

'Aren't you? Never mind, perhaps you'll find someone else.'

'What on earth do you mean? I don't want anyone else! She didn't mean anything to me – but you're my wife, and I want you to stop all this nonsense at once. You must admit, I've been very patient.'

'I expect you have, looked at from your viewpoint. I'm sure Bluebeard thought he was being perfectly reasonable, too. But you must stop thinking that I threw you out because I found out about the girl. I'd already made up my mind long before that. Wendy's only made me even more determined on a divorce, not just a separation. We've both changed, and there's no point in trying again.'

He opened and closed his mouth a couple of times like a rather dim fish and I added, 'Anyway, our marriage didn't even have going for it what I thought it had in the first place – on your side it was a sham. I'd rather be alone now.'

He looked at me with a sort of dawning horror. Had he really thought I'd dismiss Wendy as some sort of minor peccadillo, sob contritely on his shoulder, and beg him to return to me?

Certainly, patent uninterest was not what he was expecting.

'Tish, what's come over you lately? You never used to be so cold and hard – and I still love you!'

'Do you?' ('*It's love, Jim – but not as we know it!*' said Spock's voice in my head.)

In silence we sipped coffee-substitute and Bess cautiously emerged, looking pointedly at the biscuit tin. I gave her a ginger nut, and it vanished in a bite and a gulp. A bit like it does with Bob.

James heaved a long sigh. 'Uncle Lionel warned me that you'd have small provincial ideas on fidelity if you ever found out about my bit of fun. But just remember that it's not what I wanted, so don't come running back crying in a few months and expect me to take you on again.'

'No, I certainly won't!' I assured him, thinking that in a few months I will be quite incapable of running anywhere! 'And I'm glad you've taken it so well, James.'

He gave a snort. 'How on earth do you think you're going to manage? What about the mortgage, the practical arrangements? I don't think you realise just how much is involved. And what am I supposed to do about somewhere to live? I can't stay in the flat for ever.'

'I do realise what's involved, and I can manage very well as long as I don't have to give you any lump sums immediately. We can get the furniture, and car and your radio equipment and everything valued, and make an equal division. That is – I suppose you *are* going to let me have the house?'

'I suppose so,' he replied sulkily. I don't expect he thought I'd have worked it all out, and was hoping I wouldn't be able to manage financially without him.

He cast a disparaging glance around the kitchen. 'Since I've been living in the flat I've rediscovered how much more comfortable modern houses are. If we'd got back together I was going to suggest we move to a big modern, detached house in a couple of years, maybe on that new estate at Lower Nutthill.'

Move to a horrible modern box, just when I'd got my little cottage how I wanted it? Is he mad?

He continued on, oblivious. 'I suppose we can work it out to be fair to both of us – but I hope you're right about being able to manage.'

I could see he didn't really expect me to be able to, and was perhaps even counting on my running back to him soon and begging him to return.

'As long as I keep writing I won't starve to death, James,' I assured him cheerfully. 'This American contract is going to be very lucrative. Do you want any of the furniture and things? What about the wedding presents?'

He said he didn't want to burden himself with a lot of junk (our wedding presents were not junk – I wrote the list myself!) but he would like the CD player, TV, video, etc. I said that was fine (I can always rent a little TV), so long as they all came out of his share at the Reckoning – along with the car, which of course he's still got.

I insisted we go to see a solicitor I've heard of to get everything in writing and set the divorce in motion and he reluctantly agreed, then said, very seriously, 'There's just one more thing!'

I wondered what on earth could be coming. I knew that mood of sweet reason wouldn't last!

'The Shack – I can't move all that stuff until I've bought another house. Can I come here in the evenings and use it? I won't bother you. I'll use the side gate.'

I didn't really want him trailing in and out, but equally I didn't want to spoil the *entente cordiale* (such as it was) either, so I said reluctantly, 'I suppose so – though I want the whole lot moved as soon as possible, *especially* the aerial.'

He got up to go, relieved of his most pressing worry. He'd been more grieved at the idea of being parted from his radio than from me. Bess looked relieved, too. I'm glad the stupid bitch is staying. I'll get her made mine in writing, while James is still in Reasonable Mode.

I escorted him off the premises, wondering why on earth he didn't just move in with Howard and Alice and dear little Wendy. They could be one big happy family.

As I closed the gate, Nerissa skimmed to a halt in one of those flat thin sports cars, like a red credit card on wheels.

'Hi, Tish!' she called gaily, but her huge brown eyes were on James, who was transfixed, though that might have been by the car.

'Is this your husband? You didn't tell me he was *sooo* handsome!'

'Didn't I?' I said. 'Yes, this is James – James, Nerissa.'

'Actually, I wondered if I might persuade you down to the pub for a drink, Tish,' she cooed. 'Only Fergal's just so busy at the moment, and I did enjoy our little chat. But maybe you and James were just going out?'

'James is going out – I'm staying in,' I said concisely. Becoming bosom friends with Fergal's fiancée was too masochistic a prospect for me. 'Some other time, perhaps.'

'Actually, I was thinking of having a quick one at the Dog and Duck myself, if you'd settle for my company?' James offered eagerly.

'Love to,' she said promptly, then added with a glance at me, 'If Tish doesn't mind my hijacking her gorgeous husband!'

Only the best butter, I thought. But it was certainly working on James, who was halfway into the car already.

'That's all right – I've finished with him,' I told her. 'You can have him.'

As they drove off I read the expression on James's face clearly: he thought I'd be raging with jealousy, and he was also doing Fergal one in the eye by going off with his girl.

I'm not sure what Nerissa was thinking. Or *if* she was thinking.

I haven't seen James to speak to since the night he went off with Nerissa, but he pops round to the Shack most evenings. I could watch him unobserved from the bedroom, but it would be pointless because he's totally uninteresting.

Bess is now afraid of being left alone in the house in case James or the Wrekins come to drag her off again, but conversely, Toby seems much more laid-back and less snappy without James about the place.

Of course, I had Mother sobbing and incoherent on the phone, saying she'd done her best for me, and it wasn't her fault if I'd turned out a mess and ruined my life. Anyone would think I was a heroin addict turned prostitute the way she went on.

If she hadn't interfered I would probably have had a happier – if shorter – relationship with Fergal than I found in my marriage.

I love Mother, but I like her less and less as I get older . . .

However, I at last feel calm enough to go and ask her face to face why she lied about Fergal's letters and calls, without physically assaulting her (I think), and I could combine the visit with a quick look at maternity clothes.

In loose things you wouldn't know I was pregnant yet, but I don't have many loose things. The maternity clothes in magazines are all very strange, though I suppose you can't do much with something shaped like a blancmange except put a frill round it.

What *am* I going to do about the Incubus?

Come to think of it, there is nothing I can do.

I've noticed some funny sensations lately, which might be the Incubus stirring . . .

This can't be happening to me!

The hospital has pressingly invited me to go for an ante-natal check-up and a scan on 26 October. I'm to drink gallons of water and not go to the loo beforehand, but also to take an early morning sample, mid-flow, for the clinic.

Aren't these two directions somewhat conflicting? Ought I to read up on what horrors are in store? I'm dreading it.

James and I had a fairly painless meeting last week in front of a strange solicitor who seemed to find it all very amusing. A separation is being drawn up, as complicated as the division of Siamese twins, and we're going in for the quickest quickie divorce possible. (James balked a bit at this point, but mention of Little Snookums Wendy's letters seemed to work wonders.)

Just as we were about to part, James remarked out of the blue that I was looking rather fat.

I told him I'd put on weight, but thought it suited me (ho, ho!), and he said I shouldn't let myself go just because I was living alone now.

Pig!

Fergal: October 1999

'Nympho Nordic blondes in sexy sauna scandal reveal all!'

Sun

Thought they already had.

The papers must be having a Bad News Day.

Wonder why these articles never seem to bear any resemblance to events as I and the rest of the band remember them. Their fiction is always stranger than the truth.

Maybe we're inhabiting a parallel universe but not, despite what the newspapers may say, a permanently horizontal one.

Carlo's fiancée is giving him hell.

Chapter 28: Bonfire of the Vanities

Felt really sick this morning, but it was just nerves about going to the hospital. I wish I hadn't read the books and was still in a state of (semi) blissful ignorance.

First I had the scan, in a sort of grimy little Portakabin round the back of the hospital.

I was bursting, because after the mid-stream sample I thought I'd better top up a bit, as it were.

I had to strip off to my undies behind an inadequate curtain and put on a funny cotton gown. I wasn't sure if it tied at the front or the back, but mine had lost its tapes so it didn't much matter.

Then I lay on a table and had hot oil rubbed into my stomach, like a sacrificial Bride of Frankenstein, before the girl ran a probe thing over my bump. A picture formed on a TV screen, but she said nothing while she pushed it to and fro, until I eventually demanded to know whether she'd found it, or wasn't I pregnant after all?

She laughed, the heartless hag. 'Of course I've found it! Look.' And she pointed to what looked like some alien creature crawling along a sea bottom – and I have a blurry grey photo to prove it.

When I was dressed again (oily enough to stir-fry, but dressed), and had – oh joy! – been to the loo, it was time for the antenatal clinic which is, of course, miles away.

There was another long wait before I was ushered off with six others into a cubicle room where I had to strip off yet again and put on another little dressing gown.

We emerged into an inner holding pen clutching plastic bags with our clothes in, like prison camp inmates and, since the dressing gowns were all very short midget length, the only sound in the room was that of thighs unpeeling from plastic chairs.

Finally it was my turn, and I suppose the doctor spoke English, because the nurse seemed to understand what he was saying. He smiled a lot and I felt like telling him it was nothing to smile about.

After the unspeakable examination I stood in humiliated silence on the scales, had my blood pressure taken, and answered questions, some downright insulting. Do I look as if I change my bed partners every night and twice on Saturday? I don't even change my library books that often!

I was assured that everything seemed normal, and asked whether my dates were right, but unless this was the Second Coming, they had to be.

I was not to worry about that early light bleeding.

I was not to worry.

(Well, that's all right then, I thought – I'll just stop.)

On the way out, the nurse handed me about fifty leaflets on things like smoking during pregnancy, diet and sterilisation (bottles, not people – too late). Two were in Urdu.

How wonderful to emerge free into the weak October

sunshine! I don't ever want to go there again. Still, most of my appointments are with my doctor.

I suppose I could just turn up at the maternity ward when I was in labour without all this? They could hardly refuse me! I don't feel any inclination to tell anyone about the baby yet, either.

When I got home I had a long soak in the bath.

The iron pills they gave me have led to ingrowing constipation. I must get some more figs. I'm supposed to eat a balanced diet, and Bess had better have one too – since she was either expecting, or swelling in sympathy, I had the vet look at her and it's the former. How could she do this to me?

He says the puppies should arrive about the end of November, since I know when it happened, though not which awful mutt is the father!

I thought it best to descend on Mother without warning, so it was something of an anti-climax to find her out lunching again with Dr Reevey. What happened to run-off-their-feet GPs?

Granny says he specialises in diseases of the rich, but likes to practise on the National Health patients first.

She'd been watching *Gone With the Wind* on video, while eating chocolate creams, which she said was the perfect combination. To get her full attention I had to stand between her and Rhett Butler and raise my voice.

'Granny, you know when I came to stay with you that time, the summer before I started university?'

Sighing, she turned down the sound. 'Course I do. I'm

not daft! You'd split up with that nice, dark boy – the singer – Freddy.'

'Fergal. He wanted me to go on tour with him to America, and I wanted to do my degree and wait for him to come back.' I paused, puzzled. 'The degree seemed important at the time.'

'Well, didn't ask you to marry him, did he? You'd have been a hanger-on. One of them gropies.'

'Groupies. And no, he never mentioned marriage. But the thing is, Granny – I mean, I don't know if Mother's told you, but I met him again recently. He's bought the big house in the park right behind the cottage.'

'I don't hold with carryings-on and such,' she said severely, giving me her full attention.

'It's nothing like that! But we got talking and it turns out that after we split up he sent me lots of letters and even phoned me, but I never heard anything about it. Do you think Mother purposely hid them?'

'Of course she did! Didn't think he was good enough for you. She wanted a big wedding, grandchildren and you living nearby. Wouldn't have had all that if you'd gone off with Fergus, would she?'

'Fergal. No, I don't suppose she would. But thanks to her, I never got the chance to find out! I came today to have it out with her.'

'Pointless: she doesn't know the truth from fairy tales half the time. That doctor had better watch himself.'

'He isn't serious, is he?'

'Looking that way. Of course, he doesn't know she's the next thing to an alcoholic.'

'She isn't that bad!'

'I've got my photos,' Granny said, with one of her sudden, baffling changes of subject.

'What? Which photos?'

'Yes, I've got my photos. You wanted to see them. Fetch that album from the table.'

Puzzled, I did so, and she riffled through the pages until she found what she wanted.

'Here we are: Bernard and me in Russia.'

'Oh – it's what you were telling me about on the phone! You were in Russia when I was born.'

'Yes. You wanted to see them.'

'I wanted to know—'

'This is us outside the hotel. Funny people, the Russkies – seemed to think we wanted to see a lot of modern factories and hospitals, but I soon put them right.'

'I'm sure you did!' I gave up and was soon absorbed in Granny and Grandpa's Russian adventure.

When she'd turned the last page I prompted: 'And there I was when you got back home?'

'Your poor father looked quite bewildered – as well he might! But then, you were a surprise baby. We didn't think, after the mumps . . . and it were funny Valerie going off on her own down to Cornwall like that, and coming back with a baby. Bound to make talk!'

'Did she? But if she didn't know she was going to have the baby – I mean, it's possible, isn't it?' (Though my subconscious certainly knew, even if it had been told to keep it to itself.)

Granny was frowning in an effort of memory. 'I thought at the time she might have gone because she'd heard where that flighty sister of hers was – that Glenda what run off, but she said not. Just needed a holiday after nursing your father.' She sighed. 'Anyway, the certificate was right, and Valerie was like a child with a new doll. I thought at the time the cat would make a better mother, though – and I was right!'

'I'd like to see my birth certificate.'

'It'll be around somewhere. In the desk?' she said vaguely.

The big desk in the corner is where Mother stuffs any bit of paper that comes her way. Any qualms I might have had about searching it were vanquished by the thought of her destroying, probably after reading, Fergal's precious letters to me.

My life might have been totally different . . . Probably just as miserable in the end, but different!

So I began to rifle through the drawers, while Granny brought me a cup of cocoa and a chocolate biscuit and then returned to her film.

('Oh – Ashley! Ashley!')I'd drawn a blank in the drawers and with the top compartment, when I suddenly remembered the so-called secret drawer.

The moulding depressed under my fingers and the drawer slid smoothly out, revealing a bundle of thin airmail letters addressed in a bold black scrawl, and under them a birth certificate.

As I stood up with them in my trembling hands the door opened and in walked Mother.

Her face filled with a sort of aghast fearfulness when she noticed the papers in my hands, and perhaps she thought I was about to leap across the room and strangle her, because she stepped back, baby-blue eyes widening and her hands at her throat.

Then she rallied, and a weak smile struggled for birth on

312

her lips. 'Leticia darling! I wasn't expecting you, was I? Have you been here long?'

'Long enough to find the proof of your lies, Mother. You ruined my life!'

Her face crumpled. 'But I meant it all for the best, darling! He was no good. And he hadn't even been to university – only art college – which shows! He would have tossed you aside when he tired of you—'

'But I *loved* him, and it was *my* life, and *my* decision, not yours!'

'You were too young to decide. I knew you'd soon forget him and find someone more suitable – and you did: you got your degree, and married dear James.'

'Dear James of the lies and mistress?'

'Not a mistress, Leticia darling – you've got it quite wrong!'

'Knew it!' Granny stated, without taking her eyes off Rhett. 'Worked too many late nights. And never trust a man with that shade of blue eyes.'

'Why didn't you say, Granny?'

'Wouldn't have made any difference – you wouldn't have believed me.'

Maybe not, but it might have made me watch him a bit closer!

'I found letters from this girl in a box in the attic, and it's clear he's been having an affair with her since just after we moved to Nutthill – months. But he doesn't seem to think it counts, since it's just "a bit on the side", while I'm his wife and he "loves" me. I think he must be mad!'

'Surely . . .' faltered Mother, sitting down rather suddenly and turning pale, 'surely it was just a little flirtation? James wouldn't – he hasn't – I can't believe it.'

'I'm afraid I can't show you the letters any more, because I gave them to Bob to burn.' Except for a couple of Little Snookums' most lurid renderings, of course, which I am keeping in reserve.

'They must have been *old* letters, dear,' Mother said firmly, rallying. 'From before he met you. You shouldn't have read them.'

I stared speechlessly at her. I'd call her brainwashed if I thought she had one to wash.

'And is it surprising that poor James was jealous, when that Fergal moved in practically next door and he caught you holding hands with him over the fence? He just turned to Someone Else for sympathy.'

This was such a warped version of reality that it was hard to see a pattern in it.

'You're a complete fool, Valerie!' Granny declared dispassionately.

'Mother,' I said with what patience I could muster, 'I didn't know Fergal had bought the Hall, and he didn't know I lived in Nutthill. James was seeing this Wendy female ages before he moved into the Hall anyway, every time he stayed overnight with Howard. And Fergal was not holding my hand. We mean nothing to each other – you took care of that long ago!'

I found I was nervously turning the sapphire heart ring round and round on my finger. (It was now the only ring I wore.)

Granny's eyes moved suspiciously from the ring to my face: 'He's not married, is he?'

'Who, Granny?'

'That Ferdy.'

'Fergal. No, he's not the marrying kind.'

'There you are then!' cried Mother triumphantly. 'I did it for the best – you wouldn't have found lasting happiness with a man like that. Why don't you give me those old letters and I'll—'

'No – they're mine!' I clutched them to my bosom defensively.

'I just thought . . . but never mind. Mummy was only trying to spare her little girl any upset. What is it you have there with them?'

'My birth certificate. I've never really looked at it.'

A flicker of alarm – or was it just my imagination? – then a pained, forgiving smile. 'Can't you look at it here and then let Mummy keep it safe for you?'

'I think I'd like to have it, thanks. I hadn't realised until Granny told me that I was born in Cornwall.'

Glancing almost furtively at the small figure in front of the TV, Mother lowered her voice: 'That's right . . . you were my little Holiday Surprise!'

'Why are you whispering?' demanded Granny. 'It's very irritating! Go and whisper secrets somewhere else.'

'There *are* no secrets,' Mother said coldly.

'Granny, Mother was just about to tell me about when I was born in—'

'Good heavens!' Mother broke in, and sprang to her feet like a particularly agile marmoset. 'Is that the time? I must go and change. Dr Reevey's going to take me to a lovely, lovely opera.'

She knows nothing about opera, unless you count *West Side Story*, which she thought sordid.

'Flibbertigibbet!' Granny commented, as Mother rushed

out. 'She won't tell you anything, and I know, because I tried. There's *something* – but if you want to know what, you'll have to go and find out.'

'Find out what?'

'I don't know, I was in Russia,' she replied crossly.

The doorbell rang.

'That'll be Rose Durwin; she's got the day off and she always comes and plays Scrabble with me.'

'The district nurse? Is she good at Scrabble?'

'Can't tell her quagga from her quango, but she knows lots of long medical words. Let her in, will you?'

I let myself out at the same time, since I clearly was not going to learn any more that day. But I did have my certificate, my letters – and a few more tantalising doubts about my birth.

However, the certificate seemed plain enough, so the thing to do was to put it right out of my head, like Fergal's letters, which I was certainly *not* going to read: no good would come of raking over old ashes.

No good at all . . .

Dawn was breaking as I finished the last one, and so was my heart: trite but true. The letters had begun with typical Fergal arrogance, but ended in despairing pleading and then anger.

He'd cared for me that much.

It was just as well Mother wasn't still within reach!

I had to wear dark glasses when I went down to the shop, which is not usual in Nutthill at the start of November, but Mrs Deakin didn't say anything.

They're building a bonfire in the church field. Bob told

me he added the box of James's old letters to the pile, which seems appropriate. Bonfire of the vanities?

Fergal: November 1999

'SECOND PATERNITY CLAIM FOR SUPER STUD ROCCO . . .'

Sun

This is getting monotonous!

Any more of it and I'll be getting the *Trendsetter* Stallion of the Year Award next time.

It always seems to be women I'm pretty sure I've never even slept with, too.

So why do these women do it (especially in these days of DNA testing, when it's easy to prove the truth)?

Is five minutes of fame enough?

Chapter 29: The Great Castrator

It's only a few short weeks since I threw James out, and already I'm getting my life organised: Bess and I are eating good mixed diets, some of which Bob produces in the garden, I've found an accountant who promises he can work wonders with my finances, Vivyan has acquired back all rights to my earlier novels and is negotiating over them with Lovecall, and my solicitor assures me things are in train to divest myself of James permanently.

So far, so good. I'm the Captain of my ship, the Ruler of my universe, and Mistress of all I survey.

Now I must learn to drive, and fast, because I'll be absolutely stuck if I haven't passed the test before the Incubus arrives. As it is, I've been doing a lot of my shopping at Mrs D.'s, because it's so tiring lugging heavy bags around on the bus.

I asked her if she knew a patient driving instructor.

'Instructress,' she corrected, before going outside to give Bess a biscuit. She thinks Bess is wonderful now she's got used to her strange appearance. Wonder if she'd like a puppy?

She came back with paw prints on her apron. 'When it comes to patience you need a woman, and I know just the one.'

She produced a pack of trade-sized cards and shuffled them like a poker player.

'Here – Dulcie Blacklock. She's sort of a cousin, and she always gets her drivers through. And cheap too, not like those big driving schools what spend your money on fancy cars with big signs on and ads in all the papers.'

'Thanks, I'll give her a ring later.'

'Saw your husband this morning,' Mrs Deakin commiserated. 'Coming out of the Wrekins' flat, he was, with a tarty-looking blonde.'

'Tarty?'

'Leather miniskirt and white handbag: tarty. They got into his car and drove off.'

So he'd been lying about not seeing her, as well!

I shrugged. 'It's nothing to do with me any more – and he won't be my husband much longer, either, if I can help it.'

'That's the spirit!' she approved. She always knows everything. I'm almost certain she knows I'm pregnant, although she hasn't said anything.

It will be all too evident soon. I don't know how James is going to react, but I foresee scenes ahead.

I phoned Mrs Blacklock as soon as I got in. She has a deep voice and reassuring manner. My first driving lesson is on Tuesday.

Much though I love fireworks, I decided not to watch the Bonfire Night celebrations on the green because Bess gets hysterical when she hears bangs, and I didn't want her getting in a state in her condition.

Toby couldn't care less: he has now almost perfected the thundering noise the printer attached to my word processor makes overhead when it is in full flood, but that is preferable to his whistling kettle routine.

As it happened, it was James who got hysterical on Bonfire Night when charred bits of his love letters blew all over the village in the strong breeze. He accused me of making him the laughing stock of the whole neighbourhood, but I assured him he was perfectly capable of doing that himself.

When the day came for my first driving lesson I was a nervous wreck, though Mrs Blacklock was very good: big and jolly, and doesn't mind repeating things over and over again.

She drove me to a quiet road, then we changed places and she showed me how to adjust the mirrors and the seat, told me what the pedals are for, and how the gears are changed. Then I started and stopped the car a couple of times.

Really, the hour passed by in a flash! She thinks she might get me to the test standard by March (the baby is due at the start of April), but it would be better if I had more than one lesson a week. I must see how things work out financially first.

She dropped me off at the bus stop: I simply had to buy something to wear! Nothing fastens properly and I look an indecent mess – and I also need a new bra, since I've acquired a bust like Britannia. My stomach seems to have popped out practically overnight, like a giant mushroom.

Maternity garments, strangely, are designed for middle-aged women with a penchant for pussy-cat bows and pie-crust collars. There wasn't much choice even in the specialist shops.

Eventually I bought a pair of dungarees, a big baggy sweat-shirt, and the pattern and material for more dungarees. I hate sewing (apart from patchwork, but that, like Topsy, just growed), but I'm not paying a fortune for clothes I won't wear afterwards.

Maternity bras are all horrid, too, and either white or that colour laughingly described as 'flesh pink'. Most had ingenious devices for opening the front of the cups, and looked like something you might buy in a Sex Shop. By the time you've unhooked and undone yourself, I expect the baby will have died of starvation.

Instead I bought sports bras with stretchy, wide straps. I only want to be comfortable, after all, so what's in a label?

I really do look pregnant in my dungarees, and feel everyone in the village is looking at me and talking. Perhaps I ought to make some in patchwork and *really* give them something to talk about?

How long will it be before James finds out? I expect I ought to do the decent thing and tell him first, but I can't summon up the feeling that it has anything to do with him (or anyone else).

Mother says she's forgiven me for my unpleasant attitude on my last visit, and isn't going to mention it again. (I don't think!) If she's concealing any Dreadful Secret, extracting it will be like prising a pearl from an oyster with a plastic knife, and then finding it's a piece of grit. True Grit, maybe, but still grit.

Then she went on about Granny's mystery taxi trips.

'Why shouldn't she go out if she wants to? I expect she goes to visit old friends.'

'What old friends?' demanded Mother. 'No, she's up to something, and the worry is undermining my health. I can't carry on much longer. Not to mention the strain of having a daughter with a Broken Marriage!'

Well, that took the biscuit, because I don't suppose I'd even have met James if she hadn't concealed Fergal's letters!

And speaking of James, I've finally got round to arranging a meeting. It's to be early evening at the Dog and Duck, because I want to be on neutral ground when I tell him. He sounded very mystified.

When I arrived at the Dog and Duck, James was sitting in the corner with a drink, and I got an orange juice and went over.

'Hi,' I said, sitting down with my coat still pulled around me to hide the bump.

A little silence fell then, while I tried to think how to begin the Great Revelation, but my mind was blank. Really, I didn't want the bother of telling him at all.

'Well, what "important thing" do you want to discuss?' James asked at last rather condescendingly, and I suddenly realised that he was expecting me to beg him to come back to me!

'I'm having a baby,' I announced baldly.

His mouth fell open. 'A baby? *Whose* baby?'

'Really, James! It's yours, of course, and will be born around the beginning of April.'

'But why didn't you tell me before? So *this* is why you've been behaving so strangely!'

'I haven't been behaving strangely, and this will alter nothing between us.'

'Of course it will!' A bemused smile spread across his face. 'A baby! My son . . .'

'Daughter, I hope. I think it'll be easier to bring up a daughter alone.'

'But there's no need to *be* alone,' he exclaimed, going all spaniel-eyed and trying to hold my hand across the table. 'This alters everything, you must see that? You couldn't cope on your own, and I promise I'd be a better husband.'

Well, he certainly couldn't be a worse one.

'I can cope alone, and you've already proved I can't trust any promises you might make. I can't be bothered with it all, James. I'm perfectly happy on my own, and I just don't need you any more.'

'Well, if it's like that, I've been managing perfectly well on my own too! But you aren't going to stop me seeing my son—'

'Daughter!'

'Whichever. I can get access, you know. I might even get custody.'

I went cold. 'I'll have an abortion, then. I'm not going through all this just to have the baby taken away from me and brought up by your blond-haired floozie!'

He blenched. 'You – you wouldn't! Surely it's too late for an abortion?'

'No, I'm only about four months gone, but I won't have one if you leave me alone – and I'll let you see the baby within reason. Just don't try threatening me again!'

My protective feelings surprised even me, let alone James, and of course I wouldn't have had an abortion, even if I'd known about the baby immediately.

James was too frightened of what I might do to press me further (which shows just how little he knows me), so I left him there to his dubious celebrations.

A second later he came haring out after me, but only to hand me my fingerless mitts. As he did so, a middle-aged woman on a bicycle squealed to a stop and gazed searchingly at us, her eyes lingering on my stomach.

'All men should be castrated once they've fathered a child,' she volunteered, matter-of-factly.

'I couldn't agree more,' I responded, stunned, and she nodded and pushed off again.

One look at James's face gave me the uncontrollable giggles.

'Good God!' he exclaimed, and dashed back into the pub, perhaps fearing that the Great Castrator might return with a knife to get on with the Good Work.

Seemed like a wonderful idea to me.

Mrs Deakin says the Great Castrator must have been Loony Louie. She's perfectly sane on all subjects except this one, which has got such a grip on her mind that she had pamphlets printed about it and pushed one through every letterbox in the village, a year or two ago. I was sorry I'd missed it, but Mrs Deakin said she'd lend me hers.

She didn't congratulate me on my pregnancy directly, but advised me that the best thing a pregnant woman can do is drink a bottle of Guinness a day, for the iron content.

Sounds more fun than those horrible pills.

Just as I was going to bed, James rang, drunk as a skunk, to inform me that the baby couldn't be his since we hadn't 'had relations' (where does he get these expressions from?) at the right time.

'Have you forgotten the night of the barbecue in July?

Not that it *was* very memorable, admittedly, but that was the fatal night.'

'Oh . . .' he muttered, then there was a pause and some angry whispering off, so I guessed that this very distasteful conversation had been instigated by his floozie.

'How do I know it's not that Rocco's?'

'I wish it was! I wish the father was *anyone* other than you!' I yelled, and slammed the phone down.

My hands shook for ages afterwards. And I know I should tell Mother next, but I can't bring myself to.

Mrs Peach came crunching up the frosty path this morning and presented me with a parcel wrapped in newspaper.

'This'll do you good. It's a rabbit, fresh-killed, and I've cleaned it for you ready for the pot – women in your condition are always squeamish.'

Then she stumped off before I could gather my wits and thank her.

The newspaper was getting a bit limp, so I took it into the kitchen – but I really couldn't eat a rabbit, especially one newly killed in my honour. Ugh! And I couldn't give it to Bob this time, either, in case that got back and hurt her feelings.

Then I had a brain wave and cooked it for Bess, who was ecstatic, though I was nearly sick taking out all the fragile little bones, before I gave it to her.

While I was recovering from this, six author's copies of my last (ever) novel with Thripps arrived in the post. On the cover my pretty, dark-haired young heroine had been transformed into a raddled, red-haired, worldly hussy with a definite squint – but still, I won't have to worry about Thripps covers any more from now on.

I'm writing very well again, and new plots just spring into my mind. I jot them down quickly before I forget them. It's surprising really, with all this trauma going on, but useful. I need to write as many as possible before the Incubus arrives, because I may be a little occupied afterwards.

Margaret called today, the first time since her misguided attempt at peace negotiations, 'just for a chat'. But really, it's no use if she believes everything James tells her, despite evidence to the contrary, like Mother – but I suppose James is terribly plausible. I wonder what happened to Margaret's first husband.

She didn't stay long, and I gave her a message for James about Bess's pregnancy, because I forgot it last time I saw him. She looks distinctly heavy now round the middle, a strange thing in a Borzoi.

Mother phoned again, incoherent and tearful, complaining that I'd callously failed to inform her of my pregnancy. (Guilty as charged.) James had rectified my omission, of course, telling her he didn't want his child to be the product of a broken home, and she demanded to know why I didn't come to my senses and take him back.

'Leave her alone, you drunken fool!' Granny's voice shouted clearly in the background. 'Let her live her own life!' Or something like that.

On my next antenatal visit to the doctor (who at least isn't a *total* stranger), I took the opportunity to do some shopping at the supermarket and got a bit carried away.

As I struggled back to the bus stop, laden with four large

bags, a horn sounded imperatively and a strangely familiar little white sports car drew alongside with Fergal at the wheel, looking decidedly grim.

'Get in!' he ordered tersely.

'I'm not sure I can,' I replied doubtfully, for the seats were awfully low down and something had obviously put him in one of his rages. 'Anyway, the shopping wouldn't fit, and there's a bus due any minute, so thanks, but—'

He got out, silently relieved me of my bags, wedging them somehow in the back, then opened the passenger door.

I gave in. It was a relief to sink down into the seat, even if I never managed to climb out again.

I sneaked a glance at Fergal as he pulled out into the traffic, and thought about those letters . . . which by some association of ideas caused me to exclaim, 'This surely isn't the same Frog-eyed Sprite you had all those years ago, is it?'

'Yes, I never sold it.' He flashed an angry look at me and snapped, 'What the hell do you think you were doing, Tish?'

'Me? Doing? What – when?'

'Now! Just! Carrying great heavy bags of shopping in your condition.'

'They aren't that heavy! Anyway, I needed a few things and Mrs Deakin is a bit expensive,' I explained defensively.

'I don't know what your husband is thinking of, letting you do it.'

'He isn't letting me do anything! I do what I like, and it's no business of yours.'

'You can stop pretending you've achieved married Nirvana, Tish. Mrs Deakin told me you'd split up and are divorcing.'

Oh God! If Mrs Deakin knows all the details, everyone within a ten-mile radius of Nutthill knows.

'He can't keep his hands off other women, this nice, solid, middle-class husband your mother picked out for you?'

'It's nothing to do with you!'

'No, it isn't. But he could at least do the heavy shopping for you, since you're expecting his child.'

'I don't want his help! I'm learning to drive, anyway.'

'Since when?'

'Oh – ages,' I said airily. 'I'm expecting the test date through at any moment.'

'Who's teaching you?'

'A nice lady recommended by Mrs Deakin.'

He was silent while I seethed indignantly, but at least the inquisition seemed to be over – almost.

'Do you practise?'

I jumped. 'What?'

'Do you practise driving between lessons?'

'N-no. James has the car and anyway, I don't know anyone who'd go with me.'

'I will,' he offered, to my complete amazement.

'But I couldn't possibly drive this!'

'There's a little Mini Cooper in the garage we can use.'

'It's very kind of you, Fergal,' I said, touched, 'but—'

'No, it's not kind, it's self-preservation. I don't want another half-taught driver loose on the local roads.'

'Thanks very much! But unless your temper's improved drastically, you wouldn't make the most patient of teachers. I haven't forgotten last time.'

'I've mellowed. Let me know when you want to go out. Do you know my telephone number?'

'No.' And what's more, I've no intention of ever phoning him for this, or any other reason.

When we stopped outside my gate he scribbled it down on a bit of paper. 'There. Right, let's get this lot in.'

'You don't have to—' I began, trying to lever my bulk out of the passenger seat and failing: gravity was against me.

He came round and pulled me upright with no apparent effort. You forget how strong that misleadingly slender body is – like coiled steel under your fingers. Warm coiled steel . . .

'Go and open the door.'

He dumped everything on the kitchen table, refused a polite offer of coffee, and stalked out again, saying he had things to do.

I wondered if they involved Nerissa.

None of my business if they did.

Mrs Peach's face rose like a full moon over the dividing hedge, luminous with interest.

I'm turning into a satsuma! I even prefer them to sherbet dips now.

That was all I meant to buy from Mrs D., but I ended up with a hyacinth bulb in a growing vase shaped like something a man might be offered in hospital to pee into.

She was looking very pleased with herself, and when she'd finished wrapping my involuntary purchases, she suddenly whipped a paper bag out from under the counter.

'This is for you! You don't look like a knitter.'

Inside was a tiny, beautifully hand-knitted woolly baby jacket with white satin ribbons.

'Oh – how lovely!' I exclaimed, tears coming into my eyes. 'I don't know what to say!'

'That's all right then. I like to knit of an evening, and a

baby jacket makes a nice change from the church bazaar stuff. Don't say no more about it.'

She was pleased because she could see I was touched; there was something about that minute jacket that really first brought it home to me that I was having a baby. Not some vague, nebulous Thing, an Incubus, unwanted and troublesome, but a whole, new little person. It would need all sorts of things – and I know nothing about babies.

Rushing home, I started ransacking the baby books, but they were all more concerned with grisly things like the actual birth and cracked nipples, than what clothes it needs, and where it sleeps.

I need something a bit more practical: an Owner's Manual.

Galvanised by panic, I dashed into town next morning, as soon as I'd finished writing, to find one. I also bought a magazine for pregnant women, because it had a pattern in it for a big, baggy shirt.

I suspect I may still need these clothes afterwards, because I'll have a big, baggy body to fit into them.

The list of things you need for a newborn baby will cost a fortune and I don't know what half of them are for, but I have already made some economies. I've called the TV rental firm to remove the one I hired after James took ours, and I won't renew the licence. I can listen to the radio instead. And I've cancelled the daily paper.

Instead of watching TV I can do more writing and research, finish my dungarees off, and start making voluminous nighties for hospital. (The mere word 'hospital' gives me the shivers!)

Perhaps I should accept one of their pressing invitations

to antenatal classes, but deep inside, I really don't want to know.

Bess is behaving very strangely, and keeps trying to get inside cupboards if I leave the door open. Is this the nesting instinct? The puppies are due any minute.

When I got her a lovely big cardboard box instead and padded it out with an old blanket, she immediately dragged the bedding off and jammed herself with it down the gap at the side of the Aga.

She needn't think I'm going to let her have her puppies in such a narrow space. I wouldn't be able to see whether she was all right or not.

She growled at me when I put the blanket back in the box. Her nerves must be playing her up.

I know the feeling.

Fergal: November 1999

> '*WILD CHILD!*
> *Nerissa Bright on why Fergal Rocco*
> *is the only man for her . . .*'
>
> *Exposé* magazine

The girl's in love with publicity, not me. I've come to the conclusion she'll do or say anything to get in the public eye.

She's managed to project this image of herself as my long-standing girlfriend, on the strength of a couple of one-night stands and a few photographs of us in the same place at the same time.

Cunning, in its way, and I suppose it diverts any interest from Nutthill and Tish. I'm sick of holding off, waiting for

331

her stupid husband to realise what he's got now she's pregnant: the bastard doesn't deserve her.

And I couldn't let her struggle with that heavy shopping, could I?

Chapter 30: Pupped

Bess had her puppies last night!

I thought I heard a strange noise around midnight, and came down to find her back in the corner by the Aga, licking something small and wriggly.

I had to get a torch to see what she was doing, and then only had a quick look, because of not wanting to upset her.

There was only the one puppy, but she seemed to be straining a bit. It was all very messy, and Borzois are such a funny shape for giving birth that I called the vet.

He wasn't too pleased, but I insisted he come and help Bess, and finally he agreed, though it was over an hour until he actually arrived.

By then Bess had pretty well done everything herself, and I felt wrung out.

The vet had a quick look. 'Just what I thought. No need to call me out, she's had a perfectly normal delivery and all six are doing well. Funny-looking little blighters! You'll get my bill, plus call-out charge. Don't forget – nourishing diet.'

He paused on the threshold and added cheekily, '*Both* of you had better have a nourishing diet!'

Perhaps I'll change to a different vet.

But – *six* puppies! What am I going to do with them?

One thing's certain – they're not leaving the kitchen until they're all house-trained.

Wearily, I erected a sort of little cardboard wall around the Aga out of the rejected box to keep out any draughts, put a drink within Bess's reach, and finally dragged myself off to bed for what remained of the night.

Bess looked as mentally confused as I felt when I stumbled back downstairs, bleary-eyed, later that morning. Her half-naked, blind brood squirmed around her.

When the doorbell rang I could hardly summon the energy to answer it; someone had filled my bones with lead in the night. My hair was a tangled Medusa snarl, I hadn't so much as washed my face and was still in my old dressing gown, so of course it had to be Fergal, in a crisp blue linen shirt, looking twice as alive as most people and about twelve times as alive as me.

My recoil and attempt to shut the door were instinctive, but he got past me somehow and raised one eyebrow. 'I came to take you out driving, but I can see you're in no fit state. What's up?'

'N-nothing! Bess had six puppies last night, and I was up for most of it. I'm just tired – very, very tired.'

I swayed slightly and he removed my grasp from the door knob and shepherded me in. 'You need to go back to bed.'

'I can't – Bess needs seeing to, and Bob will be here soon, and I was going to write a list of shopping for him to get me from Mrs Deakin's – I'm nearly out of milk – and – and—'

'Go to bed,' he ordered firmly. 'Have you had any break-fast?'

'No, I've only just got up – and anyway, who are you to order me about?' I protested weakly.

'Someone has to. Do you want this baby or not?'

I burst into tears. These days I'm the nearest thing to a fountain you'll see in human form. (OK, semi-human.) 'Oh yes – yes – I do want it!' I wailed.

'Well, then' he said, exasperated. 'You'll have to take more care of yourself. Look, hush now – I didn't mean to snap at you . . .'

With his arm around me he guided me upstairs, bending to avoid the low beam as if he'd been there a hundred times before. His crisp blue shirt smelled delicious and so did he.

'Is this your room? Go on to bed. I'll feed the dog, and bring you a drink and something to eat.'

'But you can't! Why should—'

'Shut up!' he said with a thin smile, and vanished.

A few weak tears ran down my face as I sank back against the pillows, but I suppose he's right about my trying to do too much. Pregnancy does take it out of you.

I must have dozed off, and woke with the sense of time having passed, definitely feeling better.

A fragrant, mouth-watering smell wafted upstairs from the kitchen, along with a low, throaty voice singing softly.

What will Mrs Peach make of this? It will be all round the village and into James's ears in a flash that Fergal called first thing and stayed all morning . . . but at least he didn't call in the evening and stay all night, which *would* have put the cat among the pigeons, even with me in my present gross condition!

Fergal nudged the door open with his elbow and came in carrying a tray.

'You look better,' he said judiciously. 'I looked in earlier, but I thought you needed sleep more than food, so I didn't disturb you.'

Bess appeared suddenly beside him, cast me a worried, harassed look, and dashed off again in a flurry of fur.

I struggled upright and pushed the hair out of my eyes. 'Are the puppies all right?'

'Everything's all right. I've fed the dog, bribed the parrot into silence with a biscuit, told your gardener to do what he likes, got some supplies from Mrs D.'s – and this is lunch.'

He put the tray down on my knees. I'd forgotten he numbered cooking among his many and varied assets.

'It smells wonderful!'

'It's just paella, with a bit of this and that . . . There wasn't an awful lot in your kitchen, other than brown rice and lentils.'

'I'm a bit low – I meant to stock up.'

'I've stocked up. Now, eat this before it gets cold. What do you want to drink?'

'Orange juice, please. I seem to have gone off coffee, even the coffee-substitute I've been getting from the health food shop. Mrs Deakin says I should drink Guinness.'

'The Irish in me would have to agree with that. I don't see that it would do you any harm, anyway.'

'But I'm not supposed to drink alcohol.'

'Eat your lunch before it gets cold. I'm going to make that dog go out into the garden for a few minutes.'

The paella was delicious, with prawns and things in it – which I certainly hadn't had in the house. I must ask him how much the shopping came to.

I'd put down the tray and was half-nodding off again, when the sound of the front door closing jarred me awake.

336

James's voice called, 'Tish! Tish!'

I closed my eyes and opened them again resignedly. 'Yes, James – I'm up here.'

His head poked suspiciously round the door. 'What are you doing in bed at this time of day?'

'Resting. I was up all night with Bess – she had her puppies.'

'Oh?' His eyes darted about the room, and I became anxious to get rid of him before Fergal returned.

'What do you want, James?'

'Want? Oh – the commode.'

'The *commode*?'

'You never liked it. I could use it in the Shack.'

'If it means that much to you, take it. But it's a good piece of furniture and probably worth something now it's restored.'

'Yes, and *I* restored it, so it belongs to me.'

'I see! So, since I restored the house, by the same reckoning that's mine?'

'Don't be stupid! Anyway, I'll take what I like, and there isn't anything you can do about it, is there? You're going to have to watch your step, Tish, because now I've had the time to think about it, I'm not convinced this baby really is mine after all. And if not, why should you walk off with the house and everything?'

'I think you've said quite enough!' Fergal said from behind him, in a voice so cold polar bears would have shivered.

James certainly went Arctic White, and swivelled round, eyes bulging: 'You! And her – going on about my bit of fun, when all the time the sneaky little bitch was—'

Fergal's fist made contact with James's chin with a very satisfying crunch and he hit the floor with a crash that rocked the house.

Fergal hauled him back upright by the collar, stunned and gibbering with rage. But although James is stocky and solid, he's let himself run to seed (rye, mostly), and Fergal was looking lethal, so discretion took the better part of valour.

Twisting out of Fergal's grip, he backed away towards the door, fingering the mark on his chin.

'You'll be sorry about this!' he threatened me.

'Don't be silly, James. It's your own fault. You can't seriously think I've been having an affair, and with Fergal, of all people! He's hardly even been in the same country for months.'

'But I would, of course, have had no objection otherwise,' Fergal butted in helpfully.

I ignored him. 'He only called today to offer to give me some driving practice, which was kind of him, and stayed to look after things while I got some rest.'

'Yes, very kind!' sneered James, but I could see his brain cells had started to rub together again. 'Yes, OK! Sorry! Only what else was I supposed to think?'

'Almost anything else! I don't have cheap little affairs like you. I suppose Wendy has been putting these sordid ideas into your head?'

'Leave Wendy out of it!' he blustered, and then added spitefully, 'But if she saw you now, she'd realise how ludicrous the idea was.'

Miserably made aware of how I must look, with no make-up on, my hair all over the place, and wearing my old outsize Snoopy T-shirt (not to mention a mid-section the size of a medium zeppelin), I wished Fergal would hit him again.

'You should take better care of yourself,' he added, and

Fergal took a hasty step forward and seemed to be about to make my wish come true.

James thought so too, for he turned and vanished at high speed down the steep stairs, banging his head and cursing as he went, and the door slammed after him.

'Shut the bloody door!' came Toby's faint shout from the living room.

'Delightful!' Fergal remarked.

'I'm terribly sorry, Fergal.'

'What for? Marrying him? I should think you would be, Angel.'

'No, that you've been cast as the villain of the piece.'

He shrugged. 'I'm used to it.'

'He's always been jealous of you.'

'Has he?' I was pleased to see that he'd stopped looking quite so ferocious. 'Perhaps he's looking for a scapegoat. Think how much better he'd feel about his behaviour if he convinced himself you'd been having an affair, too. But he's finding it difficult, because you aren't really the type, are you, Tish? I suppose in London it was a combination of finding out your husband had been unfaithful and drink. You were just looking for comfort, and I was there.'

'Yes, that was it,' I agreed (though there was quite a bit of Frustrated Lust in there too, I'm ashamed to say). 'I – I'm sorry.'

'Always happy to oblige,' he said politely.

I think he's right about the scapegoat bit, though, if only James could convince himself it was true – or let Wendy convince him. I used to think he was a solid rock I could depend on, but now I see he's just another weak vacillating quicksand of a man.

'I'm beginning to wish this baby was anyone's except James's!' I said bitterly.

'Are you? It's yours – that's what matters.' He wandered over to the window, back to me. It's a very nice back, broad in the shoulders and tapering to narrow hips and long, long legs. 'Tish . . .'

'Mmm?' I murmured, sinking back onto the pillows.

He turned and gave me a curious smile. 'Never mind. Look, I've got a temporary housekeeper from an agency – Mrs Bell. I'll tell her to ring you next time she goes to the supermarket and you can give her a list of what you want.'

'But why should the poor woman do *my* shopping too?'

'Why not? I'm paying her enough. And I'm not having you carrying heavy bags about – it isn't good for the baby.'

'No,' I agreed. I just couldn't resent his trying to order me about any more; in fact, weak tears came to my eyes because someone cared about me enough to think of these things.

He wandered over and flicked my cheek carelessly with one finger, smiling. 'And don't take what James said to heart, Angel – you look like a ripe peach, good enough to eat!'

He can't mean it, but it was kind of him to try to make me feel better.

'I'll have to go now. Do you think you'll be all right?'

'Of course! I'm fine, and I've got a book to finish.'

'Ah yes. I enjoyed *Love Goes West*,' he said smoothly, and I was so unnerved that I forgot to ask how much my shopping had come to, or even thank him properly.

I hope James isn't going to turn vindictive about the house and everything after this – but I'm still glad Fergal hit him.

* * *

Fergal: December 1999

'GONERIL – SO FAR, SO BAD.
The unofficial pictorial history of the band . . .'
                    Trendsetter magazine

It's stuff like this that tempts me to cancel my subscription
to the cuttings agency – except I feel better knowing what's
being said about us, good or bad. (Mostly bad.)

At the moment, all I really want is a quiet life at Nutthill,
painting, writing songs, and watching out for Tish, because
God knows, her stupid husband isn't.

At least she's stopped looking at me as if I'm the Devil
incarnate – though that might change if she sees some of
the snaps in *this* little family album!

Chapter 31: The Least Little Thing

The puppies do look odd! What on earth was the father? They're all blind and deaf, with big tummies and heads, and little legs. I hope they're supposed to be like that.

Bob was so desperate to see them, I let him have a quick peep. Bess didn't mind – she likes him. He was so incoherent you'd think he was the father. I said he could have one if his mum agreed. I expect it would be as happy with Bob as anyone, as long as it got on with the Jack Russells.

At least Bess has got it all over with.

At five months, my tummy is already so tightly stretched that my navel is on the surface instead of sunk in, and the skin itches. I feel mildly uncomfortable all the time, too, and since it's turned freezing now we're into December and I can't fasten any of my coats, I've had to buy a loose, warm jacket.

I simply must have some intensive driving lessons before I'm too big to fit behind the wheel.

Nerissa called in again. It's hard to slam the door in her face when she acts as if she knows I'm her friend, but I think she came just to tell me that Fergal had gone to London.

'I thought he might have told you when he had to give

you a lift the other day. He's such a softie at heart, just can't bear to see you struggling with shopping in your condition.' Her big brown eyes lifted to my face. 'Poor you, not being able to drive when you're pregnant – and alone! Well, I think he's gone to buy me a ring, because he was so secretive. He didn't mention it, I suppose?'

I cringed at the thought of Fergal telling Nerissa he'd had to give his poor old pregnant ex-girlfriend a lift home . . .

'An engagement ring?' I tried not to sound surprised – how do I know the idea of marriage hasn't grown on him? 'No, he didn't mention it – but we hardly spoke.'

'Say, that's a nice ring *you're* wearing!' she said suddenly, gazing at my sapphire heart. 'Is it antique?'

'This old thing?' I said casually. 'Yes.' And with an effort of will I restrained myself from adding, 'And Fergal gave it to me!'

I wish Nerissa wouldn't keep appearing like this – she makes me feel huge, pathetic and old. And a nuisance . . . When Fergal's housekeeper did phone to ask if I wanted any shopping, sounding cross, I thanked her and said I'd made other arrangements. I'll find a way to manage – other women do.

Just after lunch today I was standing at the window idly eating a tangerine, when a big, dark car pulled up at my gate. It was hard to make out through the curtain of sleety rain, but the driver seemed to have got out in order to help his passenger alight.

A small, dark and solid figure advanced up the path under a large striped umbrella and I hastily disposed of the tangerine and wiped my hands. Whoever it was, they were coming here.

The visitor rang twice and knocked with the letter flap for good measure, before I got the door unlocked to discover, with amazement, a familiar, crumpled red face framed in a black sou'wester.

'What on earth . . .? Granny! Where – is Mother here, too?'

'Not flaming likely!' She pushed past me like a small wet seal, and jammed her dripping umbrella in the corner. 'I've given her the slip. Permanently. Shut the door – all the warm air's going out.'

Then she prodded me in the stomach, none too gently. 'What's all this?'

'I'm pregnant, Granny.'

'Nothing good ever came of it.'

'I've noticed.'

That seemed to be the end of the subject as far as Granny was concerned, for she moved off purposefully towards the kitchen.

'Thought as much!' she announced, flinging back the door with a crash that made me wince, and Bess in her corner whimper.

'I'll make you some tea, Granny. You'll like that better than coffee, won't you?'

'I don't like coffee – it makes me Go.' She examined the kitchen, poking in all the cupboards she could reach, and opening up the front of the Aga. 'Good stove – you should use it.'

'I don't know how.'

'Find out.'

I made the tea in the bright red pot and put out the sugar bowl. Despite being diabetic, she'd insist on having some in her tea if I didn't put it out, whereas if it was very much in evidence she probably wouldn't.

Meanwhile, she concluded her tour with a scathing inspection of Bess, cowering over her brood, and was now removing her mack and peculiar plastic overshoes – transparent with little dots of glittering gold embedded in them. The heels were the same archaic shape as the shoes inside them, which were Ladies' Extra Broad Kid, size 3.

'I love your overshoes, Granny.'

'Bought six pairs in Thompson's closing-down sale. No – leave that tea. It'll be weak as cat's pee yet.'

'Does Mother know where you are? How did you get here?'

'Does yer mother know yer out?' she parodied, and cackled. 'I came by car. Hired it. I've left a note for Valerie . . .' she mused, stirring the contents of the teapot with a spoon. 'I'll have to sell the house with her as a sitting tenant, and I won't get half as much for it.'

'Sell the house?' I had a sudden, horrible suspicion that Mother was right after all about Granny's sanity. 'But you can't do that, Granny! Where would you live? Do you need the money urgently?'

'Don't be silly, dear.' She poured herself a cup of black, treacly liquid. Her hand hovered over the sugar, then passed on to the milk. She added gallons, but it didn't make the brew noticeably paler.

'I've had enough of your mother. She doesn't want me, and I don't want her – you should understand that! What I want and deserve is a bit of peace and pleasure in my old age, and that's what I'm going to have. I've bought a cottage in Devon, and I'm off there now.'

'But, Granny! You can't be serious. How could you live alone? What about your injections and everything?'

'Won't be alone!' she said triumphantly. 'Rose Durwin – the district nurse – is coming with me.'

'Mrs Durwin? To live with you?'

'That's right. She's a widow too, and she wanted to retire early. We get on well – always have. Her daughter lives in Devon, that's why we chose it. We've been planning this for weeks.'

'Oh?'

Suddenly I thought: why not?

'It all sounds perfect, Granny! And I know you've always enjoyed Mrs Durwin's company.'

'Got a sense of humour, and likes cooking and gardening. We'll each have our own sitting rooms, so we won't get on top of each other.'

'But it must have cost a lot of money.'

'I've sold most of my jewellery – not that I was strapped for cash, mind, but it might as well be doing me some good as sitting in a safe deposit box. It'll see me out in style.'

She took a gulp of tea. 'It was a mistake trying to live with Valerie. Blood may be thicker than water, but hers is pure sherry and that doesn't count. I'm off.'

She refilled her mug. 'But I always liked you – finicky child, but turned out not too badly, considering.'

'Thank you, Granny!'

'Not that I hold with it, mind.'

'Hold with what?'

'Don't hold with it – but maybe they didn't, and anyway, what's done is done. And I always liked you, as I said, so I

346

just thought I'd pop in on my way to Devon and give you a little something.'

She fished in an enormous black bag and handed me a crumpled handkerchief. A tangle of jewellery fell out.

'I saved one or two bits I thought you'd like. Nothing very valuable, but not trumpery stuff, either.'

'Oh, Granny! I – I don't know what to say!' There was a lovely little bracelet of linked cameos, some glittering diamond earrings and a flat gold brooch that proclaimed: 'MIZPAH'.

'Don't say anything, then. I can see you like them; that's enough. You can have this –' she jangled the bracelet she always wore – 'after I'm gone. Bernard gave me the three little Fabergé eggs on it.'

Her eyes went misty for a minute, then with a sigh she came back to reality and began heaving herself to her feet. 'I'd best be off. Rose and the driver have been waiting long enough.'

'Granny, what if Mother just follows you down there? She loves Devon.'

She gave her familiar cackle. 'She'd never live in the same house as Rose – they don't get on!'

'That's true,' I said. 'But what will she do?'

'If she plays her cards right, that fool of a doctor might marry her.'

My heart lightened. 'Oh, do you really think so?'

'She'll do the "brave little woman struggling to survive with the house being sold over her head" routine to perfection – that should fetch him.'

'Granny, you are clever!'

She reclad herself in crackling black. 'Still got enough

347

brain cells to see me out,' she conceded modestly. 'But if it doesn't work out, I've put enough aside to set Valerie up in a little flat. And you can come down and visit me for a weekend when I'm settled.'

On the doorstep she opened her huge umbrella and gave me a brisk peck on the cheek. 'If Valerie phones, you don't know where I am. I'll send her the address when she's stopped foaming at the mouth.'

'All right.'

She prepared to move off. 'Mother!' she snorted suddenly. 'Hah!'

'Granny, you keep hinting things about Mother! Do you really think there's something strange about—'

But she was already vanishing into the misty rain and only odd words carried back: '. . . talk again soon . . . visit . . . bye, dear . . .'

She'd done it again! Planted more vague doubts in my mind and then toddled off before I could attempt to pin her down.

'Granny, come back!' I yelled, struggling into my wellies. But by the time I'd run down the path the big car was pulling away. She waved to me regally.

I trudged damply back in, wondering if it was one of her odd jokes, after all. But no, her sense of humour isn't that obscure.

The rain trickled down my back and the Incubus leaped like a fish in my womb. The phone rang.

Mother?

'I'll need only half a dozen eggs a fortnight now,' I told Mrs Peach on the Monday.

'Eggs is nourishing!' she stated disapprovingly.

I told her that they were only good for you in small quantities, because of cholesterol, but she said she'd never heard of it, and wouldn't feed it to her hens if she had, and anyway, eggs had never done her any harm.

However, with her lopsided face she's hardly a glowing advertisement.

She added that I ought to eat a rabbit or two a week to build me up, but I brilliantly announced that I'd suddenly gone off all meat and felt queasy just at the thought of it.

Then she stumped past me into the living room without a by-your-leave.

'Bloody hell!' shouted Toby delightedly, abandoning a half-eaten monkey nut. 'Bloody hell!'

'Cunning old bird!' crooned Mrs P. 'Who's glad to see old Mrs Peach then?'

The phone rang, so I had to leave them to their lovers' tryst.

It was Mother again, and my heart plummeted into my turquoise suede loafers. I'm desperately afraid she'll try to plant herself on me permanently now Granny's gone, though at least when I hear her prim and proper voice on the phone, I realise that some of my worst imaginings about Granny's hints are unfounded. There's something she's concealing about my birth, but I can't believe it's anything major.

'Are you still there, Leticia?' she demanded peevishly. 'I've had a letter from Granny, and she's quite safe, but completely mad! Do you know what she's done?'

Mrs P. stumped silently past me at this point and let herself out. This is quite usual – I'm thinking of charging for parrot-viewing. But I missed most of Mother's diatribe.

Mother's anger had further been exacerbated by a communication from Mr Herries, informing her that the house is to be sold over her head.

I held the phone a little way away, feeling the baby turn and kick, and thinking how odd it is to look down and see your abdomen jumping about of its own volition.

The phone was still quacking. I looked at it, then laid it gently down in its rest, and when it rang again a few moments later, I ignored it.

It rang for ages.

I'm just too tired to be bothered at the moment . . . I could sleep twenty hours out of every twenty-four, if I didn't urgently need to write quickly.

Mrs Deakin is a fund of knowledge about pregnancy and childbirth, but I wish so many of her stories were not so awful. Surely giving birth can't have that many complications? Most of the stories end with absolutely blood-chilling phrases like, '. . . and there was so much blood the nurses were wading about in white wellies'. Or even, '. . . forceps the size of a horsedoctor's!'

I'd like to have a natural childbirth, but under general anaesthetic.

Bess is not a very good mother and there's a definite smell hanging round in that corner of the kitchen. I'm dying to do it all out with disinfectant, but I must control myself until the puppies are bigger. They're really rather sweet . . .

I've had to start buying a daily paper again, just to put on the floor round the Aga (whichever publication is thickest).

Bess considers James to be a potential puppy-napper and

growls whenever he walks round to the Shack. Her fur stands on end and all the puppies whimper.

Still no address from Granny.

Fergal: December 1999

'This week I'd like all my parishioners to reflect on the text: Let him who is without sin cast the first stone . . .'
                                    Nutthill Parish Magazine

Thanks, Vicar, I need a champion.

Mrs D. has given me some idea of the kind of rumours running like wildfire through the village since I was seen coming out of Tish's cottage . . . not to mention James being seen on the same day with a bruised face.

Nerissa called just to tell me, 'How absolutely ludicrous, Fergal honey, that anyone should think you've got a thing going with your poor old pregnant girlfriend, when all you're doing is being sorry for her!'

Yeah, right.

Chapter 32: Tie-dyed

The puppies have opened their eyes! They all have identical milky blue ones: was Bess kidnapped by aliens?

Bob was enthralled by the sight and, do you know, his eyes are the same weird blue. Perhaps he's an alien too?

Bess condescended to come out for a little run with me (though neither of us is up to much running) and we met James, who was in a mood of rather shame-faced truculence. He didn't even ask how I was feeling.

Mrs Blacklock has made me send in a driving test application (the written exam comes first, but I'm not worried about that one), and I've booked extra driving lessons for after Christmas. I don't know how I'll manage if I haven't passed before the baby arrives, but as I drove along during the last lesson, I suddenly had the exhilarating feeling it could be quite fun – but then I stalled three times at the traffic lights and the feeling vanished. I wish I could always turn left.

Fergal is back; Nerissa phoned especially to tell me, though goodness knows how she got my ex-directory number, unless she'd been riffling through Fergal's address book.

'I know he's got the goods,' she said conspiratorially,

'because a friend saw him coming out of a jeweller's. But I guess I'll have to wait until Christmas.'

I hope I said the right things. I wonder if I can bear to live here with Nerissa married to Fergal and giving me a running account of their wedded bliss.

One thing is for sure – I won't be asking him to take me out for some driving practice! He only offered because he felt sorry for me, and I can manage by myself.

I can manage *everything* by myself.

Our annual Christmas card and present arrived from James's parents in South Africa, plus a long, printed, round-robin letter about nothing in particular. If James has told them about our separation or my pregnancy, they don't mention it. But at least I now understand why they don't mind not seeing him for years, as I feel much the same myself.

The present is a small watercolour of wild animals round a waterhole. There's a lot of dust, and a lion seems to be killing a zebra in the background. James can have it – it isn't my cup of tea at all.

Alice, Howard's girlfriend, called, suggesting we meet and talk over the situation regarding her sister, Wendy, and my ex-Significant Other!

I couldn't see the point, but she was pretty insistent in a vague way, like a cobweb that wouldn't brush off, so we met at a pizza place roughly halfway between us.

She was already there when I arrived, looking almost normal in jeans and a fringed Indian cotton top, tie-dyed.

The baby was asleep in a sort of plastic bucket seat next to her. It didn't look much bigger, but it had a lot of indeterminate brown hair and was wearing a Babygro also tie-dyed in mustard and a rather bilious green.

'Hi, Alice! Nice to see you again,' I said with false breeziness, and she smiled vaguely. 'Shall we order and then talk? I'm ravenous.'

I always am lately.

'Your hair is *red*!' Her mud-coloured eyes examined me with mild surprise.

'It isn't,' I replied coldly. 'Must be the light in here. James is the one with red hair.'

She blinked slowly, like something unused to bright lights, which she probably was, since Howard's electricity is always being cut off.

'I'm having the Vegetarian Special,' she offered.

'That sounds healthy – I'll have that too. And a side salad and a chocolate milkshake.'

When we'd ordered, since she still didn't seem about to burst into speech, I cast around for something to say.

'What did you call the baby? I expect James told me, but I've forgotten.' (James hadn't told me – or even whether it was male or female, come to that.)

'Mickey. We couldn't think of a name, but when I saw those Mickey Mouse bibs I knew . . .' she sighed dreamily.

'Michael?'

'No, Michael's a boy's name! We called her just – Mickey.'

'How . . . nice!'

I'm certainly glad the bibs didn't have Thumper or Pocahontas on them.

'What did you want to talk about, Alice?' I enquired, grasping the bull by the horns. (Or vegetarian nut cutlets, in Alice's case.)

'It's Wendy, my sister. She saw you at the party. She wasn't supposed to be there that night, but she came back – and she didn't *know* you were pretty because James never said, so she was jealous.'

Quelling the urge to ask how Dear James had described me to Wendy, I said: 'It was Wendy who used to make those silent phone calls to me, wasn't it?'

She nodded. 'I told her not to – it made James cross, but she even did it one night when he was there asleep, and he woke up and was *furious*.'

I began to see that Wendy had strong-armed her vacuous sister into this meeting. 'What does she want?' I asked bluntly.

Her eyes opened wider. 'James!'

'So? She can have him. *I* don't want him.'

'But she wants to *marry* him!'

You'd think the concept was obscene. Come to that, perhaps it is.

'But does James want to marry her? I mean, he has a lot of very old-fashioned ideas, you know, about there being two sorts of girls: the ones you marry and the ones you don't, and I'm afraid Wendy qualifies for the second category.'

'Marriage is an outdated ritual . . .' she murmured sadly.

'He'd have to get divorced first, anyway, Alice, and it does take some time. Can Wendy hang on to him long enough to get him to the altar, that's the question?'

'She's given up her fashion design course and everything! Daddy says she's obsessed, and he's furious.'

Obsessed with James? But I suppose if people can be obsessed with trainspotting, or collecting bits of perforated paper with pictures on . . . It just seems awfully odd of her, that's all.

Before he went to seed he did have a sort of rugged Highlander look about him, but he was never exciting – or maybe no man was exciting after Fergal?

'I still don't see what you want *me* to do, Alice. If she wants James, it's up to her.'

'But since he found out about the baby he thinks you'll want him back, because you won't be able to manage on your own. And she says he keeps talking about his son! Archaic!'

'He's a middle-class reactionary bore,' I agreed, borrowing at random from Howard's store of stock phrases. 'An *unfaithful* middle-class reactionary bore!'

Alice's eyes slid away like evasive mud puddles. 'She says the baby isn't his, that you've been seeing someone else.'

'She's wrong.'

'She says it's Fergal Rocco's.' Her eyes furtively scrutinised my face, and some sort of spark flickered in them.

So Fergal can even animate the Undead!

The faint spark died away. 'I don't suppose it was really true, though? Do you know him?'

'I did know him a bit, years ago, before he got famous.'

She lost interest. 'So it's James's baby?'

'Unless aliens did a Midwich Cuckoo on me, yes.'

We ate vegetarian pizza silently for a while and then the baby started to stir and mutter.

'So if you really don't want him . . .?' Alice had evidently been pursuing some train of thought of her own. 'What would make him marry Wendy?'

'Shot-gun?' I suggested flippantly. (Or, in James's case, *sot* gun.) 'Or she could try wearing neat little suits and smart shoes, and Big Hair . . . and have a son or two.'

'Have a son?' she echoed blankly. 'Suits?' Her lizard lips stretched over the word.

'That's how he wants his wife to look, but the sort of women he has on the side probably all look like Wendy.'

Good old Bendy Wendy.

'He thinks a solicitor's wife should be respectable and above reproach. Wendy would be a bit of a non-starter on both counts.'

Mickey now woke properly, turned red in the face, and produced an ominous smell.

Alice sighed and got up. 'I'll have to go and change her.'

I sincerely hoped she wasn't going to do it there and then! However, she set off with the little plastic bucket seat, and the smell followed her like a dog.

After fifteen minutes, when they hadn't returned, I went to the ladies to look for her.

She was the sole occupant of the pink, softly lit ante-chamber, and appeared to be offering Mickey up to the wall-mounted hand-dryer, like some kind of small sacrifice.

'What on earth are you doing, Alice?'

'Drying Mickey's hair.'

'Was it wet?'

'Yes . . . It was so nice and warm down here, and clean, and Mickey's hair needed washing, so I did it. And then I thought I'd dry it . . . The electricity's off at home, and Daddy's in Capri.'

'I – is he?'

The mad logic of all this was mind-numbing.

The baby gurgled, seeming to like the feel of the warm air blowing on her head.

'Yes. He thinks Howard should get a job.'

'What on earth *as*?'

'He's terribly clever really, Tish – he could be anything!'

'Yes, he could!' I agreed heartily. An escapee from the Planet Zog seemed the most likely.

'But actually, Howard and I are going to learn craftwork and join a commune.'

Daddy would probably end up supporting the commune as well, if any commune was mad enough to include Howard and Alice among its numbers.

The baby's hair was now dry, so we went back upstairs and collected our coats and paid the bill.

'How are you getting home?' I asked her, worrying about the baby, warm from the hand-dryer, going out into the cold December air.

'Howard's picking me up in the van.'

Just then a *frisson* of revulsion ran through the pizza house as something horrible flattened itself against the outside window.

'I think he's here,' I told her.

'Well, goodbye, Tish, and thanks for . . . for . . . you really don't want him back?'

'James? No, never ever again. If Wendy can get him, she can keep him!'

Howard leered at me, then without a word went and got back into his rusty little red van, leaving Alice to get herself and the baby in unassisted.

She put the bucket seat down on the floor by her feet in the front. I'm sure that's illegal! And surely not safe.

It's some slight comfort to realise that I'm almost certainly going to make a better mother than Alice!

I went to the antenatal clinic on my way home, where I

sat with a lot of women expecting imminent triplets. They all had an air of bovine contentment that was very irritating.

Trailed back on the bus. I'm so tired of it – I'll be glad when I can drive. Come to that, I'm so tired, full stop. And I expand visibly every day. Could I be expecting twins, and they've missed one?

I should be tethered in the sky somewhere with a slogan displayed up my side (if I've still got a side, that is).

The novelty of having puppies has definitely worn off for Bess, and she wishes they would all vanish; I only hope I don't feel the same about the baby.

Fergal: December 1999

'A Festive Fergal to warm you up for Christmas . . .'
                                    Trendsetter magazine

Ho, ho, ho little girls – have I got a surprise for you!

Chapter 33: Christmas Spirit

Oh horrors! Mother's invited herself over for Christmas!

I told her that I felt like being alone, since I had a lot of work to finish before D-day . . . or should that be B-day? No, on second thoughts, *not* B-day. But she assured me that she'd stay only a night or two, and not be any trouble, and that Dr Reevey had drawn the short straw and was working over Christmas, with his widowed sister coming down to stay, as she usually did.

Nose-out-of-joint syndrome.

I hope the romance is progressing. It would be wonderful to get her off my hands, especially to a doctor who would know how to nip her incipient alcoholism in the bud, though from what I've seen of his whisky habit, his own blood is probably ninety per cent proof.

But if she doesn't get a better offer she'll try to establish herself here permanently . . . and how do you throw your mother out? It might be more to the point if I got the vicar to come and sprinkle holy water to exorcise her, bell, book and candle. I expect she'd vanish fast enough then. Or perhaps it would be a garlic, cross and wooden stake job?

I foresee an awful Christmas.

She's arriving on Thursday, and suggested I meet her train.
'What in?' I queried.

'Well – the car, dear. I thought James might—'

'Any arrangement you make with James is your own affair. But I'm certainly not coming all the way into town on the bus in order to meet your train just to turn around and come back with you. You will have to get a taxi.'

'Leticia! Your little domestic tiff has made you very hard, dear. I'm sure poor James would come and pick me up if I asked him, and perhaps stay to dinner? After all, there's no need for you not to be friends, is there?'

'Mother,' I managed to say evenly, 'if you bring James with you, or make any attempt to meddle in my affairs by throwing us together, you'll find yourself and your bags on the doorstep.'

'I only want to do what's best for my little girl!' she faltered, and then began to sob gustily.

I said I knew what was best and I wasn't a little girl (in fact, I'm now a very *big* girl), but I supposed she could come for a couple of days if she turned up without James.

I knew they weren't real tears, but I couldn't bear it.

On the Thursday before Christmas I woke with a deep sense of foreboding, then remembered that Mother was arriving today.

I popped down to the shop to add a few extras to my stores, though I'm certainly not cooking a turkey – the little turkey crown roast I have in the freezer will do nicely just for the two of us. Bob is presenting me with bushels of Brussels sprouts, and at least I'll be sober this year when I peel them. Under the influence, I tend to pare the layers of leaves down like pass the parcel until there's almost nothing left.

Realising I hadn't even bought a Christmas present for Mother yet, I added two huge boxes of chocolates to my shopping, to Mrs Deakin's approval. One was an over-the-top satin-covered affair, like a small chest of drawers, with tassels instead of handles, which was exactly Mother's cup of tea. That will have to do.

Since a card had at last come from Granny with her new address I could now send off the silk scarf I'd bought her. I gave Mrs D. her card and posted the Wrekins' and Mrs Peach's through their letter boxes on the way home, which pretty well ended my festive preparations. I'd already got one of those doggy stockings full of treats for Bess.

For myself I'd bought a pretty and voluminous Laura Ashley nightdress, which should cover all eventualities, even ones as large as mine.

The spare bed is made, the radiator on. It still looks a bit bleak, but I don't want to encourage Mother (not that she needs it). But she'll have to think again: this room is earmarked for the nursery.

By late afternoon I'd done everything except take Bess for a decent walk, but I felt so tired it was as if I was wading through a lake of treacle.

Bob was still pottering about in the garden, having come back, for some reason. He comes and goes, I hardly notice any more, and has made himself a cosy little den in the garden shed. So I asked him if he could possibly take the stupid bitch for a walk, payment at the usual rates, and he went off with her quite happily.

It was two hours before they came back, both muddy and

happy, and Bess exhausted, and she lay on the mat in front of the Aga snoring once I'd cleaned her up. The puppies fell on her as if they'd been abandoned for a week, but she couldn't have cared less if they'd all vanished in her absence.

At four, a parcel arrived containing a strange, hand-knitted baby jacket constructed by Granny from hard woollen knots, like some miniature instrument of torture. Still, the thought was there. A brief note assured me all was well, and not to let Mother batten on to me like a leech.

As I folded it up, I heard a car draw up outside and, sure enough, it was a taxi bearing the maternal leech.

Decanted at the door with one enormous suitcase and a collection of clinking canvas holdalls, she demanded that I pay the taxi driver, since her purse was at the bottom of her handbag.

That settled, she kissed me, clasped my unwilling hands in hers and looked me up and down, all dewy-eyed. 'My little girlie isn't so little any more! And to think I'm to be a grandmother at my young age!'

There didn't seem to be any polite reply to this, so I suggested she take her case up to the spare bedroom and then we could have a hot drink.

Mother waited for me to pick up the suitcase, but when I took hold of the carriers instead she sighed and trudged upstairs after me, chipping the paint with the corners all the way up.

Over coffee in the sitting room, where she sat as far from Toby's cage as she could (the antipathy was mutual: Toby had become morose and silent as soon as he set his beady eyes on her), she launched into a diatribe against Granny and 'that scheming nurse'. Pausing to draw breath,

363

she took a sip from her cup and pulled a face. 'What type of coffee is this, dear? It has a most peculiar taste.'

'It's Coffette, "wholegrain goodness in a cup". I've gone off coffee – I don't think the Incubus likes it.'

'The what, dear?'

'The current tenant of my womb.'

'That's a very strange way of putting it, Leticia!'

'Pregnancy is a very strange state to be in. Suddenly there are two of us in here, and one keeps dictating what the other should eat and drink. Didn't you find that strange, when you were expecting me?'

She shifted uncomfortably: 'Not at all – it's all completely natural.'

'So's death, but no one says you have to enjoy that.'

'Really, I can't think what's got into you lately, Leticia.'

I looked at her, all ruffled plumage, and decided to clear the air once and for all. 'Mo— Mummy, Granny's said one or two things lately that did make me wonder if – well, whether I really *am* your natural daughter?'

She bridled angrily: 'That woman never liked me! What has she been saying? Just because I didn't look pregnant when they left – they were away months – and I was one of those rare, rare cases where I didn't know I was expecting until you actually arrived: such a surprise!'

'Was I? But why did you leave Father just after he'd recovered from the mumps and go off to Cornwall by yourself?'

'Just a holiday. I was exhausted with all that nursing. Then poor Daddy had to rush down and bring us back. Now, Leticia, I really don't want to discuss it further. You should really allow for Granny's strange sense of humour. It's very naughty of her to say that sort of thing to you.'

She gathered her ruffled plumage together huffily. 'You are my very own little girl. Now, let's just forget the whole silly thing, shall we, and talk about more important issues. How is poor James managing alone? We must see if we can clear up this teeny tiff over Christmas – the Season of Goodwill, you know!'

'Poor James is infrequently alone, and it would take more than the spirit of Christmas to make me wish to resume our marriage. A frontal lobotomy, perhaps.'

'A *what*, darling?'

'Never mind. Now, understand this once and for all, Mother: I'm perfectly happy without James and I've no wish ever to live with him again. Any attempt to meddle will only lead to your having to go home early. Right?'

Sniffling, she dabbed at her nose. 'I only want what's best for you both – and the poor little baby!'

'I know what's best. If you want to see James I'll give you the Wrekins' phone number and you can go there, or—'

'Where's the TV?' she interrupted. 'There's something I want to watch in twenty minutes.' She peered about, as if it might be hiding behind the sofa, waiting to spring out. 'Is it in the kitchen?'

'No. I haven't got one.'

'Don't be silly – of course you have. Everyone has one.'

'Not me. I did have a little rented one, but I decided to economise and do without it. But I've got the radio.'

'You are joking, aren't you?' she asked doubtfully.

'No. I really haven't got one.'

'But – Christmas, Leticia! I'll miss all the films and every-thing! And what shall I do without it?'

'I don't usually have any problems. I'm doing a lot of

writing in the evenings because I'm determined to finish two novels before the baby arrives.'

'But my programme starts soon! Really, you might have thought about your mother. Can't you hire one? I think—' She broke off as footsteps trod heavily round the house and Bess, who was in the kitchen, howled mournfully, like the Hound of the Baskervilles. 'What's that?' She looked like a frightened ferret with gold-rinsed hair.

'Only James. I'm letting him carry on using the transmitter in the Shack until he can move it.'

'James is *here*? In the garden? Oh, then perhaps I could just pop out to say hello?'

I pointed her in the right direction and off she tottered in her high heels. Then I went up and got on with my typing, and it was quite some time before I resurfaced to the sound of voices in the house . . . and I'd *warned* her not to invite James in without permission!

But when I flung open the door to the sitting room I found her alone, watching a small portable television.

'Ssh!' she whispered without getting up.

'Where on earth did you get that from?'

The credits came up and she sighed and turned. 'Those kind people James is staying with insisted I borrow the TV from the children's playroom over Christmas. So sweet!'

'Oh, really, Mother!' I protested, but there wasn't anything I could do – it would look peculiar if I snatched it back from poor Mother and marched back with it. I suppose it is kind of the Wrekins, and it certainly kept her quiet for the rest of the evening, especially after I got the bottle of sherry out. Whenever I left the room, the level sank.

Unsurprisingly, she slept late next morning (she's drinking

even more than I thought, which is rather worrying), and came down yawning and weary-eyed at eleven thirty.

She sat down heavily at the kitchen table, then gave a sudden gasp and straightened, gazing wide-eyed out of the window. 'Good heavens, there's a man in your garden – *cavorting*!'

'It's only Bob,' I soothed, handing her a cup of tea and two aspirins (her chosen breakfast), 'the gardener. He spends a lot of time here just pottering about.'

'But is he all right?' she quavered. 'He's laughing and talking, and there's no one else there.'

'He's just a bit – wanting, but terribly nice. I couldn't manage without him.'

'He's mental!' she shrieked, clutching her nylon housecoat to her throat. 'You've employed him just to spite me. You know I can't stand anything wrong with people – *nothing*! You and Granny – both out to spite me . . .'

'Don't get in a state, Mother. Bob's been working for me for months; I didn't hire him because you were coming. And he's just a bit simple and perfectly harmless. He wouldn't hurt a fly.'

As if to refute this statement, Bob swanned up to the kitchen door and pressed his nose to the glass. Mother slid off her chair and retreated, step by step, with her unwavering, bloodshot eyes fixed on him, until she fetched up against the dresser, rattling all the cups.

'Don't let him in!'

'Oh, really, Mother!' I said, exasperated, and opened the back door. 'Hello, Bob. Do you want a cup of tea?'

He proffered a bouquet of Brussels sprouts. 'Going home now. Mum says I mustn't come tomorrow. Father Christmas is coming instead!' He gave a great guffaw of laughter.

'That's right, Bob – no one works on Christmas Day.' (Except all those women cooking, serving and clearing up meals, of course – but that's all natural, like childbirth.) 'Off you go, then, but first here's a little Christmas present for the dogs.' I handed him two small parcels containing rawhide bones. 'And this one's for you, but don't open it till tomorrow.'

I tucked his present into his capacious coat pocket (a *Beano* annual and a box of Edinburgh rock) along with the envelope of wages, and off he trotted.

Mother emerged cautiously. 'Is he gone? Really, Leticia, I can't have him coming round while I'm staying here. You'll have to get rid of him.'

Oh, Mother: how you play into my hands, I thought.

'Certainly not. There are a few little things I want him to do about the house next weekend, since he can't do an awful lot in the garden when the ground's so hard.'

'Inside?' she quavered. 'But not while I'm here?'

'Oh, no – but you did say you were going home before next weekend, didn't you?'

'Anyone would think you were dying to get rid of me,' she sniffled. 'You're an unnatural child. Poor James – my heart bleeds for him!'

'Does it? Perhaps you ought to go round and commiserate with him this afternoon, then. I've a few last things to get from the shop, and then I must take Bess out before it snows.'

She looked doubtfully up at the sky. 'Do you think it will? Perhaps I ought to put my boots on.'

'Do. And perhaps you could give James this parcel.'

'Oh, Leticia! Can it be that your heart is relenting towards him? Is this a peace offering?'

'No, it's three pairs of woollen socks, so don't go all

dewy-eyed. He's very hard on the heels, and I don't suppose his bit of crumpet will have bought him anything practical.'

'He hasn't got a – a bit of crumpet, dear! That's all finished,' she assured me earnestly. 'He was just trying to make you jealous, and that cheap girl threw herself at him. And now she keeps pestering him!'

'If she's there, get her to give you her version of events. That might be interesting. Wish James a Happy Christmas from me.'

'Is that all? No message about the baby?'

I shrugged, then patted my huge and ever-expanding bump. 'Obviously it's still there. What else is there to say?'

'So hard!' she murmured sadly, trailing away in yards of ruffled lilac nylon. 'So hard!'

Spurning my offer of lunch, she tottered off as soon as she was dressed, wearing a simulated mink jacket (or 'stimulated mink', as Granny always put it), black spike-heeled Cossack boots, dangly earrings and a peevish pout. Apart from the scragginess of the legs, she looked like a prosperous tart.

Right after she'd gone two parcels addressed in Granny's hand arrived, one for Mother, the other for me. Mine felt like a book, and there was another brief epistle inside the brown-paper wrapping:

'Dear child, I hear Valerie is with you. Don't let her hang round your neck like an albatross,' she wrote, rather bafflingly.

An albatross?

'Settled in here and Rose potting', she continued – or was that 'potty'? The handwriting was a bit spidery. 'District nurse will do, but local doctor another body-snatcher. Your affectionate Grandmother.'

Well! Sighing, I examined the rest of my post, which included a big, expensive glossy card from the Wrekins. I'd pushed my cheap little card through their door. Nothing from Fergal – but then, I hadn't sent him one because after I'd written it I wasn't sure whether I should have put Nerissa's name in it too.

Right at the bottom of the heap was an invitation to take the written part of the driving test early in the New Year, so I'd better mug up the Highway Code.

Fergal: December 1999

> *'Beelzebub in our Midst!*
> *says Miss Louie Carter of Lower Nutthill,*
> *well known for her previous campaign for*
> *compulsory castration . . .'*
>
> Nutthill District Advertiser

You know, I really didn't think I was that bad! (Though I admit to having been called worse in the past.)

Does seem unfair, though, when just lately I've been trying to do the right thing regarding Tish.

Nerissa's been out and about with James a few times, looking so pleased with herself that she must think I'm jealous. I'm not, I just hope this isn't hurting Tish too much, but she must already know that he often has this other girlfriend round at the flat he's using anyway, because according to Mrs Deakin the whole village knows.

Tish looks even more beautiful pregnant, but fragile, and she needs help, whatever she says . . .

Chapter 34: Twinkle, Twinkle

Thinking about Fergal must have conjured him up, for he appeared half an hour later – and for once, thank goodness, I didn't look a total mess! I was wearing green cord trousers, a long green shirt and my hair fastened back with a silver slide.

'Hi, Tish,' he said, leaning casually against my door. 'I thought you were going to phone me about some driving practice?'

'Oh, I didn't want to bother you. Nerissa told me how busy you are, and – and – it looks like snow!'

'It's not going to snow yet, I've got an hour to spare, and there's all the park to practise in without anything to hit.' He cocked a quizzical eyebrow as I hesitated. 'Coming? What's the matter? Scared?'

'Of course not! I'll get my coat.'

I stuffed his card in my pocket, scribbled a quick note for Mother and went out, feeling sick with terror. He drove us into the park where we changed places. The Mini has very similar controls to Mrs Blacklock's car, but perhaps they all have? I've never really looked.

Knowing Fergal's temper of old, I flinched every time I

scrunched the gears or stalled, but the explosion never came and slowly I began to relax – perhaps he *had* mellowed.

Narrow little roads meandered over the estate, up and down the rolling grass and around the stands of trees. I did some three-point turns, lots of reversing, and a few emergency stops, only one involving a cow and it wasn't hurt at all, just gave me a deeply offended look before wandering off.

'Gosh, I'm doing thirty!' I exclaimed, skimming along a nice straight stretch.

'Watch the sharp bend after those trees,' warned Fergal quietly, and I gave a galvanic start that wobbled two wheels onto the grass: I'd forgotten he wasn't Mrs Blacklock for a minute!

'Steady! You're doing fine. The roads around Nutthill may be safe yet.'

'Thank you!'

'Carry on down here to the left, past the house, to the main road, and then you can drive us back to the cottage.'

I was highly gratified that he trusted me to drive him on the public roads, but hoped we wouldn't meet anything, since I can't overtake even stationary vehicles yet.

Then we came round the bend and I had my first sight of Greatness Hall.

We glided to a stop while I just stared and stared. I heard Fergal put the handbrake on.

Long, low and mellow, icy sunshine glittered from the mullioned windows, while at each end of this central seventeenth-century hall, funny little turrets had been added like incongruous ears.

'Oh, what a gorgeous house!'

'I think so, especially now I've had all the tacky later embellishments removed. But I rather liked the vulgar turrets, and I'm leaving the Victorian ballroom out the back too, because I'm turning it into a recording studio.'

'Yes, Mrs Deakin told me,' I replied absently: I couldn't tear my eyes away. 'It isn't a bit like I imagined it – it looks so lived in and cosy.'

'That's what I thought the first time I saw it. And the reason I flew back from Japan midway through the tour was to exchange contracts, rather than risk losing it. I'll show you round when I come back.'

'Back from where?' I blurted, then could have bitten my tongue.

'London – family Christmas.'

'Oh, of course.'

I'm sure Mother's neighbours are still talking about the Christmas when the Roccos rented the house next door, and what seemed like the whole, voluble populations of Italy and Ireland had met and melded all over the house and spilled out into the garden by sheer force of numbers. I'd gone in shyly with Fergal and been instantly absorbed into the noisy warm atmosphere . . . rather different from Christmas with Mother.

'I'm going as soon as I've dropped you off,' he added.

'Oh, Fergal, you shouldn't have let me delay you.'

'You should know by now, Angel, that I never do anything unless I want to,' he said shortly. His mouth relaxed a bit. 'You need the practice, and I didn't intend starting off until later. Actually, you aren't too bad.'

'Thank you!'

'Apart from that little trick you have of trying to change my right knee instead of the gear lever.'

I crunched the gears and set off again with a jerk.

'I have to pass the test before the baby arrives,' I told him, 'but there's no reason for you to feel you have to help me. I can manage fine on my own. Mrs Blacklock is a good instructor.'

'Practice helps, and you needn't go all stiff-lipped: what are friends for? Speaking of which, Mrs Bell says you refused her offer to get your shopping?'

'She isn't employed to look after me as well as you. I'm doing most of my shopping at Mrs Deakin's now, even if it is a bit more expensive. I give Bob a list and he collects it.' I sighed. 'I don't know what I did without Bob! He's so willing once he understands what you want.'

The drive divided in front of the house and Fergal directed me left, but as I began decorously to turn the corner a familiar small red sports car shot round it and screamed to a halt in a spray of gravel with the bonnet only an inch or two from mine. Nerissa stared at me through the windscreen.

I was glad I'd been practising emergency stops.

Fergal let his breath out in a hiss, and glancing sideways I noted signs of rising temper: something about the way all the angular planes of his face tightened, and a white look about the nostrils.

It had been a bit thoughtless of Nerissa to hurtle round the bend that fast, but I didn't want to be the cause of any argument between them, so as she got out and sauntered over to my side of the car, I wound the window down and prepared to try to smooth things over.

A breath of air almost as chill as her eyes invaded my shrinking lungs.

'My, my! Turned instructor, Fergal honey?' she cooed, all

Southern Belle. 'I don't think there's much you can teach *Tish*!'

I was taken aback by her uncalled-for venom, and felt the Incubus cringe when she turned her Gorgon smile on me. 'You sure are enormous, darling! Is it hard getting behind the wheel, or does it all sort of flow, like an amoeba?'

I felt like a big, ugly blob, which must have been her intention, though I don't know why she thought she needed to put me down. You can't feel less attractive than I do at the moment and she must know that Fergal is only being sorry for me, or helping me for old times' sake, or a combination of the two.

'What the hell were you doing coming round the corner that fast?' Fergal demanded stormily. 'You could have hurt Tish if you'd crashed into us!'

Nerissa fluttered her long dark eyelashes and pouted. 'I was in a hurry to see you, Fergal! Mom and Pop are expecting you tomorrow for dinner, but I thought you might just come back with me now and spend Christmas Eve too?'

'No dice, Nerissa. I told you I'm spending Christmas with my family as usual.'

'But, darling! They surely wouldn't begrudge you one Christmas with me.' A thought seemed to strike her and she brightened. 'Say, I haven't met your mom and pop yet, have I? Don't you think it's about time I did? I could come with you and—'

'No,' he said flatly.

'But I could—'

'No!' he said with finality. 'Now, will you move over and let us pass? Tish needs to get home.'

If looks could kill I'd be a big bubbling blob on the tarmac.

'I'll just go in and wait for you then, Fergal honey.'

'Pointless. I've put my cases in the other car and I'm leaving as soon as I get back from Tish's. Goodbye, Nerissa.'

He brutally abandoned any interest in her. 'Right, Tish, could you edge past, do you think? Reverse a bit first.'

'I think so, if I go partly on the grass.'

'That's OK, just take it easy.'

Mercifully I reversed without doing anything embarrassing and, as I began to crawl past her, Nerissa wailed despairingly: 'But, Fergal! I've got a present for you!'

'God, she must have been a limpet in her last incarnation,' Fergal muttered.

The car rocked back onto the even gravel and we set slowly off. I concentrated hard on getting us back in one piece.

Practically the whole population of Nutthill seemed to be out and about, from Mrs D. outside her shop to Margaret, and I felt a self-conscious glow edge up from my shirt as I drove sedately past and pulled up outside the cottage.

Fergal woke from a silent reverie. I suppose it's restful to be with a woman you know is just an old friend and clearly incapable of chasing you anywhere, even if she wanted to. (Which she doesn't . . . All right, *sometimes* she does, but she isn't going to!)

I expect he'll make up his quarrel with Nerissa. She's so young and pretty, and he seems to have given her the idea he wanted to marry her, so he can't blame her for being persistent. But if not, there are more of them out there just like her.

He helped me – the Great Amoeba – out of the car (I suppose Nerissa did have a point), and I thanked him and handed over his Christmas card.

'Will you wish your family Happy Christmas from me? If they remember me, that is.'

'Once seen, never forgotten!' he said lightly enough, but then gripped my shoulders rather painfully and scowled down. 'I only hope you're going to look after yourself and not overdo things while your mother's staying.'

'I certainly won't do that. I seem to have become incredibly lazy – or selfish – I'm not sure which.'

'You're entitled to be lazy. Is everything all right with the baby?'

'Yes, the doctor seems quite pleased – it's a good size and moves about a lot.'

'That's good. Do everything they tell you to.'

'I'm sorry I was the cause of you quarrelling with Nerissa.'

He shrugged. 'She could have hurt you – and I don't like assumptions being made about me. I never had any intention of going anywhere except London for Christmas, you know.'

'Oh?' (I don't think Nerissa had quite got the hang of that!)

'And then I'm straight off to Italy afterwards, to bring my aunt Maria back to housekeep permanently for me. What shall I bring *you* back?'

He was joking, of course, but I was glad to see he'd cheered up again. 'Oh, bring me some nice warm sunshine!' I said lightly.

It was starting to get dark, but it was ages before Mother came back carrying a card and a parcel from James. At least she'd missed Fergal, which was something to be thankful for.

The card was large and sentimental, neither of which applied to James, and the message said, 'Let's see if we can patch up our differences for the sake of the baby.'

Honestly – Mother must have been encouraging him again. She was eagerly watching me now.

'You will see him, won't you? It's so sad at a time like this, and with a baby coming and everything. He's sorry he was jealous, and he knows you aren't the sort of girl who would have a sordid affair. Oh, and we're invited to the Wrekins' for drinks after dinner, and I thought you might—'

'No,' I said firmly.

'No?' She looked huffy. 'I'm certainly going and so is James, and I can assure you that that girl Wendy won't be there! She's a thing of the past.'

'I saw her coming out of the flat not a week ago.'

'Oh, no, dear – that must have been one of Margaret's friends. James hasn't seen her for months.'

'It makes no difference. You go and have a good time.'

'I wish you would try to be a little less cold, darling – it's only a habit you've got into. Now, call me Mummy like my little girl always does.'

I sighed: here we go again! 'You go, Mummy, and tell Margaret thanks, but no thanks. She'll understand. James may come round tomorrow afternoon for a drink, if he wants to, but definitely no reconciliation.'

She brightened. 'Well, I suppose that's something. Now, what's for dinner? The walk has given me quite an appetite and the Wrekins were having lamb. I could smell it.'

'Savoury lentil casserole and brown rice.'

When she discovered I wasn't joking she was inclined to sulk and pick at her food. She said the brown rice hurt her teeth, and there were stones in the casserole, which there weren't, because I picked over the lentils very carefully.

She did ample justice to the mince pies and cream, though.

So did I, come to that, and felt quite bloated afterwards. There isn't space left to put food now that the Incubus is spreading into every last crevice of my abdominal cavity. I suppose I should be grateful it lets me breathe.

After supper Mother went to change into something unsuitable (pink and blue chiffon), and came down a bit unsteadily, with flushed cheeks.

'Look, Mother,' I said, picking my words carefully. 'You haven't had too much to drink today, have you? It isn't healthy to overdo the alcohol, especially at your age.'

'There's nothing wrong with my age that a glass of sherry can't cure!' she said pompously, and then giggled. 'Or a Martini! Ray Wrekin mixes a mean Martini. What a shame you can't have a little drinkie – and Christmas, too!'

'One of us has to be sober enough to cook Christmas dinner tomorrow. You look very smart, but isn't that glittery eyeshadow a bit much?'

'So old-fashioned, my little girl! Do brighten yourself up when you come to the midnight carol service.'

'The carol service?'

'Of course. The Wrekins asked me to go with them, but I said I was sure my little girlie would want to come with me. But not in those trousers – so unfeminine!'

How can you look unfeminine when you're grossly pregnant? It's a contradiction in terms!

'Mother, I really don't want to go.'

'Nonsense! I do think you might make an effort when it means so much to me.'

Her eyes swam with maudlin tears and already her shiny red lipstick had begun to weave its way up the lines around her mouth, making it look like a muddy river estuary.

'Don't cry, Moth— Mummy. I'll come if you really want me to, but I'd much rather just go to bed. Look, I'll meet you in the church porch just before the service – how about that? You can walk there with the Wrekins.'

When she'd gone I had a leisurely bath and, as I emerged feeling rested and relaxed, I heard the sound of carol singers.

I turned out the light immediately! It's not that I'm mean, it's just that I didn't want to freeze on the doorstep in my dressing gown, with my hair in wet rat-tails.

When I peeped through the window children were gathering outside, so I flattened myself against the wall . . . unfortunately, the wrong bit of wall, for I inadvertently clicked on the light switch with my shoulder blade, illuminating my strange stance to the singers outside. I managed a sickly grin and a wave.

'Jingle Bells' wavered, then steadied. I sidled round the door into the hall, fumbled in my bag for some money, and thrust it through the half-open door with a: 'Very nice – thank you! Good night!'

They had just embarked on 'Away in a Manger', but tailed off, muttered, and then trod crisply away down the path.

I had to dampen my hair before I could do anything with it.

Mother was awaiting me in the church porch, inclined to sing 'Twinkle, Twinkle Little Star' in a sort of baby lisp, so I tried to persuade her to come home instead, but she clung to the porch door indignantly, still singing.

I'd had much the same struggle with Toby, earlier, when he'd let himself out of his cage again and ravaged the curtain tieback tassel.

'You come along in with me, dearie!' Mrs Deakin said

firmly, coming alongside and taking Mother's arm. I took the other and we got her into a seat at the back.

We made quite a noise and several heads turned, including the Wrekins', who smiled and waved. There was a row of other drunks at the back with us, but Mrs Deakin kindly said she'd stay next to Mother since she had a good view down the aisle and could ensure that at least Mother didn't fall into it.

'Twinkle, twinkle, twinkle,' sang Mother more quietly. 'Twinkle, twinkle, twinkle.' Then she broke off and said blearily, 'James!'

It was, too, and I think he meant to sit with us, except that luckily there was no room, so he ended up on the opposite side of the aisle. This was probably just as well considering how furious I was with him for letting Mother come to church in such a state.

Mrs Deakin said afterwards that she didn't know when she'd enjoyed a service more, and pointed out a girl slipping out of the back of the church wearing a black fur jacket, short leather skirt and boots. She had long hair and fat thighs: Wendy!

'Like a play on the telly it's been, what with her trying to catch your husband's eye, and him trying to catch yours!'

I hadn't been aware of it, being preoccupied with trying to keep Mother from springing up like a Jack-in-the-box at inappropriate moments. At least she'd now quieted to a semi-comatose state. At the gate I thanked Mrs Deakin for her help and supported my tottering parent away down the dark lane. I wish she would wear sensible footwear.

A few fat flakes of snow fell, and it was very cold. I longed for bed and a hot-water bottle with my entire being.

Mrs Peach passed us and said good evening, but didn't

stop, which I was thankful for. I expect she was in church too, but up front with the godly.

I made Mother take her boots and coat off at the door, then left her while I put hot-water bottles into both our beds and got ready. When I came down in my dressing gown, she was muttering about ungrateful children and a little drinkie before bedtime, but I told her she must just look after herself.

Fergal: December 1999

> 'Friends, new and old, will all be welcome to the midnight carol service . . .'
>
> *Nutthill Parish Magazine*

The kindly vicar came up to the hall especially to assure me that I'd be welcome at the carol service, though clearly he sees me as the black sheep among his flock. Still, maybe next year I'll go and see if I'm struck by a Damascene conversion on the spot.

This was the first time I'd ever set off for the big family Christmas with a reluctant heart and it felt heavier with every mile that separated me from Nutthill. I hope Tish looks after herself in my absence, because that ghastly mother of hers is unlikely to think of anyone except herself. And that husband of hers . . . I'd like to teach him the hard way that, in my code, single men mess around with other women, but married men don't. Tish's mother screwed up: I'd have made a much better husband than James, that's for sure, even if appearances were to the contrary.

Tish . . .

Chapter 35: Uncertain Appetites

All the lights were still blazing away downstairs when I got up on Christmas morning – later than usual since I'd been listening to the radio, drinking Coffette from the Teasmade, and eating chocolates with gooey centres out of the spare box I'd got from Mrs Deakin, which I'd decided to award to myself.

There was no sound other than snoring from the spare room, so I thought it would be lunchtime, at least, before Mother emerged.

Outside everything was lightly frosted with snow: very Christmas-cardish. Bess and I had a quick stroll – she didn't like getting snow on her feet, and kept trying to lift them all off the ground simultaneously with the obvious result.

Back home I switched on the radio for the Christmas programmes and gave Bess her stocking. She disembowelled it all over the kitchen, but wouldn't let the pups near it. Toby got a peeled satsuma and half a Jaffa cake, which would glue his beak up nicely for a bit. Then I put the turkey roast in its tin and prepared the vegetables.

Mother came down much later in unusual silence, except for complaining of a headache, so I gave her two aspirins, wished her Happy Christmas and recommended a walk.

She gave me a look and continued sitting hunched over the kitchen table drinking gallons of weak sugary tea, while I lunched on Christmas cake and four satsumas. Then I suggested we go into the living room and open our presents.

Granny's to me was a book of helpful hints on divorce, which Mother said was further evidence of her senility, but that was after she'd opened her own present and found thermal underwear.

'But it's just the thing for this weather, Mother.'

'Don't be silly, dear – it's the kind of thing old women wear!'

'I think this sort of lacy vest top is very pretty. If you don't like it, I'll have it.'

When she unwrapped my box of chocolates, she said, 'Thank you, darling. I suppose you've been too busy lately to think of Poor Little Me!'

Her present to me was, as always, a small bottle of an expensive scent that I particularly dislike. I kissed her cheek and thanked her.

After that I reluctantly ripped off the glossy paper enclosing James's offering, to reveal an indecently large bottle of ridiculously expensive perfume, which quite took me aback, and made Mother miffed because her little bottle looked nothing beside it.

'Oh blast! What am I going to do with this?'

'But – aren't you *pleased*, Leticia?'

'Pleased? It must have cost the earth! I can't possibly accept it.'

'But surely it must touch your heart, his spending all that money on this lovely perfume?'

'No – it's vulgar! And impersonal.' But I could see she

didn't understand. I put the bottle on the dresser. 'I'll give it back when he comes round later.'

'But you can't. He'll be terribly hurt!'

'I can't do anything else, Mother.'

While I put the finishing touches to dinner, she sat in front of the TV eating her chocolates and destroying her liver.

The table looked very festive with the holly and fir cone decoration I'd made, and a red cloth. I'd done roast potatoes and all the trimmings, but Mother was predictably outraged that I hadn't bought an enormous turkey.

'But it's such an economy – you can cut at it for days, and there's always something to eat if visitors come round.'

'I get sick of it by the second day, and I'm not expecting visitors.'

'James!'

'Let him eat cake.'

'Really, it's no wonder you couldn't keep him with an attitude like that.'

'Oh, do you think so? But I'm sure Blondie isn't a cordon-bleu chef either – unless she's feeding a different appetite.'

'Leticia!'

'Have some Christmas pudding, Mother, but mind you don't choke on the silver charms – that wouldn't be lucky.'

We both found one and she insisted on keeping hers to put on her charm bracelet although already she rattles like the Ghost of Christmas Past. I don't know how she can lift her wrist.

After the meal we lay about in front of the Wrekins' telly, replete, with Bess, who'd escaped her maternal duties yet again. It was snug, even though outside the snow was falling and the sky a strange, unearthly colour.

The Incubus was kicking and protesting at the amount of food pressing on its swimming space and I wished it would have a nice long sleep until digestion had done its bit.

Mother watched the film, while I fell asleep part-way through reading *Quick Divorce Solutions*, and woke later when she was talking on the phone to her beau; he seems pretty keen and apparently calls her at least once every day!

I heaved myself up and went to make some ham sandwiches, and had just brought them in on a tray with mince pies, fruit, and chocolate finger biscuits (with Mother still bemoaning the lack of turkey), when James arrived.

They both spurned my coffee in favour of something stronger.

James followed me out to the kitchen afterwards, though he didn't offer to carry anything. 'I'd forgotten about the puppies!' he exclaimed, but when he made as if to go nearer Bess growled and looked defensive, so he had to content himself with peering at them from a distance.

'Funny-looking things! Do you know what the father is?'

'I'm beginning to suspect it's that enormous Old English sheepdog that's always roaming round the village.'

'Good God! You'll never get rid of them if it is. Perhaps you ought to have them put down?'

'I certainly will not! I'll find homes for them.'

He sat down at the table, and the light showed all the lines and wrinkles that were forming, and the way his skin seemed to be coming detached from the craggy bones of his face. It gave me some idea of what he'd look like as an old man if he didn't cut down on the self-indulgence – and it wouldn't be a pretty sight.

'Oh – thanks,' he said unenthusiastically as I put a cup and more mince pies in front of him. 'But I couldn't eat another thing.'

I did, though. I think he was just put off by the darkness of the wholemeal pastry.

'How are you feeling? Is the baby all right?'

I looked at him in surprise. 'Caring James' was a new manifestation. 'Fine – it should arrive at the beginning of April.' (April the first, actually, but I refuse to contemplate that possibility!)

He sighed. 'I suppose you wouldn't consider having another shot at the marriage? I've been considering things a lot and it would be different this time. I still think you were a bit hasty, but Wendy must have been a shock.'

'She was certainly a surprise.' I selected another mince pie. 'Lots of fruit and thin pastry!'

'What?'

'The mince pies: that's how I like them. And our marriage is all in the past, as far as I'm concerned. What you get up to with Wendy, or anyone else, isn't my concern any more.'

'Yes, but that's just it – now you've thrown me out, she keeps trying to move in with me permanently and hinting that when I get the divorce I should marry her.'

'Why don't you and Wendy just live with Alice and Howard?'

'Alice seems to think it would be better if Wendy moved in with me – I think she wants Howard to herself.'

'What for, to experiment on?'

He gave me one of his uncomprehending blinks and carried on plaintively, 'In any case, I don't want to live with her anywhere, you know that.'

'Do I?'

'Of course – I want us to be together again.'

'There is no "us". There never really was.' My bowels of compassion remained unstirred. 'Sorry, James, you'll have to sort it out yourself. The divorce goes ahead.'

'Alice says her father knows Uncle Lionel,' he said, even more gloomily.

'Then perhaps she might have the makings of a solicitor's wife after all,' I suggested brightly, and he glowered. It would be one solution. Then afterwards, Wendy could eat him alive like a female spider. Tidy.

'Look, why not just tell her you don't want to see her any more, if you mean it, James? You're a big boy now.'

'You don't know Wendy.'

'Well, there is that to be thankful for, I suppose.'

He got himself into this mess and he can find his way out . . . if he really wants out. I don't know how much of what he says is true any more.

Anyway, I then compounded his happiness by returning his present and he got mad and said he would give it to Wendy instead. I kindly pointed out that she would think he was really serious if he gave her such an expensive gift.

'Let's not argue about it, James,' I said. 'It's Christmas, after all.'

'Look, if I swap the bottle for a smaller one, would that be all right?' he said more reasonably.

'Yes – fine. But the smallest size, mind.'

We went back to Mother, who was snoring in front of the TV, and I crammed half a box of chocolates in on top of everything else, which put an end to the Incubus's gymnastics for one night.

James had to help me get Mother upstairs, then turned maudlin on the doorstep. I pushed him out into the cold, cold snow: that would sober him.

Fergal rang me just as I was going up to bed myself, to wish me Happy Christmas, and I could hear the sound of family revelry in the background.

'Look after yourself,' he said and then I thought he added, 'and I wish you were here . . .' but I must have imagined that, for he said breezily, 'See you in 2000, Angel!' and rang off.

Chapter 36: Guilt-edged

I felt exhausted by Boxing Day and made Mother go down to Mrs Deakin's (who'd said she'd be opening the shop for a couple of hours), for a few things we'd run out of. She was gone for absolutely ages, so God knows what she'd been telling her! My name will be on everyone's lips by nightfall (if it isn't already).

I began my new novel: *The Sweet Wine of Love*, which is about a young English girl touring Europe, who loses all her money and has to find a job picking grapes. There she meets a young man who is really the son of a comte, only he has to prove himself in the fields to inherit the money . . .

Though I didn't see much of Mother, I could hear the TV booming away: she must be going deaf.

Apparently Dr Reevey called, too – it must be love! He's probably her last hope of salvation before alcoholism. After Bess's last run of the evening the phone rang and I thought it might be him again . . . or even Fergal, but when I picked it up and said, 'Hello?' there was no reply other than a silence like an old, rather tiresome, acquaintance.

'What do you want, Wendy?' I asked wearily. 'He isn't here, you know.'

There was a long, snuffling sigh. (Something to do with having a nose like a piglet, I suppose.) 'But he said he was going to see you yesterday and he hasn't come back yet.'

'He did come here for a couple of hours, but I haven't seen him since.'

'You could be just saying that!'

'For goodness' sake! Look, Wendy, I'm too tired for this sort of conversation and I'm off to bed – alone. I neither know nor care where James is.'

'How do I know if you're telling the truth? You told Alice you wanted a divorce, but James says you don't.'

Fumes of sleep were drifting round inside my skull like clouds, but I attempted to focus. 'Wendy, the divorce was my idea, and my solicitor is already dealing with it.'

'But James says—' she bleated.

'I don't care what James says. Hasn't he already proved himself a prize liar by deceiving me with you over the last year? I don't care about James, full stop! Right?'

'I hope you mean that – because at least when I have *my* baby he'll know he's the father!' she said viciously, then slammed down the phone.

Wendy pregnant? Alice must have taken that advice I gave her seriously! I should have known she didn't have a sense of humour. Wendy must have moved fast . . . I wonder if she'll also take the rest of my advice about smart little suits and big hair.

What will James do now – if it's true, that is, for Wendy is probably at least as big a liar as he is?

But if it is, then the Incubus might have a half-sibling . . . half-baby, half-Pekinese.

I had a driving lesson booked for next day and it went

quite well, especially my reversing and three-point turns. Must have been that practice with Fergal. But I'm beginning to find sitting tensely for an hour a bit uncomfortable with my increasing bulk; come to that, any position for doing *anything* is getting uncomfortable. Like one of those prisoners in a little cage who can neither stand nor lie down – a Little Ease. There's certainly little ease in pregnancy.

I'm certain now that Bess's puppies are half Old English sheepdog (or Durex Dog, as Mrs Deakin once put it, though I don't think she knew she was making a mistake). At least she's got it all over with – *and* got her figure back!

The puppies are like large, shambling, disparate bits of shaggy rug, though at least they can all now manage to stagger out onto the newspaper to perform. A certain smell still lingers, however many times I change the papers and disinfect the floor.

Bess has long since abandoned any attempt to clean up after them, though she does show interest in eating their expensive puppy food. So much for the maternal instinct.

Bob has picked out the puppy he wants: the one with the four unmatching legs and a walleye. It may improve as it gets older. Mrs Sloggit sent a note saying he could have one, and I've told him he can take it home when it's eight weeks old.

Bess will be delighted.

Mrs Deakin reported (via Dulcie Blacklock) loud shouting outside the Wrekins' flat in the early hours of the day after Boxing Day, followed by the departure of Wendy in her white Volkswagen Polo. (Bag with Baggage.) So, all the time James was trying to persuade me to take him back, he knew she was waiting for him at the flat!

I wonder where he went after he left here. Could Nerissa have wafted him away to console her for Fergal's absence? (I mean, just how desperate can you get?)

I know where he was tonight – the Dog and Duck with Mother, because he brought her back late. He had to – from the sound of it she'd never have made it alone. But at least she found the door key I gave her, so I didn't have to get out of bed.

James came round early in a belligerent mood, to 'talk to me seriously' about Mother's drinking, which he blames entirely on the worry caused by our marital break-up. He didn't believe me when I said it'd been creeping up for over a decade, and said I ought to have her to live with me, since it would also put a stop to my 'goings-on with that long-haired pop singer'.

He said the whole village was talking about how I'd been seen out in Fergal's car, and his visits to the cottage.

The village – and James – must have good, if strange, imaginations, that's all I can say. I mean, do I look as if I'm in the middle of a torrid affair with someone?

I told him he was a complete cretin, and while he must know the baby's his, it was nothing to do with him if I was having an affair with Fergal, or anyone else, now we're separated.

'And before you start on *my* morals, where were you for the two nights after Christmas? Off with someone else, while your mistress awaited you in the flat?'

He went puce and slammed out.

After he'd gone Mother finally emerged, and I tactfully reminded her to wear something warm for the journey home.

She showed a tendency to cry into the home-made tangerine marmalade.

It didn't seem to have much effect on her departure, though, for it was lunchtime before she finally got dressed and resurfaced her face, and even then she simply drifted into the kitchen and settled down again with tea and cake, while the times of two trains she could have taken came and went.

Finally I asked, point-blank, 'Do you want me to pack for you, Mo— Mummy, or will you do it yourself?'

Instead of replying she suddenly swooped down on the puppies, and emerged with one of the little creatures in her bony hands.

It whimpered, and I saw that it was my favourite – but I was afraid to snatch it back since she was quite capable of hanging on to it until it parted in the middle. (If she'd been at the Judgement of Solomon she'd have said, 'Ok, split it down the middle – but I want the left side, mind!' whether it was her baby or not.)

'You know,' she fluted, 'I think I'll take this sweet little mite back with me. I need some company now I'm all alone.'

'I'm afraid it's too young – and in any case they're all spoken for.'

'Not all, surely! No one will want this one, will they? I only chose it because I thought I should take the ugly one off your hands.'

The puppy whimpered again, and Bess began stalking towards her, growling menacingly. I was quite impressed.

Mother hurriedly put the puppy down and backed away with an uncertain laugh. 'Well, it was just an idea after all.'

'What time is your train?'

'Really, darling, anyone would think you wanted to get rid of me! I've hardly been here five minutes, and I was only thinking last night that I mustn't let myself be hurt, or driven away by any little fancies you had about . . . well, about your arrival, darling.'

She made my birth sound like a train: 'The baby now arriving at bed one . . .'

'And it's so silly! Everyone says how like me you are.'

Good heavens! If I thought I resembled Mother in any way I would stick my head in the oven. (Not the Aga, because even if it was working I expect it would only slow-cook it.)

'And a girl really needs her mother at a time like this. It'll be New Year's Eve in a few days, and the new millennium – you can't possibly be alone for that. The Wrekins are having a party and they invited— '

'No,' I broke in flatly. 'I'm totally unexcited about the new millennium – I have other things on my mind – and I certainly don't feel like going to any parties, especially at the Wrekins'!'

'But *I* could go and, after all, there's no reason for me to hurry home. It's terribly unpleasant having people coming to look over the house and trying to deduce how long I'm going to live, or if they could buy me out,' Mother complained. She paused breathlessly and smiled. 'So I'll stay here with you until the birth. You need me more than you realise.'

Like a hole in the head.

'Mother, I like living alone, and if I need any help I'll arrange for it. But thank you for offering. And you haven't considered Dr Reevey – he's missing you already, isn't he?'

'Yes . . . but no sacrifice is too great for my little girlie!'

'I don't want your sacrifice, Mother. Now, I'd better ring

for the taxi, hadn't I? Or you'll miss the next train, too. Hadn't you better bring your things down?'

She plumped down into a chair and, as I dialled, dabbed her eyes cautiously with a lace-edged handkerchief. 'Unfeeling child!'

I put down the receiver: 'The taxi's coming. I won't come to the station with you, if you don't mind – I'm feeling rather tired.'

'A *taxi* when James would have taken me for nothing! And after all, it's a lot of money, and—'

'I'll pay for the taxi. Now, have you got your things together? What about your suitcase?'

'I haven't brought it down – it's so heavy!'

'You managed to carry it up there all right, and it should be easier coming down. Now, do you need a carrier bag for your other bits and pieces? I've got an enormous one some-where. I'll go round and see what you've forgotten.'

She dragged her suitcase down while I tossed various odds and ends into the bag. She'd managed to scatter her belong-ings into every corner of the house.

When I'd finished I found her wrapping up a bottle and some sandwiches in the kitchen. 'Just a little something for me to eat in my cold, empty house tonight!' she explained with a brave smile and I added another bottle of sherry and a large box of chocolate biscuits to the bag, with tears in my eyes, even though I'd just overheard her making a telephone assignation with the Laughing Cowboy.

It was unfortunate for her that the taxi arrived just then, for in my weakened state she might have worked on me to let her stay a bit longer from sheer guilt, the creation of which is her speciality.

I tucked her into the back of the taxi and gave her the fare, then guilt struck again I pressed another note I could ill afford into her hand and begged her to have a proper meal en route. You'd think she was journeying to Siberia, not the London suburbs.

The taxi finally vanished with Mother sobbing into the money, and I trudged back up the path with guilty tears rolling down my face and thankfully closed the front door.

But once I'd tidied the house and stripped the bed I felt much happier and settled down to pig out on the last of the Christmas cake and satsumas.

It was just as well I'd decided to have an early night, because Bob was knocking at the door at the crack of dawn, wanting to see his pup. I yelled down at him from the window to go away until a decent hour of the morning.

His face fell and he wandered off. He didn't go home, though, because I heard the sound of a spade crashing into the frozen earth at the bottom of the garden. He seemed to be trying to dig a trench, perhaps to dispose of my enormous bulk in (but if so, he will have to wait for the thaw).

I called him in later and gave him a cup of tea while he played with the puppies. He has four spoons of sugar in his tea and can eat a whole packet of biscuits in five minutes by putting two in his mouth at once and swallowing them with a gulp of tea.

He informed me that four of the puppies are girls, and two boys, and I didn't ask how he could tell.

'Is yours a little boy or a little girl puppy, Bob?'

'Un's a bitch,' he replied, holding the chosen puppy nose to nose until they both went cross-eyed.

'Oh. And what are you going to call her?'

'Maggie.'

His huge hands held the squirming puppy quite gently and she seemed to have taken to him.

'Maggie? That's nice. I've never met a dog called Maggie before.' After Goldie the goldfish I'd been expecting something more like Doggo or Bitchie.

'Dad said . . .' He wrinkled his brow in an effort of recollection. 'Dad said Maggie was a good name for a bitch.'

Maggie peed down his jumper at this point, but he didn't seem to mind.

I might put a notice in Mrs D.'s window about the rest of the litter: 'Free to good homes. Peculiar and potentially huge puppies, who will demolish your home and eat all your money in Half-breed Chum.'

I'm terribly tempted to keep my favourite . . . so I'll just have to go on reminding myself it'll probably grow up into an even bigger fool than Bess.

Fergal: December 1999

Fergal Rocco's Christmas Wish List!
                              Trendsetter magazine

If I'd been able to put what I really, really wanted on that list, it would have set a few cats among the pigeons!

Number one would have been that Nerissa'd finally get the message that our relationship – such as it was – came to an end a long time ago.

You can probably guess the rest of the list . . .

My sister Lucia was in Italy with her husband and children, so I visited her (and got some excellent sisterly advice) before going on to Rome to collect my aunt Maria and bring her back to Greatness: I intend living a sober and respectable life from now on, and with Aunt Maria around there won't be much chance to stray back into my old habits, even if I'm tempted to.

And since meeting Tish again, that hasn't happened.

Maybe I'm just getting old.

Chapter 37: The Sweet Wine of Love

The Sweet Wine of Love progresses very well since Christmas, considering the disruption of Mother's visit and the fact that all my mental functions want to lie down and hibernate. (Also, I keep getting the urge to transform the little bedroom with bunny stencils.)

I saw Margaret in the village, and she was making tentative overtures, though it is very difficult with James practically living in her house . . . but anyway, after some thought, I phoned her up and invited her round for coffee tomorrow. Knowing her Guilty Secret sort of makes me even.

I wonder if Wendy has dropped her bombshell and moved in permanently? But I don't think she can have or Mrs D. would have known by now. Was she lying?

There were to be fireworks on the village green at midnight on New Year's Eve, not to mention a broadcast to the nation from London on TV (had I still had one), but I felt profoundly uninterested.

Instead, I celebrated the advent of the new millennium by half-guiltily drinking a small bottle of Guinness and then retiring to bed with a box of hazelnut whirls and a good book. I'd already unplugged the phone, to avoid any possibility of drunk and maudlin midnight calls from Mother or James, and, apart from the occasional pop of fireworks in the distance, was undisturbed.

Oh, the joys of living alone – or *almost* alone, for of course the Incubus dictates my taste in foods, my internal capacity for consumption, and the length of time between trips to the loo.

Margaret came round as arranged next morning, looking a little jaded after her party, and I took her into the living room, where Toby still slept with his head under one wing, groaning gently.

There was a difficult silence once we'd wished each other a Happy New Year, until she suddenly said she was sorry for her previous attitude and confessed that she'd been deceived by James and wouldn't have been his Peace Envoy if she'd known the full extent of his infidelity.

She understood how I felt because she'd been through it herself: apparently her first husband had thought that a *ménage à trois* consisting of Margaret, himself and his pretty young secretary, Sharon, was quite a sensible proposition.

Unfortunately Sharon also thought so, and when she moved in, Margaret moved out. Men have some very strange ideas.

She and Ray are going to get married when her divorce becomes absolute in March.

'Ray has taught me that there *are* Good Men,' she explained, in her Awfully Nice Golden Syrup voice. 'You may feel bitter now, but Mr Right is still out there somewhere.'

'Then I hope he's got a tent, because he'll be out there a long time.'

'If it's any consolation, I'm sure James is sorry he's lost you – he doesn't *really* care for Wendy at all.'

'He may not care for her, but it doesn't stop her spending most nights in the flat.'

She flushed. 'Oh dear, that sort of thing does get noticed! But it's not the way it seems – he told her he didn't want to see her any more, but she just turns up anyway. I didn't bargain for all this when I let him have the flat.'

'Throw him out!' I suggested helpfully.

'You don't mean that. And he isn't really any bother – it's just this Wendy.'

'What's she like?'

'Only twenty, but a bit hard. And she isn't interested in women at all – if there aren't any men about she just slumps and looks bored.'

'Polite!'

'Mmm . . . and she eats and drinks anything that comes within reach. I don't think she's pretty really, either. If you cut off all that blonde hair she'd look just like a Pug.'

'That's funny, I thought she looked like a Pekinese! It's the nose and the slight pop eyes. And a bit tarty, with those little short leather skirts.'

'She always wears that sort of thing, and when she sits down her thighs merge into one fatty blob.'

'I heard about the scene she made outside the flat when James didn't come back over Christmas.'

'I think all Nutthill heard it – it was certainly in the *Nutthill Advertiser*! The police came, though by then Wendy had gone off in her car – but she's back again now.'

'She phoned me late on Boxing Day to ask if James was still here.'

'How incredibly brass-faced of her!'

'Not one of Nature's more sensitive little plants,' I agreed. 'I wonder where he was. I only hope he hasn't got another girlfriend somewhere.'

'Someone did say they'd seen him get into a red sports car like that one Fergal Rocco's girlfriend has – Nerissa,' she suggested tentatively.

'Well, they *have* met, and I did wonder . . . Only it seems a bit unlikely. If she's set her sights on Fergal Rocco, she's not going to settle for James! But he might have someone else; he's probably bored with Wendy. What puzzles me is what Wendy sees in him. Her sister, Alice, who lives with one of James's oldest friends, asked me to meet her a few weeks ago, to talk it all over.'

'No! Does she look like Wendy?' Margaret leaned forward eagerly. 'What did she say?'

'Alice looks like something you might find under a rock if you were particularly unlucky, and she said that Wendy wants to marry James. She must be mad!'

'But I'm sure James doesn't want to marry *her*.'

'He'll have to sort his own problems out – I've got enough of my own. I suppose you don't want a puppy?'

The din from the kitchen was now reaching ear-splitting proportions, and I took Margaret in and showed her the brood: it was just as noisy in the living room, since Toby had woken up and decided to treat us to his impersonation of my Amstrad printer.

I don't think Margaret is a bird person, going by the nervous glances she'd given Toby even while he was harm-lessly asleep, but she was certainly a doggy one.

'Oh, what darlings!' she cried, plumping down onto her

knees among the damp newspapers, heedless of her immaculate navy wool skirt. 'Particularly this one. Look at her cute little face!'

'*His* cute little face, according to Bob. There are six, but one is spoken for already.'

She cuddled the little monstrosity in her arms. 'I'm surprised this one hasn't gone – it's so adorable! I wonder if the children would like a dear little puppy.'

My conscience prompted me. 'I think the father was an Old English sheepdog . . . and they aren't house-trained yet.'

'May can cope, I'm sure,' she said confidently.

'You think about it and let me know in a day or two, Margaret. You can't take it until it's eight weeks, anyway.'

She clutched the acquiescent bundle to her bosom. 'But someone else might see him! I *will* have him! You'll keep him for me, won't you?'

'If you're quite sure. Will you know which is which?'

'Yes – mine has that funny black patch over one eye, and a kink in its tail.'

'So it has, that will be easy to remember, and I'll make a note of it, too. Don't worry, I won't let anyone else have him.'

That decided, we adjourned back to the living room with more coffee (Margaret said she thought the health version 'interesting' – she has such lovely manners), where I bribed Toby into silence with a biscuit.

There, she regaled me with a couple of the usual gynaecological horror stories, to which I'm becoming immune, and enquired after my health.

I said I was quite well, considering the strain on my system, and then she asked me if I'd started buying baby things yet. 'Only one of my friends wants to get rid of all hers, and it's like new.'

'Oh, I don't know really . . .' I began doubtfully.

'Everything came from Harrods. She wasn't very well during the pregnancy so she just ordered everything the sales assistant recommended on the phone.'

'Really?' Harrods second-hand seems somehow different! 'I expect she'll want a lot of money, though?'

'Only a hundred pounds – she needs the space more than the cash. There's a cot, high chair, crib, lots of clothes . . .'

'I'm definitely interested,' I said firmly, because I wouldn't even get a new cot with a hundred pounds!

'I almost said I'd have it myself,' she confided, 'only really, I've got everything.'

'Are you . . .?' (Is *everybody*?)

She nodded happily. 'In June! But don't tell anyone yet – Ray and I want to get married first. So I'll tell my friend you'd like the things, shall I? After all, if there's anything you don't want you can resell it, can't you?'

'Yes, please,' I said.

This agreed, we had some further chat about pregnancy's more undesirable aspects (though actually, I haven't come across any desirable ones yet) and then she gave me her no-fail recipe for Hasty Buns, which are a sort of little no-knead bread rolls that even I could make successfully (though she tactfully didn't put it like that). Then off she went, leaving me feeling better for having had a good talk to someone other than Mrs Deakin.

And I'm sure she would have mentioned it if Wendy had announced her pregnancy; so that was either a lie or a threat.

But there's already a lot of it going round . . .

Another year, another antenatal check-up.

The doctor said all was well and asked me if I'd been attending the antenatal classes. When I confessed that I hadn't, she advised me to go to at least one, and I suppose I really ought to – but later. First I must turn the spare bedroom into a nursery, book extra driving lessons . . . and time is marching along.

I'm just into the last trimester of pregnancy; soon the baby will be here and I'll be A Mother. Do all children love their mothers, and all mothers their children? I think mine would have been just as happy with a Tiny Tears doll!

I expect I'll feel the correct emotions because, after all, I've grown to love Bess (and even Toby, despite his attempts to bite the hand that feeds him), and I didn't like dogs very much. Or I thought I didn't, because Mother never let me have one, so I'd had no experience of them.

I'll be glad to get the birth over with. I'd like to feel energetic again, and see my feet when I look down. I'd like to lie back without heartburn and stand without my legs aching and my back going numb. I'd like to get in the bath without the water damming up behind me.

I'd like the feeling of someone's loving arms around me.

I'd like to drink alcohol.

I'm reaching straight for the bottle after the birth. With Mother's example before me I'll never be an alcoholic, it's just I keep having this craving for champagne.

I'd also like to know Mother's guilty secret (which, if it is a skeleton in the cupboard, is likely to be that of a very small rodent). But I *need* to know it, for my baby's sake.

Peggy lives in Cornwall. Could I ask her to dig around a bit? Time I brought her up to date with the situation, anyway!

Fergal: January 2000

'*TOO MUCH CHRISTMAS CHEER?*
Police called out to dawn village disturbance.'
                                        Nutthill District Advertiser

The local paper had been delivered along with the rest of the mail, and that front-page headline caught my eye. At least it wasn't me making the scandals this time . . .

I wanted to rush right round and check that Tish was OK, and not upset by all this, but I restrained myself. Leaving Aunt Maria unpacking, I went down to the village shop to get all the news from Mrs Deakin first.

The gardener, who'd been looking after the cat, brought Twinkletoes back just as I was on my way out, and I was halfway to the shop before I realised I hadn't warned Aunt Maria about the cat's strange feet . . .

Chapter 38: Unlicensed Behaviour

Lumbered up to the postbox today with Bess. I hadn't been out very far for a few days because it's been so icy and I was afraid of falling. What's happened to my centre of gravity?

Mrs Deakin updated me with the current gossip, including that Fergal had arrived back the previous afternoon, bringing his auntie with him. I felt strangely miffed that he hadn't rung me to tell me he was back . . . though why on earth should he?

When I got home, I had to squeeze past a van parked right across the drive, and found a strange man peering through my letter box.

'Can I help you?' I enquired coldly, restraining Bess from giving him an effusive and messy greeting.

He straightened abruptly and turned a sharp, vole-like face towards me. His whiskers practically twitched.

'Mrs Drew? I'm from the TV Licensing authority, and it appears –' here he scrutinised a red plastic clipboard – 'that you don't have a TV licence!'

I opened the door and pushed Bess through, and she bounded off up the hall, scattering rugs.

'That's right, I haven't got one.'

He goggled at me: 'You haven't got a licence? That's a very serious offence, you do realise?'

'But only if you have a television set, surely?' I replied, puzzled.

'You – you haven't got a television?'

'No.'

This was obviously too novel an idea to take in all at once. 'A portable? An old black and white?'

'No television of any kind.' Thank goodness the Wrekins' had gone back!

'Having a TV without a licence can lead to a very heavy fine,' he assured me earnestly.

'So I believe. Now, I'm afraid you must excuse me – goodbye!' And I slammed the door on his baffled face.

After a while I heard the van drive past.

I dismissed it from my mind and went to do some work on the book, then gave in to my inner urgings and started to paint the nursery a pale terracotta (suitable for a boy or a girl), until I was rudely interrupted by a sudden eruption of yelling and scuffling from the back garden.

Dropping the brush I raced down to discover Fergal holding in a vice-like grip a small, shaken man with a red clipboard.

It reminded me of the day Bob caught the rat.

Fergal gave his captive a shake. 'This creep was staring in at the windows! Some kind of Peeping Tom. Do you know him?'

'I wouldn't say know him, exactly – he's the TV Licensing inspector who called earlier.'

Fergal relaxed his grip enough for the man to draw a choking breath.

'That's right!' he croaked. 'Just doing my job! And I could get you for assault, Mr – Mr—'

'Rocco. You're welcome to try. Do you usually sneak round peering in at windows?'

'I was checking that there's no TV on the premises!'

'Isn't that what detector vans are for?'

'She might have switched it off! Everyone has at least one TV these days.'

'*Do* you have one, Tish?'

'No. James took ours and then I rented one for a bit, but I sent it back ages ago as an economy and didn't renew the licence.'

'There, you see? No TV. Now, push off and if I ever find you're round here again I'll give you some real grounds for assault!'

The man smoothed his ruffled collar and tie and began to back off. 'There's no call to be violent. And if there is a TV, the detector vans will get it in the end!'

Fergal made a move forward and the TV Licensing man took to his heels with a squawk and fled.

'Thank you, Fergal. What a very persistent man!'

'That's all right.' He frowned at me. 'But are you really so short of money that you've had to give up TV?'

'It wasn't such a sacrifice. I hardly ever watched it anyway, because I was writing instead. I don't miss it.'

He was still frowning. 'Seriously, Tish, are you finding it difficult to make ends meet on your own?'

'Of course not! I'm simply being careful until I see how I stand, but really, I'm fine.'

He followed me into the kitchen, where Bess and the puppies were still snoring behind their cardboard barrier, oblivious of the rumpus. 'I've had to make a few cuts, but you don't realise just how popular an author I am! It's only that it doesn't come in neat monthly amounts, and that makes it a bit difficult to calculate everything.'

'Your husband will have to pay maintenance for the baby.'

'I wouldn't accept his money – I can manage on my own. And if he doesn't want to acknowledge the baby, then that's fine by me too. In fact, I'd prefer it! All this vacillation about who's the father whenever Wendy's been having a go at him is very wearing.'

It was warm in the kitchen. Fergal unzipped his heavy Italian leather jacket and hung it on the back of a chair before sitting down and subjecting me to one of his jade-green scrutinies. 'You're taking on a lot. Is James behaving himself?'

'Reasonably. He's having too many problems with his girlfriend to give me much bother . . . and— Oh damn!' I exclaimed, suddenly remembering, 'I didn't put the lid back on the paint tin, and the brush will have dried!'

'Which paint tin?'

'I was just painting the baby's room.'

'I don't think you should be doing that. All that stretching, and the fumes!'

'I don't see why not – I'm not ill, after all, and I'm being very careful. Anyway, it has to be done. *I* can't afford to just send for the decorators when I feel like it.'

'Then I'll do it,' he stated calmly, taking the wind out of my sails. 'Which room is it?'

'Don't be silly, you'd get paint all over you – and besides, I can manage. I'll do it a bit at a time, and—'

And I might as well have saved my breath, because he *did*

paint the room, getting hardly a splash on himself in the process.

He liked the terracotta paint and the stencils, so I showed him the stencilled floor in my little workroom. He was very taken with the drifts of leaves, and the row of leaves I'd clipped across the window on nylon line, so the light shone through.

We went back into the nursery, and while he painted and I admired the way the muscles on his back rippled under his thin black T-shirt (I'm only human after all) he told me about his Christmas, and about bringing his aunt Maria back to the Hall. She speaks very good English, having been the housekeeper to an English lady in Pisa for years.

Then I found myself, by some sort of natural progression, telling him about Wendy and Alice and everything – all the details. It was wonderful to get it all off my chest, and even more wonderful to find someone who thought Alice washing her baby's hair in the ladies' loo at the pizza house just as funny as I did. We always did laugh at the same things . . . when we weren't arguing about everything else, that is!

It was all very cathartic – I haven't felt so good in ages! I don't know why I told him, except that I trust him, I suppose, now I know he didn't really abandon me all those years ago. And when we're chatting like this, I forget everything he's reputed to have got up to since then. Anyway, if you believed it all, he'd have to be some kind of monster.

The monster looked up just then and said, 'Your divorce should be making some progress by now if it's uncontested – have you chased your solicitor up?'

'No. I suppose I ought to.' It would be good to be legally parted from the Party of the First Part.

'The sooner the better,' he said, and smiled at me. It's unfair to have a smile like that.

But at least he still cared enough about me to be interested in what was happening. Which reminded me of something I'd often wondered about. 'Fergal, did you know I'd be at that dinner in London – and how did you find out I was staying in the hotel overnight?'

He looked a little sheepish, an unusual expression for him. 'After I saw you at my exhibition I began to wonder sometimes how you were doing – if you were happy – so I decided to find out.'

'Find out? How?'

'I hired this man I know who's an enquiry agent. He found out about the novels, and then I asked if you'd be at the hotel that night, because I thought I might as well collect my award and catch up on things with you myself.'

We'd certainly caught up on things.

I stared at him speechlessly for a minute, then found my tongue. 'An enquiry agent! Isn't that going a bit far? And – oh, I see! James really was being followed that time! And me too? I didn't notice.' A suspicion crossed my mind. 'Did you know about James and that Wendy before I did?'

'No – I called him off before all that, and before you moved to Nutthill, too. I knew about the photocopier, though, but I couldn't tell you, could I? Especially once I knew you were pregnant. I thought he might just settle down after that.'

I sat down on a chair. 'You really didn't know I was living down here when you bought the Hall?'

'No, strangely enough. Nerissa found the house – it's near her parents' home. But I bought it because I fell in love with it. It was a shock when I saw you at the fête, and you didn't look too pleased to see me either.'

'Of course I wasn't. I'd been fairly successfully pretending to myself that London never happened.' I sighed and gave up; I expect it would never have crossed his mind anyway that it would make any difference to me, having an ex-boyfriend living nearby. Why should it? And it was nice of him to have wondered how I was, though a detective seemed to be going a bit far.

'I'd probably have told you about it at the hotel, if I'd had a chance, but casual conversation didn't seem to be on the agenda.'

I looked at him doubtfully. He grinned and went past me carrying the paint tin and brush.

He stowed them in the cellar, then I left him in the living room with Bess making shameless advances and Toby muttering morosely (he's gone off men since the whisky incident), and went to make him some coffee.

He called out that he was just fetching something from the car, and when I took the tray in there was a big, Christmas-wrapped parcel on the coffee table, beside a flat cardboard box.

He smiled. 'Belated Happy Christmas! I said I'd bring you something back from Italy.'

'But I thought you were joking! Oh, Fergal, you shouldn't have.' I went all hot and embarrassed, and the tray wobbled in my hands.

He relieved me of it and set it down. 'I wanted to – and it's not just for you. Open it.'

There were two parcels inside the wrapping. One contained an oversized fine cream sweatshirt emblazoned across the front with the word 'Bambino', and the other, three disarming little baby stretch suits in pastel harlequin patterns. I fingered their velvety texture. 'Oh, Fergal – they're perfect! And I love the sweatshirt.'

'Good. The box is from my sister Lucia. It's a dress she bought for herself last time she was expecting, and then decided didn't suit her. I thought it would suit *you*. Lucia hopes you don't mind it not being new.'

But I stopped listening then, for folding back the tissue paper revealed a green stretch velvet maternity dress that certainly never came from any British maker. It was sort of Renaissance style, with a low neckline and soft full folds falling from just under the bust. The long sleeves were full, too, and the high waistline elasticised.

'Fergal, it must have cost a fortune! And I'm sure your sister's never worn it once.'

'Don't you like it? I thought you might, somehow.'

'It's wonderful! But—'

'But nothing – unless you're too proud to accept something someone else has worn?'

I clutched it to me. 'Oh, no, I'm not! I just can't believe she didn't want this lovely dress. Will you thank her very much for me?'

I was practically blubbing by now, and wished I had something – anything – to give him in return. Then a brain wave struck me. 'I won't be a minute,' I told him, and went out to the kitchen.

Returning, I thrust the smallest puppy into his surprised arms. 'Happy Christmas, Fergal!'

'It's for me?' he said, trying to avoid a tongue like a yard of wet flannel.

'Yes – it's my favourite, but you can have one of the others if you want to choose your own.'

He regarded his present with a twitching lip: 'No, this one is perfect, thanks.'

'You can't take it yet, though. It's too young. But you can get ready for it, can't you?'

'I think I'll have to!' he said in rather a choked voice. 'Er . . . you don't happen to know who – or what – the father was?'

'Old English sheepdog.'

'That should be an interesting mixture. I'll have to think up a suitable name!'

His green eyes, brimming with amusement, met mine and suddenly I giggled.

'You don't have to have it if you don't want it. I do realise they're hideously ugly and will be enormous! It's just that I love this one, but I think I'll have enough to do with Bess and a baby, and I know you like dogs.'

'I definitely do want it. It's mine! What wonderful presents you give me – first the many-toed cat, now a giant puppy. The parrot isn't pregnant too, by any chance?'

'I sincerely hope not – it's male.'

'Thank goodness for that!'

Rising, he handed me the pup, who whimpered a bit at being parted from his warm chest, which I could empathise with.

'Do you want to have some driving practice tomorrow? I'm not doing anything in the afternoon, and I said I'd show you round the Hall. You can meet Aunt Maria, too.'

'Well, I – I'd like that, thanks,' I found myself saying, hoping I wasn't being a nuisance. And what would Aunt

Maria make of his exceedingly pregnant friend? 'But won't Nerissa mind?'

'Nerissa, I'm glad to say, has gone off in a huff, and is currently trying to make me jealous by flaunting a succession of her conquests around, including your husband.'

'I'm terribly sorry, Fergal!'

He shrugged, seemingly unbothered, then kissed me enthusiastically on both cheeks in a rather foreign (though pleasant) way, wished me a belated Happy New Year, and said he'd be round to pick me up about one.

The minute he was out of the house I rushed upstairs and tried on the sweatshirt (which is fun) and the dress.

The dress is so comfortable I may spend the rest of my life in it. It's also the first garment I've worn for months that actually suits me. The neckline shows off my bosom, of which I have more than usual, and the colour makes my skin look very white.

I put the baby things in my room to wait until the paint smell in the nursery has evaporated, feeling quite light-hearted. Must be the relief at having unburdened myself to someone.

Fergal: January 2000

'This week, I'd like you all to reflect on the subject of family values, in these difficult times . . .'
                                    Nutthill Parish Magazine

I looked across the room to where my aunt was engrossed in *Love Goes West*, with Twinkletoes draped over one shoulder like a vintage fur wrap.

'Maria, you've read a lot of romantic fiction, haven't you? Are these typical?'

She put her forefinger on the page and looked up in some surprise. 'Typical? They are very good! I would like to read them in the Italian, though, if they have been translated. And the heroes, have you noticed Fergal how they are all big and dark and bad, like you?'

'I'm not bad,' I protested. But she was right, there was something horribly familiar about the heroes. 'I've read three of Tish's books now, and the men in them are all complete bastards until something horrible happens to them. Then they see the error of their ways – and the true worth of the heroine – and go all humble and undeserving.'

Maria shrugged. 'It is the usual thing, only your friend, she does it very well. This one in *Love Goes West*, he is mean and arrogant, so he does not deserve the heroine until he has suffered. Yes, he must suffer very much, and change, and then she will have him after all.'

'But why, if he is such a complete bastard? He isn't going to stay humble for long, is he?'

'She loves him. She believes her love will change him, of course.' She looked at me as if I was totally stupid.

'The rake reformed,' I said sardonically, but she'd gone back to her book.

It strikes me that Tish gets a great deal of pleasure from making her heroes suffer!

Chapter 39: Dress Optional

I was wearing the green dress next day when Fergal came to collect me – but I had (very reluctantly) taken it off in the interval!

We whizzed round the park for a bit, with my confidence increasing since there was no other traffic to worry about. Fergal cheered me with tales of Maria's driving. He said she was hell on wheels, and would soon be careering about the countryside in one of the Minis. (He has two, and a Morris Traveller a bit like the vicar's, and some old motor bikes.)

When we went into the house the kitten, now very much larger, came running up to Fergal with its tail held high, mewing, followed by a small, plump, middle-aged lady with coiled black hair and lots of dark eye make-up.

When Fergal had divested me of my coat the dark-ringed eyes scanned me in seeming surprise. 'But you are beautiful! Fergal, you do not tell me that she is beautiful.'

Pink with embarrassment I muttered something about being the size of an elephant.

'She thinks she can't be pregnant and beautiful,' he interpreted. 'But it suits her.'

'You discompose your friend,' Maria pointed out sternly.

'Take her over the house if you must – no, I will not come – but I will have coffee ready in the little room with the big fire. You will need it.'

'The library.'

'Why a library, when there are no books in it? But it is warm.'

'It's going to have books in it, and the whole house is warm since the central heating was sorted out, Maria. Also, I think Tish might prefer something other than coffee.'

'Yes. I'm terribly sorry, but I've gone off it, and I don't drink tea.'

'The hot milk? The English cocoa? I make it well, the English cocoa.'

'Cocoa would be lovely, thanks.'

The house was also lovely – darkish, because there was a lot of glossy wood panelling, but not too big to feel like a home. In one room some paintings had been let into the panelling, and Fergal pointed to one.

'I bought those portraits with the house and look – see her left hand? I only noticed yesterday.'

The painting was of a young, fair-haired girl, elaborately dressed. She was holding a fan half open, and on her finger was my ring.

'It's the same one, isn't it?' He took my hand and compared it.

'But, Fergal, it must be an heirloom.' I would have given it back then and there if his hand wasn't still enclosing mine.

'If it is, then it isn't mine. No, it belongs to you, and it suits you.'

I do love it . . . and since I flogged my wedding and engagement rings and bought with the proceeds a small pair of heart-shaped sapphire earrings to match it, it would be a pity to lose it.

We ended the tour with the new recording studio, built in part of the former ballroom. Then, with a strangely self-conscious air, he threw open a door and I walked past him into an artist's studio with great canvases full of colour everywhere, and the spicy smell of linseed oil and paint.

Astonishment struck me dumb. After all, I hadn't had a proper chance to look at the paintings in the gallery that time, and now here I was, faced with something pretty amazing . . . quite a lot of the pictures featuring images of a red-headed woman.

'It's not been easy, trying to paint when I've been away with the band so much,' he said rather defensively. 'It's not easy getting your work taken seriously when you're famous – or infamous – for something else, either. But it's part of the reason I want to settle down – to paint more.'

I walked round the studio wonderingly. I mean, I knew he could paint, he got a first-class honours degree and an MA in Fine Art before he took to the music highway, but these were very different from the way he used to paint.

Suddenly I thought: why shouldn't they be? He's matured in more ways than one. And then I had the oddest sensation of the old Fergal and the new one overlapping and melding. I blurted without thinking first (as usual), 'Fergal, in Rome – with the nuns. Did you really—'

'No!' he interrupted, scowling blackly.

'Oh. What about that time in Sweden, with the six—'

Noticing that his mouth was closing like a trap, I shut up suddenly. But for the first time I began to believe that the wildness of his lifestyle had been exaggerated, for publicity purposes, if nothing else. Not all of it. I don't think he's been a saint for the last few years – far from it. But he couldn't have been doing *all* those wild and crazy things and still have produced so much brilliant work.

'They're wonderful, absolutely wonderful!' I enthused. 'They look a bit familiar too, especially this one.'

I'd stopped in front of an enormous canvas on which numbers and letters seemed to be leaping and diving like fish across the surface.

'I've been exhibiting under a different name. One of these won the John Moore's competition last year.'

'That's it! It was in the Sunday papers. "Reclusive painter shuns limelight"! Reclusive – you!'

He grinned. 'I only wanted to be taken seriously.'

'You will be. Anyone would have to take you seriously when they see these!'

His eyes met mine, glowing with a bright green light, and he took a step towards me.

There was a faint cry from the house and he started. 'Maria! We've been ages. Come on.'

Taking my hand he towed me briskly back to the library where he sat back and watched, amused, as Maria (as she asked me to call her) pumped me mercilessly about the baby, my pregnancy symptoms, diet and all the rest of it.

Actually, she was very practical and gave me some good advice, though her statement that I was not to worry about the actual birth, because the Good God would not send me any more pain than I could bear, was not *that* reassuring.

When she went out with the tray, Fergal moved next to me on the sofa before the crackling fire.

'Right!' he said, taking my hands in his, 'you told me most

of your worries yesterday, but I can see there's still something bothering you. What is it?'

I don't know how he guessed. 'Well, yes, there is something, but I'm sure you didn't buy a quiet country retreat just to have other people's problems dumped in your lap!'

'You're not "other people", Tish, you should know that.'

I looked doubtfully at him. Surely he must be tiring of my sordid little affairs by now?

'What are friends for, after all, if not to share your troubles with? And don't ever think you're a nuisance. You can't imagine how relaxing it is to be with a woman who isn't struck dumb by wonder and amazement at my very presence.'

He left out lust.

And little did he know I occasionally felt all three and found myself thinking: wow! I'm alone with Fergal Rocco! until he merged back into the familiar, everyday (though no less gorgeous) Fergal.

'Maria didn't seem awed and amazed.'

'She's seen me grow up. But that's what I mean – family, old friends' (that's me, just an old friend) 'see me as I am, not as the dangerous character I'm hyped up to be. Which reminds me,' he added gloomily, 'Hello! magazine want to do a feature on me and my new house.'

'That sounds terribly domestic. But you don't have to do it if you don't want to, do you?'

'I won't. But it means that everyone knows where I've moved to.' He sighed. 'It had to come sooner or later. There were a couple of fans hanging round the gate yesterday.'

'You aren't likely to have hordes of screaming fans besieging you at your gates, are you?'

'Hardly, but there always seemed to be a few hanging round my house in London. Some have been to so many concerts I recognise them. They're all right. It's just the odd ones, who try and get in the house, and the reporters short of a good story . . . I suppose I should be grateful I've *got* fans, or I wouldn't have all this.'

'There is that. And if there weren't any women hanging about drooling over you, you'd probably start worrying in case you'd lost your charms!' I said tartly, and he grinned.

'Drooling!'

'They do. Haven't you ever seen the close-ups of your audiences? But anyway, you can keep the gates locked, can't you? Aren't they electronic?'

'Yes, though I haven't had to use them so far. I'll give you one of the controls – it works on the back gates, too.'

'Thank you!' I said, surprised. 'But I won't want to be barging in disturbing you all the time.'

'Disturb me any time you like,' he said, and smiled. 'I'll need the company when the fans stop drooling!'

I don't suppose they ever will . . . but he's so kind to me. In fact, he seems to be quite fond of me, and I don't know why that thought is depressing!

'We seem to have wandered off the original subject, Tish: what's bothering you?'

'Oh – it's the silliest thing really. Just something Granny keeps hinting about.' And I told him what she'd said . . . or, perhaps, *not* said.

It was amazing how quickly he managed to pick out the salient points. 'It is a bit strange that your conventional mother departed solo on a long holiday to Cornwall and came home with a new baby. But having an unexpected baby might have been enough to make her go all prim and proper when the subject came up, you know.'

'That's what I thought. But I'd just like to know for sure – probably something to do with being pregnant myself. I wrote to my friend Peggy in Cornwall and she promised to dig around, but she hasn't found anything out yet.'

He put a comforting arm round me. 'If there's anything to know, I'll find out.'

I looked up at him, startled. '*You* will?'

'You can't go down to Cornwall at the moment, and that's the place to find out, but I'll send someone down – a professional.'

'A professional – your detective?'

'That's the one!' He grinned unrepentantly.

'Won't it be terribly expensive, though?'

'It's pretty straightforward. I'll organise it, and you can pay me back later. It'll probably cost less than trying to do it yourself, and really, I don't think there's very much in it.'

'I suppose you're right,' I conceded gratefully.

'Then leave it to me. I'll need your birth certificate, but I'll photocopy it and give it back.'

'Yes, of course,' I replied, thinking how easy it would be to become reliant on him, and just how big a mistake that would be. After all, I know now that I can look after myself, financially and otherwise. I don't need anyone else. It's just that he seems to have inserted his dynamic presence into all the little crevices of my life . . .

I looked up, which was a mistake, because he was smiling down into my eyes from inches away, which tended to dislocate my brain functions (such as they are at the moment).

'I'd love to see the pictures of Granny in Russia,' he said unexpectedly, and grinned.

'I'll try and get copies. She's wearing the most enormous fur hat pulled down over her eyes, and Grandpa has one with ear flaps. Do you know what she said to the guard at Lenin's tomb? "I've seen better looking things laid out on marble slabs at the fish shop."'

We were both laughing when there was a sudden commotion in the hall and the door was flung open. Nerissa stood framed in the doorway looking like Playmate of the Month, in a very long open coat over a very short dress.

'How cosy!' she drawled.

I suppose it did all look rather intimate and my first, almost guilty, reaction was to try and snatch my hand from Fergal's. His grip tightened and the arm about my shoulders pulled me closer.

Maria pushed past Nerissa, dark eyes snapping angrily. 'I told her you do not want to see her, you are not to be disturbed, but she goes right past me!'

'It's all right, Maria. Nerissa hasn't been house-trained yet. Strangely enough, I was just saying to Tish that I'll have to start using the security gates or uninvited guests will be barging in all the time.'

Nerissa's cheeks turned a hot red. 'That's not much of a welcome!' Then, with a visible effort, she softened her approach. 'Fergal, honey! You aren't usually this cold. I don't know what's got into you, but you sure must be pining for a little fun!'

She let her coat fall further open, revealing her perfect figure clad, more or less, in clinging white. 'It must be so-o boring for you here – I was going to say alone – but the next best thing, anyway!'

426

'It's neither boring nor lonely since my aunt came to live with me.'

Nerissa stared incredulously at Maria, having obviously discounted her as some sort of foreign help. Then she rallied and dragged in the cavalry, calling, 'James, have you seen? Your dear little wife is here, too!'

His face loomed out of the cool dark tank of the hall like a strange fish and goggled at me over her shoulder.

'*Tish!*' His eyes bulged so much he reminded me of Wendy. 'You're wearing a dress!'

'I'm not a transvestite, James. Why shouldn't I wear a dress?'

'Did you come here just to criticise Tish's taste in clothes, or do you both have some other reason?' enquired Fergal coldly, but James, reddening angrily, only had eyes for me.

'You never wore a dress when *I* wanted you to wear one,' he said pettishly. 'I suppose *he* likes you in a dress. Did he buy it?'

'For goodness' sake, what does it matter?' Nerissa exclaimed furiously. 'Isn't it obvious you've been taken for a ride? Why else should he take so much interest in your wife when she's in that condition if it isn't his? Well, all I can say is: I don't admire your taste, Fergal! Come on, James.'

And out she swept.

It was a pretty good exit. Perhaps she's a *Gone With the Wind* addict, like Granny.

James lingered, seemed about to say something else, but was yanked away by an invisible hand. The door slammed and a minute later a car revved up loudly and shot off in a scattering of gravel.

'That won't have done the drive a lot of good,' Fergal remarked.

'It will rake over,' Maria replied absently. She was eyeing me thoughtfully, almost with a hint of speculation.

'That was your husband, yes?'

'Ex-husband. Well, almost.'

'With Fergal's girlfriend?'

'Ex-girlfriend,' Fergal said helpfully. 'Though not even that, really.'

'Ah!' There was a pause. 'And the baby?' she hinted delicately.

'My husband's,' I said regretfully.

'Nerissa has a poisonous tongue, and your James looked ready to believe every word,' Fergal said.

'Not *my* James,' I said wearily. 'And I suppose he's going to change his mind about the baby again. He's like a revolving door.'

I explained (or tried to explain) to Maria: 'My husband was unfaithful to me for months with a girl – not Nerissa – so I'm divorcing him. Fergal and I are just old friends and we hadn't seen each other for years until recently.'

'The English are all mad,' Maria said sadly. 'Why should your husband stray when he has a young, beautiful wife? That Nerissa, she is a bitch! Your husband is a fool if he lets such a one lead him by the nose.'

'He's still involved with this other girl, too, and I don't suppose Nerissa is seriously interested in him.'

'Just came to flaunt him in front of me,' Fergal agreed. He didn't seem to mind in the least. Plenty more fish in the sea, I suppose.

Maria sighed again. 'I go to cook the dinner. You are staying? I will make a nourishing sauce with the pasta, and—'

'No – no, I can't stay, thank you very much!' I said hastily.

'I must get back and see to my dog, and I have work to do tonight.'

'I hope you are eating well. The sauce, it will freeze. Fergal will bring you some.'

He rose and pulled me to my feet. 'Good idea. Come on then, Tish, if you won't stay, you can drive me back if you aren't too tired?'

I was tired, but drove back anyway. I need the practice.

I haven't told him – or anyone else – that I'm taking the written driving test tomorrow. It's not that one I'm worried about, though!

Fergal has given me a little remote control for the electric gates, and taken my birth certificate away with him.

Next day on my way into town I came face to face with Wendy for the first time. I think she must have been lying in wait for me just inside Margaret's hedge, because she bounced out into my path and stood there like a pugnacious Peke.

'I got him!' she announced triumphantly, subjecting me to the same scrutiny I was giving her, since up till then we had been ships that pass in the night. Or telephones that say nothing in the night.

She made James sound like an infectious disease.

'So you did, Wendy. Nice to see endeavour receive the reward it deserves.'

There was suspicion and a hint of anger in her piggy little blue eyes. 'I suppose you think you can keep a man like Fergal Rocco?' she said spitefully.

'You can't keep anyone if they want to go, Wendy, even if you butter their feet like a straying cat's. But you ought to bear in mind that James's record for faithfulness is pretty dodgy.'

I shifted my bulk from foot to foot and added thoughtfully, 'As Shakespeare said about Desdemona, "She has deceived her father, and may thee." Only of course she didn't, but Iago saw the weakness there. Like all those politicians who drop their trousers at the least temptation – if their wives can't trust them, their constituents certainly can't.'

I warmed to the theme, having never really thought it through before. 'Reminds me of that thing where a man asks a girl if she'll sleep with him for a million pounds, and she can't resist that and agrees. Then he says: "Madam, we've established *what* you are, now let's negotiate a *price*."'

Wendy seemed to have gone into a trance, for her pink rosebud mouth hung open and her eggshell-blue eyes were glazed and vacant. Then without another word she turned and wobbled off on high heels that had worn down to the metal spikes and which tilted her at a drunken angle.

I must point out to Mother that this is how she will end up if she doesn't halt her sartorial decline.

For some reason this encounter put me in a good mood, and I came out of the Test Centre later feeling quietly confident that I'd passed.

Wish I felt the same about the actual driving test.

Fergal: January 2000

'ROCKER BROKE MY HEART
says heiress Nerissa Bright, after finding singer boyfriend, Fergal Rocco, with another woman on eve of announcing their engagement . . .'

                                                                Exposé magazine

Which engagement? I haven't had any kind of engagement (not even a sexual one) with Nerissa for *months*!

I suppose this is all part of her little fantasy . . . and to make her look good with her friends, but at least she didn't take vindictiveness to the point of naming Tish as the Other Woman. Perhaps she knew I'd wring her stupid neck if she did.

The phone's been ringing off the hook, but I've told Maria not to answer it, just let the machine pick up: there's no point in my trying to defend myself in the press at this stage in my life. A dignified silence is the best I can do.

Tish looked like a ripe Renaissance beauty in that green dress, and I so want to paint her like that . . .

Chapter 40: Sold a Pup

Mother's birthday coming round again made me think about her last one, to which I can date the rot setting into my marriage. (Of course, the termites were already nibbling at the foundations, but I didn't realise that at the time.) How unbearably smug I was in my little safe world, with my perfect marriage, dream cottage and reliable, trustworthy, dependable husband!

If James can be so devious, yet Fergal, who looks about as reliable and domesticated as a tiger, turns out to be a staunch and caring friend, how am I ever to judge anyone? But even Fergal's capable of dropping a girlfriend without a qualm, it seems, after giving her the idea he was serious about her. (She couldn't possibly have meant *me* in that article, could she? But if not, did she really find Fergal with another girl?)

I'm much better off building a life alone, and I've written down my Four-Part Plan for Happiness. (Or if happiness is too much to hope for, I'll settle for peace.)

1) Divest myself of James permanently.
2) Find out if there's a secret about my birth, so I can stop worrying about the Incubus.

3) Find a lovely cottage somewhere else – perhaps Cornwall or Devon near Granny or Peggy – which will make it easier to leave this one.
4) Make it clear to Fergal that once I move I don't expect to keep in touch with him.

When I phoned Mother to ask how she wanted to celebrate her birthday, she said rather stiffly that Dr Reevey was taking her out to dinner and a show, but she expected she would see me before too long, and thank you for the Interflora basket.

Considering I'd braced myself to endure a large chunk of her undiluted company I was strangely disconcerted by this rebuff.

I wish something would come of her beau. Perhaps I should ask him if his intentions are honourable.

She said there were some people interested in buying the house, too, so if he doesn't propose soon Granny will have to come clean and set Mother up in a little flat after all.

The key to Mother's huffiness came at the end of our conversation, when she suddenly burst out with, 'I simply couldn't believe it of you, Leticia!'

'Believe what?'

'James told me – he didn't mean to, but he was so upset, the poor boy! I assured him he'd misinterpreted an innocent situation, but I'm afraid you're falling under the influence of that Evil Man again.'

'Evil Man? Do you mean Fergal? Oh, I see! You've had the St James version of finding me all alone – except for the presence of Fergal's Aunt Maria, I suppose, but let's not quibble – in his house at tea time!'

'With his arm around you,' Mother quavered.

'Yes!' I giggled insanely. (Or perhaps I'm the only sane one left?) 'Decadent, isn't it!'

'How can you be so shameless? Could what James said about you and That Man be true?'

'It comes to something when even your own mother would rather believe your philandering husband is innocent, while you are a tart!' (But not the Tart of the First Part.) 'You ought to know me better, and so ought James, if he wasn't so blinded by misplaced jealousy. I suppose he did mention that he was with a girl when he turned up at Fergal's – and not Little Snookums Wendy, either.'

'I don't know what to believe!' she quavered. 'But I can tell you now that James won't have you back. You've burned your boats!'

'Oh, whoopi-doo!'

'There's no need to take that attitude. Worry over this has completely ruined my birthday. And have you seen what That Man has been up to now? Shameless!'

'Mother, stop worrying and imagining things. Go out with your boyfriend and enjoy yourself.'

'Boyfriend! At my age you don't have boyfriends!'

'You aren't fifty yet, and you don't look a day over forty,' I lied valiantly, to perk her up.

'Don't I really? I'm sure you are flattering me, darling! Though Duncan says I'm a giddy little thing.'

'Does he?' I managed to say politely. 'Well, have a lovely time, and don't stay out too late.'

She's easily distracted: from high tragedy to farce in a ten-minute conversation. I only hope her play tonight is half as good.

* * *

Another spin in the Mini with Fergal, but this time I drove round the countryside and we had tea in a pretty little village about fifteen miles away.

I told him I was sure he didn't want to be seen in public with a grossly pregnant woman, but he said I was beautiful and he was proud to be seen with me.

He can't mean it, but it's very thoughtful and kind of him to say it, all the same.

Two customers asked for his autograph just as we were leaving, but no one bothered him until then, which I thought very civilised.

I know I ought to try to distance myself from him, but it's very hard to say no when he just turns up, usually now with food packages from Maria, who seems to make enough of everything for ten people and send me half.

I'm not complaining: my freezer is now full of delicious food, which comes with lightly translated cooking instructions. And he says that if I don't take it she'll make him eat it all, and he'll quickly become twice the man Meat Loaf is.

Later I went down to ask Mrs Deakin if she knew anyone who'd like a puppy, and she said to let her think about it for a day or two, and she wished she could see them.

'Why don't you come tonight when the shop shuts?' I suggested.

'I can't tonight – it's the WI. I'll come tomorrow, though, if you don't mind. I do love a nice puppy!'

I didn't tell her they weren't nice. She'll find that out soon enough.

'Dulcie Blacklock says your driving's coming on a treat,' she remarked with a sly look. 'Must be all that practice in Mr Rocco's funny little car with the checked roof.'

'It does help. It's very kind of him to spare the time when he's so busy up at the Hall.'

'That Italian woman come in, and near made me scrub the carrots before she bought them – said she wasn't paying for mud!' she said admiringly.

I wish *I* had Maria's gall.

'She's coming to the WI with me tonight. The lady she used to Do for told her it was a traditional English ladies' club.'

'I hope she enjoys it.'

'She seems a respectable body,' conceded Mrs D. regretfully: clearly there would be no goings-on up at the Hall with Maria in residence. 'There's your ex going past.'

'James? This is early for him to be back.'

'How's the divorce, dear?'

'Coming along nicely. Isn't it amazing how quickly you can get an uncontested one through?'

The sooner the better now. Can James – or Nerissa – really believe Fergal Rocco is interested in having a fling with me in this condition – or any condition? He could have anybody (and probably has).

I lumbered home with my bit of shopping and had just made a cup of cocoa for Bob, who was lurking in his shed doing God knows what, when the Shack door slammed and James came stamping across to the house.

There are more men lurking in sheds in my garden than in any D.H. Lawrence novel.

I thought he'd carry on round the corner of the house, so he nearly received the contents of Bob's mug in his face when I turned and bumped into him in the doorway. (OK, my stomach bumped into him, but I was right behind it.)

He recoiled, and I could see he was in a vile temper because of his scarlet face and the giveaway twitching vein in his temple.

'Bob!' I called, before he could speak. 'Bob!'

Bob shambled out, accompanied by the two Jack Russells and a strong smell of damp sacking. I handed him the cocoa and half a packet of ginger nuts.

'Everything all right, Bob?'

He paused in blowing the top of his cocoa and stared incuriously at James, who was seething with repressed impatience and temper like a minor volcano.

'Snoddrops,' he said after a minute.

I fended a puppy back from the open door with my foot. 'Snoddrops – I mean, snowdrops – in the garden? Are they out?'

'No,' Bob said.

'You mean, I've got snowdrops, but they haven't got flowers on yet?'

'Snoddrops,' he agreed, and demonstrated the size of his mouth by inserting a whole ginger nut into it and revolving it slowly like some strange lip-plate. Then he poured cocoa on top and chomped it down.

You could hangar an aeroplane in a mouth like that.

Then he smiled with amiable vacuity and wandered back off towards the shed with his cocoa and little dogs.

'Are you mad employing someone like that? He could be a dangerous lunatic!'

'I only know one of those,' I told him coldly. 'You sound just like Mother. Bob's totally harmless and a good gardener. He must have just picked it up from watching his father and grandfather.'

'I don't know why we're talking about Bob. And I don't know how you can look me in the face after the other night! By God, I'm beginning to believe what everyone's been telling me about you!'

'Everyone being Nerissa and Wendy?' I sighed. 'Do you want the whole village to share this, or would you care to come in and harangue me privately? Only I need to sit down.'

He followed me just over the threshold, then halted dramatically and pointed an accusing finger. 'Wendy's pregnant, her father and Uncle Lionel are trying to force me to marry her, and it's all your fault!'

Isn't everything? Why didn't Mother just have me christened Eve and have done with it?

This time I was determined not to burden Fergal with my boring problems. As it was, he drove me to the solicitor's despite my protests. He's so sweet to me already that I keep telling him I feel I'm presuming on his good nature, but he says he hasn't got one.

Just because we once went out with each other doesn't mean he has to feel obliged to look after me now.

We set off, but he could somehow tell that I was seething over something, for after a bit we pulled into a quiet lay-by where, I'm ashamed to say, with minimal persuasion, I described James's visit – and his ultimatum.

'Wendy's pregnant. You know, it must be due about the same time as Margaret Wrekin's. Oh – you don't know the Wrekins, do you?'

'No. Go on, though. So the baby's real?'

'So it seems, and James blames me, because she took the advice I gave her sister seriously! And Alice and Wendy's

438

father is Something Big in the City, and knows James's uncle, who's the head of the firm. So now he knows about the baby they've got together to pressure James into getting the divorce sorted out and marrying Wendy quickly.'

'Shot-gun weddings have always been popular,' Fergal pointed out.

'Yes, but not with the bridegroom! James says this is my fault – first for wanting to divorce him, secondly for telling Wendy to get pregnant, and thirdly and worst, for carrying on with you – sorry, Fergal! – thus making it impossible for him to avoid marriage with Wendy by nobly insisting on not divorcing me, in case I came to my senses and wanted him back.'

'*Your* fault? None of this is your fault!'

'The best is yet to come: he then said he'd contest the divorce unless, on top of the division of property we've already agreed on, I give him ten thousand pounds.'

'The bastard! He's no right to make demands like that.' It was as well James wasn't within reach just then, or he might have had his face rearranged in an unfamiliar pattern.

'I know, Fergal, but I've been thinking about it ever since and I just want to get my divorce and be rid of him, even if I have to pay through the nose to do it. He said he wanted the money as consolation for having to marry Wendy – which bodes well for their future happiness! And her father's going to buy them one of those new detached houses in Lower Nutthill.'

Fergal looked thoughtful. 'My immediate reaction was to go round and break both his legs, but it might just be worth paying him off and getting rid of him.'

'If I can! But I don't have that sort of money to hand, although Granny might loan it to me if I ask her.'

'*I'll l*end you the money.'

My eyes smarted. 'That's so kind of you, Fergal. But I couldn't possibly! I mean, with James already thinking the baby's yours half the time, not to mention the village, I mean, it would look as if . . .'

He shrugged. 'Why should anyone know? I wouldn't tell them. You can pay me interest if it makes you feel better. And you're well into your new novel, aren't you?'

'*The Sweet Wine of Love,*' I said absently. 'Yes.'

'So you needn't feel under any obligation to me – it isn't going to put you into my evil clutches, and I won't try to exercise my droit de seigneur.'

'Really, Fergal! What a thing to say,' I protested primly, and looked down at my bump, which shifted visibly under the scrutiny. Impulsively, I took his hand and placed it on the Incubus, who obligingly gave him a good kick. I laughed at his surprised face.

'Does it do that all the time?'

'No, thank goodness. It's quite painful – but when it stops for too long I worry.'

'I think that kick signified approval for the loan, don't you? So, between the three of us, are we agreed?'

I nodded, and he dropped a chaste kiss on my forehead. 'Sealed with a kiss! But don't worry – that's as droit as my seigneur is going to get!'

I wasn't worrying, but I didn't say so.

The solicitor thought I should fight for every farthing I could screw out of James, but I suppose I'm her client and that's her job.

She soon saw that to me the priority was simply to get

rid of him, a clean divorce, and she thinks the first stage will be through in about six weeks. Then we have to wait for it to be made absolute and that's it.

She's communicating all this to James, and drawing up a new agreement specifying a time limit for moving the Shack and aerial.

Far from distancing myself from Fergal, I now find I'm under an even greater obligation to him, and I wish there was something I could do to repay him. But probably the best thing I can do is remove myself from his orbit after the baby arrives, so he doesn't feel he has to take any more responsibility for me.

Mrs Deakin came round in the evening to see the puppies and, to be honest, with all that going on I'd quite forgotten she was coming. I showed her what I'd done to the house first, and she said it would be very nice when I could afford carpet and wallpaper, despite my assurance that the effect was intentional.

She was absolutely amazed by the puppies. 'Well, I never! And look at the size of them!'

'Yes,' I agreed regretfully. 'They're going to be vast, and I've got to find homes for three of them still. Mr Rocco is having one, and Bob, and Margaret Wrekin is having this one – isn't it sweet? I love the way its eyes cross.'

Mrs Deakin leaned down and tickled one under the chin. 'I might think of someone who would want one,' she said vaguely. 'Half-Bourgeois, half—'

'Durex,' I said irresistibly.

'Oh, yes.'

Bess then astounded me by performing the first intel-ligent action of her life: taking the biggest puppy, the one who made her life a misery by his constant demands for attention (just like a man!) by the scruff, she dragged it across to Mrs D. and deposited it hopefully at her feet, where it chewed thoughtfully on her pinny while lambently eyeing her.

She picked it up, and I knew she was lost when it snuggled its head under her chin and gave a long, blissful sigh.

'After all,' she said, as if trying to convince herself, 'everyone's got a Labrador, but there aren't many half-Bourgeois about!'

'That's very true!' I agreed.

'And it would be nice to have the company of an evening. I can get the food wholesale.'

'That's an advantage.'

'And I've still got old Bozo's lead and basket.'

'Even better. But are you sure you've got time for such a big dog? And it *is* going to be big.'

'That Bob – I've seen him walking Bess sometimes. Well, he can walk mine, too, if I'm busy. I don't suppose he'll mind.'

Bob could make quite a good thing out of this!

Mrs D. is going to try to think who might take the other two. I hope she doesn't change her mind about hers.

Margaret kindly ran me to my next antenatal visit.

All the doctor did was take my blood pressure, laugh, and say that if I got any bigger I would have to have the door taken out when I went to hospital.

Margaret said I looked OK to her, and then we had a mooch around some antique shops and a pub lunch before she dropped me back home, which made a nice change.

When I got back I found my driving test date on the mat: 4 February at nine thirty.

It was just as well the letter came after I got back from my appointment or my blood pressure would've been skyhigh. Fergal said to look on the first test as a practice run, but he doesn't have the pressing sense of urgency I do. He phoned because his private eye is coming to the Hall tomorrow to report. Fergal doesn't hang about when he decides to do something!

I wonder what – if anything – the detective has found out? Probably just that Mother is Mother, and the pregnancy has unhinged me.

What with that and the test to look forward to, I'm a jangle of nerves.

The detective, a small innocuous-looking man, was called Mr Rooney (but not another Mickey – I asked). He didn't look at all familiar to me – I'm surprised James spotted him. 'Shall I go or stay?' enquired Fergal.

'Stay, of course!' I said immediately. 'You know all about it, and if Mr Rooney has found anything out I want you to hear it too.'

I looked nervously at the detective. '*Have* you found anything out?'

'Well, I'm satisfied that I've got to the bottom of the matter, yes, but you must understand that after such a length of time it was impossible to find any hard evidence.'

'If you're satisfied you know what happened, that's good enough,' Fergal said, taking my hand in a warm, hard grip. 'Go on.'

'It seems that Mrs Norwood went down to Cornwall

because her sister was staying there in a rented cottage, in the last stages of pregnancy.'

'Glenda!' I exclaimed. 'Mother never mentions her because she ran off with someone when she was sixteen, or at least that's why I thought she never mentioned her. Do you mean,' I added slowly as it sank in, 'that Glenda was my real mother?'

I didn't, strangely enough, feel that shocked; after Granny's hints it all seemed to fall into place.

Mr Rooney nodded. 'Yes, it seems pretty certain, although what confuses things is that *your* parents' names appear on your birth certificate.'

'But I don't understand.'

'Glenda called herself Mrs Norwood when she went into the cottage hospital to have you, and I think she was already planning to leave you with her sister when she did so, though whether with her knowledge and agreement or not is unclear. Mrs Norwood may have responded to a call for help, and then been left, literally, holding the baby.'

'Me!'

'Yes. Glenda seems to have left suddenly within a week of your birth, and Mr Norwood arrived almost immediately to take his wife and yourself home. Even after this length of time, some of the local inhabitants remember the goings-on as being a little out of the ordinary.'

I should think they might! I sat back, and found Fergal looking anxiously at me.

'I hope this hasn't been too much of a shock, Tish?'

'No,' I said a little shakily. 'It's a lot better than some of the things that occurred to me since Granny sowed the seeds of doubt in my mind, I can tell you. You know, I even had visions of Mother snatching some stranger's baby! At least

444

this keeps it in the family.' A doubt struck me. 'Except for the father, I suppose. I don't know who he was. And I don't know where Glenda is, either.'

'Shall I make a few more enquiries and see if I can find out what happened to her?'

'Would you like that, Tish?' asked Fergal.

'Oh, yes, please. I don't suppose Mother will tell me if she knows, though surely, whatever happened, Glenda would want to know what happened to her baby. How could she just dump me on her sister and vanish like that?'

'She was very young,' pointed out Mr Rooney. 'And she perhaps thought it would be better for you to grow up as her sister's child.'

'Perhaps,' I said, but still, I can't imagine just handing the Incubus to someone else when it's born and walking away.

The frustrating thing is that Mother could tell me All but I'm sure when I try to get the details from her she'll hysterically deny everything.

The effort is beyond me at the moment; I feel a great inertia creeping over me like a marshmallow avalanche.

Fergal: January 2000

Exclusive interview with Goneril's manager:
Final tour not to be their last, after all . . .

Hywel at it again, but his tactics aren't going to work any more than Nerissa's ever did, because no amount of saying something to the press will make it true.

I'll be glad when Tish has finally divorced James and more

than happy to help her achieve that, now I know what kind of man he is. That might sound strange coming from me, but he never deserved her. I don't think *I* deserve her either, but if it wasn't for Lucia's advice to take things slowly . . .

Chapter 41: Green-Eyed Men

Mrs Blacklock came in to see the puppies before my lesson. She didn't want one, she just couldn't believe Mrs Deakin's description of them.

She emerged ten minutes later covered in dog hair and drool, the bewildered future owner of one of the last two puppies, which just leaves the one with the enormous ears and permanent worried expression.

Next week I'm having driving lessons every afternoon, and what with all the practice I'm getting with Fergal I should be ready for the test (or as ready as I'll ever be) .

My solicitor phoned in the afternoon to say the cheque (from Fergal!) has been duly handed over to James, and the agreement signed: the divorce is proceeding.

Just as I put the phone down on that glad news a van drew up and disgorged a mountain of the baby equipment I'd bought through Margaret.

There was an amazing amount of it – it filled the hall and spilled over into the front garden. Boxes and boxes, plus odd items of furniture. Surely one little baby doesn't need so much? Mrs Peach's curtains were twitching like mad!

I was still dazedly surveying the piles of stuff when a large unfamiliar car drew up and Fergal got out, followed by a younger, less angular version of himself – his brother Carlo.

Carlo waded through the boxes and kissed me with enthusiasm on both cheeks and the mouth.

'Tish! You look wonderful!'

He'd started in to kiss me all over again when Fergal's icy voice just behind us snapped, 'Put her down, Carlo!'

'Hands off?' Carlo enquired with a grin, and set me back on my feet (breathless).

Fergal ignored this, and turned the glacial stare on me. 'You shouldn't be standing about in this cold wind! And what *is* all this stuff?'

'Baby equipment. I bought it from a friend of a friend, but I wasn't expecting quite so much!'

'Looks like we got here at just the right time,' Carlo said. 'We came to ask you to dinner – Maria said we weren't to take no for an answer.'

'That's very kind, but I'll be pretty busy today, trying to find somewhere to put everything . . .' I said helplessly.

'It'll look much less when it's unpacked,' Fergal assured me. 'We'll take it upstairs and do that.'

I was so glad to see he was coming out of the bad mood he'd arrived in that I didn't argue when he wouldn't let me carry even one little box.

He was right about it seeming less unpacked, too – but not that much. There was a cot, high chair, baby bath, bedding, clothes . . . and what would fans of Goneril think if they could see their idols now, assembling a cot like a giant three-dimensional jigsaw puzzle?

I stowed things away in the little wardrobe unit and the drawers of the baby-changing table, which was a pale mint green, like most of the rest of the equipment. It goes well with the stencilled trees, and I thought I'd get a rug and some curtains in a colour scheme that will draw it all together.

Carlo and Fergal flattened the empty cartons and took them outside, so by the time they'd finished I'd practically got a complete nursery – and a nasty surprise for the refuse collectors.

All it needed now was a baby. A shiver went down my spine. Wasn't it tempting fate, or bad fairies, or something, to have everything waiting? But you can't leave it until the baby actually arrives!

'I could do with more drawers, and perhaps a wardrobe,' I mused. 'I saw one in a magazine like a little striped beach tent.'

'You have the basics so you can afford one or two extras,' Fergal agreed, setting the wicker bassinet on to its stand while Carlo suspended a musical mobile above the cot.

'Did you really only give a hundred pounds for all this?' he added.

'Yes – she must be so rich she doesn't care! I like all this pale green, don't you? But I could get tired of shell-pink baby clothes.'

'So will the baby if it's a boy,' Carlo pointed out, lying on the floor to see the effects of the mobile from underneath with the lights and music working. 'This is fun!'

'You'd better have a little chat with Sara, then,' Fergal suggested. 'He's getting married,' he explained to me.

'Congratulations, Carlo!'

Carlo rose to his feet, smiling. 'Thank you. I'd let you kiss me, but I'm afraid of Fergal!'

'Fool!' his brother said amiably, his earlier bad mood

seeming to have worn off completely. 'But have you thought of the damage domestic bliss will do to your image? The fans will desert you in droves.'

'Me!' exclaimed Carlo. 'What about—'

A look from Fergal silenced him, so I'll never know what indiscretions he was about to give away.

The room was transformed, and Carlo was right – it had been fun. But it was getting late, so I gave them a drink out of my modest cache (Guinness, cooking sherry, or Guinness) and left them phoning Maria while I went to change.

I put on The Dress and brushed the Barrett Browning ringlets into loose waves, and by the time I got back downstairs Carlo was nursing the last unclaimed puppy on his knee with a familiar bemused expression on his handsome face.

'But how on earth will you exercise the thing in London, Carlo?' Fergal was objecting practically.

'I live opposite the park, and anyway, we're going to buy a country cottage.'

'You'll need two – one for the dog!'

The puppy had really taken to Carlo and didn't want to let him go. I had to promise he could take it back with him tomorrow – it *is* almost eight weeks old – and we rescued one of the bigger cartons to transport it in.

Carlo flirted with me so outrageously at dinner that even Fergal had to laugh, and Maria said he should be ashamed of himself, and what would his fiancée say?

She fussed over me so much that on the way home I asked Fergal if she really thought it *was* his baby after all.

'Of course.'

'I'm terribly sorry, Fergal!'

'What for? I'm beginning to feel as if it's mine, too!'

He was only joking, but it's true he's done more for the baby than James has.

Early next morning Carlo called in on his way back to town to collect the puppy, and as we padded out the carton with crumpled paper and an old towel he stunned me by remarking, 'I'm really glad you and Fergal have got back together again, Tish.'

I sat back on my heels and stared at him. 'Carlo, we aren't – we haven't – got back together like that! We're just friends, and he's been so good to me, even though I must have been a nuisance with all my boring problems and the pregnancy and everything. I even caused a quarrel between him and that girl Nerissa he was seeing.'

'Nerissa?' he dismissed her with a shrug. 'She's nothing – a smokescreen for the gossip columns, if that. And I don't think he's bored. Remember how he snapped my head off just for kissing you yesterday?'

I went scarlet. 'Don't be silly, Carlo! He was just in a temper about something. He couldn't possibly think about me that way – especially now!'

'He loves children, and you know that he wouldn't let the baby not being his make any difference to him.'

'No, not if he did feel like that about me . . . but he doesn't! You've got it wrong.'

Carlo looked unconvinced. 'It'll be interesting to see if his lyrics cheer up, now.'

'What on earth do you mean?'

'You must have realised that a lot of his songs are about you?' He sang a few lines of 'Red-Headed Woman' in a voice nearly as husky as Fergal's.

'No, of course not – I don't believe you! Besides,' I added tartly, 'I haven't got red hair.'

'You haven't listened to the words very closely then.'

'I haven't listened at all if I could help it – it was too painful to hear his voice after we split up.'

'I'll send you some CDs down – you listen to them!'

'But even if you're right about that – which I'm sure you can't be – you're quite, quite wrong about his having any feelings for me now except friendship and – and pity.'

'You're impossible!' he said, but he smiled. 'Come on, let's get this monster loaded into the car.'

We jammed the box in front of the passenger seat where the puppy could see Carlo. It couldn't get out, because the sides were too high – just.

He would be all right as long as it didn't grow on the way there.

I gave him some puppy food, and then Bess and I stood side by side and saw them off. She wagged her tail as the car vanished from sight.

After he'd gone I found it hard to settle to anything. How on earth could Carlo make such a mistake?

And perhaps some of his earlier lyrics *were* about me, which is rather touching, but then – most of the heroes in my books are black-haired, green-eyed men!

It would be strange to think we'd been each other's muses throughout the years we were apart.

* * *

452

Fergal: February 2000

'*THE FROCK THAT'S OUT TO SHOCK*
Ex-girlfriend of Fergal Rocco reveals almost all
at the party of the season.'

Exposé magazine

Pop isn't going to like that one, but at least he can't blame my bad influence this time.

In any case, I hope I've always known the difference between the outrageous and the vulgar.

But at least if she is calling herself my ex-girlfriend, she must surely have given up on me.

Carlo came down for a flying visit – I knew he'd guessed what was going on, from one or two things I'd said over Christmas, and was worried about me. And then, stupidly, I felt so jealous when he kissed Tish!

We had a good evening, though, and when I'd taken Tish home again Carlo said he could see how things were with me and he wished me luck. I think I'll need it . . .

I don't know what his fiancée is going to think of that puppy!

Chapter 42: Mirror, Signal, Manoeuvre

Bob was hovering around the garden at the crack of dawn to collect his puppy on the day they were eight weeks old, but I was prepared for him this time. He'd been getting steadily more excited all week.

His face was blissful, and I was deeply touched when he stood up holding his puppy and assured Bess that he would 'look after 'un proper!' (Not that she cared.)

Then he vanished with it, and was seen no more for the rest of the day.

Margaret came for hers with a smart, purpose-made cardboard container and stayed for a long chat. I showed her the nursery and she admired the colour scheme, and had a few helpful ideas about what else I needed. Then she asked me if I would help her choose the colour scheme of her nursery later.

'Wendy's moved in with James permanently now, so I got Ray to ask him to leave as soon as possible. She wouldn't look so smug if she knew how often James has been seen about with that Nerissa.'

'What one earth does Nerissa see in him?' I exclaimed.

'Well, he's rather attractive,' Margaret mused, to my amazement. 'You must have thought so yourself at one time.'

'I suppose so. And his being older than me didn't seem to matter at first. But Nerissa is very young. He could almost be her father – or Wendy's!'

I could see there was something else she was concealing, and after a bit of pumping she told me that the entire village was now watching me and Fergal with the sort of acute interest normally only accorded to the TV soaps. They're practically taking bets on the father of the Incubus since James aired his doubts in the pub one night while under the influence, the creep.

'Just because Fergal is sorry for me, and helping me for old times' sake, it doesn't make him the father of my child. He's a good friend and nothing more.' (Unfortunately.)

'Is he?' she said doubtfully. 'It's just that you hear such terrible stories about him – though he could have reformed, couldn't he?'

'You can't believe everything you see in the press!'

'No . . . I suppose not. Did he really – you know – that time in Rome, with the six nuns and—'

'No!' I said shortly.

'Oh?' she sounded disappointed.

We got on to the subject of driving tests, and she said to immediately put in for a re-test if I failed first time, because she passed on her fifth, having worn them down by persistence. Then she staggered off down the drive, listing to starboard, with the puppy in its carrier.

Later, Mrs Deakin and Dulcie Blacklock came together to collect their puppies: mutual support, I suppose. Suddenly the kitchen looked quite empty.

Bess kept staring at the last puppy as if hoping *it* would vanish, too.

Fergal came to dinner, and I did wholewheat pasta with a seafood sauce from the freezer, care of Maria, which must have made it home from home except for the pasta being darker.

After Carlo's remarks I felt a bit shy at first even though I know he's got it wrong, but the feeling soon wore off. Afterwards Fergal washed up while I put my feet up (under protest – I'd hardly been slaving over a hot stove for hours). Then he asked if he could do some drawings of me and we sat there peacefully for an hour or so, exchanging the odd word. It was very comfortable . . . companionable, even.

Later I distracted Bess with a biscuit while Fergal removed the last puppy.

I needn't have bothered, really, because Bess thought it was a fair exchange, and didn't even look for it when I let her out again.

Tomorrow I'm going to give that corner by the Aga a jolly good clean-out.

After I'd finished disinfecting the kitchen I phoned Mother on impulse and told her I'd discovered that her sister, Glenda, was my real mother. I thought the initial approach might be easier by phone.

There was a small, stunned silence, and then she quavered, 'Don't be silly, darling. Of course I'm your real mummy!'

'But, Mother—'

'It's so upsetting when you say this sort of thing, Leticia, and I don't want to hear any more about it,' she said repressively.

'Mother, I don't want to upset you, but I need to know. Couldn't we just talk about it?'

456

'I absolutely refuse to discuss the topic further!' she said, hysteria in her voice.

I sighed. 'All right – but do you know where Glenda's living now? It would be nice to get in touch with my only aunt.' (My giddy aunt? My mad mother?)

'No. We washed our hands of her. She was never any good. It broke Father's heart when she ran away like that, and drove him to an early death.'

'I always thought he was an alcoholic, and that was why you—'

'Broken heart!' she screeched, and began to sob gustily. 'If you loved me you wouldn't go upsetting me by raking all this up now!'

I had a feeling she did know where Glenda was, but wasn't going to tell me. I spent some time soothing her down.

I expect Mr Rooney will find Glenda.

I've had a solid week of driving lessons and am too shattered to think straight! Fergal has taken me out driving practically every morning, too.

The only diversion has been the reports coming in from the Devil Puppy Owners' Club suggesting they're literally eating their new homes, so I was interested in hearing that Margaret's vet had advised her to buy a sort of giant cage in which to incarcerate the little horror when necessary. Apparently this helps with house-training too, since you line it with white fleece, and they don't soil their bedding.

I immediately spread the news of this discovery to the other owners. Fergal said Carlo's fiancée would be eternally grateful, and Maria had insisted he go out and purchase one of these things immediately.

On the day of the test I woke with the words Mirror, Signal, Manoeuvre on my lips (and Bess, blissfully puppyless, on the bed beside me).

Mrs Blacklock gave me a quick pep talk, then left me in the clutches of a short, bearded, morose man with a clipboard. He remained steadfastly monosyllabic all the way through, which had the unfortunate effect of making me babble like an idiot.

At one point a squirrel ran across the road and I said idiotically, 'Oh, look! Isn't it sweet? Do you think that's a lucky omen?' But he just scowled down at his clipboard and scribbled something. Probably, 'This woman is a moron.'

But as far as I could see I hadn't done anything wrong at all, even the three-point turn and the hill start went perfectly, and I didn't go over the kerb when I reversed.

So I felt quite confident at the end, my spirits rising as he put the lid back on the pen. It was quite a shock when he calmly said, 'I'm afraid you haven't reached test standard yet, Mrs Drew.'

'Ms,' I corrected automatically, but most of the rest of what he was saying was lost in the despair. If I failed when I did everything right, how was I ever to pass?

Mrs Blacklock slid in beside me after he'd gone and handed me a tissue. Apparently he's a misogynistic martinet.

He should be put against a wall, hung with nuts, and have squirrels fired at him.

The official reasons for my failure are that I went too slowly and over-cautiously at junctions, and also too fast and incautiously at junctions. And I didn't use the mirror enough.

'But I did!' I wailed.

'Then you must turn your head more.' She demonstrated, looking as if she was watching tennis. Then she made me post off my next test application on the way home.

'But I'll never get one before the baby arrives!'

'You often get cancellations at short notice and the baby's not due till April, is it? You'll make it – I always get my drivers through. The longest they've had to wait is the third test, and she was so nervous she needed Valium before the driving lessons.'

This cheered me a bit.

Margaret phoned to see what happened, commiserated, then told me by way of distraction that James is pleading to be allowed to stay in the flat until he and Wendy can move into the new house that Wendy's father is buying.

'So it looks like he's being forced into the marriage, doesn't it? But he's staying out more and more, and we can hear them arguing at night. Do you know, Wendy looks very pregnant already, and fed up.'

'Perhaps she's the type who bloats out immediately.'

'Perhaps. Her sister, Alice, and that Howard came round the other day. Aren't they peculiar? Howard is creepy!'

'Never mind, you'll never have to see them again once James is out of your flat.'

'The sooner the better, really. I want to get it knocked through and converted into a nursery.'

The second I'd put the phone down after that conversation it rang again, with Fergal this time.

He said I'm a good driver and will pass next time, but I could only just hear him over the strange background noise, which he said was the puppy trying to play with the kitten, who was a bit reluctant. Maria thought the puppy was adorable, but needed feeding up, so it was probably shortly going to be spherical, with cosmopolitan food tastes.

I've resumed my weekly driving lessons, and twice now I've been up to the Hall and driven the Mini all over the estate on my own. This is quite legal as long as I don't leave Fergal's land.

There isn't much temptation to go anywhere else – wherever I go I seem to see enormously pregnant women. Where have they all come from? Are we all going to pop our pods at once like in some sci-fi film?

There's less than two months to go now (if the Incubus arrives on time), and I've had enough of it. To add to my happiness the hospital have sent for me again, so I suppose I may as well accept their pressing invitation to attend an antenatal class afterwards with a tour of the labour ward thrown in.

Maria drove me to the hospital, and she does drive like a maniac – Fergal was right. When she illustrates what she's saying with her hands, which is often, she strays across to the other side of the road.

Fergal has gone to London to make a video promoting the single from the new album, *Out of the Dark*. I wonder if he'll be drawn back by the bright lights. It must seem awfully tame here after all that globe-trotting, though he says it isn't.

Maria left me at the hospital and went shopping, promising to return in a couple of hours.

I was poked, prodded and tested, and it was all horrible, but everything was going well.

Then I was directed across to the hut where the antenatal classes take place and found it full of grossly pregnant teenagers lying about on rubber mats like so many beached whales.

I felt huge, awkward and old.

The small whiskered Scot in charge informed me severely that I was very late for the classes, and should have been attending them for weeks, but I told her I'd only come for the tour of the labour ward.

However, she insisted on me joining in first, and I had to lie down, do funny exercises and breathe (though I do that all the time), which would help with the Pain.

How can breathing help with pain? And if it does, why aren't we taught it at school so we don't need aspirin for headaches?

After this she passed round a rubber mask for us all to try. It smelled of dentists. You get gas and air from it, which also helps with the Pain.

There was too much mention of the Pain and I was glad I hadn't been to any of the other classes, especially the one where they show a film of an actual birth.

Finally we got a brisk tour of a very antiseptic ward full of new mothers with babies in fish tanks by each bed, and a peep into an unoccupied, sterile and very hot labour room, which gave me the shivers.

Afterwards the class instructor said severely that she expected to see me the following week.

Dream on.

I'm not going near that hospital again now until the birth.

Maria, who was sitting in the car reading a magazine, said I should have the baby at home and she would help me, but

461

I think I've left it a bit late for that, and what if something went wrong?

I wonder if Fergal and Maria would look after Toby and Bess while I'm in hospital.

If Fergal comes back . . .

Fergal: February 2000

'It's new! It's wicked! The new single from Goneril – and the video you've all been waiting for – on screen now!'
                                          Top of the Pops

Surrounded with beautiful, half-naked women (and a lot of dry ice to cover our modesty, though none of us were as near-naked as we looked), all I wanted to do was escape back to Nutthill.

Not that I've any objection to being surrounded by pretty girls, and nor have the rest of the band, though Carlo went all self-conscious because Sara came to keep an eye on him.

I didn't need anyone to keep an eye on me, because all the time I was staring at the camera I was imagining Tish watching me, wearing her best militant disapproving angel expression.

Chapter 43: Out of the Dark

Fergal called in on his way home from London and said it was twice as dirty and tedious as it ever was, and he resented every minute he spent away from Greatness. The only good thing was that he'd found a buyer for his London house.

He went to a party with Carlo and Sara where he saw Nerissa, with James in tow! I suppose he's simply filling in an idle moment for her – these are certainly not the sort of circles he usually moves in. Fergal said Nerissa pointedly ignored him, though he didn't seem bothered by it at all.

Perhaps he met someone else there; probably hordes of sophisticated, beautiful, thin young girls positively threw themselves at him, though he didn't mention them.

He left the CDs Carlo promised me, and I've listened to them all. I think some of the lyrics are beautiful but sad – and some are just plain angry! Perhaps a few of the early ones may be about me, but I'm sure the later ones aren't, because I wouldn't have stuck in his memory that long.

Fergal's current album is called *Out of the Dark*, and he said I wouldn't like the promotional video because he's surrounded by about sixty ash-blonde girls.

I don't know why he thinks that.

'Just bear in mind,' he said gravely, 'that I only look as if I've got no clothes on.'

I'm not sure if he was joking or not.

Since he came back Maria reports that he spends hours in the studio painting, and leaves coloured tacky fingerprints on the doors. But that's better, she says, than having wild parties with drugs and Goings-On. She often pops down for a little chat in the afternoons, and so does Margaret, and since they first met they've got on well together.

Toby, who's been eavesdropping on our conversations, suddenly startled me one day by exclaiming, '*Mamma mia!*' He's done it several times since, but it's preferable to several of his other utterances.

On my last lesson with Mrs Blacklock she said she was just putting the final gloss on my driving technique, and then described how her puppy ate her bright green and magenta mittens (sounds like they were of Mrs Deakin's making) and then spent ten embarrassing minutes getting rid of them in the vet's waiting room.

It hurts me to laugh like that.

Fergal was right – I don't like the promotional video for his new album, and it's just all plain old jealousy.

Dark, gorgeous, and apparently naked, he's rising up from a positive sea of writhing (and also near-nude) ash-blonde girls, with his hands resting on the pommel of a strategically placed sword. Around the edge reclined the rest of the band, similarly devoid of clothing, like so many satiated Roman Emperors. They didn't have swords, but the camera angles were artful and there were clouds of dry ice.

Carlo looked pretty good, actually . . .

All done in the best possible taste.

Wonder if any of these thin, young blondes were at the party where Fergal saw James.

My birthday – and I almost forgot. Thirty-one seems ancient, though it did make me reflect on how very young Glenda was when she had me – and Mother, when she assumed the role (whether voluntarily or not).

She phoned to wish me Happy Birthday, sounding preoccupied: perhaps her boyfriend is showing signs of making an honest woman of her at last? I wish he would, then I wouldn't have to worry about her so much.

I thanked her for her present – a book called *Beautiful Thoughts for Mothers-To-Be* – though, actually, morning sickness would have been preferable.

My back aches, my legs ache, and I have perpetual heartburn. Apart from that, I'm fine.

Granny sent me the most wonderful old-rose-coloured velvet house-gown, the entire works of Beatrix Potter in a tiny wooden bookcase, and a small, multicoloured pot like a mad sea urchin from Rose Durwin (who *is* potting, not potty – such a relief).

Her letter ignored my last one in which I told her what I'd discovered from Mr Rooney, except for a brief postscript: 'I knew there was something! Typical! Love, Granny.'

I thought that was it for the birthday revels, though as it happened Fergal has invited me to dinner and to keep him company tonight, while Maria's at the WI. The first words he spoke when he picked me up were, 'Happy Birthday!'

So I was glad I'd put on The Dress and taken the trouble

to make myself look nice (or as nice as possible under the circumstances). I don't know how he remembered.

We ate by candlelight in the library (which now has bookshelves and some books) and afterwards he brought in a birthday cake Maria had made, shaped like a book with the title iced on the cover: *Love Goes West*.

'It's lovely, Fergal! Maria is so clever – and kind. But I wonder why she chose that book?'

'I chose it. It was the first one I read, and when I realised the hero was me, I knew you'd never quite got me out of your system.'

He was standing right next to me and I looked indignantly up at him. 'Fergal Rocco! Just because the hero is dark and—'

'I especially like the bit where the hero suddenly pulls the heroine into his arms.' He suited the action to the words. 'Snarls: "You're mine – don't you know that!" and kisses her . . . like this.'

As soon as his lips touched mine it was like stepping into a time warp: my eyes closed, my arms went round him, and all sorts of feelings I didn't think pregnant women had any more surged about.

When he finally lifted his head I tried to pull away, embarrassed by my reaction, but he didn't release me, just looked down at me with one of his more unnerving smiles.

'Will you marry me?' he said huskily.

'What?'

For a minute my mind reeled; then, soberingly, came the realisation that my all-too-eager response to his kiss had made him think I was taking it seriously, and he was trying not to hurt my feelings.

'Don't be silly, Fergal!' I scolded shakily. 'You shouldn't

joke about things like that – what if I thought you meant it?'

'I'm not joking. I didn't mean to say it, but—'

'Of course you are! You can't possibly be in love with me – especially when I'm in this condition!'

'Can't I?'

'No! And anyway,' I added irrelevantly, 'I'm still married.'

'Not for much longer.'

'No, and I'm really looking forward to being single again!' I assured him brightly, just in case he had any lingering doubts. 'I do value our friendship, though. You know that, don't you, Fergal?'

'What are you upset about, then?' he said softly.

I brushed my eyes with the back of my hand and wished he'd release me: close proximity was numbing my thought processes. (Nothing else, just the thought processes.)

'I'm not upset: it's j-just that you have b-been so kind and thoughtful. But you really don't have to worry about me, or feel responsible.'

'I do feel responsible – I want to look after you.' His beautiful mouth curved into the sort of smile that would melt a Gorgon. It certainly liquefied me.

Then his eyes narrowed and his arms tightened round me: 'I'd like—'

The front door slammed and the brisk clatter of Maria's high heels sounded on the hall floor.

'Damn!' he said, and let me go. I sank rather limply back into the nearest chair.

Now I'll never know what he'd like! Still, it's unlikely to be the same thing as I would. I'm quite ashamed of myself.

It's as well Maria came in just then. If she noticed anything amiss she was too polite to show it, and when Fergal said he'd take me home she pressed me to take a piece of the birthday cake with me.

My bit of icing said 'GOES', which was appropriate.

Fergal was very quiet on the short drive, probably from sheer relief that I hadn't taken him up on his impulsive offer, but when he'd helped me out of the car he handed me a small package.

'Just a little something from an old friend,' he said rather ironically. 'Happy Birthday, Angel!' and he kissed me quickly before I could thank him for the present – or the evening. (Or the kiss, come to that, which I could still be wearing indelibly imprinted on my lips tomorrow, like a stigma.)

I'm now the owner of a pair of Renaissance-style earrings to match my dress, with baroque pearls and green stones that look suspiciously like emeralds.

They also look extremely expensive, but it would take a braver woman than me to toss Fergal Rocco's presents back in his face.

After an almost sleepless night I got up vowing to put the events of the previous evening out of my head. My hormones are obviously in a state of turmoil at the moment. All right, I admit it – they've been in a state of turmoil ever since Fergal re-entered my orbit. I still have strong feelings for him, and I expect I always will, but that doesn't mean I can't live a perfectly happy and fulfilled life on my own . . . does it?

Anyway, I've got my new driving test date to distract me: 2 March. I hope I can fit behind the steering wheel.

I was still sitting about after reading this (why does

pregnancy affect your mind? I feel as if I've been hit on the head by a brick half the time!) when my soon-to-be ex-spouse called and abruptly informed me that his father was on the way over from South Africa on a business trip.

'I'm sure that's absolutely riveting, James, but what's it got to do with me?'

'He doesn't know we've split up.'

'Tell him, then! He's your father, after all. And you can also inform him about your impending second marriage to dear Wendy.'

'That's just it – I can't tell him. He's set off, and I don't know where to get hold of him. All I know is, he's arriving on the second.'

'Arriving where?' I asked with a sense of foreboding.

'The cottage,' he said sulkily.

'That's all I need! If he does arrive he'll find himself sitting on the doorstep, because I've a driving test that day.'

'Can't you postpone it?'

'No, I can't postpone it! If you've been stupid enough not to tell him you can hang around in your Shack all day and head him off. And you'd better check with Margaret that it's all right for him to stay in the flat while he's here.'

'I'm too busy to spend the day hanging around waiting!' he said indignantly.

'So am I – and he's not *my* father!'

'Perhaps your Fancy Man can wait in for him, then,' he said nastily. 'He seems to come and go as he pleases now.'

Honestly – Fancy Man! I got the sudden giggles, making things worse.

After a bit more of this sort of unproductive exchange he said he'd ring his stepmother and try to get an address for

469

his father en route so he could redirect him. This is not my problem, and I'm certainly not putting his father up.

Mr Rooney is now in Canada in pursuit of Glenda, Fergal says! I was amazed, and also afraid his bill would be huge until Fergal said he hadn't just gone over on my business, he was doing something for him too, and we'd sort it out later.

Still, now Lovecall has started releasing my previous novels in America I should be all right (so long as they sell)! And Vivyan has just read *The Sweet Wine of Love* and adores it.

I've been brightly cheerful with Fergal since my birthday so he knows I didn't take him seriously. He's looking a bit brooding. I hope he isn't getting bored with country life. Or with me and my tedious problems.

Fergal: March 2000

> '*ROCKER IN LOVE TANGLE SCANDAL!*
> *Lead singer of Goneril, Fergal Rocco, broke engagement*
> *for pregnant ex-girlfriend, Mrs Leticia Drew, better known*
> *as romantic novelist Marian Plentifold.*
> *Heartbroken heiress Nerissa Bright reveals all.*'
>
> *Sun*

I wouldn't have seen this if the *Sun* hadn't been pushed through my door instead of that of the lodge . . .

That girl's got more imagination than I gave her credit for, but I'd still like to wring her stupid neck – the next thing, reporters are going to be turning up in droves, bothering Tish, and that's the last thing she needs at a time like this.

470

It's her driving test today, too . . .

I'll warn her about the article later, when that's over – I don't suppose she reads the *Sun*, so it should be safe enough till then.

It's ironic that I only want to protect her, yet everything I do seems to make her life more difficult!

Chapter 44: Aftershock

March the second, day of the second driving test, dawned bright and clear. I had a driving lesson first, and felt much calmer than last time. The fact that I'd received a letter a few days before informing me I'd passed the written segment of the test had helped my confidence. I was determined that even if a white rhino crossed the road in front of me I would just Mirror, Signal and Manoeuvre round it.

It did unnerve me a bit that it was the same examiner, but he looked petrified when I squeezed my enormous bulk behind the steering wheel. I expect he was afraid I would give birth in the driver's seat just out of spite if he failed me.

I did everything in grim and concentrated silence, and at the end he just flatly told me I'd passed and hopped hastily out.

I could hardly take it in!

Now all I need is a car I can fit a baby and a Borzoi into.

Once I'd recovered from the shock of passing I began to notice I was having niggly little pains and backache – probably from the tension. The backache's not new, but the pains were.

My first thought after Mrs Blacklock dropped me off was

to phone Fergal and tell him I'd passed, but I was distracted by finding Mother on the doorstep, bursting with glad tidings of her own: Dr Reevey has proposed at last!

The relief was so stupendous I had to go and lie down for half an hour while the new, sunnier version of Mother was slapping a sandwich meal together in the kitchen, which she proposed washing down with Asti Spumante.

I don't suppose a small glass of that will do the Incubus much harm at this stage.

Dr Reevey – Duncan – dropped her off, and is to collect her this evening. I'll have to restrain myself from thanking him on my knees, because I'd never get up again.

'Leticia! It's ready!' called Mother gaily.

'Coming!' I said, hoisting myself up rather reluctantly, since the pains were still there. They must be those practice ones you get, a sort of warning of the joys to come, although the Incubus isn't due for weeks yet.

Just as I reached the bottom of the stairs the phone went off practically in my ear, making me (and the Incubus) jump. 'I'll get it, Mother!' I called and picked it up.

'Hello?'

'Tish? This is James,' he said tersely.

'Oh. Did you manage to get in touch with your father?'

'He's here – at the office. Has been since early this morning. Uncle Lionel and I have been explaining the whole situation to him.'

'What situation?'

'Our situation: how you forced me to leave when that pop singer moved into the village, and the scandalous way you've been behaving with him since then, despite carrying my child.'

473

His child? Had he done another of his revolving-door acts? 'Now look here!' I began indignantly, but he just steam-rollered inexorably on.

'Have you seen today's *Sun*?'

'No, of course I haven't. I've been out all day and anyway—'

'"Rocker in Village Love Tangle Scandal,"' he read out. '"Fickle Fergal broke my heart, says Nerissa Bright as he dumps her for heavily pregnant girlfriend Mrs Leticia Drew . . ."'

'What?'

'It's the last straw. Father and Uncle Lionel are sure that once you've had the baby I'll have very strong grounds for gaining custody. I'm not having my son brought up by that degenerate, drug-crazed, promiscuous—'

There was a crash as the phone dropped from my numb fingers. My ears rang and the wall seemed to be swaying towards me.

The baby – I'd have to move right away now. Perhaps to Granny? And Fergal – I had to see him. He had to tell them he'd never see me again, or I'd lose the baby!

I was flooded with panic and despair – and the knowledge that deep down part of me had been cherishing dreams that Fergal, despite everything, still loved me.

I had to see Fergal.

Through the glass door panel my dazed eyes saw a small van pull up, and two men get out. One was hoisting a camera onto his shoulder, and both were unmistakably pressmen . . .

I was out of the kitchen door past Mother like a sprinter hearing a starting gun, just registering her stunned face. Somehow I found myself over the fence and plodding – my top speed even when desperate these days – towards the Hall, through the darkening, rainy, dismal evening.

'Keep the baby, never see Fergal again. See Fergal again, lose the baby,' droned a monotonous voice in my head.

Independence didn't seem so desirable now it was being forced on me. More like banishment.

It was just about dark as I trudged towards the house, and light was spilling warmly through the open front door, illuminating a small car parked outside.

A girl got out – slender and dark – and Fergal came down the steps and enfolded her in his arms.

I must have stood there in the shadows until they went back into the house laughing and talking, with the rain dripping coldly down my face and the back of my neck and gluing the clothes to my shivering body. Then I turned and numbly walked away.

Chapter 45: Issues

The hospital cubicle was small, hot and glitteringly white, and I seemed to be looking at it down the wrong end of a telescope.

What was I doing here? I seemed to remember running through the wet, dark night, trying to find – to find . . .

A sudden series of rippling pains began to run through me. 'Fergal!' I gasped, panicking, and his concerned face bent over me.

'I'm here, Tish! Don't try to fight it.' His hand took mine and I clung to it as if I were drowning, which I was: drowning in pain.

'How did I – what am I doing here?'

'The gardener found you near the lodge, soaking wet and cold, but by the time I arrived you'd fainted. What made you run out like that, without a coat or anything? Were you trying to get to me?'

Memories stirred . . . horrible memories.

'The baby!'

I tried to sit up, and he gently but firmly pushed me down again. 'The baby will be fine.'

'Oh God!' It all came back to me: 'The baby can't be

476

coming yet – and James will – James says—' I grasped the hand that was gently pushing hair away from my face and shook it. 'Fergal – you have to phone James and tell him I'm moving away from Nutthill. Tell him you're never going to see me again! You *have* to tell him, or I'll lose the baby.'

'It'll be all right, Angel, believe me,' he assured me soothingly. 'Four weeks isn't that early – and forget whatever James has been saying. What he says or thinks doesn't matter.'

'But, Fergal – you don't understand!'

A blonde nurse strode briskly in, stopped dead and stared at him, open-mouthed. 'Aren't you . . .?'

'No!' he said baldly. 'Get a doctor, will you?'

'Yes you are!' said the nurse playfully. 'You're Fergal Rocco! Fancy that! I knew you lived locally now, but—'

'I think I'm about to have this baby!' I uttered through clenched teeth.

'Nonsense, dear!' she said brightly, without a glance in my direction.

My waters burst like Niagara. I wondered if there was really a baby left in there, or if it had washed out with the flood?

'My God!' exclaimed the nurse, rapidly checking me. 'You *are* having the baby.'

'It's not due until April,' I protested, but forces beyond my control had taken over.

'Well, it's arriving now.'

And suddenly I was whipped off on a dizzying ride to the labour ward, and into one of the hot, horrid, high-tech labour rooms, with people running about like disturbed ants.

I never let go of Fergal's hand once – it was the only safe thing in a dangerous world. (And might have to be surgically removed later.)

'Don't fight it, Mrs Rocco – go with it,' the nurse now urged me.

All the way up she'd been saying, 'Don't push! Don't push!'

'You've changed your tune, and I'm not Mrs R—' I began, then gasped as a different sort of pain made its way through me as if it was going somewhere. I thought I'd better go with it.

'Perhaps you'd rather go out, Mr Rocco?'

'No!' I tightened my grip even more. 'Don't leave me, Fergal, I need you!'

He looked pale but determined. 'It's all right, I'm not going anywhere.'

'I can see the baby's head,' the doctor said. 'Breathe gently, Mrs Rocco – shallow breaths! Haven't you been doing your breathing exercises?'

'No – I could already breathe without them. Oooh!'

With a sort of slithering and burning sensation the Incubus surfed into the light on the remains of the waters.

'Oh, well done, Angel!' Fergal exclaimed, and hugged me.

'Is it – is it all right? It must be too small, it . . .' I choked, unable to look.

'Hush, it's all right, darling,' he soothed, wiping my face gently with a cool damp cloth. 'They're just checking the baby – listen!'

There was a sort of muted whimpering, then a nurse turned, smiling, and brought across a tiny, blanket-wrapped bundle. 'Congratulations, Mrs Rocco! It's a girl!'

'Shouldn't she be in an incubator?'

'Not at all. She's a big healthy baby!'

'But I—'

'Give her to me.' Fergal reached out and gently took the

baby, but I looked the other way: even if she was all right, there was no point in getting attached to her if she was going to be wrenched away from me by James. A tear formed under my eyelids and trickled slowly down.

I felt Fergal sit down on the side of the bed.

'Tish, there's absolutely nothing wrong with her – she's beautiful,' he said tenderly.

'She looks just like her daddy!' the blonde nurse cooed sentimentally.

'Tish,' he coaxed, in the voice I found hard to resist. 'Just look at her?'

Slowly my head turned until I met a blue, innocent gaze ... and was enraptured. She was perfect – and she was *mine!*

I held out my arms and Fergal placed her in them, smiling.

'I don't suppose anyone's got a camera?'

Someone produced an instant one, and snaps were taken of me with the baby, Fergal and me with the baby, the midwife and doctor with the baby, and the blonde nurse and the midwife, rather carried away, with Fergal.

Then he and the baby were temporarily removed and, after a short messy interval with the afterbirth and being cleaned up, I was moved into a little private room which he must have arranged, because I certainly hadn't.

The midwife said it was one of the easiest births she's ever seen. I wouldn't want to go through a difficult one, if that's an easy one ... though there is a most peculiar empty feeling now that the Incubus and I are separated.

She was wheeled back in, asleep, followed by a grinning, exhilarated, crumpled Fergal. 'Do you know what they've put on her wrist bracelet? Baby Rocco!'

'Fergal,' I began, then broke off to yawn hugely. Great

waves of tiredness were trying to suck me under, and suddenly sleep seemed more important than anything else. Only I knew there was something I had to tell him first, to make him do . . .

The bed sank as he sat on it and took my hand. 'What is it? You ought to get some sleep, Tish.'

My drowsy gaze focused on our joined hands, his marked by rising bruises.

'Oh, your poor hand! Did I do that? I'm sorry.'

'It's nothing – I wish I could have taken some of the pain for you.' He frowned. 'I always wanted lots of children, but I didn't realise . . . How could I ask you to go through that again?'

'Don't be silly!' I muttered sleepily. 'She's worth it, isn't she? And you won't let them – they won't take her away from me, will they?'

'Take her away from you? Over my dead body!'

A tired, disembodied little voice that I vaguely recognised as my own explained what James had threatened, and that was why I didn't want to hold her, because if I loved her and lost her . . . a tear trickled down. It was already too late – I did love her. And that newspaper headline, and the reporters . . . it all came tumbling out.

'I'm sorry about the newspaper. I saw it this morning, and then Lucia came down with a copy this evening, to show me in case I hadn't seen it.'

'Lucia?'

'She's over to visit my parents, and she wanted to break it to me gently – she knows my temper – but I'd already seen it and I was going to warn you about it later. And Angel, you know I won't let anyone take the baby away from you.

I promise you, James won't be able to take her. She's mine, don't forget – it says so on the bracelet!'

'And the baby . . . I don't understand why—'

'Don't worry about it any more tonight – we'll talk about it tomorrow. Everything will be all right.'

My eyes began inexorably closing.

'My night things are in a case in my bedroom.'

'I'll go and fetch them.'

'Bess and Toby . . .'

'Can go up to the Hall with Maria.'

'My mother! She was there! She'll—'

'It was your mother who rang me and told me you were missing. I was just going out to look for you when the gardener found you at the gate. I phoned Maria up after we got here and she'll have let her know you're safe.'

'Fergal?' There was something else I needed to remember, something to ask.

'Leave it all to me,' he said, kissing me lightly. 'Go to sleep and don't worry about anything. I'll see you tomorrow.'

Tomorrow . . .

Chapter 46: Alignments

I was woken at some unearthly hour of the morning. There was no sign of the baby, but a nurse assured me she was fine and would be brought up later.

'You won't give her to anyone else, will you?' I asked urgently, and she gave me a strange look on the way out and said, 'All our babies are properly tagged and there's no possibility of error.'

She was gone before I could explain.

My hospital bag was by the bed, mute evidence that Fergal had been back in the night. I only hope he'd found time to have some sleep.

Attired in my own nightie and with my hair brushed, I almost passed as a member of the human race again, except that my breasts felt, and looked, like a big hard pair of water wings worn back-to-front.

Then a nurse brought the baby back and showed me how to feed and wind her, and change the nappy on her fragile little body.

'She's so tiny! I'm afraid to hurt her.'

'She's not so tiny!' she assured me, laughing. 'She's seven pounds – quite a good weight.'

I stared at her, realising just what it was that had been niggling at the back of my mind. 'Isn't that rather a lot for a baby who's a month early?'

'A month early! Wherever did you get that idea? She's a full-term baby.' She laughed heartily. 'You've got your dates wrong. Now, I'll just leave her with you, but ring if you want anything.'

I didn't reply, too busy calculating a month back from the barbecue and coming up with a conclusion that made my brain reel.

Did I want anything? Yes! I wanted to get my hands on Fergal Rocco.

Preferably when I got my full strength back.

I stared down thoughtfully at my dark-haired daughter, and her big blue eyes seemed to stare right back. She was a strangely long, elegant baby, rather than a pudgy, squished up little bundle, and Mother would say she looked foreign . . . but at least she hadn't got red hair!

No wonder Fergal was so certain James couldn't take her away from me.

When, later, I made my painful way to the loo (where my crushed organs had forgotten the most basic functions), I discovered a whole ward of new mothers who seemed to be wearing large, hard water wings, worn the wrong way round.

This isn't mentioned in any of the books I've read.

'There's a man outside who says he's your husband,' said a small dark nurse, sticking her head in. She looked puzzled. 'But his name is Drew.'

'So is mine at the moment, and I suppose he's technically still my husband.'

'But Mr Rocco? Isn't the baby—'

'I don't want to see him!'

'Mr Rocco?' she said doubtfully.

'No! Mr Drew!'

'Oh – I see.'

It was pretty obvious she didn't. She asked hesitantly: 'Will you see your mother – Mrs Norwood?'

'I suppose so,' I said wearily. I might as well get it over with. 'There isn't an older Mr Drew out there too, is there?'

She thought I was mad, and perhaps I was a bit yesterday, but today I was feeling more and more sane. Perhaps that's a sign of madness?

'No – just the one. Your husband – er – Mr Rocco phoned . . .' She sighed dreamily and went into a trance.

'Did he?'

'His voice on the phone was so sex—' She bit off the word and blushed scarlet. 'He said you weren't to worry about anything, and he'd be here later.'

'I won't see him!'

'Mr Rocco?'

'Mr Rocco,' I agreed.

She went out, looking back at me as if I were insane. Perhaps I am at that, but at least there won't be room for postnatal depression.

Mother tottered in, looking pale and fragile. 'Darling!'

She laid her powdered cheek against mine. 'How could you frighten me so! I was so worried when you just ran out like that. I even rang Fergal because I thought you might have gone there. It *would* have to be him who found you!'

She sounded as if she'd rather I hadn't been found at all.

'That foreign woman phoned and said you were safe, and

then *he* came and told me you'd had the baby and took Bess, Toby and your case away in his car! I was so upset that poor Duncan stayed all night – in separate rooms, of course,' she added primly.

'Of course,' I agreed.

'And I phoned James at the Wrekins' this morning to tell him – he should know, after all! And he wants to see you. But now I must see my granddaughter at last! Does she look like you? You were such a pretty baby, darling.'

She got up, peered into the crib, and added doubtfully, '– a pretty baby just like this one. But she's very *dark*, dear, isn't she?'

'I don't think their hair stays the same colour.'

She took another furtive peek at the baby. 'What are you going to call her, Leticia?'

That's the one thing I haven't thought of! 'Incubus' wouldn't look well on the birth certificate, but 'Cuckoo' is a distinct possibility.

'I don't know, Mother, I'll have to think about it. What made Glenda choose Leticia?'

She looked at me and her lip trembled. 'I – I had a baby doll called that when I was a little girl, and Glenda said she thought you looked like it. But it means "gladness", darling.'

She subsided into a chair and said slightly defensively, 'And Daddy and I *were* glad, when we got over the shock!'

'So you didn't plan on adopting me when you went down there?'

'No – oh, no!' she quavered, blotting blue mascara with the edge of her silk scarf. 'I felt I had to go and help her when she sent the telegram saying she was about to have

485

you, but then one morning she'd gone and left a note and your birth certificate, and I could see she'd planned it.'

Now it was all coming out I decided to keep prodding her. 'So I was forced on you?'

'Well, of course it *was* a shock, darling, at first, but Daddy came straight down even though he was still far from well, and we decided to take you home as our own. Daddy was worried that we wouldn't have any children after the mumps, and as it happened we didn't!' She straightened up and added more brightly, 'So it all turned out for the best, didn't it?'

'But didn't Glenda get in touch? Don't you know where she is?'

She shook her head and a last, blue-tinged droplet fell off her eyelashes. 'Oh, no. We were afraid at first that she'd want you back, but after about a year she wrote asking for money to go abroad, and after Daddy sent it we never heard from her again.'

It was a bit hurtful to be so unwanted by my real mother. But then, hadn't Mother been my real mother in every way, to the best of her ability? Poor Mother, afraid I might be snatched away, and with little hope of any children of her own.

'I'm glad you've told me, Mo— Mummy.'

'You don't mind?'

'Of course I *mind*, but I'm grateful to you and Daddy. You're my real parents.'

Mother, catharsis achieved, was preparing to sweep it all under the carpet. 'I don't think we need to mention it again, do we? You're my little girlie and that's all that matters, isn't it?'

I winced, but she was adjusting her make-up in her

compact mirror and didn't notice. Then she sneaked another glance at the sleeping infant, who was wearing a singularly Etruscan smile for a newborn, and suggested timidly: 'What about James?'

What about James? 'Oh, I suppose I'll have to see him eventually,' I said wearily, 'but not yet. I'll deal with him later.' And at least now I wouldn't have to worry about his threats.

'That Italian woman's looking after Toby and the dog up at the Hall, so Duncan thinks he might as well take me home now.'

'Yes, the hospital are keeping me in for a week, mostly because they say I'm anaemic, so you might as well.'

'I'll come back after that, if you need me.'

I thanked her and said I would bear it in mind, and she tottered off with one last dazed backwards look at the baby.

Three minutes later James burst through the door in Manic Mode, though the reek of whisky just made it before him.

'Where is she?' he demanded aggressively. 'I'm entitled to see her, aren't I? You needn't think I've changed my mind about custody, either! What does Valerie mean by saying it would be better if I didn't see her?'

Thank you, Mother!

I pressed my bedside buzzer as he veered across to the plastic tank and stared down into it.

His face began to go red and the vein started its ominous twitch. I wanted to leap out of bed and snatch the Incubus up, except that I can't leap anywhere at the moment. But I started to ease myself down as quickly as I could.

Then his eyes fell on the wrist tag, which still read 'Baby Rocco', and he went berserk.

'It's bloody his!' he bellowed, advancing menacingly on me this time. 'I was right all along, wasn't I?'

I began to shuffle back over to the far side of the bed, wondering if I could fell him with the carafe before he strangled me.

'Calm down, James! I didn't know – I still don't know for sure.'

Fergal walked in, and everything suddenly went still and held its breath, as though someone had pressed the freeze button.

'Leave her alone,' he told James coolly. 'You've done enough harm, sending her into labour with your threats. She *didn't* know the baby was mine. *I* didn't know the baby was mine until I saw her. I took advantage of her at the hotel when she'd drunk herself senseless after seeing you with your lover.'

'Fergal!'

'A likely story!' sneered James. 'You've been having an affair right under my nose and she would have palmed the baby off on me if she could.'

'No I wouldn't!' I protested indignantly. 'That's the last thing I would have done if I'd known.'

But I might as well have saved my breath for all the notice they took of me.

'There was no affair, though I'd every intention of taking Tish off you once I found out you didn't deserve her. When I thought she was expecting your baby I held back to give you another chance, but you blew it – and just as well, because the baby's mine!'

'Just a minute!' I exclaimed. 'She's *mine*, no one else's!'

'I'd have brought her up as mine anyway,' Fergal continued calmly.

'What do you mean?' blustered James. 'What right have you—'

'I intend marrying Tish.'

The Incubus moved restlessly in her sleep and whimpered a little.

A security guard appeared in the doorway, big and solid, with the little dark nurse next to him.

'That's the man!' She pointed to James. 'He's drunk, and he just burst in here and started shouting. The whole ward could hear him!'

'But I'm her husband!' began James.

'Ex,' Fergal told him, eyes like glacier splinters. 'Your divorce is through: time to leave.'

Baffled, the guard looked from Fergal's calm implacability to James's red, angry face and made his decision.

'I'm afraid I'll have to ask you to leave the hospital, sir,' he said, taking a firm grip on James's arm.

James opened and shut his mouth a couple of times like a dying guppy, then let himself be led away.

'You can go too,' I told Fergal without looking in his direction. 'You may have taken advantage of me, and then lied to me about it, but that doesn't mean you've any claim on my baby!'

'Our baby!' he said softly, sitting on the side of the bed and putting his arms around me. 'Isn't it wonderful? And I really didn't lie to you – I didn't realise she was mine until I saw her. I never thought I'd be grateful for faulty goods! Or maybe, in the heat of the moment . . .?'

My God! Escaped Fergal Rocco sperm are probably even now establishing a breeding colony in the hotel's air conditioning system! Angrily I tried to push him away, tears flooding my eyes. 'How could you, Fergal? You must have seen what a state I was in that night.'

'Angel, you knew exactly what you were doing, drunk or sober! I lied to James when I said I took advantage of you.'

I stared indignantly at him.

'I resisted as long as humanly possible,' he assured me gravely, 'but, as you know, I'm no saint. You took advantage of me.'

'I took advantage – how dare you, Fergal Rocco? The whole situation was your fault, pouncing on me outside my room like that.' If my arms hadn't felt like limp string I'd have hit him.

'I only intended talking to you. Admittedly I was a bit angry at the way you tried to avoid me earlier, but as soon as I got you in there you wouldn't let me go. You practically had the clothes off my back before I closed the door!'

'I – I did not!' I protested weakly.

'You can't have forgotten?'

'Shut up!'

'And although you didn't say very *much* you said it clearly enough. "Yes – oh yes, Fergal!" that kind of thing. I didn't realise how much you'd drunk.' He grinned.

I went scarlet. 'I didn't know what I was doing! You must have known that! You should have resisted.'

'You seemed to know exactly what you were doing – and I'm not made of stone, darling! And I wasn't exactly thinking clearly at the time either, because as soon as I touched you I knew that I loved and wanted you just as much as ever.'

I looked down and discovered I'd twisted the bedspread into a screw. 'You are only saying that because the baby's yours.'

'What do I have to do to make you believe me?' he exploded, giving me a small shake. 'I've already asked you to marry me once. And what's more,' he added fiercely, 'when I kissed you on your birthday I knew you loved me too! You didn't need to get tanked up *that* time to respond to me.'

'You arrogant, conceited snake in the grass,' I snarled.

He pulled me closer and kissed me.

'I don't want to marry anyone!' I gasped when I came up for air. 'How could I ever trust—'

The nurse came in, squawked, and left hastily, but I'd just discovered something interesting.

After the birth I thought I'd never, ever, want to make love again. But now I just possibly might . . . in a year or so, say, when my internal organs have rearranged themselves into a more familiar alignment.

Fergal held me close and tenderly stroked my hair. 'I don't want anyone except you,' he murmured huskily. 'If you'd only come to America with me in the first place—'

'Oh, yes, and hung around in the background while you sowed your wild oats with the groupies, or whoever else took your fancy? That would have been wonderful!'

'There wouldn't have been anyone else. And why are we arguing about old history? You know you can trust me, Tish. I want a family, to settle down – I want you!'

'No you don't – you said I was prissy!'

'I love your prissy, immaculate little ways.' His voice went deeper, and even throatier. 'And I think it's time you cleaned me up and hung me out to dry, don't you?'

He grinned wickedly, but I hardened my heart – he wasn't getting off that easily.

'I'll think about your kind offer,' I said primly.

'Think fast. Your mother's suddenly decided she wants us to marry. She's been reading your mail again, that's how I knew about the divorce coming through. I'm getting a special licence.'

'She doesn't even like you! And anyway, just because the baby's dark, it doesn't mean—'

'She's a Rocco.' He got up and went to peer into the crib. 'Bet she's going to have green eyes!'

'They're blue.'

'All babies' eyes are blue – they'll change.'

I looked helplessly at him. 'Fergal, why do you want me? You could have anyone.'

He has an interestingly sudden way of stopping arguments. 'We're getting married.'

'I'm never getting married again,' I said crossly with my head on his shoulder. 'I like being independent, and I'm going to live in the cottage with the baby and write my novels.'

'Don't you think it might be a bit crowded in the cottage?'

'What do you mean?'

'You, me, the baby, two dogs, one parrot, a cat – and Maria!'

'*Maria!*'

'You don't think she's going to lose the chance to get her hands on the baby, do you? She's been knitting for weeks! And how are you going to write more wonderful books about me if there's no one to look after Baby Rocco?'

I sank back against the pillow with as much dignity as I could muster and said faintly, 'I think I need to rest.'

'I'll see you later. Is there anything you want me to bring?'

'Champagne!' I snapped, and he laughed and went away.

* * *

Fergal: March 2000

*'First sensational pictures of Fergal Rocco and
Leticia Drew with their baby girl . . .'*

Exposé magazine

Must have been one of the nurses – money spoke louder than ethics. But I forgive her. I forgive everybody, I'm so happy.

I knew the baby was mine the minute I set eyes on her, I don't know how. If only I'd known all along, I'd have done things very differently, and to hell with her husband.

I love Tish. I always have and I always will, and it's a relief to stop pretending I don't, when really I want to marry her and earn the right to look after her for ever.

And she loves me too, even if she's a little mad at me at the moment.

The amount of publicity all this has generated is going to come as a shock to her when she leaves the safe world of the hospital, but I've plans to deal with that . . . and after all, I've already kidnapped her dog and parrot!

Maria says she is now running a menagerie, rather than a house.

Chapter 47: Photo Finish

It was highly ingenious the way reporters tried to find a way into the hospital, even to the extent of trying to bribe the nurses.

In the end we had a sort of minor press conference, on the understanding that they would then leave us in peace for a bit.

The photograph of Fergal, the baby and me was rather nice, though I'm sure I don't remember him saying anything like the things they attributed to him in the article.

My agent is ecstatic – he rang to say my book sales are rocketing since the news broke and sent a huge flower arrangement to the hospital. (I'm having writing withdrawal symptoms.)

James has vanished from the scene entirely, since he now has other things on his mind – Wendy's in here too, having been rushed in a couple of days after me.

Makes you think, doesn't it?

She must have had her little lapse about the same time as I conceived, hence the urgency to get rid of me and induce James to marry her, I suppose. And when I told Alice that

James wanted sons, she must have thought announcing her pregnancy was a sure card.

And the nurse says it *is* a boy at that, so perhaps it is.

Wendy and sprog had been moved to the main ward when I next minced through on my way to the bathroom. (Take it from me, normal methods of locomotion are out when someone's been practising embroidery on your credentials.)

She was wearing the usual back-to-front water wings and a glum expression.

Moved by something of a spirit of fellow feeling – and sheer unbridled curiosity – I veered across.

'Hi, Wendy,' I said. 'Congratulations.'

Stooping, I looked down into her baby's cross, pink face.

There was no mistaking that aubergine-shaped nose, now rendered in minute incongruity in the crumpled, screwed-up face.

He looked exactly like Howard.

'Well,' Granny's welcome voice said sternly down the telephone, a call orchestrated by Fergal. 'I suppose it'll all come out in the wash.'

'What will, Granny?'

'All that mess. Mind you, I never liked him, and at least that Frodo's a real man.'

'Fergal.'

'And I blame your mother.'

'She did her best,' I said, to my own surprise. 'Granny, you did get my letter, didn't you, explaining about Glenda, and how I'm . . .' This was really difficult, and I swallowed painfully before going on in a rush, 'I'm not really related to you at all, Granny!'

'Of course you are, you great daft ha'porth. It's ozzymoses.'

'Who?'

'Ozzymoses. That thing where it all sort of seeps in. You've been around me long enough to absorb some Thorpe into you.'

'Osmosis?'

'That's what I said. Anyway, you're the only kind of grand-daughter I've got, so you'll just have to make the best of it.'

I began to feel better. 'I think I can live with that, Granny.'

'Rose and I'll hire a car and come and see you soon. When's the wedding?'

'I don't know yet. I haven't—'

'Get on with it. Your mother's marrying that doctor too, thank goodness, so at least she'll be off your hands.'

'Yes. I'm going to be a bridesmaid.'

'Better be a bride first. That Fingal phoned me up.'

'Fergal?'

'He's a charmer and no mistake. Said everything was his fault, but he wanted to settle down with you and be a good husband.'

I shuddered. 'That's what I thought James was. I don't want another one of those.'

'Better have a bad one then,' she pointed out practically.

Fergal: March 2000

'LOVE WAS TOO STRONG FOR US,'
says Fergal Rocco of rock group Goneril, who is to wed
divorcée and mother of his child Leticia Drew, 31 . . .'

Sun

Maria said she'd told Tish that I'd make a model husband and father.

'I told her: he will not want his little girl to see pictures in the papers of her papa doing naughty things with other ladies, will he?'

'What did she say to that?'

Maria frowned. 'I did not quite understand the idiom, but it was something about wearing your guts for garters if you did anything like that in future . . . does that make sense?'

I nodded. I didn't need the warning: you can accuse me of many things, but being as stupid as her last husband isn't going to be one of them.

Chapter 48: Besieged

This week in hospital has given me some time to think, if nothing else – and clearly life isn't ever going to be the same again – thank God.

Of course, everything isn't perfect – the *world* isn't perfect (and I certainly won't be taking out any shares in rubber goods either . . .) – but it's as near as it's going to get.

Mr Rooney found Glenda in Canada. She's now a high-powered businesswoman, divorced, with no other children, and although she sent her best wishes, she doesn't feel that she's any place in my life. Nor, it sounds like to me, any real interest in me. I'd still like one day to meet her, more for curiosity's sake than anything. I've written asking her for any details she can remember about my real father (apparently chance-met at a pop concert: Ill Met by Moonlight?), but more for the sake of the baby than anything.

Mother, predictably, is still impossible, but now she'll soon be someone else's responsibility. They're planning a June wedding and she wants me to be a bridesmaid, which is the strangest idea she's thought of yet. Margaret wants me to be

Matron of Honour at hers, too, so you can see I'm much in demand.

Wendy doesn't want me to be anything at hers. (I wonder if you can get leather wedding dresses.)

The hospital, my cottage, and the gates of the Hall are all still under siege by reporters waiting for me to take the baby home.

Home . . .

I admit I did cry when Fergal said it was impossible for me to go back to the cottage since reporters and cameramen line every perimeter like rabid triffids, but secretly I was relieved, too. The thought of having the sole responsibility for a tiny baby was throwing me into a panic, now it was actually time to leave the warm cocoon of hospital.

Not that I could have kept Fergal away anyway.

Maria says he's decorated a room at the Hall exactly like the nursery at the cottage, and moved everything up there – what Granny would call a 'fate acumply'. And he's made me a study in one of the little tower rooms with a view of the park, and filled it with great drifts of my golden autumn leaves.

Maria was horrified!

The animals are settling in well together, and Bob is looking after the cottage and its garden for me until we decide what to do with it. (A weekend retreat for Carlo and Sara is on the cards – I quite like the thought of that.)

Maria also says the baby is the most beautiful one she's ever seen (so do I, but as her mother I can't go around saying that kind of thing!), and gave me the idea for her name when she said she was a late Valentine.

Valentina.

It sounds very romantic, and has made me think of a wonderful plot for a new novel.

But if the hero doesn't have black hair, green eyes and a very short fuse, Fergal says he'll want to know the reason why!

If you've enjoyed *Good Husband Material*, why not try some of Tish's recipes?

Recipes

Apple Chutney

Ingredients
1lb/450g cooking apples
8oz/225g sultanas
6oz/175g shallots or onions
1 rounded tsp ground ginger
7oz/200g sugar – brown muscovado gives a good flavour
1 tsp salt
1 pint/600ml malt vinegar

Method
Peel, core and chop the apples and place in a large bowl with the sultanas. Finely chop the onion and mix in, together with all the remaining ingredients.

Cover the bowl and leave to stand for one hour.

Put the mixture into a large heavy non-reactive pan bring it slowly to a boil, uncovered, and then turn the heat down and simmer for thirty minutes or so, stirring frequently, until the mixture is thick and brown.

Allow to cool slightly and then spoon into warm, dry, sterilised jars and cover with a waxed disc and seal. Leave to mature for 3 months before opening.

Chewy Fig Fingers

Ingredients
4oz/100g dried figs (the soft, ready-to-eat ones are easiest)
4oz/100g sunflower seeds
rice paper or sesame seeds

Method
Chop the figs into little pieces, discarding the stalks and any hard bits. Put into a food processor and blend to a thick paste, or you can mash them up by hand.

Mix in the sunflower seeds. Make a 'sandwich' of the paste by rolling it flat between two layers of rice paper, then cut into bars. As an alternative, form the fig paste into little logs or balls and roll them into sesame seeds sprinkled onto a plate, to coat.

Store the bars or logs in a box in the fridge, or a cool place, between layers of greaseproof paper until needed.

Hasty Buns

These little bread rolls are akin to scones and are best eaten warm, split and buttered.

Ingredients
1lb/450g plain flour
1 tsp salt (optional)
2tsps baking powder
2oz/50g butter
1 egg, lightly beaten
¼ pint/150ml milk

Method
Preheat the oven to 425°F, 220°C, Gas Mark 7. Grease a baking tray.

Sieve the flour into a mixing bowl and add the baking powder and salt.

Add the butter, using the rubbing-in method.

Mix the milk and beaten egg together, keeping a little bit of the egg back to glaze the rolls with.

Quickly stir the egg and milk mixture into the dry ingredients and then gather it together into a stiff, stretchy dough. (Have a little extra milk on hand, in case it needs a drop or two more, but add cautiously – you don't want a sticky mass.)

Divide into about sixteen little rolls or balls. Place on the baking tray, brush tops with the last of the beaten egg, and bake in middle of oven for ten to fifteen minutes.

To find out more about Trisha and her warm, wise and and witty books, visit her website www. trishaashley.com or become a fan of her Facebook page Trisha Ashley Books. You can also say hello on Twitter @trishaashley